Praise for *H...*

"A splendid novel. Not only is it ... about dragons, it's a very clever one and fits neatly into the historical niche this author has used. The plot was excellent, extraordinary in that the reader has no idea where it's leading—which is always fun. Let's hope this is the first of many from Naomi Novik. She'll be one to watch."
—ANNE MCCAFFREY

"One of the best books I've read in years—a truly new approach. Lots of fun and cleverly thought out ideas. *His Majesty's D... ...* a de..."

"Wo... witty... acco... conf... as a ... a re... limit... enga... *Black...*"

"Rea... McCa... *Majes...* ... Novik beautifully renders an eighteenth-century Europe in which both naval buffs and dragon lovers will be keen to immerse themselves."
—ALAN DEAN FOSTER,
author of the Pip & Flinx series

"[A] refreshingly original fantasy adventure. It has tense action, strong characters, and an intriguing new world for the reader to explore. I can't wait to read the other books in the series."
—MARTHA WELLS, author of *The Wizard Hunters*

His Majesty's

Dragon

NAOMI NOVIK

DEL
REY

BALLANTINE BOOKS • NEW YORK

His Majesty's Dragon is a work of fiction. All incidents and dialogue, and all characters with the exception of some well-known historical and public figures, are products of the author's imagination and are not to be construed as real. Where real-life historical or public figures appear, the situations, incidents, and dialogues concerning those persons are entirely fictional and are not intended to depict actual events or to change the entirely fictional nature of the work. In all other respects, any resemblance to persons living or dead is entirely coincidental.

A Del Rey Mass Market Original

Copyright © 2006 by Naomi Novik
Excerpt from *Throne of Jade* by Naomi Novik copyright © 2006 by Naomi Novik

Published in the United States by Del Rey Books, an imprint of The Random House Publishing Group, a division of Random House, Inc., New York. Originally published in Great Britian as *Temeraire* by Voyager, an imprint of HarperCollins Publishers, London.

DEL REY is a registered trademark and the Del Rey colophon is a trademark of Random House, Inc.

This book contains an excerpt from the forthcoming book *Throne of Jade* by Naomi Novik. This excerpt has been set for this edition only and may not reflect the final content of the forthcoming edition.

Interior art: © Gayle Marquez

ISBN 0-345-48128-3

Printed in the United States of America

www.delreybooks.com

OPM   9   8   7   6   5   4   3   2   1

for Charles
sine qua non

His Majesty's
Dragon

I

Chapter 1

THE DECK OF the French ship was slippery with blood, heaving in the choppy sea; a stroke might as easily bring down the man making it as the intended target. Laurence did not have time in the heat of the battle to be surprised at the degree of resistance, but even through the numbing haze of battle-fever and the confusion of swords and pistol-smoke, he marked the extreme look of anguish on the French captain's face as the man shouted encouragement to his men.

It was still there shortly thereafter, when they met on the deck, and the man surrendered his sword, very reluctantly: at the last moment his hand half-closed about the blade, as if he meant to draw it back. Laurence looked up to make certain the colors had been struck, then accepted the sword with a mute bow; he did not speak French himself, and a more formal exchange would have to wait for the presence of his third lieutenant, that young man being presently engaged belowdecks in securing the French guns. With the cessation of hostilities, the remaining Frenchmen were all virtually dropping where they stood; Laurence noticed that there were fewer of them than he would have expected for a frigate of thirty-six guns, and that they looked ill and hollow-cheeked.

Many of them lay dead or dying upon the deck; he

shook his head at the waste and eyed the French captain with disapproval: the man should never have offered battle. Aside from the plain fact that the *Reliant* would have had the *Amitié* slightly outgunned and outmanned under the best of circumstances, the crew had obviously been reduced by disease or hunger. To boot, the sails above them were in a sad tangle, and that no result of the battle, but of the storm which had passed but this morning; they had barely managed to bring off a single broadside before the *Reliant* had closed and boarded. The captain was obviously deeply overset by the defeat, but he was not a young man to be carried away by his spirits: he ought to have done better by his men than to bring them into so hopeless an action.

"Mr. Riley," Laurence said, catching his second lieutenant's attention, "have our men carry the wounded below." He hooked the captain's sword on his belt; he did not think the man deserved the compliment of having it returned to him, though ordinarily he would have done so. "And pass the word for Mr. Wells."

"Very good, sir," Riley said, turning to issue the necessary orders. Laurence stepped to the railing to look down and see what damage the hull had taken. She looked reasonably intact, and he had ordered his own men to avoid shots below the waterline; he thought with satisfaction that there would be no difficulty in bringing her into port.

His hair had slipped out of his short queue, and now fell into his eyes as he looked over. He impatiently pushed it out of the way as he turned back, leaving streaks of blood upon his forehead and the sun-bleached hair; this, with his broad shoulders and his severe look, gave him an unconsciously savage appearance as he surveyed his prize, very unlike his usual thoughtful expression.

Wells climbed up from below in response to the summons and came to his side. "Sir," he said, without waiting to be addressed, "begging your pardon, but Lieutenant Gibbs says there is something queer in the hold."

"Oh? I will go and look," Laurence said. "Pray tell this gentleman," he indicated the French captain, "that he must give me his parole, for himself and his men, or they must be confined."

The French captain did not immediately respond; he looked at his men with a miserable expression. They would of course do much better if they could be kept spread out through the lower deck, and any recapture was a practical impossibility under the circumstances; still he hesitated, drooped, and finally husked, *"Je me rends,"* with a look still more wretched.

Laurence gave a short nod. "He may go to his cabin," he told Wells, and turned to step down into the hold. "Tom, will you come along? Very good."

He descended with Riley on his heels, and found his first lieutenant waiting for him. Gibbs's round face was still shining with sweat and emotion; he would be taking the prize into port, and as she was a frigate, he almost certainly would be made post, a captain himself. Laurence was only mildly pleased; though Gibbs had done his duty reasonably, the man had been imposed on him by the Admiralty and they had not become intimates. He had wanted Riley in the first lieutenant's place, and if he had been given his way, Riley would now be the one getting his step. That was the nature of the service, and he did not begrudge Gibbs the good fortune; still, he did not rejoice quite so wholeheartedly as he would have to see Tom get his own ship.

"Very well; what's all this, then?" Laurence said now; the hands were clustered about an oddly placed bulkhead towards the stern area of the hold, neglecting the work of cataloguing the captured ship's stores.

"Sir, if you will step this way," Gibbs said. "Make

way there," he ordered, and the hands backed away
from what Laurence now saw was a doorway set inside
a wall that had been built across the back of the hold; recently, for the lumber was markedly lighter than the surrounding planks.

Ducking through the low door, he found himself in a
small chamber with a strange appearance. The walls had
been reinforced with actual metal, which must have added
a great deal of unnecessary weight to the ship, and the
floor was padded with old sailcloth; in addition, there
was a small coal-stove in the corner, though this was not
presently in use. The only object stored within the room
was a large crate, roughly the height of a man's waist
and as wide, and this was made fast to the floor and
walls by means of thick hawsers attached to metal rings.

Laurence could not help feeling the liveliest curiosity,
and after a moment's struggle he yielded to it. "Mr.
Gibbs, I think we shall have a look inside," he said, stepping out of the way. The top of the crate was thoroughly
nailed down, but eventually yielded to the many willing
hands; they pried it off and lifted out the top layer of
packing, and many heads craned forward at the same
time to see.

No one spoke, and in silence Laurence stared at the
shining curve of eggshell rising out of the heaped straw;
it was scarcely possible to believe. "Pass the word for
Mr. Pollitt," he said at last; his voice sounded only a little strained. "Mr. Riley, pray be sure those lashings are
quite secure."

Riley did not immediately answer, too busy staring;
then he jerked to attention and said, hastily, "Yes, sir,"
and bent to check the bindings.

Laurence stepped closer and gazed down at the egg.
There could hardly be any doubt as to its nature, though
he could not say for sure from his own experience. The
first amazement passing, he tentatively reached out and

touched the surface, very cautiously: it was smooth and hard to the touch. He withdrew almost at once, not wanting to risk doing it some harm.

Mr. Pollitt came down into the hold in his awkward way, clinging to the ladder edges with both hands and leaving bloody prints upon it; he was no kind of a sailor, having become a naval surgeon only at the late age of thirty, after some unspecified disappointments on land. He was nevertheless a genial man, well liked by the crew, even if his hand was not always the steadiest at the operating table. "Yes, sir?" he said, then saw the egg. "Good Lord above."

"It is a dragon egg, then?" Laurence said. It required an effort to restrain the triumph in his voice.

"Oh, yes indeed, Captain, the size alone shows that." Mr. Pollitt had wiped his hands on his apron and was already brushing more straw away from the top, trying to see the extent. "My, it is quite hardened already; I wonder what they can have been thinking, so far from land."

This did not sound very promising. "Hardened?" Laurence said sharply. "What does that mean?"

"Why, that it will hatch soon. I will have to consult my books to be certain, but I believe that Badke's *Bestiary* states with authority that when the shell has fully hardened, hatching will occur within a week. What a splendid specimen, I must get my measuring cords."

He bustled away, and Laurence exchanged a glance with Gibbs and Riley, moving closer so they might speak without being overheard by the lingering gawkers. "At least three weeks from Madeira with a fair wind, would you say?" Laurence said quietly.

"At best, sir," Gibbs said, nodding.

"I cannot imagine how they came to be here with it," Riley said. "What do you mean to do, sir?"

His initial satisfaction turning gradually into dismay as he realized the very difficult situation, Laurence stared at the egg blankly. Even in the dim lantern light, it shone with the warm luster of marble. "Oh, I am damned if I know, Tom. But I suppose I will go and return the French captain his sword; it is no wonder he fought so furiously after all."

Except of course he did know; there was only one possible solution, unpleasant as it might be to contemplate. Laurence watched broodingly while the egg was transferred, still in its crate, over to the *Reliant:* the only grim man, except for the French officers. He had granted them the liberty of the quarterdeck, and they watched the slow process glumly from the rail. All around them, smiles wreathed every sailor's face, private, gloating smiles, and there was a great deal of jostling among the idle hands, with many unnecessary cautions and pieces of advice called out to the sweating group of men engaged in the actual business of the transfer.

The egg being safely deposited on the deck of the *Reliant,* Laurence took his own leave of Gibbs. "I will leave the prisoners with you; there is no sense in giving them a motive for some desperate attempt to recapture the egg," he said. "Keep in company, as well as you can. However, if we are separated, we will rendezvous at Madeira. You have my most hearty congratulations, Captain," he added, shaking Gibbs's hand.

"Thank you, sir, and may I say, I am most sensible—very grateful—" But here Gibbs's eloquence, never in great supply, failed him; he gave up and merely stood beaming widely on Laurence and all the world, full of great goodwill.

The ships had been brought abreast for the transfer of the crate; Laurence did not have to take a boat, but only sprang across on the up-roll of the swell. Riley and the rest of his officers had already crossed back. He gave the order to make sail, and went directly below, to wrestle with the problem in privacy.

But no obliging alternative presented itself overnight. The next morning, he bowed to necessity and gave his orders, and shortly the midshipmen and lieutenants of the ship came crowding into his cabin, scrubbed and nervous in their best gear; this sort of mass summons was unprecedented, and the cabin was not quite large enough to hold them all comfortably. Laurence saw anxious looks on many faces, undoubtedly conscious of some private guilt, curiosity on others; Riley alone looked worried, perhaps suspecting something of Laurence's intentions.

Laurence cleared his throat; he was already standing, having ordered his desk and chair removed to make more room, though he had kept back his inkstand and pen with several sheets of paper, now resting upon the sill of the stern windows behind him. "Gentlemen," he said, "you have all heard by now that we found a dragon egg aboard the prize; Mr. Pollitt has very firmly identified it for us."

Many smiles and some surreptitious elbowing; the little midshipman Battersea piped up in his treble voice, "Congratulations, sir!" and a quick pleased rumble went around.

Laurence frowned; he understood their high spirits, and if the circumstances had been only a little different, he would have shared them. The egg would be worth a thousand times its weight in gold, brought safely to shore; every man aboard the ship would have shared in the bounty, and as captain he himself would have taken the largest share of the value.

The *Amitié*'s logs had been thrown overboard, but her hands had been less discreet than her officers, and Wells had learned enough from their complaints to explain the delay all too clearly. Fever among the crew, becalmed in the doldrums for the better part of a month, a leak in her water tanks leaving her on short water rations, and then at last the gale that they themselves had so recently weathered. It had been a string of exceptionally bad luck, and Laurence knew the superstitious souls of his men would quail at the idea that the *Reliant* was now carrying the egg that had undoubtedly been the cause of it.

He would certainly take care to keep that information from the crew, however; better by far that they not know of the long series of disasters which the *Amitié* had suffered. So after silence fell again, all Laurence said was simply, "Unfortunately, the prize had a very bad crossing of it. She must have expected to make landfall nearly a month ago, if not more, and the delay has made the circumstances surrounding the egg urgent." There was puzzlement and incomprehension now on most faces, though looks of concern were beginning to spread, and he finished the matter off by saying, "In short, gentlemen, it is about to hatch."

Another low murmur, this time disappointed, and even a few quiet groans; ordinarily he would have marked the offenders for a mild later rebuke, but as it was, he let them by. They would soon have more cause to groan. So far they had not yet understood what it meant; they merely made the mental reduction of the bounty on an unhatched egg to that paid for a feral dragonet, much less valuable.

"Perhaps not all of you are aware," he said, silencing the whispers with a look, "that England is in a very dire situation as regards the Aerial Corps. Naturally, our handling is superior, and the Corps can outfly any other nation of the world, but the French can outbreed us two to one, and it is impossible to deny that they have better variety in their bloodlines. A properly harnessed dragon is worth at least a first-rate of one hundred guns to us, even a common Yellow Reaper or a three-ton Winchester, and Mr. Pollitt believes from the size and color of the egg that this hatchling is a prime specimen, and very likely one of the rare large breeds."

"Oh!" said Midshipman Carver, in tones of horror, as he took Laurence's meaning; he instantly went crimson as eyes went to him, and shut his mouth tight.

Laurence ignored the interruption; Riley would see Carver's grog stopped for a week without having to be told. The exclamation had at least prepared the others. "We must at least make the attempt to harness the beast," he said. "I trust, gentlemen, that there is no man here who is not prepared to do his duty for England. The Corps may not be the sort of life that any of us has been raised to, but the Navy is no sinecure either, and there is not one of you who does not understand a hard service."

"Sir," said Lieutenant Fanshawe anxiously: he was a young man of very good family, the son of an earl. "Do you mean—that is, shall we all—"

There was an emphasis on that *all* which made it obviously a selfish suggestion, and Laurence felt himself go near purple with anger. He snapped, "We all shall, indeed, Mr. Fanshawe, unless there is any man here who is too much of a coward to make the attempt, and in that case that gentleman may explain himself to a court-martial when we put in at Madeira." He sent an angry glare around the room, and no one else met his eye or offered a protest.

He was all the more infuriated for understanding the sentiment, and for sharing it himself. Certainly no man not raised to the life could be easy at the prospect of suddenly becoming an aviator, and he loathed the necessity of asking his officers to face it. It meant, after all, an end to any semblance of ordinary life. It was not like sailing, where you might hand your ship back to the Navy and be set ashore, often whether you liked it or not.

Even in times of peace, a dragon could not be put into dock, nor allowed to wander loose, and to keep a full-grown beast of twenty tons from doing exactly as it pleased took very nearly the full attention of an aviator and a crew of assistants besides. They could not really be managed by force, and were finicky about their handlers; some would not accept management at all, even when new-hatched, and none would accept it after their first feeding. A feral dragon could be kept in the breeding grounds by the constant provision of food, mates, and comfortable shelter, but it could not be controlled outside, and it would not speak with men.

So if a hatchling let you put it into harness, duty forever after tied you to the beast. An aviator could not easily manage any sort of estate, nor raise a family, nor go into society to any real extent. They lived as men apart, and largely outside the law, for you could not punish an aviator without losing the use of his dragon. In peacetime they lived in a sort of wild, outrageous libertinage in small enclaves, generally in the most remote and inhospitable places in all Britain, where the dragons could be given at least some freedom. Though the men of the Corps were honored without question for their courage and devotion to duty, the prospect of entering their ranks could not be appealing to any gentleman raised up in respectable society.

Yet they sprang from good families, gentlemen's sons handed over at the age of seven to be raised to the life, and it would be an impossible insult to the Corps to have anyone other than one of his own officers attempt the harnessing. And if one had to be asked to take the risk, then all; though if Fanshawe had not spoken in so unbecoming a way, Laurence would have liked to keep Carver out of it, as he knew the boy had a poor head for heights, which struck him as a grave impediment for an aviator. But in the atmosphere created by the pitiful request, it would seem like favoritism, and that would not do.

He took a deep breath, still simmering with anger, and spoke again. "No man here has any training for the task, and the only fair means of assigning the duty is by lot. Naturally, those gentlemen with family are excused. Mr. Pollitt," he said, turning to the surgeon, who had a wife and four children in Derbyshire, "I hope that you will draw the name for us. Gentlemen, you will each write your name upon a sheet here, and cast it into this bag." He suited word to deed, tore off the part of the sheet with his own name, folded it, and put it into the small sack.

Riley stepped forward at once, and the others followed suit obediently; under Laurence's cold eye, Fanshawe flushed and wrote his name with a shaking hand. Carver, on the other hand, wrote bravely, though with a pale cheek; and at the last Battersea, unlike virtually all the others, was incautious in tearing the sheet, so that his piece was unusually large; he could be heard murmuring quietly to Carver, "Would it not be famous to ride a dragon?"

Laurence shook his head a little at the thoughtlessness of youth; yet it might indeed be better were one of the younger men chosen, for the adjustment would be easier. Still, it would be hard to see one of the boys sacrificed to the task, and to face the outrage of his family. But the same would be true of any man here, including himself.

Though he had done his best not to consider the consequences from a selfish perspective, now that the fatal moment was at hand he could not entirely suppress his own private fears. One small bit of paper might mean the wreck of his career, the upheaval of his life, disgrace in his father's eyes. And, too, there was Edith Galman to think of; but if he were to begin excusing his men for some half-formed attachment, not binding, none of them would be left. In any case, he could not imagine excusing himself from this selection for any reason: this was not something he could ask his men to face, and avoid himself.

He handed the bag to Mr. Pollitt and made an effort to stand at his ease and appear unconcerned, clasping his hands loosely behind his back. The surgeon shook the sack in his hand twice, thrust his hand in without looking, and drew out a small folded sheet. Laurence was ashamed to feel a sensation of profound relief even before the name was read: the sheet was folded over once more than his own entry had been.

The emotion lasted only a moment. "Jonathan Carver," Pollitt said. Fanshawe could be heard letting out an explosive breath, Battersea sighing, and Laurence bowed his head, silently cursing Fanshawe yet again; so promising a young officer, and so likely to be useless in the Corps.

"Well; there we have it," he said; there was nothing else to be done. "Mr. Carver, you are relieved of regular duty until the hatching; you will instead consult with Mr. Pollitt on the process to follow for the harnessing."

"Yes, sir," the boy responded, a little faintly.

"Dismissed, gentlemen; Mr. Fanshawe, a word with you. Mr. Riley, you have the deck."

Riley touched his hat, and the others filed out behind him. Fanshawe stood rigid and pale, hands clasped behind his back, and swallowed; his Adam's apple was prominent and bobbed visibly. Laurence made him wait sweating until his steward had restored the cabin furniture, and then seated himself and glared at him from this position of state, enthroned before the stern windows.

"Now then, I should like you to explain precisely what you meant by that remark earlier, Mr. Fanshawe," he said.

"Oh, sir, I didn't mean anything," Fanshawe said. "It is only what they say about aviators, sir—" He stumbled to a stop under the increasingly militant gleam in Laurence's eye.

"I do not give a damn what they say, Mr. Fanshawe," he said icily. "England's aviators are her shield from the air, as the Navy is by sea, and when you have done half as much as the least of them, you may offer criticism. You will stand Mr. Carver's watch and do his work as well as your own, and your grog is stopped until further notice: inform the quartermaster. Dismissed."

But despite his words, he paced the cabin after Fanshawe had gone. He had been severe, and rightly so, for it was very unbecoming in the fellow to speak in such a way, and even more to hint that he might be excused for his birth. But it was certainly a sacrifice, and his conscience smote him painfully when he thought of the look on Carver's face. His own continued feelings of relief reproached him; he was condemning the boy to a fate he had not wanted to face himself.

He tried to comfort himself with the notion that there was every chance the dragon would turn its nose up at Carver, untrained as he was, and refuse the harness. Then no possible reproach could be made, and he could deliver it for the bounty with an easy conscience. Even if it could only be used for breeding, the dragon would still do England a great deal of good, and taking it away from the French was a victory all on its own; personally he would be more than content with that as a resolution, though as a matter of duty he meant to do everything in his power to make the other occur.

The next week passed uncomfortably. It was impossible not to perceive Carver's anxiety, especially as the week wore on and the armorer's attempt at the harness began to take on a recognizable shape, or the unhappiness of his friends and the men of his gun-crew, for he was a popular fellow, and his difficulty with heights was no great secret.

Mr. Pollitt was the only one in good humor, being not very well informed as to the state of the emotions on the ship, and very interested in the harnessing process. He spent a great deal of time inspecting the egg, going so far as to sleep and eat beside the crate in the gunroom, much to the distress of the officers who slept there: his snores were penetrating, and their berth was already crowded. Pollitt was entirely unconscious of their silent disapproval, and he kept his vigil until the morning when, with a wretched lack of sympathy, he cheerfully announced that the first cracks had begun to show.

Laurence at once ordered the egg uncrated and brought up on deck. A special cushion had been made for it, out of old sailcloth stuffed with straw; this was placed on a couple of lockers lashed together, and the egg gingerly laid upon it. Mr. Rabson, the armorer, brought up the harness: it was a makeshift affair of leather straps held by dozens of buckles, as he had not known enough about the proportions of dragons to make it exact. He stood waiting with it, off to the side, while Carver positioned himself before the egg. Laurence ordered the hands to clear the space around the egg to leave more room; most of them chose to climb into the rigging or onto the roof of the roundhouse, the better to see the process.

It was a brilliantly sunny day, and perhaps the warmth and light were encouraging to the long-confined hatchling; the egg began to crack more seriously almost as soon as it was laid out. There was a great deal of fidgeting and noisy whispering up above, which Laurence chose to ignore, and a few gasps when the first glimpse of movement could be seen inside: a clawed wing tip poking out, talons scrabbling out of a different crack.

The end came abruptly: the shell broke almost straight down the middle and the two halves were flung apart onto the deck, as if by the occupant's impatience. The dragonet was left amid bits and pieces, shaking itself out vigorously on the pillow. It was still covered with the slime of the interior, and shone wet and glossy under the sun; its body was a pure, untinted black from nose to tail, and a sigh of wonder ran throughout the crew as it unfurled its large, six-spined wings like a lady's fan, the bottom edge dappled with oval markings in grey and dark glowing blue.

Laurence himself was impressed; he had never seen a hatchling before, though he had been at several fleet actions and witnessed the grown dragons of the Corps striking in support. He did not have the knowledge to identify the breed, but it was certainly an exceedingly rare one: he did not recall ever seeing a black dragon on either side, and it seemed quite large, for a fresh-hatched creature. That only made the matter more urgent. "Mr. Carver, when you are ready," he said.

Carver, very pale, stepped towards the creature, holding out his hand, which trembled visibly. "Good dragon," he said; the words sounded rather like a question. "Nice dragon."

The dragonet paid him no attention whatsoever. It was occupied in examining itself and picking off bits of shell that had adhered to its hide, in a fastidious sort of way. Though it was barely the size of a large dog, the five talons upon each claw were still an inch long and impressive; Carver looked at them anxiously and stopped an arm's length away. Here he stood waiting dumbly; the dragon continued to ignore him, and presently he cast an anxious look of appeal over his shoulder at where Laurence stood with Mr. Pollitt.

"Perhaps if he were to speak to it again," Mr. Pollitt said dubiously.

"Pray do so, Mr. Carver," Laurence said.

The boy nodded, but even as he turned back, the dragonet forestalled him by climbing down from its cushion and leaping onto the deck past him. Carver turned around with hand still outstretched and an almost comical look of surprise, and the other officers, who had drawn closer in the excitement of the hatching, backed away in alarm.

"Hold your positions," Laurence snapped. "Mr. Riley, look to the hold." Riley nodded and took up position in front of the opening, to prevent the dragonet's going down below.

But the dragonet instead turned to exploring the deck; it flicked out a long, narrow forked tongue as it walked, lightly touching everything in its reach, and looked about itself with every evidence of curiosity and intelligence. Yet it continued to ignore Carver, despite the boy's repeated attempts to catch its attention, and seemed equally uninterested in the other officers. Though it did occasionally rear up onto its hind legs to peer at a face more closely, it did as much to examine a pulley, or the hanging hourglass, at which it batted curiously.

Laurence felt his heart sinking; no one could blame him, precisely, if the dragonet did not show any inclination for an untrained sea-officer, but to have a truly rare dragonet caught in the shell go feral would certainly feel like a blow. They had arranged the matter from common knowledge, bits and pieces out of Pollitt's books, and from Pollitt's own imperfect recollection of a hatching which he had once observed; now Laurence feared there was some essential step they had missed. It had certainly seemed strange to him when he learned that the dragonet should be able to begin talking at once, freshly hatched. They had not found anything in the texts describing any specific invitation or trick to induce the dragonet to speak, but he should certainly be blamed, and blame himself, if it turned out there had been something omitted.

A low buzz of conversation was spreading as the officers and hands felt the moment passing. Soon he would have to give it up and take thought to confining the beast, to keep it from flying off after they fed it. Still exploring, the dragon came past him; it sat up on its haunches to look at him inquisitively, and Laurence gazed down at it in unconcealed sorrow and dismay.

It blinked at him; he noticed its eyes were a deep blue and slit-pupiled, and then it said, "Why are you frowning?"

Silence fell at once, and it was only with difficulty that Laurence kept from gaping at the creature. Carver, who must have been thinking himself reprieved by now, was standing behind the dragon, mouth open; his eyes met Laurence's with a desperate look, but he drew up his courage and stepped forward, ready to address the dragon once more.

Laurence stared at the dragon, at the pale, frightened boy, and then took a deep breath and said to the creature, "I beg your pardon, I did not mean to. My name is Will Laurence; and yours?"

No discipline could have prevented the murmur of shock which went around the deck. The dragonet did not seem to notice, but puzzled at the question for several moments, and finally said, with a dissatisfied air, "I do not have a name."

Laurence had read over Pollitt's books enough to know how he should answer; he asked, formally, "May I give you one?"

It—or rather he, for the voice was definitely masculine—looked him over again, paused to scratch at an apparently flawless spot on his back, then said with unconvincing indifference, "If you please."

And now Laurence found himself completely blank.

He had not given any real thought to the process of harnessing at all, beyond doing his best to see that it occurred, and he had no idea what an appropriate name might be for a dragon. After an awful moment of panic, his mind somehow linked dragon and ship, and he blurted out, "Temeraire," thinking of the noble dreadnought which he had seen launched, many years before: that same elegant gliding motion.

He cursed himself silently for having nothing thought out, but it had been said, and at least it was an honorable name; after all, he was a Navy man, and it was only appropriate— But he paused here in his own thoughts, and stared at the dragonet in mounting horror: of course he was not a Navy man anymore; he could not be, with a dragon, and the moment it accepted the harness from his hands, he would be undone.

The dragon, evidently perceiving nothing of his feelings, said, "Temeraire? Yes. My name is Temeraire." He nodded, an odd gesture with the head bobbing at the end of the long neck, and said more urgently, "I am hungry."

A newly hatched dragon would fly away immediately after being fed, if not restrained; only if the creature might be persuaded to accept the restraint willingly would he ever be controllable, or useful in battle. Rabson was standing by gaping and appalled, and had not come forward with the harness; Laurence had to beckon him over. His palms were sweating, and the metal and leather felt slippery as the man put the harness into his hands. He gripped it tightly and said, remembering at the last moment to use the new name, "Temeraire, would you be so good as to let me put this on you? Then we can make you fast to the deck here, and bring you something to eat."

Temeraire inspected the harness which Laurence held out to him, his flat tongue slipping out to taste it. "Very well," he said, and stood expectantly. Resolutely not thinking beyond the immediate task, Laurence knelt and fumbled with the straps and buckles, carefully passing them about the smooth, warm body, keeping well clear of the wings.

The broadest band went around the dragon's middle, just behind the forelegs, and buckled under the belly; this was stitched crosswise to two thick straps which ran along the dragon's sides and across the deep barrel of his chest, then back behind the rear legs and underneath his tail. Various smaller loops had been threaded upon the straps, to buckle around the legs and the base of the neck and tail, to keep the harness in place, and several narrower and thinner bands strapped across his back.

The complicated assemblage required some attention, for which Laurence was grateful; he was able to lose himself in the task. He noted as he worked that the scales were surprisingly soft to the touch, and it occurred to him that the metal edges might bruise. "Mr. Rabson, be so good as to bring me some extra sailcloth; we shall wrap these buckles," he said over his shoulder.

Shortly it was all done, although the harness and the white-wrapped buckles were ugly against the sleek black body, and did not fit very well. But Temeraire made no complaint, nor about having a chain made fast from the harness to a stanchion, and he stretched his neck out eagerly to the tub full of steaming red meat from the fresh-butchered goat, brought out at Laurence's command.

Temeraire was not a clean eater, tearing off large chunks of meat and gulping them down whole, scattering blood and bits of flesh across the deck; he also seemed to enjoy the intestines in particular. Laurence stood well clear of the carnage and, having observed in faintly queasy wonder for a few moments, was abruptly recalled to the situation by Riley's uncertain, "Sir, shall I dismiss the officers?"

He turned and looked at his lieutenant, then at the staring, dismayed midshipmen; no one had spoken or moved since the hatching, which, he realized abruptly, had been less than half an hour ago; the hourglass was just emptying now. It was difficult to believe; still more difficult to fully acknowledge that he was now in harness, but difficult or not, it had to be faced. Laurence supposed he could cling to his rank until they reached shore; there were no regulations for a situation such as this one. But if he did, a new captain would certainly be put into his place when they reached Madeira, and Riley would never get his step up. Laurence would never again be in a position to do him any good.

"Mr. Riley, the circumstances are awkward, there is no doubt," he said, steeling himself; he was not going to ruin Riley's career for a cowardly avoidance. "But I think for the sake of the ship, I must put her in your hands at once; I will need to devote a great deal of my attention to Temeraire now, and I cannot divide it so."

"Oh, sir!" Riley said, miserably, but not protesting; evidently the idea had occurred to him as well. But his regret was obviously sincere; he had sailed with Laurence for years, and had come up to lieutenant in his service from a mere midshipman; they were friends as well as comrades.

"Let us not be complainers, Tom," Laurence said more quietly and less formally, giving a warning glance to where Temeraire was still glutting himself. Dragon intelligence was a mystery to men who made a study of the subject; he had no idea how much the dragon would hear or understand, but thought it better to avoid the risk of giving offense. Raising his voice a little more, he added, "I am sure you will manage her admirably, Captain."

Taking a deep breath, he removed his gold epaulettes; they were pinned on securely, but he had not been wealthy when he had first made captain, and he had not forgotten, from those days, how to shift them easily from one coat to another. Though perhaps it was not entirely proper to give Riley the symbol of rank without confirmation by the Admiralty, Laurence felt it necessary to mark the change of command in some visible manner. The left he slipped into his pocket, the right he fixed on Riley's shoulder: even as a captain, Riley could wear only one until he had three years' seniority. Riley's fair, freckled skin showed every emotion plainly, and he could hardly fail to be happy at this unexpected promotion despite the circumstances; he flushed up with color, and looked as though he wished to speak but could not find the words.

"Mr. Wells," Laurence said, hinting; he meant to do it properly, having begun.

The third lieutenant started, then said a little weakly, "Huzzah for Captain Riley." A cheer went up, ragged initially, but strong and clear by the third repetition: Riley was a highly competent officer, and well liked, even if it was a shocking situation.

When the cheering had died down, Riley, having mastered his embarrassment, added, "And huzzah for—for Temeraire, lads." The cheering now was full-throated, if not entirely joyful, and Laurence shook Riley's hand to conclude the matter.

Temeraire had finished eating by this point, and had climbed up onto a locker by the railing to spread his wings in the sun, folding them in and out. But he looked around with interest at hearing his name cheered, and Laurence went to his side; it was a good excuse to leave Riley to the business of establishing his command, and putting the ship back to rights. "Why are they making that noise?" Temeraire asked, but without waiting for an answer, he rattled the chain. "Will you take this off? I would like to go flying now."

Laurence hesitated; the description of the harnessing ceremony in Mr. Pollitt's book had provided no further instructions beyond getting the dragon into harness and talking; he had somehow assumed that the dragon would simply stay where it was without further argument. "If you do not mind, perhaps let us leave it awhile longer," he said, temporizing. "We are rather far from land, you see, and if you were to fly off, you might not find your way back."

"Oh," said Temeraire, craning his long neck over the railing; the *Reliant* was making somewhereabouts eight knots in a fine westerly wind, and the water churned away in a white froth from her sides. "Where are we?"

"We are at sea." Laurence settled down beside him on the locker. "In the Atlantic, perhaps two weeks from shore. Masterson," he added, catching the attention of one of the idle hands who were not-very-subtly hanging about to gawk. "Be so good as to fetch me a bucket of water and some rags, if you please."

These being brought, he endeavored to clean away the traces of the messy meal from the glossy black hide; Temeraire submitted with evident pleasure to being wiped down, and afterwards appreciatively rubbed the side of his head against Laurence's hand. Laurence found himself smiling involuntarily and stroking the warm black hide, and Temeraire settled down, tucked his head into Laurence's lap, and went to sleep.

"Sir," Riley said, coming up quietly, "I will leave you the cabin; it would scarcely make sense otherwise, with him," meaning Temeraire. "Shall I have someone help you carry him below now?"

"Thank you, Tom; and no, I am comfortable enough here for the moment; best not to stir him unless necessary, I should think," Laurence said, then belatedly thought that it might not make it easier on Riley, having his former captain sitting on deck. Still, he was not inclined to shift the sleeping dragonet, and added only, "If you would be so kind as to have someone bring me a book, perhaps one of Mr. Pollitt's, I should be much obliged," thinking this would both serve to occupy him, and keep him from seeming too much an observer.

Temeraire did not wake until the sun was slipping below the horizon; Laurence was nodding over his book, which described dragon habits in such a way as to make them seem as exciting as plodding cows. Temeraire nudged his cheek with a blunt nose to rouse him, and announced, "I am hungry again."

Laurence had already begun reassessing the ship's supply before the hatching; now he had to revise once again as he watched Temeraire devour the remainder of the goat and two hastily sacrificed chickens, bones and all. So far, in two feedings, the dragonet had consumed his body's weight in food; he appeared already somewhat larger, and he was looking about for more with a wistful air.

Laurence had a quiet and anxious consultation with Riley and the ship's cook. If necessary, they could hail the *Amitié* and draw upon her stores: because her complement had been so badly reduced by her series of disasters, her supplies of food were more than she would need to make Madeira. However, she had been down to salt pork and salt beef, and the *Reliant* was scarcely better off. At this rate, Temeraire should eat up the fresh supplies within a week, and Laurence had no idea if a dragon would eat cured meat, or if the salt would perhaps not be good for it.

"Would he take fish?" the cook suggested. "I have a lovely little tunny, caught fresh this morning, sir; I meant it for your dinner. Oh—that is—" He paused, awkwardly, looking back and forth between his former captain and his new.

"By all means let us make the attempt, if you think it

right, sir," Riley said, looking at Laurence and ignoring the cook's confusion.

"Thank you, Captain," Laurence said. "We may as well offer it to him; I suppose he can tell us if he does not care for it."

Temeraire looked at the fish dubiously, then nibbled; shortly the entire thing from head to tail had vanished down his throat: it had been a full twelve pounds. He licked his chops and said, "It is very crunchy, but I like it well enough," then startled them and himself by belching loudly.

"Well," Laurence said, reaching for the cleaning rag again, "that is certainly encouraging; Captain, if you could see your way to putting a few men on fishing duty, perhaps we may preserve the ox for a few days more."

He took Temeraire down to the cabin afterwards; the ladder presented a bit of a problem, and in the end the dragon had to be swung down by an arrangement of pulleys attached to his harness. Temeraire nosed around the desk and chair inquisitively, and poked his head out of the windows to look at the *Reliant*'s wake. The pillow from the hatching had been placed into a double-wide hanging cot for him, slung next to Laurence's own, and he leapt easily into it from the ground.

His eyes almost immediately closed to drowsy slits. Thus relieved of duty and no longer under the eyes of the crew, Laurence sat down with a thump in his chair and stared at the sleeping dragon, as at an instrument of doom.

He had two brothers and three nephews standing between himself and his father's estate, and his own capital was invested in the Funds, requiring no great management on his part; that at least would not be a matter of difficulty. He had gone over the rails a score of times in battle, and he could stand in the tops in a gale without a bit of queasiness: he did not fear he would prove shy aboard a dragon.

But for the rest—he was a gentleman and a gentleman's son. Though he had gone to sea at the age of twelve, he had been fortunate enough to serve aboard first- or second-rate ships-of-the-line for the most part of his service, under wealthy captains who kept fine tables and entertained their officers regularly. He dearly loved society; conversation, dancing, and friendly whist were his favorite pursuits; and when he thought that he might never go to the opera again, he felt a very palpable urge to tip the laden cot out the windows.

He tried not to hear his father's voice in his head, condemning him for a fool; tried not to imagine what Edith would think when she heard of it. He could not even write to let her know. Although he had to some extent considered himself committed, no formal engagement had ever been entered upon, due first to his lack of capital and more recently to his long absence from England.

He had done sufficiently well in the way of prize-money to do away with the first problem, and if he had been set ashore for any length of time in the last four years, he most likely would have spoken. He had been half in mind to request a brief leave for England at the end of this cruise; it was hard to deliberately put himself ashore when he could not rely upon getting another ship afterwards, but he was not so eligible a prospect that he imagined she would wait for him over all other suitors on the strength of a half-joking agreement between a thirteen-year-old boy and a nine-year-old girl.

Now he was a poorer prospect indeed; he had not the slightest notion how and where he might live as an aviator, or what sort of a home he could offer a wife. Her family might object, even if she herself did not; certainly it was nothing she had been led to expect. A Navy wife might have to face with equanimity her husband's frequent absences, but when he appeared she did not have to uproot herself and go live in some remote covert, with a dragon outside the door and a crowd of rough men the only society.

He had always entertained a certain private longing for a home of his own, imagined in detail through the long, lonely nights at sea: smaller by necessity than the one in which he had been raised, yet still elegant; kept by a wife whom he could trust with the management of their affairs and their children both; a comfortable refuge when he was at home, and a warm memory while at sea.

Every feeling protested against the sacrifice of this dream; yet under the circumstances, he was not even sure he could honorably make Edith an offer which she might feel obliged to accept. And there was no question of courting someone else in her place; no woman of sense and character would deliberately engage her affections on an aviator, unless she was of the sort who preferred to have a complacent and absent husband leaving his purse in her hands, and to live apart from him even while he was in England; such an arrangement did not appeal to Laurence in the slightest.

The sleeping dragon, swaying back and forth in his cot, tail twitching unconsciously in time with some alien dream, was a very poor substitute for hearth and home. Laurence stood and went to the stern windows, looking over the *Reliant*'s wake, a pale and opalescent froth streaming out behind her in the light from the lanterns; the ebb and flow was pleasantly numbing to watch.

His steward Giles brought in his dinner with a great clatter of plate and silver, keeping well back from the dragon's cot. His hands trembled as he laid out the service; Laurence dismissed him once the meal was served and sighed a little when he had gone; he had thought of asking Giles to come along with him, as he supposed even an aviator might have a servant, but there was no use if the man was spooked by the creatures. It would have been something to have a familiar face.

In solitude, he ate his simple dinner quickly; it was only salt beef with a little glazing of wine, as the fish had gone into Temeraire's belly, and he had little appetite in any case. He tried to write some letters, afterwards, but it was no use; his mind would wander back into gloomy paths, and he had to force his attention to every line. At last he gave it up, looked out briefly to tell Giles he would take no supper this evening, and climbed into his own cot. Temeraire shifted and snuggled deeper within the bedding; after a brief struggle with uncharitable resentment, Laurence reached out and covered him more securely, the night air being somewhat cool, and then fell asleep to the sound of the dragon's regular deep breathing, like the heaving of a bellows.

Chapter 2

THE NEXT MORNING, Laurence woke when Temeraire proceeded to envelop himself in his cot, which turned round twice as he tried to climb down. Laurence had to unhook it to disentangle him, and he burst out of the unwound fabric in hissing indignation. He had to be groomed and petted back into temper, like an affronted cat, and then he was at once hungry again.

Fortunately, it was not very early, and the hands had met with some luck fishing, so there were still eggs for his own breakfast, the hens being spared another day, and a forty-pound tunny for the dragon's. Temeraire somehow managed to devour the entire thing and then was too heavy to get back into his cot, so he simply dropped in a distended heap upon the floor and slept there.

The rest of the first week passed similarly: Temeraire was asleep except when he was eating, and he ate and grew alarmingly. By the end of it, he was no longer staying below, because Laurence had grown to fear that it would become impossible to get him out of the ship: he had already grown heavier than a cart-horse, and longer from tip to tail than the launch. After consideration of his future growth, they decided to shift stores to leave the ship heavier forward and place him upon the deck towards the stern as a counterbalance.

The change was made just in time: Temeraire only barely managed to squeeze back out of the cabin with his wings furled tightly, and he grew another foot in diameter overnight by Mr. Pollitt's measurements. Fortunately, when he lay astern his bulk was not greatly in the way, and there he slept for the better part of each day, tail twitching occasionally, hardly stirring even when the hands were forced to clamber over him to do their work.

At night, Laurence slept on deck beside him, feeling it his place; as the weather held fair, it cost him no great pains. He was increasingly worried about food; the ox would have to be slaughtered in a day or so, with all the fishing they could do. At this rate of increase in his appetite, even if Temeraire proved willing to accept cured meat, he might exhaust their supplies before they reached shore. It would be very difficult, he felt, to put a dragon on short commons, and in any case it would put the crew on edge; though Temeraire was harnessed and might be in theory tame, even in these days a feral dragon, escaped from the breeding grounds, could and occasionally would eat a man if nothing more appetizing offered; and from the uneasy looks no one had forgotten it.

When the first change in the air came, midway through the second week, Laurence felt the alteration unconsciously and woke near dawn, some hours before the rain began to fall. The lights of the *Amitié* were nowhere to be seen: the ships had drawn apart during the night, under the increasing wind. The sky grew only a little lighter, and presently the first thick drops began to patter against the sails.

Laurence knew that he could do nothing; Riley must command now, if ever, and so Laurence set himself to keeping Temeraire quiet and no distraction to the men. This proved difficult, for the dragon was very curious about the rain, and kept spreading his wings to feel the water beating upon them.

Thunder did not frighten him, nor lightning; "What makes it?" he only asked, and was disappointed when Laurence could offer him no answer. "We could go and see," he suggested, partly unfolding his wings again, and taking a step towards the stern railing. Laurence started with alarm; Temeraire had made no further attempts to fly since the first day, being more preoccupied with eating, and though they had enlarged the harness three times, they had never exchanged the chain for a heavier one. Now he could see the iron links straining and beginning to come open, though Temeraire was barely exerting any pull upon it.

"Not now, Temeraire, we must let the others work, and watch from here," he said, gripping the nearest side-strap of the harness and thrusting his left arm through it; though he realized now, too late, that his weight would no longer be an impediment, at least if they went aloft together, he might be able to persuade the dragon to come back down eventually. Or he might fall; but that thought he pushed from his mind as quickly as it came.

Thankfully, Temeraire settled again, if regretfully, and returned to watching the sky. Laurence looked about with a faint idea of calling for a stronger chain, but the crew were all occupied, and he could not interrupt. In any case, he wondered if there were any on board that would serve as more than an annoyance; he was abruptly aware that Temeraire's shoulder topped his head by nearly a foot, and that the foreleg which had once been as delicate as a lady's wrist was now thicker around than his thigh.

Riley was shouting through the speaking-trumpet to issue his orders. Laurence did his best not to listen; he could not intervene, and it could only be unpleasant to hear an order he did not like. The men had already been through one nasty gale as a crew and knew their work; fortunately the wind was not contrary, so they might go scudding before the gale, and the topgallant masts had already been struck down properly. So far all was well, and they were keeping roughly on their eastern heading, but behind them an opaque curtain of whirling rain blotted out the world, and it was outpacing the *Reliant*.

The wall of water crashed upon the deck with the sound of gunfire, soaking him through to the skin immediately despite his oilskin and sou'wester. Temeraire snorted and shook his head like a dog, sending water flying, and ducked down beneath his own hastily opened wings, which he curled about himself. Laurence, still tucked up against his side and holding to the harness, found himself also sheltered by the living dome. It was exceedingly strange to be so snug in the heart of a raging storm; he could still see out through the places where the wings did not overlap, and a cool spray came in upon his face.

"That man who brought me the shark is in the water," Temeraire said presently, and Laurence followed his line of sight; through the nearly solid mass of rain he could see a blur of red-and-white shirt some six points abaft the larboard beam, and something like an arm waving: Gordon, one of the hands who had been helping with the fishing.

"Man overboard," he shouted, cupping his hands around his mouth to make it carry, and pointed out to the struggling figure in the waves. Riley gave one anguished look; a few ropes were thrown, but already the man was too far back; the storm was blowing them before it, and there was no chance of retrieving him with the boats.

"He is too far from those ropes," Temeraire said. "I will go and get him."

Laurence was in the air and dangling before he could object, the broken chain swinging free from Temeraire's neck beside him. He seized it with his loose arm as it came close and wrapped it around the straps of the harness a few times to keep it from flailing and striking Temeraire's side like a whip; then he clung grimly and tried only to keep his head, while his legs hung out over empty air with nothing but the ocean waiting below to receive him if he should lose his grip.

Instinct had sufficed to get them aloft, but it might not be adequate to keep them there; Temeraire was being forced to the east of the ship. He kept trying to fight the wind head-on; there was a hideous dizzying moment where they went tumbling before a sharp gust, and Laurence thought for an instant that they were lost and would be dashed into the waves.

"With the wind," he roared with every ounce of breath developed over eighteen years at sea, hoping Temeraire could hear him. "Go with the wind, damn you!"

The muscles beneath his cheek strained, and Temeraire righted himself, turning eastwards. Abruptly the rain stopped beating upon Laurence's face: they were flying with the wind, going at an enormous rate. He gasped for breath, tears whipping away from his eyes with the speed; he had to close them. It was as far beyond standing in the tops at ten knots as that experience was beyond standing in a field on a hot, still day. There was a reckless laughter trying to bubble out of his throat, like a boy's, and he only barely managed to stifle it and think sanely.

"We cannot come straight at him," he called. "You must tack—you must go to north, then south, Temeraire, do you understand?"

If the dragon answered, the wind took the reply, but he seemed to have grasped the idea. He dropped abruptly, angling northwards with his wings cupping the wind; Laurence's stomach dived as on a rowboat in a heavy swell. The rain and wind still battered them, but not so badly as before, and Temeraire came about and changed tacks as sweetly as a fine cutter, zigzagging through the air and making gradual progress back in a westerly direction.

Laurence's arms were burning; he thrust his left arm through the breast-band against losing his grip, and unwound his right hand to give it a respite. As they drew even with and then passed the ship, he could just see Gordon still struggling in the distance; fortunately the man could swim a little, and despite the fury of the rain and wind, the swell was not so great as to drag him under. Laurence looked at Temeraire's claws dubiously; with the enormous talons, if the dragon were to snatch Gordon up, the maneuver might as easily kill the man as save him. Laurence would have to put himself into position to catch Gordon.

"Temeraire, I will pick him up; wait until I am ready, then go as low as you can," he called; then he lowered himself down the harness slowly and carefully to hang down from the belly, keeping one arm hooked through a strap at every stage. It was a terrifying progress, but once he was below, matters became easier, as Temeraire's body shielded him from the rain and wind. He pulled on the broad strap which ran around Temeraire's middle; there was perhaps just enough give. One at a time he worked his legs between the leather and Temeraire's belly, so he might have both his hands free, then slapped the dragon's side.

Temeraire stooped abruptly, like a diving hawk. Laurence let himself dangle down, trusting to the dragon's aim, and his fingers made furrows in the surface of the water for a couple of yards before they hit sodden cloth and flesh. He blindly clutched at the feel, and Gordon grabbed at him in turn. Temeraire was lifting back up and away, wings beating furiously, but thankfully they could now go with the wind instead of fighting it. Gordon's weight dragged on Laurence's arms, shoulders, thighs, every muscle straining; the band was so tight upon his calves that he could no longer feel his legs below the knee, and he had the uncomfortable sensation of all the blood in his body rushing straight into his head. They swung heavily back and forth like a pendulum as Temeraire arrowed back towards the ship, and the world tilted crazily around him.

They dropped onto the deck ungracefully, rocking the ship. Temeraire stood wavering on his hind legs, trying at the same time to fold his wings out of the wind and keep his balance with the two of them dragging him downwards from the belly-strap. Gordon let go and scrambled away in panic, leaving Laurence to extract himself while Temeraire seemed about to fall over upon him at any moment. His stiff fingers refused to work on the buckles, and abruptly Wells was there with a knife flashing, cutting through the strap.

His legs thumped heavily to the deck, blood rushing back into them; Temeraire similarly dropped down to all fours again beside him, the impact sending a tremor through the deck. Laurence lay flat on his back and panted, for the moment not caring that rain was beating full upon him; his muscles would obey no command. Wells hesitated; Laurence waved him back to his work and struggled back onto his legs; they held him up, and the pain of the returning sensation eased as he forced them to move.

The gale was still blowing around them, but the ship was now set to rights, scudding before the wind under close-reefed topsails, and there was less of a feel of crisis upon the deck. Turning away from Riley's handiwork with a sense of mingled pride and regret, Laurence coaxed Temeraire to shift back towards the center of the stern where his weight would not unbalance the ship. It was barely in time; as soon as Temeraire settled down once again, he yawned enormously and tucked his head down beneath his wing, ready to sleep for once without making his usual demand for food. Laurence slowly lowered himself to the deck and leaned against the dragon's side; his body still ached profoundly from the strain.

He roused himself for only a moment longer; he felt the need to speak, though his tongue felt thick and stupid with fatigue. "Temeraire," he said, "that was well done. Very bravely done."

Temeraire brought his head out and gazed at him, eye-slits widening to ovals. "Oh," he said, sounding a little uncertain. Laurence realized with a brief stab of guilt that he had scarcely given the dragonet a kind word before this. The convulsion of his life might be the creature's fault, in some sense, but Temeraire was only obeying his nature, and to make the beast suffer for it was hardly noble.

But he was too tired at the moment to make better amends than to repeat, lamely, "Very well done," and pat the smooth black side. Yet it seemed to serve; Temeraire said nothing more, but he shifted himself a little and tentatively curled up around Laurence, partly unfurling a wing to shield him from the rain. The fury of the storm was muffled beneath the canopy, and Laurence could feel the great heartbeat against his cheek; he was warmed through in moments by the steady heat of the dragon's body, and thus sheltered he slid abruptly and completely into sleep.

* * *

"Are you quite sure it is secure?" Riley asked anxiously. "Sir, I am sure we could put together a net, perhaps you had better not."

Laurence shifted his weight and pulled against the straps wrapped snugly around his thighs and calves; they did not give, nor did the main part of the harness, and he remained stable in his perch atop Temeraire's back, just behind the wings. "No, Tom, it won't do, and you know it; this is not a fishing-boat, and you cannot spare the men. We might very well meet a Frenchman one of these days, and then where would we be?" He leaned forward and patted Temeraire's neck; the dragon's head was doubled back, observing the proceedings with interest.

"Are you ready? May we go now?" he asked, putting a forehand on the railing. Muscles were already gathering beneath the smooth hide, and there was a palpable impatience in his voice.

"Stand clear, Tom," Laurence said hastily, casting off the chain and taking hold of the neck-strap. "Very well, Temeraire, let us—" A single leap, and they were airborne, the broad wings thrusting in great sweeping arcs to either side of him, the whole long body stretched out like an arrow driving upwards into the sky. He looked downwards over Temeraire's shoulder; already the *Reliant* was shrinking to a child's toy, bobbing lonely in the vast expanse of the ocean; he could even see the *Amitié* perhaps twenty miles to the east. The wind was enormous, but the straps were holding, and he was grinning idiotically again, he realized, unable to prevent himself.

"We will keep to the west, Temeraire," Laurence called; he did not want to run the risk of getting too close to land and possibly encountering a French patrol. They had put a band around the narrow part of Temeraire's neck beneath the head and attached reins to this, so Laurence might more easily give Temeraire direction; now he consulted the compass he had strapped into his palm and tugged on the right rein. The dragon pulled out of his climb and turned willingly, leveling out. The day was clear, without clouds, and a moderate swell only; Temeraire's wings beat less rapidly now they were no longer going up, but even so the pace was devouring the miles: the *Reliant* and the *Amitié* were already out of sight.

"Oh, I see one," Temeraire said, and they were plummeting down with even more speed. Laurence gripped the reins tightly and swallowed a yell; it was absurd to feel so childishly gleeful. The distance gave him some more idea of the dragon's eyesight: it would have to be prodigious to allow him to sight prey at such a range. He had barely time for the thought, then there was a tremendous splash, and Temeraire was lifting back away with a porpoise struggling in his claws and streaming water.

Another astonishment: Temeraire stopped and hovered in place to eat, his wings beating perpendicular to his body in swiveling arcs; Laurence had had no idea that dragons could perform such a maneuver. It was not comfortable, as Temeraire's control was not very precise and he bobbed up and down wildly, but it proved very practical, for as he scattered bits of entrails onto the ocean below, other fish began to rise to the surface to feed on the discards, and when he had finished with the porpoise he at once snatched up two large tunnys, one in each forehand, and ate these as well, and then an immense swordfish also.

Having tucked his arm under the neck-strap to keep himself from being flung about, Laurence was free to look around himself and consider the sensation of being master of the entire ocean, for there was not another creature or vessel in sight. He could not help but feel pride in the success of the operation, and the thrill of flying was extraordinary: so long as he could enjoy it without thinking of all it was to cost him, he could be perfectly happy.

Temeraire swallowed the last bite of the swordfish and discarded the sharp upper jaw after inspecting it curiously. "I am full," he said, beating back upwards into the sky. "Shall we go and fly some more?"

It was a tempting suggestion; but they had been aloft more than an hour, and Laurence was not yet sure of Temeraire's endurance. He regretfully said, "Let us go back to the *Reliant*, and if you like we may fly a bit more about her."

And then racing across the ocean, low to the waves now, with Temeraire snatching at them playfully every now and again; the spray misting his face and the world rushing by in a blur, but for the constant solid presence of the dragon beneath him. He gulped deep draughts of the salt air and lost himself in simple enjoyment, only pausing every once and again to tug the reins after consulting his compass, and bringing them at last back to the *Reliant*.

Temeraire said he was ready to sleep again after all, so they made a landing; this time it was a more graceful affair, and the ship did not bounce so much as settle slightly lower in the water. Laurence unstrapped his legs and climbed down, surprised to find himself a little saddle-sore; but he at once realized that this was only to be expected. Riley was hurrying back to meet them, relief written clearly on his face, and Laurence nodded to him reassuringly.

"No need to worry; he did splendidly, and I think you need not worry about his meals in future: we will manage very well," he said, stroking the dragon's side; Temeraire, already drowsing, opened one eye and made a pleased rumbling noise, then closed it again.

"I am very glad to hear it," Riley said, "and not least because that means our dinner for you tonight will be respectable: we took the precaution of continuing our efforts in your absence, and we have a very fine turbot which we may now keep for ourselves. With your consent, perhaps I will invite some members of the gunroom to join us."

"With all my heart; I look forward to it," Laurence said, stretching to relieve the stiffness in his legs. He had insisted on surrendering the main cabin once Temeraire had been shifted to the deck; Riley had at last acquiesced, but he compensated for his guilt at displacing his former captain by inviting Laurence to dine with him virtually every night. This practice had been interrupted by the gale, but that having blown itself out the night before, they meant to resume this evening.

It was a good meal and a merry one, particularly once the bottle had gone round a few times and the younger midshipmen had drunk enough to lose their wooden manners. Laurence had the happy gift of easy conversation, and his table had always been a cheerful place for his officers; to help matters along further, he and Riley were fast approaching a true friendship now that the barrier of rank had been removed.

The gathering thus had an almost informal flavor to it, so that when Carver found himself the only one at liberty, having devoured his pudding a little more quickly than his elders, he dared to address Laurence directly, and tentatively said, "Sir, if I may be so bold as to ask, is it true that dragons can breathe fire?"

Laurence, pleasantly full of plum duff topped by several glasses of a fine Riesling, received the question tolerantly. "That depends upon the breed, Mr. Carver," he answered, putting down his glass. "However, I think the ability extremely rare. I have only ever seen it once myself: in a Turkish dragon at the battle of the Nile, and I was damned glad the Turks had taken our part when I saw it work, I can tell you."

The other officers shuddered all around and nodded; few things were as deadly to a ship as uncontrolled fire upon her deck. "I was on the *Goliath* myself," Laurence went on. "We were not half a mile distant from the *Orient* when she went up, like a torch; we had shot out her deck-guns and mostly cleared her sharpshooters from the tops, so the dragon could strafe her at will." He fell silent, remembering: the sails all ablaze and trailing thick plumes of black smoke; the great orange-and-black beast diving down and pouring still more fire from its jaws upon them, its wings fanning the flames; the terrible roaring which was only drowned out at last by the explosion, and the way all sound had been muted for nearly a day thereafter. He had been in Rome once as a boy, and there seen in the Vatican a painting of Hell by Michelangelo, with dragons roasting the damned souls with fire; it had been very like.

There was a general moment of silence, imagination drawing the scene for those who had not been present. Mr. Pollitt cleared his throat and said, "Fortunately, I believe that the ability to spit poison is more common among them, or acid; not that those are not formidable weapons in their own right."

"Lord, yes," Wells said, to this. "I have seen dragon-spray eat away an entire mainsail in under a minute. But still, it will not set fire to a magazine and make your ship burst into flinders under you."

"Will Temeraire be able to do that?" Battersea asked, a little round-eyed at these stories, and Laurence started; he was sitting at Riley's right hand, just as if he had been invited to the gunroom for dinner, and for a moment he had almost forgotten that instead he was a guest in his former cabin, and upon his former ship.

Fortunately, Mr. Pollitt answered, so Laurence could

take a moment to cover his confusion. "As his breed is not one of those described in my books, we must wait for the answer until we reach land and can have him properly identified; even if he is of the appropriate kind, most likely there would be no manifestation of such an ability until he has his full growth, which will not be for some months to come."

"Thank heavens," Riley said, to a general round of laughing agreement, and Laurence managed to smile and raise a glass in Temeraire's honor with the rest of the table.

Afterwards, having said his good nights in the cabin, Laurence walked a little unsteadily back towards the stern, where Temeraire lay in solitary splendor, the crew having mostly abandoned that part of the deck to him as he had grown. He opened a gleaming eye as Laurence approached and lifted a wing in invitation. Laurence was a little surprised at the gesture, but he took up his pallet and ducked under into the comfortable warmth. He unrolled the pallet and sat down upon it, leaning back against the dragon's side, and Temeraire lowered the wing again, making a warm sheltered space around him.

"Do you think I will be able to breathe fire or spit poison?" Temeraire asked. "I am not sure how I could tell; I tried, but I only blew air."

"Did you hear us talking?" Laurence asked, startled; the stern windows had been open, and the conversation might well have been audible on deck, but somehow it had not occurred to him that Temeraire might listen.

"Yes," Temeraire said. "The part about the battle was very exciting. Have you been in many of them?"

"Oh, I suppose so," Laurence said. "Not more than many other fellows." This was not entirely true; he had an unusually large number of actions to his credit, which had seen him to the post-list at a relatively young age, and he was accounted a fighting-captain. "But that is how we found you, when you were in the egg; you were aboard the prize when we took her," he added, indicating the *Amitié*, her stern lanterns presently visible two points to larboard.

Temeraire looked out at her with interest. "You won me in a battle? I did not know that." He sounded pleased by the information. "Will we be in another one soon? I would like to see. I am sure I could help, even if I cannot breathe fire yet."

Laurence smiled at his enthusiasm; dragons notoriously had a great deal of fighting spirit, part of what made them so valuable in war. "Most likely not before we put into port, but I dare say we will see enough of them after; England does not have many dragons, so we will most likely be called on a great deal, once you are grown," he said.

He looked up at Temeraire's head, presently raised up to gaze out to sea. Relieved of the pressing concern of feeding him, Laurence could give thought now to the other meaning of all that strength behind his back. Temeraire was already larger than some full-grown dragons of other breeds, and, in his inexperienced judgment, very fast. He would indeed be invaluable to the Corps and to England, fire-breath or no. It was not without pride that he thought to himself there was no fear Temeraire would ever prove shy; if he had a difficult duty ahead of him, he could hardly have asked for a worthier partner.

"Will you tell me some more of the battle of the Nile?" Temeraire said, looking down. "Was it just your ship and the other one, and the dragon?"

"Lord, no, there were thirteen ships-of-the-line for our side, with eight dragons from the Third Division of the Aerial Corps in support, and another four dragons from the Turks," Laurence said. "The French had seventeen and fourteen for their part, so we were outnumbered, but Admiral Nelson's strategy left them wholly taken aback," and as he continued, Temeraire lowered his head and curled more closely about him, listening with his great eyes shining in the darkness, and so they talked quietly together, long into the night.

Chapter 3

❧

THEY ARRIVED AT Funchal a day short of Laurence's original three-week estimate, having been sped along their way by the gale, with Temeraire sitting up in the stern and eagerly watching from the moment the island had come into view. He caused something of an immediate sensation on land, dragons not ordinarily to be seen riding into harbor upon small frigates, and there was a small crowd of spectators gathered upon the docks as they came into port, although by no means coming very close to the vessel.

Admiral Croft's flagship was in port; the *Reliant* was nominally sailing under his command, and Riley and Laurence had privately agreed that the two of them should report together to acquaint him with the unusual situation. The signal *Captain report aboard* flag went up on the *Commendable* almost the instant they had dropped anchor, and Laurence paused for only a moment to speak with Temeraire. "You must remain aboard until I return, remember," he said, anxiously, for while Temeraire was never willfully disobliging, he was easily distracted by anything new and of interest, and Laurence did not have a great deal of confidence in his restraint while surrounded by so much of a new world to explore. "I promise you we shall fly over the whole island when I come back; you shall see all you like, and in the meantime Mr. Wells will bring you a nice fresh veal and some lamb, which you have never had."

Temeraire sighed a little, but inclined his head. "Very well, but do hurry," he said. "I would like to go up to those mountains. And I could just eat those," he added, looking at a team of carriage horses standing nearby; the horses stamped nervously as though they had heard and understood perfectly well.

"Oh, no, Temeraire, you cannot just eat anything you see on the streets," Laurence said in alarm. "Wells will bring you something straightaway." Turning, he caught the third lieutenant's eye, and conveyed the urgency of the situation; then with a final dubious glance, he went down the gangplank and joined Riley.

Admiral Croft was waiting for them impatiently; he had evidently heard something of the fuss. He was a tall man and a striking one, the more so for a raking scar across his face and the false hand which was attached to the stump of his left arm, its iron fingers operated by springs and catches. He had lost the limb shortly before his promotion to flag rank, and since had put on a great deal of weight; he did not rise when they came into his stateroom, but only scowled a little and waved them to chairs. "Very well, Laurence, explain yourself; I suppose this has something to do with the feral you have down there?"

"Sir, that is Temeraire; he is not feral," Laurence said. "We took a French ship, the *Amitié*, three weeks ago yesterday; we found his egg in their hold. Our surgeon had some knowledge of dragonkind; he warned us that it would hatch shortly, and so we were able to arrange— that is to say, I harnessed him."

Croft sat up abruptly and squinted at Laurence, then at Riley, only then taking notice of the change in uniform. "What, yourself? And so you— Good Lord, why didn't you put one of your midshipmen to the thing?" he demanded. "This is taking duty a little far, Laurence; a fine thing when a naval officer chooses to jump ship for the Corps."

"Sir, my officers and I drew lots," Laurence said, suppressing a flare of indignation; he had not desired to be lauded for his sacrifice, but it was a little much to be upbraided for it. "I hope no one would ever question my devotion to the service; I felt it only fair to them that I should share the risk, and in the event, though I did not draw the lot, there was no avoiding it; he took a liking to me, and we could not risk him refusing the harness from another hand."

"Oh, hell," Croft said, and relapsed into his chair with a sullen expression, tapping the fingers of his right hand against the metal palm of the left, a nervous gesture, and sat silently except for the small clinking noise which his fingernails made upon the iron. The minutes dragged, while Laurence alternated between imagining a thousand disasters which Temeraire might precipitate in his absence, and worrying what Croft might do with the *Reliant* and Riley.

At last Croft started, as if waking up, and waved his good hand. "Well, there must be some sort of bounty; they can hardly give less for a harnessed creature than a feral one, after all," he said. "The French frigate, a man-of-war, I suppose, no merchantman? Well, she looks likely enough, I am sure she will be brought into the service," he added, good humor apparently restored, and Laurence realized with mingled relief and irritation that the man had only been calculating his admiral's share in his head.

"Indeed, sir, she is a very trim craft; thirty-six guns," he said politely, keeping several other things which he might have said to himself; he would never have to report to this man again, but Riley's future still hung in the balance.

"Hm. You have done as you ought, Laurence, I am sure; though it is a pity to lose you. I suppose you shall like to be an aviator," Croft said, in tones that made it quite plain he supposed no such thing. "We have no division of the Corps locally, though; even the dispatch-carrier only comes through once a week. You will have to take him to Gibraltar, I imagine."

"Yes, sir, though the trip must wait until he has more growth; he can stay aloft for an hour or so without much trouble, but I do not like to risk him on a long flight just yet," Laurence said firmly. "And in the meantime, he must be fed; we have only managed to get by so long with fishing, but of course he cannot hunt here."

"Well, Laurence, that is no lookout of the Navy's, I am sure," Croft said, but before Laurence could be really taken aback by this petty remark, the man seemed to realize how ill it sounded, and amended his words. "However, I will speak to the governor; I am sure we can arrange something. Now then, the *Reliant*, and of course the *Amitié*, we must take some thought for them."

"I should like to point out that Mr. Riley has been in command of the *Reliant* since the harnessing, and that he has handled her exceptionally well, bringing her safely to port through a two-days' gale," Laurence said. "He fought very bravely in the action which won us the prize, as well."

"Oh, I am sure, I am sure," Croft said, turning his finger in circles again. "Who do you have in the *Amitié*?"

"My first lieutenant, Gibbs," Laurence said.

"Yes, of course," Croft said. "Well, it is a bit much of you to hope to make both your first and second lieutenants post in such a way, Laurence, you must see that. There are not so many fine frigates out there."

Laurence had great difficulty in keeping his countenance; the man was clearly looking for some excuse to give himself a plum to deal out to one of his own favorites. "Sir," he said, icily, "I do not quite take your meaning; I hope you are not suggesting that I had myself put in harness in order to open a vacancy. I assure you my only motive was to secure to England a very valuable dragon, and I would hope that their Lordships will see it in such a way."

It was as close as he would come to harping on his own sacrifice, and a good deal closer than he would have preferred to come, without Riley's welfare at stake. But it had its effect; Croft seemed struck by the reminder, and the mention of the Admiralty; at least he hemmed and hawed and retreated, and dismissed them without saying anything final about removing Riley from command.

"Sir, I am deeply indebted to you," Riley said, as they walked together back towards the ship. "I only hope you will not have caused difficulties for yourself by pressing the matter so; I suppose he must have a great deal of influence."

Laurence at the moment had little room for any emotion but relief, for they had come to their own dock, and Temeraire was still sitting on the deck of the ship; although that looked more like an abattoir at the moment, and the area around his chops more red than black. The crowd of spectators had entirely dispersed. "If there is any blessing to the whole business, Tom, it is that I no longer need to give much thought to influence; I do not suppose it can make any difference to an aviator," he answered. "Pray have no concern for me. Should you mind if we were to walk a little faster? I think he has finished eating."

Flying did a great deal more to soothe his ruffled temper; it was impossible to be angry with the whole island of Madeira spread out before him and the wind in his hair, and Temeraire excitedly pointing out new things of interest, such as animals, houses, carts, trees, rocks, and anything else which might catch his eye; he had lately worked out a method of flying with his head partly turned round, so that he might talk to Laurence even while they flew. By mutual agreement, he perched at last upon an empty road that ran along at the edge of a deep valley; a bank of clouds was rolling thickly down the green southern slopes, clinging to the ground in a peculiar way, and he sat to watch their movement in fascination.

Laurence dismounted; he was still growing used to riding and was glad to stretch his legs after an hour in the air. He walked about for a while now, enjoying the view, and thought to himself that the next morning he would bring something to eat and drink on their flight; he would rather have liked a sandwich, and a glass of wine.

"I would like another one of those lambs," Temeraire said, echoing his own thoughts. "They were very tasty. Can I eat those over there? They look even larger."

There was a handsome flock of sheep grazing placidly on the far side of the valley, white against the green. "No, Temeraire; those are sheep, mutton," Laurence said. "They are not as good, and I think they must be someone's property, so we cannot go snatching them. But perhaps I will see if I cannot arrange for the shepherd to set one aside for you for tomorrow, if you would like to come back here."

"It seems very strange that the ocean is full of things that one can eat as one likes, and on land everything seems to be spoken for," Temeraire said, disappointed. "It does not seem quite right; they are not eating those sheep themselves, after all, and I am hungry now."

"At this rate, I suppose I shall be arrested for teaching you seditious thinking," Laurence said, amused. "You sound positively revolutionary. Only think, perhaps the fellow who owns those is the same one we will ask to give us a nice lamb for your dinner tonight; he will hardly do so if we steal his sheep."

"I would rather have a nice lamb now," Temeraire muttered, but he did not go after one of the sheep, and instead returned to examining the clouds. "May we go over to those clouds? I would like to see why they are moving like that."

Laurence looked at the shrouded hillside dubiously, but he more and more disliked telling the dragon no when he did not have to; it was so often necessary. "We may try it if you like," he said, "but it seems a little risky; we could easily run up against the mountainside and be brought by the lee."

"Oh, I will land below them, and then we may walk up," Temeraire said, crouching low and putting his neck to the ground so Laurence could scramble back aboard. "That will be more interesting in any case."

It was a little odd to go walking with a dragon, and very odd to outdistance one; Temeraire might take one step to every ten paces of Laurence's, but he took them very rarely, being more occupied in looking back and forth to compare the degree of cloud cover upon the ground. Laurence finally walked some distance ahead and threw himself down upon the slope to wait; even under the heavy fog, he was comfortable, thanks to the heavy clothing and oilskin cloak which he had learned from experience to wear while flying.

Temeraire continued to creep very slowly up the hill, interrupting his studies of the clouds now and again to look at a flower, or a pebble; to Laurence's surprise, he paused at one point and dug a small rock out of the ground, which he then brought up to Laurence with apparent excitement, pushing it along with the tip of a talon, as it was too small for him to pick up in his claws.

Laurence hefted the thing, which was about the size of his fist; it certainly was curious, pyrite intergrown with quartz crystal and rock. "How did you come to see it?" he said with interest, turning it over in his hands and brushing away more of the dirt.

"A little of it was out of the ground and it was shining," Temeraire said. "Is that gold? I like the look of it."

"No, it is just pyrite, but it is very pretty, is it not? I suppose you are one of those hoarding creatures," Laurence said, looking affectionately up at Temeraire; many dragons had an inborn fascination with jewels or precious metals. "I am afraid I am not rich enough a partner for you; I will not be able to give you a heap of gold to sleep on."

"I should rather have you than a heap of gold, even if it were very comfortable to sleep on," Temeraire said. "I do not mind the deck."

He said it quite normally, not in the least as though he meant to deliver a compliment, and immediately went back to looking at his clouds; Laurence was left gazing after him in a sensation of mingled amazement and extraordinary pleasure. He could scarcely imagine a similar feeling; the only parallel he could conceive from his old life would be if the *Reliant* had spoken to say she liked to have him for her captain: both praise and affection, from the highest source imaginable, and it filled him with fresh determination to prove worthy of the encomium.

"I am afraid I cannot help you, sir," the old fellow said, scratching behind his ear as he straightened up from the heavy volume before him. "I have a dozen books of draconic breeds, and I cannot find him in any of them. Perhaps his coloration will change when he gets older?"

Laurence frowned; this was the third naturalist he had

consulted over the past week since landing in Madeira, and none of them had been able to give him any help whatsoever in determining Temeraire's breed.

"However," the bookseller went on, "I can give you some hope; Sir Edward Howe of the Royal Society is here on the island, taking the waters; he came by my shop last week. I believe he is staying in Porto Moniz, at the north-western end of the island, and I am sure he will be able to identify your dragon for you; he has written several monographs on rare breeds from the Americas and the Orient."

"Thank you very much indeed; I am glad to hear it," Laurence said, brightening at this news; the name was familiar to him, and he had met the man in London once or twice, so that he need not even scramble for an introduction.

He went back out into the street in good humor, with a fine map of the island and a book on mineralogy for Temeraire. The day was particularly fine, and the dragon was presently sprawled out in the field which had been set aside for him some distance outside the city, sunning himself after a large meal.

The governor had been more accommodating than Admiral Croft, perhaps due to the anxiety of his populace over the presence of a frequently hungry dragon in the middle of their port, and had opened the public treasury to provide Temeraire with a steady supply of sheep and cattle. Temeraire was not at all unhappy with the change in his diet, and he was continuing to grow; he would no longer have fit on the *Reliant*'s stern, and he was bidding fair to become longer than the ship itself. Laurence had taken a cottage beside the field, at small expense due to its owner's sudden eagerness to be nowhere nearby, and the two of them were managing quite happily.

He regretted his own final removal from the ship's life

when he had time to think of it, but keeping Temeraire exercised was a great deal of work, and he could always go into the town for his dinner. He often met Riley or some of his other officers; too, he had some other naval acquaintances in the town, and so he rarely passed a solitary evening. The nights were comfortable as well, even though he was obliged to return to the cottage early due to the distance; he had found a local servant, Fernao, who, although wholly unsmiling and taciturn, was not disturbed by the dragon and could prepare a reasonable breakfast and supper.

Temeraire generally slept during the heat of the day, while he was gone, and woke again after the sun had set; after supper Laurence would go to sit outside and read to him by the light of a lantern. He had never been much of a reader himself, but Temeraire's pleasure in books was so great as to be infectious, and Laurence could not but think with satisfaction of the dragon's likely delight in the new book, which spoke in great detail about gemstones and their mining, despite his own complete lack of interest in the subject. It was not the sort of life which he had ever expected to lead, but so far, at least, he had not suffered in any material way from his change of status, and Temeraire was developing into uncommonly good company.

Laurence stopped in a coffeehouse and wrote Sir Edward a quick note with his direction, briefly explaining his circumstances and asking for permission to call. This he addressed to Porto Moniz, then sent off with the establishment's post-boy, adding a half-crown to speed it along. He could have flown across the island much more quickly, of course, but he did not feel he could simply descend upon someone with no warning with a dragon in tow. He could wait; he still had at least a week of liberty left to him before a reply would come from Gibraltar with instructions on how to report for duty.

But the dispatch-rider was due tomorrow, and the thought recalled him to an omitted duty: he had not yet written to his father. He could not let his parents learn of his altered circumstances from some secondhand account, or in the *Gazette* notice which should surely be printed, and with a sense of reluctant obligation he settled himself back down with a fresh pot of coffee to write the necessary letter.

It was difficult to think what to say. Lord Allendale was not a particularly fond parent and was punctilious in his manners. The Army and Navy he thought barely acceptable alternatives to the Church for an impoverished younger son; he would no more have considered sending a son to the Corps than to a trade, and he would certainly neither sympathize nor approve. Laurence was well aware that he and his father disagreed on the score of duty; his father would certainly tell him it had been his duty to his name to stay well away from the dragon, and to leave some misguided idea of service out of the matter.

His mother's reaction he dreaded more; for she had real affection for him, and the news would make her unhappy for his sake. Then, also, she was friendly with Lady Galman, and what he wrote would certainly reach Edith's ears. But he could not write in such terms as might reassure either of them without provoking his father extremely; and so he contented himself with a stilted, formal note that laid out the facts without embellishment, and avoided all appearance of complaint. It would have to do; still he sealed it with a sense of dissatisfaction before carrying it to the dispatch post by hand.

This unpleasant task completed, he turned back for the hotel in which he had taken a room; he had invited Riley and Gibbs along with several other acquaintances to join him for dinner, in recompense of earlier hospitality from them. It was not yet two o'clock, and the shops were still open; he looked in the windows as he walked to distract himself from brooding upon the likely reaction of his family and nearest friends, and paused outside a small pawnbroker's.

The golden chain was absurdly heavy, the sort of thing no woman could wear and too gaudy for a man: thick square links with flat disks and small pearl drops hanging from them, alternated. But for the metal and gems alone he imagined it must be expensive; most likely far more than he should spend, for he was being cautious with his funds now that he had no future prospect of prize-money. He stepped inside anyway and inquired; it was indeed too dear.

"However, sir, perhaps this one would do?" the proprietor suggested, offering a different chain: it looked very much the same, only with no disks, and perhaps slightly thinner links. It was nearly half the price of the first; still expensive, but he took it, and then felt a little silly for it.

He gave it to Temeraire that night anyway, and was a little surprised at the happiness with which it was received. Temeraire clutched the chain and would not put it aside; he brooded over it in the candlelight while Laurence read to him, and turned it this way and that to admire the light upon the gold and the pearls. When he slept at last, it remained entwined with his talons, and the next day Laurence was obliged to attach it securely to the harness before Temeraire would consent to fly.

The curious reaction made him even more glad to find an enthusiastic invitation from Sir Edward awaiting him when they returned from their morning flight. Fernao brought the note out to him in the field when they landed, and Laurence read it aloud to Temeraire: the gentleman would receive them whenever they liked to come, and he could be found at the seashore near the bathing pools.

"I am not tired," Temeraire said; he was as curious to know his breed as Laurence. "We may go at once, if you like."

He had indeed been developing more and more endurance; Laurence decided they could easily stop and rest if needed, and climbed back aboard without even having shifted his clothing. Temeraire put out an unusual effort and the island whipped by in great sweeps of his wings, Laurence crouching low to his neck and squinting against the wind.

They spiraled down to the shore less than an hour after lifting away, scattering bathers and seashore vendors as they landed upon the rocky shore. Laurence gazed after them in dismay for a moment, then frowned; if they were foolish enough to imagine that a properly harnessed dragon would hurt them, it was hardly his fault, and he patted Temeraire's neck as he unstrapped himself and slid down. "I will go and see if I can find Sir Edward; stay here."

"I will," said Temeraire absently; he was already peering with interest into the deep rocky pools about the shore, which had odd stone outcroppings and very clear water.

Sir Edward did not prove very difficult to find; he had noticed the fleeing crowd and was already approaching, the only person in view, by the time Laurence had gone a quarter of a mile. They shook hands and exchanged pleasantries, but both of them were impatient to come to the real matter at hand, and Sir Edward assented eagerly as soon as Laurence ventured to suggest they should walk back to Temeraire.

"A most unusual and charming name," Sir Edward said, as they walked, unconsciously making Laurence's heart sink. "Most often they are given Roman names, extravagant ones; but then most aviators go into harness a great deal younger than you, and have a tendency to puff themselves up. There is something quite absurd about a two-ton Winchester called Imperatorius. Why, Laurence, however did you teach him to swim?"

Startled, Laurence looked, then stared: in his absence, Temeraire had gone into the water and was now paddling himself about. "Lord, no; I have never seen him do it before," he said. "How can he not be sinking? Temeraire! Do come out of the water," he called, a little anxious.

Sir Edward watched with interest as Temeraire swam towards them and climbed back up onto shore. "How extraordinary. The internal air-sacs which permit them to fly would, I imagine, make a dragon naturally buoyant, and having grown up on the ocean as he has, perhaps he would have no natural fear of the element."

This mention of air-sacs was a piece of new information to Laurence, but the dragon was joining them, so he saved the further questions that immediately sprang to mind. "Temeraire, this is Sir Edward Howe," Laurence said.

"Hello," said Temeraire, peering down with interest equal to that with which he was observed. "I am very pleased to meet you. Can you tell me what breed I am?"

Sir Edward did not seem nonplussed by this direct approach, and he made a bow in reply. "I hope I will be able to give you some information, indeed; may I ask you to be so kind as to move some distance up the shore, perhaps by that tree which you see over there, and spread your wings, so we may better see your full conformation?"

Temeraire went willingly, and Sir Edward observed his motion. "Hm, very odd, not characteristic at all, the way he holds his tail. Laurence, you say his egg was found in Brazil?"

"As to that, I cannot properly tell you, I am afraid," Laurence said, studying Temeraire's tail; he could see nothing unusual, but of course he had no real basis for comparison. Temeraire carried his tail off the ground, and it lashed the air gently as he walked. "We took him from a French prize, and she was most recently come from Rio, judging by the markings on some of her water casks, but more than that I cannot say. The logs were thrown overboard as we took her, and the captain very naturally refused to give us any information about where the egg was discovered. But I assume it could not have come from much further, due to the length of the journey."

"Oh, that is by no means certain," Sir Edward said. "There are some subspecies which mature in the shell for upwards of ten years, and twenty months is a common average. Good Lord."

Temeraire had just spread out his wings; they were still dripping water. "Yes?" Laurence asked hopefully.

"Laurence, my God, those wings," Sir Edward cried, and literally ran across the shore towards Temeraire. Laurence blinked and went after him, and caught up to him only by the dragon's side. Sir Edward was gently stroking one of the six spines that divided the sections of Temeraire's wings, gazing at it with greedy passion. Temeraire had craned his head about to watch, but was keeping otherwise still, and did not seem to mind having his wing handled.

"Do you recognize him, then?" Laurence asked Sir Edward tentatively; the man looked quite overwhelmed.

"Recognize? Not, I assure you, in the sense of ever having seen his kind before; there can scarcely be three living men in Europe who have, and on the strength of this one glance I am already furnished with enough material for an address to the Royal Society," Sir Edward answered. "But the wings are irrefutable, and the number of talons: he is a Chinese Imperial, although of which line I certainly cannot tell you. Oh, Laurence, what a prize!"

Laurence gazed at the wings, bemused; it had not occurred to him before that the fan-like divisions were unusual, nor the five talons which Temeraire had upon each foot. "An Imperial?" he said, with an uncertain smile; he wondered for a moment if Sir Edward was practicing a joke on him. The Chinese had been breeding dragons for thousands of years before the Romans had ever domesticated the wild breeds of Europe; they were violently jealous of their work, and rarely permitted even grown specimens of minor breeds to leave the country. It was absurd to think that the French had been trundling an Imperial egg across the Atlantic in a thirty-six-gun frigate.

"Is that a good breed?" Temeraire asked. "Will I be able to breathe fire?"

"Dear creature, the very best of all possible breeds; only the Celestials are more rare or valuable, and were you one of those, I suppose the Chinese would go to war over our having put you into harness, so we must be glad you are not," Sir Edward said. "But though I will not rule it out entirely, I think it unlikely you will be able to breathe fire. The Chinese breed first for intelligence and grace; they have such overwhelming air superiority they do not need to seek such abilities in their lines. Japanese dragons are far more likely among the Oriental breeds to have any special offensive capabilities."

"Oh," said Temeraire glumly.

"Temeraire, do not be absurd, it is the most famous news anyone could imagine," Laurence said, beginning to believe at last; this was too far to carry a joke. "You are quite certain, sir?" he could not help asking.

"Oh yes," Sir Edward said, returning to his examination of the wings. "Only look at the delicacy of the membrane; the consistency of the color throughout the body, and the coordination between the color of the eyes and the markings. I should have seen he was a Chinese breed at once; it is quite impossible that he should have come from the wild, and no European or Incan breeder is capable of such work. And," he added, "this explains the swimming as well: Chinese beasts often have an affinity for water, if I recall correctly."

"An Imperial," Laurence murmured, stroking Temeraire's side in wonder. "It is incredible; they ought to have convoyed him with half their fleet, or sent a handler to him rather than the reverse."

"Perhaps they did not know what they had," Sir Edward said. "Chinese eggs are notoriously difficult to categorize by appearance, other than having the texture of fine porcelain. I do not suppose, by the by, that you have any of the eggshell preserved?" he asked wistfully.

"Not I, but perhaps some of the hands may have saved a bit," Laurence said. "I would be happy to make inquiry for you; I am deeply indebted to you."

"Not at all; the debt is entirely on my side. To think that I have seen an Imperial—and spoken with one!" He bowed to Temeraire. "In that, I may be unique among Englishmen, although le Comte de la Pérouse wrote in his journals of having spoken with one in Korea, in the palace of their king."

"I would like to read that," Temeraire said. "Laurence, can you get a copy?"

"I will certainly try," Laurence said. "And sir, I would be very grateful if you could recommend some texts to my attention; I would be glad of any knowledge of the habits and behaviors of the breed."

"Well, there are precious few resources, I am afraid; you will shortly be more of an expert than any other European, I imagine," Sir Edward said. "But I will certainly give you a list, and I have several texts I would be happy to lend you, including the journals of La Pérouse.

If Temeraire does not mind waiting here, perhaps we can walk back to my hotel and retrieve them; I am afraid he would not fit very comfortably in the village."

"I do not mind at all; I will go swimming again," Temeraire said.

Having taken tea with Sir Edward and collected a number of books from him, Laurence found a shepherd in the village willing to take his money, so he could feed Temeraire before their return journey. He was forced to drag the sheep down to the shore himself, however, with the animal bleating wildly and trying to get away long before Temeraire even came into view. Laurence ended up having to carry it bodily, and it took its final revenge by defecating upon him just before he flung it down at last in front of the eager dragon.

While Temeraire feasted, he stripped to the skin and scrubbed his clothing as best he could in the water, then left the wet things on a sunny rock to dry while the two of them bathed together. Laurence was not a particularly good swimmer himself, but with Temeraire to hold on to, he could risk the deeper water where the dragon could swim. Temeraire's delight in the water was infectious, and in the end Laurence too succumbed to playfulness, splashing the dragon and plunging under the water to come up on his other side.

The water was beautifully warm, and there were many outcroppings of rock to crawl out upon for a rest, some large enough for both of them; when he at last led Temeraire back onto the shore, several hours had gone by, and the sun was sinking rapidly. He was guiltily glad the other bathers had stayed away; he would have been ashamed to be seen frolicking like a boy.

The sun was warm on their backs as they winged across the island back to Funchal, both of them brimming with satisfaction, with the precious books wrapped in oilskin and strapped to the harness. "I will read to you from the journals tonight," Laurence was saying, when he was interrupted by a loud, bugling call ahead of them.

Temeraire was so startled he stopped in mid-air, hovering for a moment; then he roared back, a strangely tentative sound. He launched himself forwards again, and in a moment Laurence saw the source of the call: a pale grey dragon with mottled white markings upon its belly and white striations across its wings, almost invisible against the cloud cover; it was a great distance above them.

It swooped down very quickly and drew alongside them; he could see that it was smaller than Temeraire, even at his present size, but it could glide along on a single beat of its wings for much longer. Its rider was wearing grey leather that matched its hide, and a heavy hood; he unhooked several clasps on this and pushed it to hang back off his head. "Captain James, on Volatilus, dispatch service," he said, staring at Laurence in open curiosity.

Laurence hesitated; a response was obviously called for, but he was not quite sure how to style himself, for he had not yet been formally discharged from the Navy, nor formally inducted into the Corps. "Captain Laurence of His Majesty's Navy," he said finally, "on Temeraire; I am at present unassigned. Are you headed for Funchal?"

"Navy—? Yes, I am, and I expect you had better be as well, after that introduction," James said; he had a pleasant-looking long face, but Laurence's reply had marred it by a deep frown. "How old is that dragonet, and where did you get him?"

"I am three weeks and five days out of the shell, and Laurence won me in a battle," Temeraire said, before

Laurence could reply. "How did you meet James?" he asked, addressing the other dragon.

Volatilus blinked large milky blue eyes and said, in a bright voice, "I was hatched! From an egg!"

"Oh?" said Temeraire, uncertainly, and turned his head around to Laurence with a startled look. Laurence shook his head quickly, to keep him silent.

"Sir, if you have questions, they can be best answered on the ground," he said to James, a little coldly; there had been a peremptory quality he did not like in the other man's tone. "Temeraire and I are staying just outside the town; do you care to accompany us, or shall we follow you to your landing grounds?"

James had been looking with surprise at Temeraire, and he answered Laurence with a little more warmth, "Oh, let us go to yours; the moment I set down officially, I will be mobbed with people wanting to send parcels; we will not be able to talk."

"Very well; it is a field to the south-west of the city," Laurence said. "Temeraire, pray take the lead."

The grey dragon had no difficulty keeping up, though Laurence thought Temeraire was secretly trying to pull away; Volatilus had clearly been bred, and bred successfully, for speed. English breeders were gifted at working with their limited stocks to achieve specific results, but evidently intelligence had been sacrificed in the process of achieving this particular one.

They landed together, to the anxious lowing of the cattle that had been delivered for Temeraire's dinner. "Temeraire, be gentle with him," Laurence said quietly. "Some dragons do not have very good understanding, like some people; you remember Bill Swallow, on the *Reliant*."

"Oh, yes," Temeraire said, equally low. "I understand now; I will be careful. Do you think he would like one of my cows?"

"Would he care for something to eat?" Laurence asked James, as they both dismounted and met on the ground. "Temeraire has already eaten this afternoon; he can spare a cow."

"Why, that is very kind of you," James said, thawing visibly. "I am sure he would like it very much, wouldn't you, you bottomless pit," he went on affectionately, patting Volatilus's neck.

"Cows!" Volatilus said, staring at them with wide eyes.

"Come and have some with me, we can eat over here," Temeraire said to the little grey, and sat up to snatch a pair of the cows over the wall of the pen. He laid them out in a clean grassy part of the field, and Volatilus eagerly trotted over to share when Temeraire beckoned.

"It is uncommonly generous of you, and of him," James said, as Laurence led him to the cottage. "I have never seen one of the big ones share like that; what breed is he?"

"I am not myself an expert, and he came to us without provenance; but Sir Edward Howe has just today identified him as an Imperial," Laurence said, feeling a little embarrassed; it seemed like showing off, but of course it was just plain fact, and he could not avoid telling people.

James stumbled over the threshold on the news and nearly fell into Fernao. "Are you—oh, Lord, you are not joking," he said, recovering and handing his leather coat off. "But how did you find him, and how did you come to put him into harness?"

Laurence himself would never have dreamed of interrogating a host in such a way, but he concealed his opinion of James's manners; the circumstances surely warranted some leeway. "I will be happy to tell you," he said, showing the other man into the sitting room. "I should like your advice, in fact, on how I am to proceed. Will you have some tea?"

"Yes, although coffee if you have it," James said, pulling a chair closer to the fire; he sprawled into it with his leg slung over the arm. "Damn, it's good to sit for a minute; we have been in the air for seven hours."

"Seven hours? You must be shattered," Laurence said, startled. "I had no idea they could stay aloft that long."

"Oh, bless you, I have been on fourteen-hour flights," James said. "I shouldn't try it with yours, though; Volly can stay up beating his wings once an hour, in fine weather." He yawned enormously. "Still, it's no joke, not with the air currents over the ocean."

Fernao came in with coffee and tea, and once they were both served, Laurence briefly described Temeraire's acquisition and harnessing for James, who listened in open amazement while drinking five cups of coffee and eating through two platefuls of sandwiches.

"So as you see, I am at something of a loss; Admiral Croft has written a dispatch to the Corps at Gibraltar asking for instructions regarding my situation, which I trust you will carry, but I confess I would be grateful for some idea of what to expect," he finished.

"You're asking the wrong fellow, I'm afraid," James said cheerfully, draining a sixth cup. "Never heard of anything like it, and I can't even give you advance warning about training. I was told off for the dispatch service by the time I was twelve, and on Volly by fourteen; you'll be doing heavy combat with your beauty. But," he added, "I'll spare you any more waiting: I'll pop over to the landing grounds, get the post, and take your admiral's dispatch over tonight. I shouldn't be surprised if you have a senior cap over to see you before dinnertime tomorrow."

"I beg your pardon, a senior what?" Laurence said,

forced to ask in desperation; James's mode of speaking had grown steadily looser with the coffee he consumed.

"Senior captain," James said. He grinned, swung his leg down, and climbed out of the chair, standing up on his toes to stretch. "You'll make an aviator; I almost forget I'm not talking to one."

"Thank you; that is a handsome compliment," Laurence said, though privately he wished James would have made more of an effort to remember. "But surely you will not fly through the night?"

"Of course; no need to lie about here, in this weather. That coffee has put the life back in me, and on a cow Volly could fly to China and back," he said. "We'll have a better berth over on Gibraltar anyway. Off I go," and with this remark he walked out of the sitting room, took his own coat from the closet, and strolled out the door whistling, while Laurence hesitated, taken aback, and only belatedly went after him.

Volly came bounding up to James with a couple of short fluttering hops, babbling to him excitedly about cows and "Temrer," which was the best he could do at Temeraire's name; James petted him and climbed back up. "Thanks again; will see you on my rounds if you do your training at Gibraltar," he said, waved a hand, and with a flurry of grey wings they were a quickly diminishing figure in the twilight sky.

"He was very happy to have the cow," Temeraire said after a moment, standing looking after them beside Laurence.

Laurence laughed at this faint praise and reached up to scratch Temeraire's neck gently. "I am sorry your first meeting with another dragon was not very auspicious," he said. "But he and James will be taking Admiral Croft's message to Gibraltar for us, and in another day or two I expect you will be meeting more congenial minds."

* * *

James had evidently not been exaggerating in his estimate, however; Laurence had just set out for town the next afternoon when a great shadow crossed over the harbor, and he looked up to see an enormous red-and-gold beast sailing by overhead, making for the landing grounds on the outskirts of the town. He at once set out for the *Commendable*, expecting any communication to reach him there, and none too soon; halfway there a breathless young midshipman tracked him down, and told him that Admiral Croft had sent for him.

Two aviators were waiting for him in Croft's stateroom: Captain Portland, a tall, thin man with severe features and a hawksbill nose, who looked rather dragon-like himself, and Lieutenant Dayes, a young man scarcely twenty years of age, with a long queue of pale red hair and pale eyebrows to match, and an unfriendly expression. Their manner was as aloof as reputation made that of all aviators, and unlike James they showed no signs of unbending towards him.

"Well, Laurence, you are a very lucky fellow," Croft said, as soon as Laurence had suffered through the stilted introductions, "We will have you back in the *Reliant* after all."

Still in the process of considering the aviators, Laurence paused at this. "I beg your pardon?" he said.

Portland gave Croft a swift contemptuous glance; but then the remark about luck had certainly been tactless, if not offensive. "You have indeed performed a singular service for the Corps," he said stiffly, turning to Laurence, "but I hope we will not have to ask you to continue that service any further. Lieutenant Dayes is here to relieve you."

Laurence looked in confusion at Dayes, who stared back with a hint of belligerence in his eye. "Sir," he said slowly; he could not quite think, "I was under the impression that a dragon's handler could not be relieved: that he had to be present at its hatching. Am I mistaken?"

"Under ordinary circumstances, you are correct, and it is certainly desirable," Portland said. "However, on occasion a handler is lost, to disease or injury, and we have been able to convince the dragon to accept a new aviator in more than half of such cases. I expect here that his youth will render Temeraire," his voice lingered on the name with a faint air of distaste, "even more amenable to the replacement."

"I see," Laurence said; it was all he could manage. Three weeks ago, the news would have given him the greatest joy; now it seemed oddly flat.

"Naturally we are grateful to you," Portland said, perhaps feeling some more civil response was called for. "But he will do much better in the hands of a trained aviator, and I am sure that the Navy cannot easily spare us so devoted an officer."

"You are very kind, sir," Laurence said formally, bowing. The compliment had not been a natural one, but he could see that the rest of the remark was meant sincerely enough, and it made perfect sense. Certainly Temeraire would do better in the hands of a trained aviator, a fellow who would handle him properly, the same way a ship would do better in the hands of a real seaman. It had been wholly an accident that Temeraire had been settled upon him, and now that he knew the truly extraordinary nature of the dragon, it was even more obvious that Temeraire deserved a partner with an equal degree of skill. "Of course you would prefer a trained man in the position if at all possible, and I am happy if I have been of any service. Shall I take Mr. Dayes to Temeraire now?"

"No!" Dayes said sharply, only to fall silent at a look from Portland.

Portland answered more politely, "No, thank you, Captain; on the contrary, we prefer to proceed exactly as if the dragon's handler had died, to keep the procedure as close as possible to the set methods which we have devised for accustoming the creature to a new handler. It would be best if you did not see the dragon again at all."

That was a blow. Laurence almost argued, but in the end he closed his mouth and only bowed again. If it would make the process of transition easier, it was only his duty to keep away.

Still, it was very unpleasant to think of never seeing Temeraire again; he had made no farewell, said no last kind words, and to simply stay away felt like a desertion. Sorrow weighed on him heavily as he left the *Commendable,* and it had not dissipated by evening; he was meeting Riley and Wells for dinner, and when he came into the parlor of the hotel where they were waiting for him, it was an effort to give them a smile and say, "Well, gentlemen, it seems you are not to be rid of me after all."

They looked surprised; shortly they were both congratulating him enthusiastically, and toasting his freedom. "It is the best news I have heard in a fortnight," Riley said, raising a glass. "To your health, sir." He was very clearly sincere despite the promotion it would likely cost him, and Laurence was deeply affected; consciousness of their true friendship lifted the grief at least a little, and he was able to return the toast with something approaching his usual demeanor.

"It does seem they went about it rather strangely, though," Wells said a little later, frowning over Laurence's brief description of the meeting. "Almost like an insult, sir, and to the Navy, too; as though a naval officer were not good enough for them."

"No, not at all," Laurence said, although privately he did not feel very sure of his interpretation. "Their concern is for Temeraire, I am sure, and rightly so, as well as for the Corps; one could scarcely expect them to be glad at the prospect of having an untrained fellow on the back of so valuable a creature, any more than we would like to see an Army officer given command of a first-rate."

So he said, and so he believed, but that was not very much of a consolation. As the evening wore on, he grew more rather than less conscious of the grief of parting, despite the companionship and the good food. It had already become a settled habit with him to spend the nights reading with Temeraire, or talking to him, or sleeping by his side, and this sudden break was painful. He knew that he was not perfectly concealing his feelings; Riley and Wells gave him anxious glances as they talked more to cover his silences, but he could not force himself to a feigned display of happiness which would have reassured them.

The pudding had been served and he was making an attempt to get some of it down when a boy came running in with a note for him: it was from Captain Portland; he was asked in urgent terms to come to the cottage. Laurence started up from the table at once, barely making a few words of explanation, and dashed out into the street without even waiting for his overcoat. The Madeira night was warm, and he did not mind the lack, particularly after he had been walking briskly for a few minutes; by the time he reached the cottage he would have been glad of an excuse to remove his neck-cloth.

The lights were on inside; he had offered the use of the establishment to Captain Portland for their convenience, as it was near the field. When Fernao opened the door for him, he came in to find Dayes with his head in his hands at the dinner table, surrounded by several other young men in the uniform of the Corps, and Portland standing by the fireplace and gazing into it with a rigid, disapproving expression.

"Has something happened?" Laurence asked. "Is Temeraire ill?"

"No," Portland said shortly, "he has refused to accept the replacement."

Dayes abruptly pushed up from the table and took a step towards Laurence. "It is not to be borne! An Imperial in the hands of some untrained Navy clodpole—" he cried. He was stifled by his friends before anything more could escape him, but the expression had still been shockingly offensive, and Laurence at once gripped the hilt of his sword.

"Sir, you must answer," he said angrily, "that is more than enough."

"Stop that; there is no dueling in the Corps," Portland said. "Andrews, for God's sake put him to bed and get some laudanum into him." The young man restraining Dayes's left arm nodded, and he and the other three pulled the struggling lieutenant out of the room, leaving Laurence and Portland alone, with Fernao standing wooden-faced in the corner still holding a tray with the port decanter upon it.

Laurence wheeled on Portland. "A gentleman cannot be expected to tolerate such a remark."

"An aviator's life is not only his own; he cannot be allowed to risk it so pointlessly," Portland said flatly. "There is no dueling in the Corps."

The repeated pronouncement had the weight of law, and Laurence was forced to see the justice in it; his hand relaxed minutely, though the angry color did not leave his face. "Then he must apologize, sir, to myself and to the Navy; it was an outrageous remark."

Portland said, "And I suppose you have never made nor listened to equally outrageous remarks made about aviators, or the Corps?"

Laurence fell silent before the open bitterness in Portland's voice. It had never before occurred to him that aviators themselves would surely hear such remarks and resent them; now he understood still more how savage that resentment must be, given that they could not even make answer by the code of their service. "Captain," he said at last, more quietly, "if such remarks have ever been made in my presence, I may say that I have never been responsible for them myself, and where possible I have spoken against them harshly. I have never willingly heard disparaging words against any division of His Majesty's armed forces; nor will I ever."

It was now Portland's turn to be silent, and though his tone was grudging, he did finally say, "I accused you unjustly; I apologize. I hope that Dayes, too, will make his apologies when he is less distraught; he would not have spoken so if he had not just suffered so bitter a disappointment."

"I understood from what you said that there was a known risk," Laurence said. "He ought not have built his expectations so high; surely he can expect to succeed with a hatchling."

"He accepted the risk," Portland said. "He has spent his right to promotion. He will not be permitted to make another attempt, unless he wins another chance under fire; and that is unlikely."

So Dayes was in the same position which Riley had occupied before their last voyage, save perhaps with even less chance, dragons being so very rare in England. Laurence still could not forgive the insult, but he understood the emotion better; and he could not help feeling pity for the fellow, who was after all only a boy. "I see; I will be happy to accept an apology," he said; it was as far as he could bring himself to go.

Portland looked relieved. "I am glad to hear it," he said. "Now, I think it would be best if you went to speak to Temeraire; he will have missed you, and I believe he was not pleased to be asked to take on a replacement. I hope we may speak again tomorrow; we have left your bedroom untouched, so you need not shift for yourself."

Laurence needed little encouragement; moments later he was striding to the field. As he drew near, he could make out Temeraire's bulk by the light of the half-moon: the dragon was curled in small upon himself and nearly motionless, only stroking his gold chain between his foreclaws. "Temeraire," he called, coming through the gate, and the proud head lifted at once.

"Laurence?" he said; the uncertainty in his voice was painful to hear.

"Yes, I am here," Laurence said, crossing swiftly to him, almost running at the end. Making a soft crooning noise deep in his throat, Temeraire curled both forelegs and wings around him and nuzzled him carefully; Laurence stroked the sleek nose.

"He said you did not like dragons, and that you wanted to be back on your ship," Temeraire said, very low. "He said you only flew with me out of duty."

Laurence went breathless with rage; if Dayes had been in front of him he would have flown at the man bare-handed and beaten him. "He was lying, Temeraire," he said with difficulty; he was half-choked by fury.

"Yes; I thought he was," Temeraire said. "But it was not pleasant to hear, and he tried to take away my chain. It made me very angry. And he would not leave, until I put him out, and then you still did not come; I thought maybe he would keep you away, and I did not know where to go to find you."

Laurence leaned forward and laid his cheek against the soft, warm hide. "I am so very sorry," he said. "They persuaded me it was in your best interests to stay away and let him try; but I should have seen what kind of a fellow he was."

Temeraire was quiet for several minutes, while they stood comfortably together, then said, "Laurence, I suppose I am too large to be on a ship now?"

"Yes, pretty much, except for a dragon transport," Laurence said, lifting his head; he was puzzled by the question.

"If you would like to have your ship back," Temeraire said, "I will let someone else ride me. Not him, because he says things that are not true; but I will not make you stay."

Laurence stood motionless for a moment, his hands still on Temeraire's head, with the dragon's warm breath curling around him. "No, my dear," he said at last, softly, knowing it was only the truth. "I would rather have you than any ship in the Navy."

II

Chapter 4

✦

"No, throw your chest out deeper, like so." Laetificat stood up on her haunches and demonstrated, the enormous barrel of her red-and-gold belly expanding as she breathed in.

Temeraire mimicked the motion; his expansion was less visually dramatic, as he lacked the vivid markings of the female Regal Copper and was of course less than a fifth of her size as yet, but this time he managed a much louder roar. "Oh, there," he said, pleased, dropping back down to four legs. The cows were all running around their pen in manic terror.

"Much better," Laetificat said, and nudged Temeraire's back approvingly. "Practice every time you eat; it will help along your lung capacity."

"I suppose it is hardly news to you how badly we need him, given how our affairs stand," Portland said, turning to Laurence; the two of them were standing by the side of the field, out of range of the mess the dragons were about to make. "Most of Bonaparte's dragons are stationed along the Rhine, and of course he has been busy in Italy; that and our naval blockades are all that is keeping him from invasion. But if he gets matters arranged to his satisfaction on the Continent and frees up a few aerial divisions, we can say hail and farewell to the blockade at Toulon; we simply do not have enough dragons of our own here in the Med to protect Nelson's fleet. He will have to withdraw, and then Villeneuve will go straight for the Channel."

Laurence nodded grimly; he had been reading the news of Bonaparte's movements with great alarm since the *Reliant* had put into port. "I know Nelson has been trying to lure the French fleet out to battle, but Villeneuve is not a fool, even if he is no seaman. An aerial bombardment is the only hope of getting him out of his safe harbor."

"Which means there is no hope, not with the forces we can bring to it at present," Portland said. "The Home Division has a couple of Longwings, and they might be able to do it; but they cannot be spared. Bonaparte would jump on the Channel Fleet at once."

"Ordinary bombing would not do?"

"Not precise enough at long range, and they have poisoned shrapnel guns at Toulon. No aviator worth a shilling would take his beast close to the fortifications." Portland shook his head. "No, but there is a young Longwing in training, and if Temeraire will be kind enough to hurry up and grow, then perhaps together they might shortly be able to take the place of Excidium or Mortiferus at the Channel, and even one of those two might be sufficient at Toulon."

"I am sure he will do everything in his power to oblige you," Laurence said, glancing over; the dragon in question was on his second cow. "And I may say that I will do the same. I know I am not the man you wished in this place, nor can I argue with the reasoning that would prefer an experienced aviator in so critical a role. But I hope that naval experience will not prove wholly useless in this arena."

Portland sighed and looked down at the ground. "Oh, hell," he said. It was an odd response to make, but Portland looked anxious, not angry, and after a moment

he added, "There is just no getting around it; you are
not an aviator. If it were simply a question of skill or
knowledge, that would mean difficulties enough, but—"
He stopped.

Laurence did not think, from the tone, that Portland
meant to question his courage. The man had been more
amiable this morning; so far, it seemed to Laurence that
aviators simply took clannishness to an extreme, and
once having admitted a fellow into their circle, their cold
manners fell away. So he took no offense, and said, "Sir,
I can hardly imagine where else you believe the difficulty
might lie."

"No, you cannot," Portland said, uncommunica-
tively. "Well, and I am not going to borrow trouble; they
may decide to send you somewhere else entirely, not to
Loch Laggan. But I am running ahead of myself: the real
point is that you and Temeraire must get to England for
your training soonest; once you are there, Aerial Command can best decide how to deal with you."

"But can he reach England from here, with no place
to stop along the way?" Laurence asked, diverted by
concern for Temeraire. "It must be more than a thousand miles; he has never flown further than from one
end of the island to the other."

"Closer to two thousand, and no; we would never
risk him so," Portland said. "There is a transport coming over from Nova Scotia; a couple of dragons joined
our division from it three days ago, so we have its position pretty well fixed, and I think it is less than a hundred miles away. We will escort you to it; if Temeraire
gets tired, Laetificat can support him for long enough to
give him a breather."

Laurence was relieved to hear the proposed plan, but
the conversation made him aware how very unpleasant
his circumstances would be until his ignorance was
mended. If Portland had waved off his fears, Laurence

would have had no way of judging the matter for himself. Even a hundred miles was a good distance; it would take them three hours or more in the air. But that at least he felt confident they could manage; they had flown the length of the island three times just the other day, while visiting Sir Edward, and Temeraire had not seemed tired in the least.

"When do you propose leaving?" he asked.

"The sooner, the better; the transport is headed away from us, after all," Portland said. "Can you be ready in half an hour?"

Laurence stared. "I suppose I can, if I have most of my things sent back to the *Reliant* for transport," he said dubiously.

"Why would you?" Portland said. "Laet can carry anything you have; we shan't weigh Temeraire down."

"No, I only mean that my things are not packed," Laurence said. "I am used to waiting for the tide; I see I will have to be a little more beforehand with the world from now on."

Portland still looked puzzled, and when he came into Laurence's room twenty minutes later he stared openly at the sea-chest that Laurence had turned to this new purpose. There had hardly been time to fill half of it; Laurence paused in the act of putting in a couple of blankets to take up the empty space at the top. "Is something wrong?" he asked, looking down; the chest was not so large that he thought it would give Laetificat any difficulty.

"No wonder you needed the time; do you always pack so carefully?" Portland said. "Could you not just throw the rest of your things into a few bags? We can strap them on easily enough."

Laurence swallowed his first response; he no longer needed to wonder why the aviators looked, to a man, rumpled in their dress; he had imagined it due to some advanced technique of flying. "No, thank you; Fernao will take my other things to the *Reliant,* and I can manage perfectly well with what I have here," he said, putting the blankets in; he strapped them down and made all fast, then locked the chest. "There; I am at your service now."

Portland called in a couple of his midwingmen to carry the chest; Laurence followed them outside, and was witness, for the first time, to the operation of a full aerial crew. Temeraire and he both watched with interest from the side as Laetificat stood patiently under the swarming ensigns, who ran up and down her sides as easily as they hung below her belly or climbed upon her back. The boys were raising up two canvas enclosures, one above and one below; these were like small, lopsided tents, framed with many thin and flexible strips of metal. The front panels which formed the bulk of the tent were long and sloped, evidently to present as little resistance to the wind as possible, and the sides and back were made of netting.

The ensigns all looked to be below the age of twelve; the midwingmen ranged more widely, just as aboard a ship, and now four older ones came staggering with the weight of a heavy leather-wrapped chain they dragged in front of Laetificat. The dragon lifted it herself and laid it over her withers, just in front of the tent, and the ensigns hurried to secure it to the rest of the harness with many straps and smaller chains.

Using this strap, they then slung a sort of hammock made of chain links beneath Laetificat's belly. Laurence saw his own chest tossed inside along with a collection of other bags and parcels; he winced at the haphazard way in which the baggage was stowed, and was doubly grateful that he had been careful in his packing: he was confident they might turn his chest completely about a dozen times without casting his things into disarray.

A large pad of leather and wool, perhaps the thickness of a man's arm, was laid on top of all, then the hammock's edges were drawn up and hooked to the harness as widely as possible, spreading the weight of the contents and pressing them close to the dragon's belly. Laurence felt a sense of dissatisfaction with the proceedings; he privately thought he would have to find a better arrangement for Temeraire, when the time came.

However, the process had one significant advantage over naval preparations: from beginning to end it took fifteen minutes, and then they were looking at a dragon in full light-duty rig. Laetificat reared up on her legs, shook out her wings, and beat them half a dozen times; the wind was strong enough to nearly stagger Laurence, but the assembled baggage did not shift noticeably.

"All lies well," Laetificat said, dropping back down to all fours; the ground shook with the impact.

"Lookouts aboard," Portland said; four ensigns climbed on and took up positions at the shoulders and hips, above and below, hooking themselves on to the harness. "Topmen and bellmen." Now two groups of eight midwingmen climbed up, one going into the tent above, the other below: Laurence was startled to perceive how large the enclosures really were; they seemed small only by virtue of comparison with Laetificat's immense size.

The crews were followed in turn by the twelve riflemen, who had been checking and arming their guns while the others rigged out the gear. Laurence noticed Lieutenant Dayes leading them, and frowned; he had forgotten about the fellow in the rush. Dayes had offered no apology; now most likely they would not see one another for a long time. Perhaps it was for the best; Laurence was not sure that he could have accepted the apology, after hearing Temeraire's story, and as it was impossible to call the fellow out, the situation would have been uncomfortable to say the least.

The riflemen having boarded, Portland walked a complete circuit around and beneath the dragon. "Very good; ground crew aboard." The handful of men remaining climbed into the belly-rigging and strapped themselves in; only then did Portland himself ascend, Laetificat lifting him up directly. He repeated his inspection on the top, maneuvering around on the harness with as much ease as any of the little ensigns, and finally came to his position at the base of the dragon's neck. "I believe we are ready; Captain Laurence?"

Laurence belatedly realized he was still standing on the ground; he had been too interested in the process to mount up himself. He turned, but before he could clamber onto the harness, Temeraire reached out carefully and put him aboard, mimicking Laetificat's action. Laurence grinned privately and patted the dragon's neck. "Thank you, Temeraire," he said, strapping himself in; Portland had pronounced his improvised harness adequate for the journey, although with a disapproving air. "Sir, we are ready," he called to Portland.

"Proceed, then; smallest goes aloft first," Portland said. "We will take the lead once in the air."

Laurence nodded; Temeraire gathered himself and leapt, and the world fell away beneath them.

Aerial Command was situated in the countryside just south-east of Chatham, close enough to London to permit daily consultation with the Admiralty and the War Office; it had been an easy hour's flight from Dover, with the rolling green fields he knew so well spread out below like a checkerboard, and London a suggestion of towers in the distance, purple and indistinct.

Although the dispatches had long preceded him to England and he must have been expected, Laurence was not called to the office until the next morning. Even then he was kept waiting outside Admiral Powys's office for nearly two hours. At last the door opened; stepping inside, he could not help glancing curiously from Admiral Powys to Admiral Bowden, who was sitting to the right of the desk. The precise words had not been intelligible out in the hall, but he could not have avoided overhearing the loud voices, and Bowden was still red-faced and frowning.

"Yes, Captain Laurence, do come in," Powys said, waving him in with a fat-fingered hand. "How splendid Temeraire looks; I saw him eating this morning: already close on nine tons, I should say. You are to be most highly commended. And you fed him solely on fish the first two weeks, and also while on the transport? Remarkable, remarkable indeed; we must consider amending the general diet."

"Yes, yes; this is beside the point," Bowden said impatiently.

Powys frowned at Bowden, then continued, perhaps a little too heartily, "In any case, he is certainly ready to begin training, and of course we must do our best to bring you up to the mark as well. Of course we have confirmed you in your rank; as a handler, you would be made captain anyway. But you will have a great deal to do; ten years' training is not to be made up in a day."

Laurence bowed. "Sir, Temeraire and I are both at your service," he said, but with reserve; he perceived in both men the same odd constraint about his training that Portland had displayed. Many possible explanations for that constraint had occurred to Laurence during the two weeks aboard the transport, most of them unpleasant. A boy of seven, taken from his home before his character had been truly formed, might easily be forced to accept treatment which a grown man would never endure, and yet of course the aviators themselves would consider it necessary, having gone through it themselves; Laurence could think of no other cause that would make them all so evasive about the subject.

His heart sank further as Powys said, "Now then; we must send you to Loch Laggan," for it was the place Portland had mentioned, and been so anxious about. "There is no denying that it is the best place for you," Powys went on. "We cannot waste a moment in making you both ready for duty, and I would not be surprised if Temeraire were up to heavy-combat weight by the end of the summer."

"Sir, I beg your pardon, but I have never heard of the place, and I gather it is in Scotland?" Laurence asked; he hoped to draw Powys out.

"Yes, in Inverness-shire; it is one of our largest coverts, and certainly the best for intensive training," Powys said. "Lieutenant Greene outside will show you the way, and mark a covert along the route for you to spend the night; I am sure you will have no difficulty in reaching the place."

It was clearly a dismissal, and Laurence knew he could not make any further inquiry. In any event, he had a more pressing request. "I will speak to him, sir," he said. "But if you have no objection, I would be glad to stop the night at my family home in Nottinghamshire; there is room enough for Temeraire, and deer for him to eat." His parents would be in town at this time of year, but the Galmans often stayed in the country, and there might be some chance of seeing Edith, if only briefly.

"Oh, certainly, by all means," Powys said. "I am sorry I cannot give you a longer furlough; you have certainly deserved it, but I do not think we can spare the time: a week might make all the difference in the world."

"Thank you, sir, I perfectly understand," Laurence said, and so bowed and departed.

Armed by Lieutenant Greene with an excellent map

showing the route, Laurence began his preparations at once. He had taken some time in Dover to acquire a collection of light bandboxes; he thought that their cylindrical shape might better lie against Temeraire's body, and now he transferred his belongings into them. He knew he made an unusual sight, carrying a dozen boxes more suitable for ladies' hats out to Temeraire, but when he had strapped them down against Temeraire's belly and seen how little they added to his profile, he could not help feeling somewhat smug.

"They are quite comfortable; I do not notice them at all," Temeraire assured him, rearing up on his back legs and flapping to make certain they were well seated, just as Laetificat had done back in Madeira. "Can we not get one of those tents? It would be much more comfortable for you to ride out of the wind."

"I have no idea how to put it up, though, my dear," Laurence said, smiling at the concern. "But I will do well enough; with this leather coat they have given me, I will be quite warm."

"It must wait until you have your proper harness, in any case; the tents require locking carabiners. Nearly ready to go, then, Laurence?" Bowden had come upon them and interjected himself into the conversation without any notice. He joined Laurence standing before Temeraire's chest and stooped a little to examine the bandboxes. "Hm, I see you are bent on turning all our customs upside down to suit yourself."

"No, sir, I hope not," Laurence said, keeping his temper; it could not serve to alienate the man, for he was one of the senior commanders of the Corps, and might well have a say in what postings Temeraire received. "But my sea-chest was awkward for him to bear, and these seemed the best replacement I could manage on short notice."

"They may do," Bowden said, straightening up. "I

hope you have as easy a time putting aside the rest of your naval thinking as your sea-chest, Laurence; you must be an aviator now."

"I am an aviator, sir, and willingly so," Laurence said. "But I cannot pretend that I intend to put aside the habits and mode of thinking formed over a lifetime; whether I intended it or no, I doubt it would even be possible."

Bowden fortunately took this without anger, but he shook his head. "No, it would not. And so I told—well. I have come to make something clear: you will oblige me by refraining from discussing, with those not in the Corps, any aspects of your training. His Majesty sees fit to give us our heads to achieve the best performance of our duty; we do not care to entertain the opinions of outsiders. Do I make myself clear?"

"Perfectly," Laurence said grimly; the peculiar command bore out all his worst suspicions. But if none of them would come out and make themselves plain, he could hardly make an objection; it was infuriating. "Sir," he said, making up his mind to try again to draw out the truth, "if you would be so good as to tell me what makes the covert in Scotland more suitable than this for my training, I would be grateful to know what to expect."

"You have been ordered to go there; that makes it the only suitable place," Bowden said sharply. Yet then he seemed to relent, for he added, in a less harsh tone, "Laggan's training master is especially adept at bringing inexperienced handlers along quickly."

"Inexperienced?" Laurence said, blankly. "I thought an aviator had to come into the service at the age of seven; surely you do not mean that there are boys already handling dragons at that age."

"No, of course not," Bowden said. "But you are not the first handler to come from outside the ranks, or without as much training as we might care for. Occasionally a hatchling will have a fit of distemper, and we must take anyone we can get it to accept." He gave a sudden snorting laugh. "Dragons are strange creatures, and there is no understanding them; some of them even take a liking to sea-officers." He slapped Temeraire's side, and left as abruptly as he had come; without a word of parting, but in apparently better humor, and leaving Laurence hardly less perplexed than before.

The flight to Nottinghamshire took several hours, and afforded him more leisure than he liked to consider what awaited him in Scotland. He did not like to imagine what Bowden and Powys and Portland all expected him to disapprove so heartily, and he still less liked to try to imagine what he should do if he found the situation unbearable.

He had only once had a truly unhappy experience in his naval service: as a freshly made lieutenant of seventeen he had been assigned to the *Shorewise,* under Captain Barstowe, an older man and a relic of an older Navy, where officers had not been required to be gentlemen as well. Barstowe was the illegitimate son of a merchant of only moderate wealth and a woman of only moderate character; he had gone to sea as a boy in his father's ships and been pressed into the Navy as a foremast hand. He had displayed great courage in battle and a keen head for mathematics, which had won him promotion first to master's-mate, then to lieutenant, and even by a stroke of luck to post-rank, but he had never lost any of the coarseness of his background.

What was worse, Barstowe had been conscious of his own lack of social graces, and resentful of those who, in his mind, made him feel that lack. It was not an unmerited resentment: there were many officers who looked askance and murmured at him; but he had seen in Laurence's easy and pleasing manners a deliberate insult, and he had been merciless in punishing Laurence for them. Barstowe's death of pneumonia three months into the voyage had possibly saved Laurence's own life, and at the least had freed him from an endless daze of standing double or triple watches, a diet of ship's biscuit and water, and the perils of leading a gun-crew composed of the worst and most unhandy men aboard.

Laurence still had an instinctive horror when he thought of the experience; he was not in the least prepared to be ruled over by another such man, and in Bowden's ominous words about the Corps taking anyone a hatchling would accept, he read a hint that his trainer or perhaps his fellow trainees would be of such a stamp. And while Laurence was not a boy of seventeen anymore, nor in so powerless a position, he now had Temeraire to consider, and their shared duty.

His hands tightened on the reins involuntarily, and Temeraire looked around. "Are you well, Laurence?" he asked. "You have been so quiet."

"Forgive me, I have only been woolgathering," Laurence said, patting Temeraire's neck. "It is nothing. Are you tiring at all? Should you like to stop and rest awhile?"

"No, I am not tired, but you are not telling the truth: I can hear you are unhappy," Temeraire said anxiously. "Is it not good that we are going to begin training? Or are you missing your ship?"

"I find I am become transparent before you," Laurence said ruefully. "I am not missing my ship at all, no, but I will admit I am a little concerned about our training. Powys and Bowden were very odd about the whole thing, and I am not sure what sort of reception we will meet in Scotland, or how we shall like it."

"If we do not care for it, surely we can just go away again?" Temeraire said.

"It is not so easy; we are not at liberty, you know," Laurence said. "I am a King's officer, and you are a King's dragon; we cannot do as we please."

"I have never met the King; I am not his property, like a sheep," Temeraire said. "If I belong to anyone, it is you, and you to me. I am not going to stay in Scotland if you are unhappy there."

"Oh dear," Laurence said; this was not the first time Temeraire had showed a distressing tendency to independent thought, and it seemed to only be increasing as he grew older and started to spend more of his time awake. Laurence was not himself particularly interested in political philosophy, and he found it sadly puzzling to have to work out explanations for what to him seemed natural and obvious. "It is not ownership, exactly; but we owe him our loyalty. Besides," he added, "we would have a hard time of it keeping you fed, were the Crown not paying for your board."

"Cows are very nice, but I do not mind eating fish," Temeraire said. "Perhaps we could get a large ship, like the transport, and go back to sea."

Laurence laughed at the image. "Shall I turn pirate king and go raiding in the West Indies, and fill a covert with gold from Spanish merchant ships for you?" He stroked Temeraire's neck.

"That sounds exciting," Temeraire said, his imagination clearly caught. "Can we not?"

"No, we are born too late; there are no real pirates anymore," Laurence said. "The Spanish burned the last pirate band out of Tortuga last century; now there are only a few independent ships or dragon-crews, at most, and those always in danger of being brought down. And you would not truly like it, fighting only for greed; it is not the same as doing one's duty for King and country, knowing that you are protecting England."

"Does it need protecting?" Temeraire asked, looking down. "It seems all quiet, as far as I can see."

"Yes, because it is our business and the Navy's to keep it so," Laurence said. "If we did not do our work, the French could come across the Channel; they are there, not very far to the east, and Bonaparte has an army of a hundred thousand men waiting to come across the moment we let him. That is why we must do our duty; it is like the sailors on the *Reliant*, who cannot always be doing just as they like, or the ship will not sail."

In response to this, Temeraire hummed in thought, deep in his belly; Laurence could feel the sound reverberating through his own body. Temeraire's pace slowed a little; he glided for a while and then beat back up into the air in a spiral before leveling out again, very much like a fellow pacing back and forth. He looked around again. "Laurence, I have been thinking: if we must go to Loch Laggan, then there is no decision to be made at present; and because we do not know what may be wrong there, we cannot think of something to do now. So you should not worry until we have arrived and seen how matters stand."

"My dear, this is excellent advice, and I will try to follow it," Laurence said, adding, "but I am not certain that I can; it is difficult not to think of."

"You could tell me again about the Armada, and how Sir Francis Drake and Conflagratia destroyed the Spanish fleet," Temeraire suggested.

"Again?" Laurence said. "Very well; although I will begin to doubt your memory at this rate."

"I remember it perfectly," Temeraire said with dignity. "But I like to hear you tell it."

What with Temeraire making him repeat favorite sections and asking questions about the dragons and ships which Laurence thought even a scholar could not have answered, the rest of the flight passed without giving him leisure to worry any further. Evening was far advanced by the time they finally closed in upon his family's home at Wollaton Hall, and in the twilight all the many windows glowed.

Temeraire circled over the house a few times out of curiosity, his pupils open very wide; Laurence, peering down himself, made a count of lit windows and realized that the house could not be empty; he had assumed it would be, the London Season being still in full train, but it was now too late to seek another berth for Temeraire. "Temeraire, there ought to be an empty paddock behind the barns, to the south-east there; can you see it?"

"Yes, there is a fence around it," Temeraire said, looking. "Shall I land there?"

"Yes, thank you; I am afraid I must ask you to stay there, for the horses would certainly have fits if you came anywhere near the stables."

When Temeraire had landed, Laurence climbed down and stroked his warm nose. "I will arrange for you to have something to eat as soon as I have spoken with my parents, if they are indeed home, but that may take some time," he said apologetically.

"You need not bring me food tonight; I ate well before we left, and I am sleepy. I will eat some of those deer over there in the morning," Temeraire said, settling himself down and curling his tail around his legs. "You should stay inside; it is colder here than Madeira was, and I do not want you to fall sick."

"There is something very curious about a six-week-old creature playing nursemaid," Laurence said, amused; yet even as he spoke, he could hardly believe Temeraire was so young. Temeraire had seemed in most respects mature straight out of the shell, and ever since hatching he had been drinking up knowledge of the world with such enthusiasm that the gaps in his understanding were vanishing with astonishing speed. Laurence no longer thought of him as a creature for whom he was responsible, but rather as an intimate friend, already the dearest in his life, and one to be depended upon without question. The training lost a little of its dread for Laurence as he looked up at the already-drowsing Temeraire, and Barstowe he put aside in his memory as a bugbear. Surely there could be nothing ahead which they could not face together.

But his family he would have to face alone. Coming to the house from the stable side, he could see that his first impression from the air had been correct: the drawing room was brightly lit, and many of the bedrooms had candlelight in them. It was certainly a house party, despite the time of year.

He sent a footman to let his father know he was home, and went up to his room by the back stairs to change. He would have liked a bath, but he thought he had to go down at once to be civil; anything else might smack of avoidance. He settled for washing his face and hands in the basin; he had brought his evening rig, fortunately. He looked strange to himself in the mirror, wearing the new bottle-green coat of the Corps with the gold bars upon the shoulders in place of epaulettes; it had been bought in Dover, having been partly made for another man and adjusted hastily while Laurence waited, but it fit well enough.

More than a dozen people were assembled in the drawing room, besides his parents; the idle conversation died down when he entered, then resumed in hushed voices and followed him through the room. His mother came to meet him; her face was composed but a little fixed in its expression, and he could feel her tension as he bent to kiss her cheek. "I am sorry to descend on you unannounced in this fashion," he said. "I did not expect to find anyone at home; I am only here for the night, and bound for Scotland in the morning."

"Oh, I am sorry to hear it, my dear, but we are very happy to have you even briefly," she said. "Have you met Miss Montagu?"

The company were mostly long-standing friends of his parents whom he did not know very well, but as he had suspected might be the case, their neighbors were among the party, and Edith Galman was there with her parents. He was not sure whether to be pleased or unhappy; he felt he ought to be glad to see her, and for the opportunity which would otherwise not have come for so long; yet there was a sense of a whispering undercurrent in the glances thrown his way by the whole company, deeply discomfiting, and he felt wholly unprepared to face her in so public a setting.

Her expression as he bowed over her hand gave him no hint of her feelings: she was of a disposition not easily ruffled, and if she had been startled by the news of his coming, she had already recovered her poise. "I am glad to see you, Will," she said, in her quiet way, and though he could not discover any particular warmth in her voice, he thought at least she did not seem angry or upset.

Unfortunately, he had no immediate opportunity to exchange a private word with her; she had already been engaged in conversation with Bertram Woolvey, and with her customary good manners, she turned back once they had completed their greetings. Woolvey made him a polite nod, but did not make any move to yield his place. Though their parents moved in the same circles, Woolvey had not been required to pursue any sort of occupation, being his father's heir, and lacking any interest in politics, he spent his time hunting in the country or playing for high stakes in town. Laurence found his conversation monotonous, and they had never become friends.

In any event, he could not avoid paying his respects to

the rest of the company; it was difficult to meet open stares with equanimity, and the only thing less welcome than the censure in many voices was the note of pity in others. By far the worst moment was coming to the table where his father was playing whist; Lord Allendale looked at Laurence's coat with heavy disapproval and said nothing to his son at all.

The uncomfortable silence which fell upon their corner of the room was very awkward; Laurence was saved by his mother, who asked him to make up a fourth in another table, and he gratefully sat down and immersed himself in the intricacies of the game. His table companions were older gentlemen, Lord Galman and two others, friends and political allies of his father; they were dedicated players and did not trouble him with much conversation beyond what was polite.

He could not help glancing towards Edith from time to time, though he could not catch the sound of her voice. Woolvey continued to monopolize her company, and Laurence could not help but dislike seeing him lean so close and speak to her so intimately. Lord Galman had to gently call his attention back to the cards after his distraction delayed them; Laurence apologized to the table in some embarrassment and bent his head over his hand again.

"You are off to Loch Laggan, I suppose?" Admiral McKinnon said, giving him a few moments in which to recapture the thread of play. "I lived not far from there, as a boy, and a friend of mine lived near Laggan village; we used to see the flights overhead."

"Yes, sir; we are to train there," Laurence said, making his discard; Viscount Hale, to his left, continued the play, and Lord Galman took the trick.

"They are a queer lot over there; half the village goes into service, but the locals go up, the aviators don't come down, except now and again to the pub to see one

of the girls. Easier than at sea for that, at least, ha, ha!"
Having made this coarse remark, McKinnon belatedly
recalled his company; he glanced over his shoulder in
some embarrassment to see if any of the ladies had overheard, and dropped the subject.

Woolvey took Edith in to supper; Laurence unbal-
anced the table by his presence and had to sit on the far
side, where he could have all the pain of seeing their
conversation with none of the pleasure of participating
in it. Miss Montagu, on his left, was pretty but sulky-
looking, and she neglected him almost to the point of
rudeness to speak to the gentleman on her other side, a
heavy gamester whom Laurence knew by name and reputation rather than personally.

To be snubbed in such a manner was a new experience for him and an unpleasant one; he knew he was no
longer a marriageable man, but he had not expected this
to have so great an impact upon his casual reception,
and to find himself valued less than a wastrel with blown
hair and mottled red cheeks was particularly shocking.
Viscount Hale, on his right, was only interested in his
food, so Laurence found himself sitting in almost complete silence.

Still more unpleasantly, without conversation of his
own to command his attention, Laurence could not help
overhearing while Woolvey spoke at length and with
very little accuracy on the state of the war and England's
readiness for invasion. Woolvey was ridiculously enthusiastic, speaking of how the militia would teach Bonaparte a lesson if he dared to bring across his army.
Laurence was forced to fix his gaze upon his plate to
conceal his expression. Napoleon, master of the Continent, with a hundred thousand men at his disposal, to
be turned back by militia: pure foolishness. Of course, it
was the sort of folly that the War Office encouraged, to

preserve morale, but to see Edith listening to this speech approvingly was highly unpleasant.

Laurence thought she might have kept her face turned away deliberately; certainly she made no effort to meet his eye. He kept his attention for the most part fixed upon his plate, eating mechanically and sunk into uncharacteristic silence. The meal seemed interminable; thankfully, his father rose very shortly after the women had left them, and on returning to the drawing room, Laurence at once took the opportunity to make his apologies to his mother and escape, pleading the excuse of the journey ahead.

But one of the servants, out of breath, caught him just outside the door of his room: his father wanted to see him in the library. Laurence hesitated; he could send an excuse and postpone the interview, but there was no sense in delaying the inevitable. He went back downstairs slowly nevertheless, and left his hand on the door just a moment too long: but then one of the maids came by, and he could not play the coward anymore, so he pushed it open and went inside.

"I wonder at your coming here," Lord Allendale said the moment the door had shut: not even the barest pleasantry. "I wonder at it indeed. What do you mean by it?"

Laurence stiffened but answered quietly, "I meant only to break my journey; I am on my way to my next posting. I had no notion of your being here, sir, or having guests, and I am very sorry to have burst in upon you."

"I see; I suppose you imagined we would remain in London, with this news making a nine days' wonder and spectacle of us? Next posting, indeed." He surveyed Laurence's new coat with disdain, and Laurence felt at once as poorly dressed and shabby as when he had suffered such inspections as a boy brought in fresh from playing in the gardens. "I am not going to bother reproaching you. You knew perfectly well what I would think of the whole matter, and it did not weigh with you: very well. You will oblige me, sir, by avoiding this house in future, and our residence in London, if indeed you can be spared from your animal husbandry long enough to set foot in the city."

Laurence felt a great coldness descend on him; he was very tired suddenly, and he had no heart at all to argue. He heard his own voice almost as if from a distance, and there was no emotion in it at all as he said, "Very good, sir; I shall leave at once." He would have to take Temeraire to the commons to sleep, undoubtedly scaring the village herd, and buy him a few sheep out of his own pocket in the morning if possible or ask him to fly hungry if not; but they would manage.

"Do not be absurd," Lord Allendale said. "I am not disowning you; not that you do not deserve it, but I do not choose to enact a melodrama for the benefit of the world. You will stay the night and leave tomorrow, as you declared; that will do very well. I think nothing more needs to be said; you may go."

Laurence went back upstairs as quickly as he was able; closing the door of his bedroom behind him felt like allowing a burden to slip off his shoulders. He had meant to call for a bath, but he did not think he could bear to speak to anyone, even a maid or a footman: to be alone and quiet was everything. He consoled himself with the reminder that they could leave early in the morning, and he would not have to endure another formal meal with the company, nor exchange another word with his father, who rarely rose before eleven even in the country.

He looked at his bed a moment longer; then abruptly he took an old frock coat and a worn pair of trousers from his wardrobe, exchanged these for his evening dress, and went outside. Temeraire was already asleep, curled neatly about himself, but before Laurence could slip away again, one of his eyes half-opened, and he lifted his wing in instinctive welcome. Laurence had taken a blanket from the stables; he was as warm and comfortable as he could wish, stretched upon the dragon's broad foreleg.

"Is all well?" Temeraire asked him softly, putting his other foreleg protectively around Laurence, sheltering him more closely against his breast; his wings half-rose, mantling. "Something has distressed you. Shall we not go at once?"

The thought was tempting, but there was no sense in it; he and Temeraire would both be the better for a quiet night and breakfast in the morning, and in any case he was not going to creep away as if ashamed. "No, no," Laurence said, petting him until his wings settled again. "There is no need, I assure you; I have only had words with my father." He fell silent; he could not shake the memory of the interview, his father's cold dismissiveness, and his shoulders hunched.

"Is he angry about our coming?" Temeraire asked.

Temeraire's quick perception and the concern in his voice were like a tonic for his weary unhappiness, and it made Laurence speak more freely than he meant to. "It is an old quarrel at heart," he said. "He would have had me go into the Church, like my brother; he has never counted the Navy an honorable occupation."

"And is an aviator worse, then?" Temeraire said, a little too perceptive now. "Is that why you did not like to leave the Navy?"

"In his eyes, perhaps, the Corps is worse, but not in mine; there is too great a compensation." He reached up to stroke Temeraire's nose; Temeraire nuzzled back affectionately. "But truly, he has never approved my choice of career; I had to run away from home as a boy for him to let me go to sea. I cannot allow his will to govern me, for I see my duty differently than he does."

Temeraire snorted, his warm breath coming out as small trails of smoke in the cool night air. "But he will not let you sleep inside?"

"Oh, no," Laurence said, and felt a little embarrassed to confess the weakness that had brought him out to seek comfort in Temeraire. "I only felt I would rather be with you, than sleep alone."

But Temeraire did not see anything unusual in it. "So long as you are quite warm," he said, resettling himself carefully and sweeping his wings forward a little, to encircle them from the wind.

"I am very comfortable; I beg you to have no concern," Laurence said, stretching out upon the broad, firm limb, and drawing the blanket around himself. "Good night, my dear." He was suddenly very tired, but with a natural physical fatigue: the bone-deep, painful weariness was gone.

He woke very early, just before sunrise, as Temeraire's belly rumbled strongly enough for the sound to rouse them both. "Oh, I am hungry," Temeraire said, waking up bright-eyed, and looked eagerly over at the herd of deer milling nervously in the park, clustered against the far wall.

Laurence climbed down. "I will leave you to your breakfast, and go to have my own," he said, giving Temeraire's side one final pat before turning back to the house. He was in no fit state to be seen; fortunately, with the hour so early, the guests were not yet about, and he was able to gain his bedroom without any encounter which might have rendered him still more disreputable.

He washed briskly, put on his flying dress while a manservant repacked his solitary piece of baggage, and went down as soon as he thought acceptable. The maids were still laying the first breakfast dishes out upon the sideboard, and the coffeepot had just been laid upon the table. He had hoped to avoid all the party, but to his surprise, Edith was at the breakfast table already, though she had never been an early riser.

Her face was outwardly calm, her clothing in perfect order and her hair drawn up smoothly into a golden knot, but her hands betrayed her, clenched together in her lap. She had not taken any food, only a cup of tea, and even that sat untouched before her. "Good morning," she said, with a brightness that rang false; she glanced at the servants as she spoke. "May I pour for you?"

"Thank you," he said, the only possible reply, and took the place next to her; she poured coffee for him and added half a spoonful of sugar and cream each, exactly to his tastes. They sat stiffly together, neither eating nor speaking, until the servants finished the preparations and left the room.

"I hoped I might have a chance to speak with you before you left," she said quietly, looking at him at last. "I am so very sorry, Will; I suppose there was no other alternative?"

He needed a moment to understand she meant his going into harness; despite his anxieties on the subject of his training, he had already forgotten to view his new situation as an evil. "No, my duty was clear," he said, shortly; he might have to tolerate criticism from his father on the subject, but he would not accept it from any other quarter.

But in the event, Edith only nodded. "I knew as soon as I heard that it would be something of the sort," she said. She bowed her head again; her hands, which had been twisting restlessly over each other, stilled.

"My feelings have not altered with my circumstances," Laurence said at last, when it was clear she would say nothing more. He felt he already had received his answer, by her lack of warmth, but she would not say, later on, that he had not been true to his word; he would let her be the one to put an end to their understanding. "If yours have, you need merely say a word to silence me." Even as he made the offer, he could not help but feel resentment, and he could hear an unaccustomed coldness creeping into his voice: a strange tone for a proposal.

She drew a quick, startled breath, and said almost fiercely, "How can you speak so?" For a moment he hoped again; but she went on at once to say, "Have I ever been mercenary; have I ever reproached you for following your chosen course, with all its attendant dangers and discomforts? If you had gone into the Church, you would certainly have had any number of good livings settled upon you; by now we could have been comfortable together in our own home, with children, and I should not have had to spend so many hours in fear for you away at sea."

She spoke very fast, with more emotion than he was used to seeing in her, and spots of color standing high on her cheeks. There was a great deal of justice in her remarks; he could not fail to see it, and be embarrassed at his own resentment. He half-reached out his hand to her, but she was already continuing: "I have not complained, have I? I have waited; I have been patient; but I have been waiting for something better than a solitary life, far from the society of all my friends and family, with only a very little share of your attention. My feelings are just as they have always been, but I am not so reckless or sentimental as to rely on feeling alone to ensure happiness in the face of every possible obstacle."

Here at last she stopped. "Forgive me," Laurence said, heavy with mortification: every word seemed a just reproach, when he had been pleased to think himself ill-used. "I should not have spoken, Edith; I had better have asked your pardon for having placed you in so wretched a position." He rose from the table and bowed; of course he could not stay in her company now. "I must beg you to excuse me; pray accept all my best wishes for your happiness."

But she was rising also, and shaking her head. "No, you must stay and finish your breakfast," she said. "You have a long journey ahead of you; I am not hungry in the least. No, I assure you, I am going." She gave him her hand and a smile that trembled very slightly. He thought she meant to make a polite farewell, but if that was her intention, it failed at the last moment. "Pray do not think ill of me," she said, very low, and left the room as quickly as she might.

She need not have worried; he could not. On the contrary, he felt only guilt for having felt coldly towards her even for a moment, and for having failed in his obligation to her. Their understanding had been formed between a gentleman's daughter with a respectable dowry and a naval officer with few expectations but handsome prospects. He had reduced his standing through his own actions, and he could not deny that nearly all the world would have disagreed with his own assessment of his duty in the matter.

And she was not unreasonable in asking more than an aviator could give. Laurence had only to think of the degree of his attention and affection which Temeraire commanded to realize he could have very little left to offer a wife, even on those rare occasions when he would be at liberty. He had been selfish in making the offer, asking her to sacrifice her own happiness to his comfort.

He had very little heart or appetite left for his breakfast, but he did not want to stop along his way; he filled his plate and forced himself to eat. He was not left in solitude long; only a little while after Edith had gone, Miss Montagu came downstairs, dressed in a too-elegant riding habit, something more suitable for a se-date canter through London than a country ride, which nevertheless showed her figure to great advantage. She was smiling as she came into the room, which expression turned instantly to a frown to see him the only one there, and she took a seat at the far end of the table. Woolvey shortly joined her, likewise dressed for riding; Laurence nodded to them both with bare civility and paid no attention to their idle conversation.

Just as he was finishing, his mother came down, showing signs of hurried dressing and lines of fatigue around her eyes; she looked into his face anxiously. He smiled at her, hoping to reassure, but he could see he was not very successful: his unhappiness and the reserve with which he had armored himself against his father's disapproval and the curiosity of the general company was visible in his face, with all he could do.

"I must be going shortly; will you come and meet Temeraire?" he asked her, thinking they might have a private few minutes walking, at least.

"Temeraire?" Lady Allendale said blankly. "William, you do not mean you have your dragon here, do you? Good Heavens, where is he?"

"Certainly he is here; how else would I be traveling? I left him outside behind the stables, in the old yearling paddock," Laurence said. "He will have eaten by now; I told him to make free of the deer."

"Oh!" said Miss Montagu, overhearing; curiosity evidently overcame her objections to the company of an aviator. "I have never seen a dragon; pray may we come? How famous!"

It was impossible to refuse, although he would have liked to, so when he had rung for his baggage, the four of them went out to the field together. Temeraire was sitting up on his haunches, watching the morning fog gradually burn away over the countryside; against the cold grey sky he loomed very large, even from a considerable distance.

Laurence stopped for a moment to pick up a bucket and rags from the stables, then led his suddenly reluctant party on with a certain relish at Woolvey and Miss Montagu's dragging steps. His mother was not unalarmed herself, but she did not show it, save by holding Laurence's arm a little more tightly, and stopping several paces back as he went to Temeraire's side.

Temeraire looked at the strangers with interest as he lowered his head to be washed; his chops were gory with the remains of the deer, and he opened his jaws to let Laurence clean away the blood from the corners of his mouth. There were three or four sets of antlers upon the ground. "I tried to bathe in that pond, but it is too shallow, and the mud came into my nose," he told Laurence apologetically.

"Oh, he talks!" Miss Montagu exclaimed, clinging to Woolvey's arm; the two of them had backed away at the sight of the rows of gleaming white teeth: Temeraire's incisors were already larger than a man's fist, and with a serrated edge.

Temeraire was taken aback at first; but then his pupils widened and he said, very gently, "Yes, I talk," and to Laurence, "Would she perhaps like to come up on my back, and see around?"

Laurence could not repress an unworthy flash of malice. "I am sure she would; pray come forward, Miss Montagu, I can see you are not one of those poor-spirited creatures who are afraid of dragons."

"No, no," she said palely, drawing back. "I have trespassed on Mr. Woolvey's time enough, we must be going for our ride." Woolvey stammered a few equally transparent excuses as well, and they escaped at once together, stumbling in their haste to be away.

Temeraire blinked after them in mild surprise. "Oh, they were just afraid," he said. "I thought she was like Volly at first. I do not understand; it is not as though they were cows, and anyway I have just eaten."

Laurence concealed his private sentiment of victory and drew his mother forward. "Do not be afraid at all, there is not the least cause," he said to her softly. "Temeraire, this is my mother, Lady Allendale."

"Oh, a mother, that is special, is it not?" Temeraire said, lowering his head to look at her more closely. "I am honored to meet you."

Laurence guided her hand to Temeraire's snout, and once she made the first tentative touch to the warm hide, she soon began petting the dragon with more confidence. "Why, the pleasure is mine," she said. "And how soft! I would never have thought it."

Temeraire made a pleased low rumble at the compliment and the petting, and Laurence looked at the two of them with a great deal of his happiness restored; he thought how little the rest of the world should matter to him, when he was secure in the good opinion of those he valued most, and in the knowledge that he was doing his duty. "Temeraire is a Chinese Imperial," he told his mother, with unconcealed pride. "One of the very rarest of all dragons: the only one in all Europe."

"Truly? How splendid, my dear; I do recall having heard before that Chinese dragons are quite out of the common way," she said. But she still looked at him anxiously, and there was a silent question in her eyes.

"Yes," he said, trying to answer it. "I count myself very fortunate, I promise you. Perhaps we will take you flying someday, when we have more time," he added. "It is quite extraordinary; there is nothing to compare to it."

"Oh, flying, indeed," she said indignantly, yet she seemed satisfied on a deeper level. "When you know perfectly well I cannot even keep myself on a horse. What I should do on a dragon's back, I am sure I do not know."

"You would be strapped on quite securely, just as I am," Laurence said. "Temeraire is not a horse, he would not try to have you off."

Temeraire said earnestly, "Oh yes, and if you did fall off, I dare say I could catch you," which was perhaps not the most reassuring remark, but his desire to please was very obvious, and Lady Allendale smiled up at him anyway.

"How very kind you are; I had no idea dragons were so well-mannered," she said. "You will take prodigious care of William, will you not? He has always given me twice as much anxiety as any of my other children, and he is forever getting himself into scrapes."

Laurence was a little indignant to hear himself described so, and to have Temeraire say, "I promise you, I will never let him come to harm."

"I see I have delayed too long; shortly the two of you will have me wrapped in cotton batting and fed on gruel," he said, bending to kiss her cheek. "Mother, you may write to me care of the Corps at Loch Laggan covert, in Scotland; we will be training there. Temeraire, will you sit up? I will sling this bandbox again."

"Perhaps you could take out that book by Duncan?" Temeraire asked, rearing up. "*The Naval Trident*? We never finished reading about the battle of the Glorious First, and you might read it to me as we go."

"Does he read to you?" Lady Allendale asked Temeraire, amused.

"Yes; you see, I cannot hold them myself, for they are too small, and also I cannot turn the pages very well," Temeraire said.

"You are misunderstanding; she is only shocked to learn that I am ever to be persuaded to open a book; she was forever trying to make me sit to them when I was a boy," Laurence said, rummaging in one of his other boxes to find the volume. "You would be quite astonished at how much of a bluestocking I am become, Mother; he is quite insatiable. I am ready, Temeraire."

She laughed and stepped back to the edge of the field as Temeraire put Laurence up, and stood watching them, shading her eyes with one hand, as they drove up into the air; a small figure, vanishing with every beat of the great wings, and then the gardens and the towers of the house rolled away behind the curve of a hill.

Chapter 5

❦

THE SKY OVER Loch Laggan was full of low-hanging clouds, pearl grey, mirrored in the black water of the lake. Spring had not yet arrived; a crust of ice and snow lay over the shore, ripples of yellow sand from an autumn tide still preserved beneath. The crisp cold smell of pine and fresh-cut wood rose from the forest. A gravel road wound up from the northern shores of the lake to the complex of the covert, and Temeraire turned to follow it up the low mountain.

A quadrangle of several large wooden sheds stood together on a level clearing near the top, open in the front and rather like half a stable in appearance; men were working outside on metal and leather: obviously the ground crews, responsible for the maintenance of the aviators' equipment. None of them so much as glanced up at the dragon's shadow crossing over their work-place, as Temeraire flew on to the headquarters.

The main building was a very medieval sort of fortification: four bare towers joined by thick stone walls, framing an enormous courtyard in the front and a squat, imposing hall that sank directly into the mountaintop and seemed to have grown out of it. The courtyard was almost entirely overrun. A young Regal Copper, twice Temeraire's size, sprawled drowsing over the flagstones with a pair of brown-and-purple Winchesters even smaller than Volatilus sleeping right on his back. Three mid-sized Yellow Reapers were in a mingled heap on the opposite side of the courtyard, their white-striped sides rising and falling in rhythm.

As Laurence climbed down, he discovered the reason for the dragons' choice of resting place: the flagstones were warm, as if heated from below, and Temeraire murmured happily and stretched himself on the stones beside the Yellow Reapers as soon as Laurence had unloaded him.

A couple of servants had come out to meet him, and they took the baggage off his hands. He was directed to the back of the building, through narrow dark corridors, musty smelling, until he came out into another open courtyard that emerged from the mountainside and ended with no railing, dropping off sheer into another ice-strewn valley. Five dragons were in the air, wheeling in graceful formation like a flock of birds; the point-leader was a Longwing, instantly recognizable by the black-and-white ripples bordering its orange-tipped wings, which faded to a dusky blue along their extraordinary length. A couple of Yellow Reapers held the flanking positions, and the ends were anchored by a pale greenish Grey Copper to the left, and a silver-grey dragon spotted with blue and black patches to the right; Laurence could not immediately identify its breed.

Though their wings beat in wholly different time, their relative positions hardly changed, until the Longwing's signal-midwingman waved a flag; then they switched off smoothly as dancers, reversing so the Longwing was flying last. At some other signal Laurence did not see, they all backwinged at once, performing a perfect loop and coming back into the original formation. He saw at once that the maneuver gave the Longwing the greatest sweep over the ground during the pass while retaining the protection of the rest of the wing around it;

naturally it was the greatest offensive threat among the group.

"Nitidus, you are still dropping low in the pass; try changing to a six-beat pattern on the loop." It was the deep resounding voice of a dragon, coming from above; Laurence turned and saw a golden-hued dragon with the Reaper markings in pale green and the edges of his wings deep orange, perched on an outcropping to the right of the courtyard: he bore no rider and no harness, save, if it could be called so, a broad golden neck-ring studded with rounds of pale green jade stone.

Laurence stared. Out in the valley, the wing repeated its looping pass. "Better," the dragon called approvingly. Then he turned his head and looked down. "Captain Laurence?" he said. "Admiral Powys said you would be arriving; you come in good time. I am Celeritas, training master here." He spread his wings for lift and leapt easily down into the courtyard.

Laurence bowed mechanically. Celeritas was a midweight dragon, perhaps a quarter of the size of a Regal Copper; smaller even than Temeraire's present juvenile size. "Hm," he said, lowering his head to inspect Laurence closely; the deep green irises of his eyes seemed to turn and contract around the narrowed pupil. "Hm, well, you are a good deal older than most handlers; but that is often all to the good when we must hurry along a young dragon, as in Temeraire's case I think we must."

He lifted his head and called out into the valley again, "Lily, remember to keep your neck straight on the loop." He turned back to Laurence. "Now then. He has no special offensive capabilities showing, as I understand it?"

"No, sir." The answer and the address were automatic; tone and attitude alike both declared the dragon's rank, and habit carried Laurence along through his surprise. "And Sir Edward Howe, who identified his species, was of the opinion that it was unlikely he should develop such, though not out of the question—"

"Yes, yes," Celeritas interrupted. "I have read Sir Edward's work; he is an expert on the Oriental breeds, and I would trust his judgment in the matter over my own. It is a pity, for we could well do with one of those Japanese poison-spitters, or waterspout-makers: now that would be useful against a French Flamme-de-Gloire. But heavy-combat weight, I understand?"

"He is at present some nine tons in weight, and it is nearly six weeks since he was hatched," Laurence said.

"Good, that is very good, he ought to double that," Celeritas said, and he rubbed the side of a claw over his forehead thoughtfully. "So. All is as I had heard. Good. We will be pairing Temeraire with Maximus, the Regal Copper currently here in training. The two of them together will serve as a loose backing arc for Lily's formation—that is the Longwing there." He gestured with his head out at the formation wheeling in the valley, and Laurence, still bewildered, turned to watch it for a moment.

The dragon continued, "Of course, I must see Temeraire fly before I can determine the specific course of your training, but I need to finish this session, and after a long journey he will not show to advantage in any case. Ask Lieutenant Granby to show you about and tell you where to find the feeding grounds; you will find him in the officers' club. Come back with Temeraire tomorrow, an hour past first light."

This was a command; an acknowledgment was required. "Very good, sir," Laurence said, concealing his stiffness in formality. Fortunately, Celeritas did not seem to notice; he was already leaping back up to his higher vantage point.

Laurence was very glad that he did not know where the officers' club was; he felt he could have used a quiet week to adjust his thinking, rather than the fifteen minutes it took him to find a servant who could point him in the right direction. Everything which he had ever heard about dragons was turned upon its head: that dragons were useless without their handlers; that unharnessed dragons were only good for breeding. He no longer wondered at all the anxiety on the part of the aviators; what would the world think, to know they were trained—given orders—by one of the beasts they supposedly controlled?

Of course, considered rationally, he had long possessed proofs of dragon intelligence and independence, in Temeraire's person; but these had developed gradually over time, and he had unconsciously come to think of Temeraire as a fully realized individual without extending the implication to the rest of dragonkind. The first surprise past, he could without too much difficulty accept the idea of a dragon as instructor, but it would certainly create a scandal of extraordinary proportions among those who had no similar personal experience.

It had not been so long, only shortly before the Revolution in France had cast Europe into war again, since the proposal had been made by Government that unharnessed dragons ought to be killed, rather than supported at the public expense and kept for breeding; the rationale offered had been a lack of need at that present time, and that their recalcitrance likely only hurt the fighting bloodlines. Parliament had calculated a savings of more than ten million pounds per annum; the idea had been seriously considered, then dropped abruptly without public explanation. It was whispered, however, that every admiral of the Corps stationed in range of London had jointly descended upon the Prime Minister and informed him that if the law were passed, the entire Corps would mutiny.

He had previously heard the story with disbelief; not

for the proposal, but for the idea that senior officers—any officers—would behave in such a way. The proposal had always seemed to him wrong-minded, but only as the sort of foolish short-sightedness so common among bureaucrats, who thought it better to save ten shillings on sailcloth and risk an entire ship worth six thousand pounds. Now he considered his own indifference with a sense of mortification. Of course they would have mutinied.

Still preoccupied with his thoughts, he walked through the archway to the officers' club without attention, and only caught the ball that hurtled at his head by reflex. A mingled cheer and cry of protest both went up at once.

"That was a clear goal, he's not on your team!" A young man, barely out of boyhood, with bright yellow hair, was complaining.

"Nonsense, Martin. Certainly he is; aren't you?" Another of the participants, grinning broadly, came up to Laurence to take the ball; he was a tall, lanky fellow, with dark hair and sunburnt cheekbones.

"Apparently so," Laurence said, amused, handing over the ball. He was a little astonished to find a collection of officers playing children's games indoors, and in such disarray. In his possession of coat and neckcloth, he was more formally dressed than all of them; a couple had even taken off their shirts entirely. The furniture had been pushed pell-mell into the edges of the room, and the carpet rolled up and thrust into a corner.

"Lieutenant John Granby, unassigned," the dark-haired man said. "Have you just arrived?"

"Yes; Captain Will Laurence, on Temeraire," Laurence said, and was startled and not a little dismayed to see the smile fall off Granby's face, the open friendliness vanishing at once.

"The Imperial!" The cry was almost general, and half the boys and men in the room disappeared past them, pelting towards the courtyard. Laurence, taken aback, blinked after them.

"Don't worry!" The yellow-haired young man, coming up to introduce himself, answered his look of alarm. "We all know better than to pester a dragon; they're only going to have a look. Though you might have some trouble with the cadets; we have a round two dozen of 'em here, and they make it their mission to plague the life out of everyone. Midwingman Ezekiah Martin, and you can forget my first name now that you have it, if you please."

Informality was so obviously the usual mode among them that Laurence could hardly take offense, though it was not in the least what he was used to. "Thank you for the warning; I will see Temeraire does not let them bother him," he said. He was relieved to see no sign of Granby's attitude of dislike in Martin's greeting, and wished he might ask the friendlier of the two for guidance. However, he did not mean to disobey orders, even if given by a dragon, so he turned to Granby and said formally, "Celeritas tells me to ask you to show me about; will you be so good?"

"Certainly," Granby said, trying for equal formality; but it sat less naturally on him, and he sounded artificial and wooden. "Come this way, if you please."

Laurence was pleased when Martin fell in with them as Granby led the way upstairs; the midwingman's light conversation, which did not falter for an instant, made the atmosphere a great deal less uncomfortable. "So you are the naval fellow who snatched an Imperial out of the jaws of France. Lord, it is a famous story; the Frogs must be gnashing their teeth and tearing their hair over it," Martin said exultantly. "I hear you took the egg off an hundred-gun ship; was the battle very long?"

"I am afraid rumor has magnified my accomplishments," Laurence said. "The *Amitié* was not a first-rate at all, but a thirty-six, a frigate; and her men were nearly falling down for thirst. Her captain offered a very valiant defense, but it was not a very great contest; ill fortune and the weather did our work for us. I can claim only to have been lucky."

"Oh! Well, luck is nothing to sneeze at, either; we would not get very far if luck were against us," Martin said. "Hullo, have they put you at the corner? You will have the wind howling at all hours."

Laurence came into the circular tower room and looked around his new accommodation with pleasure; to a man used to the confines of a ship's cabin, it seemed spacious, and the large, curved windows a great luxury. They looked out over the lake, where a thin grey drizzle had started; when he opened them, a cool wet smell came blowing in, not unlike the sea, except for the lack of salt.

His bandboxes were piled a little haphazardly together beside the wardrobe; he looked inside this with some concern, but his things had been put away neatly enough. A writing desk and chair completed the furnishings, beside the plain but ample bed. "It seems perfectly quiet to me; I am sure it will do nicely," he said, unbuckling his sword and laying it upon the bed; he did not feel comfortable taking off his coat, but he could at least reduce the formality of his appearance a little by this measure.

"Shall I show you to the feeding grounds now?" Granby said stiffly; it was his first contribution to the conversation since they had left the club.

"Oh, we ought to show him the baths first, and the dining hall," Martin said. "The baths are something to see," he added to Laurence. "They were built by the Romans, you know; and they are why we are all here at all."

"Thank you; I would be glad to see them," Laurence

said; although he would have been happy to let the obviously unwilling lieutenant escape, he could not say
otherwise now without being rude; Granby might be
discourteous, but Laurence did not intend to stoop to
the same behavior.

They passed the dining hall on the way; Martin, chat-
tering away, told him that the captains and lieutenants
dined at the smaller round table, then midwingmen and
ensigns at the long rectangle. "Thankfully, the cadets
come in and eat earlier, for the rest of us would starve if
we had to hear them squalling throughout our meals,
and then the ground crews eat after us," he finished.

"Do you never take your meals separately?" Laurence
asked; the communal dining was rather odd, for officers,
and he thought wistfully that he would miss being able
to invite friends to his own table; it had been one of his
greatest pleasures, ever since he had won enough in
prize-money to afford it.

"Of course, if someone is sick, a tray will be sent up,"
Martin said. "Oh, are you hungry? I suppose you had
no dinner. Hi, Tolly," he called, and a servant crossing
the room with a stack of linens turned to look at them,
an eyebrow raised. "This is Captain Laurence; he has
just flown in. Can you manage something for him, or
must he wait until supper?"

"No, thank you; I am not hungry. I was speaking only
from curiosity," Laurence said.

"Oh, there's no trouble about it," the man Tolly said,
answering directly. "I dare say one of the cooks can cut
you a fair slice or two and dish up some potatoes; I will
ask Nan. Tower room on the third floor, yes?" He nodded and went on his way without even waiting for a
reply.

"There, Tolly will take care of you," Martin said, evidently without the least consciousness of anything out
of the ordinary. "He is one of the best fellows; Jenkins is

never willing to oblige, and Marvell will get it done, but he will moan about it so that you wish you hadn't asked."

"I imagine that you have difficulty finding servants who are not bothered by the dragons," Laurence said; he was beginning to adjust to the informality of the aviators' address among themselves, but to find a similar degree in a servant had bemused him afresh.

"Oh, they are all born and bred in the villages hereabouts, so they are used to it and us," Martin said, as they walked through the long hall. "I suppose Tolly has been working here since he was a squeaker; he would not bat an eye at a Regal Copper in a tantrum."

A metal door closed off the stairway leading down to the baths; when Granby pulled it open, a gust of hot, wet air came out and steamed in the relative cold of the corridor. Laurence followed the other two down the narrow, spiraling stair; it went down for four turns and opened abruptly into a large bare room, with shelves of stone built out of the walls and faded paintings upon the walls, partly chipped away: obvious relics of Roman times. One side held heaps of folded and stacked linens, the other a few piles of discarded clothes.

"Just leave your things on the shelves," Martin said. "The baths are in a circuit, so we come back out here again." He and Granby were already stripping.

"Have we time to bathe now?" Laurence asked, a little dubiously.

Martin paused in taking off his boots. "Oh, I thought we would just stroll through; no, Granby? It is not as though there is a need to rush; supper will not be for a few hours yet."

"Unless you have something urgent to attend to," Granby said to Laurence, so ungraciously that Martin looked between them in surprise, as if only now noticing the tension.

Laurence compressed his lips and held back a sharp word; he could not be checking every aviator who might be hostile to a Navy man, and to some extent he understood the resentment. He would have to win through it, just like a new midwingman fresh on board. "Not in the least" was all he said. Though he was not sure why they had to strip down merely to tour the baths, he followed their example, save that he arranged his clothes with more care into two neat stacks, and laid his coat atop them rather than creasing it by folding.

Then they left the room by a corridor to the left, and passed through another metal door at its end. He saw the sense in undressing as soon as they were through: the room beyond was so full of steam he could barely see past arm's length, and he was dripping wet instantly. If he had been dressed, his coat and boots would have been ruined, and everything else soaked through; on naked skin the steam was luxurious, just shy of being too hot, and his muscles unwound gratefully from the long flight.

The room was tiled, with benches built out of the walls at regular intervals; a few other fellows were lying about in the steam. Granby and Martin nodded to a couple of them as they led the way through and into a cavernous room beyond; this one was even warmer, but dry, and a long, shallow pool ran very nearly its full length. "We are right under the courtyard now, and there is why the Corps has this place," Martin said, pointing.

Deep niches were built into the long wall at regular intervals, and a fence of wrought-iron barred them from the rest of the room while leaving them visible. Perhaps half the niches were empty; the other half were padded with fabric, and each held a single massive egg. "They must be kept warm, you see, since we cannot spare the dragons to brood over them, or let them bury them near volcanoes or suchlike, as they would in nature."

"And there is no space to make a separate chamber for them?" Laurence said, surprised.

"Of course there is space," Granby said rudely; Martin glanced at him and leapt in hastily, before Laurence could react.

"You see, everyone is in and out of here often, so if one of them begins to look a bit hard we are more likely to notice it," he said hurriedly.

Still trying to rein in his temper, Laurence let Granby's remark pass and nodded to Martin; he had read in Sir Edward's books how unpredictable dragon egg hatching was, until the very end; even knowing the species could only narrow the process down to a span of months or, for the larger breeds, years.

"We think the Anglewing over there may hatch soon; that would be famous," Martin went on, pointing at a golden-brown egg, its sides faintly pearlescent and spotted with flecks of brighter yellow. "That is Obversaria's get; she is the flag-dragon at the Channel. I was signal-ensign aboard her, fresh out of training, and no beast in her class can touch her for maneuvering."

Both of the aviators looked at the eggs with wistful expressions, longingly; of course each of those represented a rare chance of promotion, and one even more uncertain than the favor of the Admiralty, which might be courted or won by valor in the field. "Have you served with many dragons?" Laurence asked Martin.

"Only Obversaria and then Inlacrimas; he was injured in a skirmish over the Channel a month ago, and so here I am on the ground," Martin said. "But he will be fit for duty again in a month, and I got a promotion out of it, so I shouldn't complain; I am just made mid-wingman," he added proudly. "And Granby here has been with more; four, is that not right? Who before Laetificat?"

"Excursius, Fluitare, and Actionis," Granby answered, very briefly.

But the first name had been enough; Laurence finally understood, and his face hardened. The fellow likely was friend to Lieutenant Dayes; at any rate, the two of them had been the equivalent of shipmates until recently, and it was now clear to him that Granby's offensive behavior was not simply the general resentment of an aviator for a naval officer shoehorned into his service, but also a personal matter, and thus in some sense an extension of Dayes's original insult.

Laurence was far less inclined to tolerate any slight for such a cause, and he said abruptly, "Let us continue, gentlemen." He allowed no further delays during the remainder of the tour, and let Martin carry the conversation as he would, without giving any response that might draw it out. They came back to the dressing room after completing the circuit of the baths, and once dressed again, Laurence said quietly but firmly, "Mr. Granby, you will take me to the feeding grounds now; then I may set you at liberty." He had to make it clear to the man that the disrespect would not be tolerated; if Granby were to make another fling, he would have to be checked, and better by far were that to occur in private. "Mr. Martin, I am obliged to you for your company, and your explanations; they have been most valuable."

"You are very welcome," Martin said, looking between Laurence and Granby uncertainly, as if afraid of what might happen if he left them alone. But Laurence had made his hint quite unmistakable, and despite the informality Martin seemed able to see that it had nearly the weight of an order. "I will see you both at supper, I imagine; until then."

In silence Laurence continued with Granby to the

feeding grounds, or rather to a ledge that overlooked them, at the far end of the training valley. The mouth of a natural cul-de-sac was visible at the far end of the valley, and Laurence could see several herdsmen there on duty; Granby explained, in a flat voice, that when signaled from the ledge, these would pick out the appropriate number of beasts for a dragon and send them into the valley, where the dragon might hunt them down and eat, so long as no training flight was in progress.

"It is straightforward enough, I trust," Granby said, in conclusion; his tone was highly disagreeable, and yet another step over the line, as Laurence had feared.

"Sir," Laurence said quietly. Granby blinked in momentary confusion, and Laurence repeated, "It is straightforward enough, *sir.*"

He hoped it would be enough to warn Granby off from further disrespect, but almost unbelievably, the lieutenant answered back, saying, "We do not stand on ceremony here, whatever you may have been used to in the Navy."

"I have been used to courtesy; where I do not receive it, I will insist at the least on the respect due to rank," Laurence said, his temper breaking loose; he glared savagely at Granby, and felt the color coming into his face. "You will amend your address immediately, Lieutenant Granby, or by God I shall have you broken for insubordination; I do not imagine that the Corps takes quite so light a view of it as one might gather from your behavior."

Granby went very pale; the sunburn across his cheeks stood out red. "Yes, *sir,*" he said, and stood sharply at attention.

"Dismissed, Lieutenant," Laurence said at once, and turned away to gaze out over the field with arms clasped behind his back until Granby had left; he did not want to even look at the fellow again. With the sustaining flush of righteous anger gone, he was tired, and miserable to have met with such treatment; in addition he now had to anticipate with dismay the consequences he knew would follow on his having checked the man. Granby had seemed on their first instant of meeting to be friendly and likable by nature; even if he were not, he was still one of the aviators, and Laurence an interloper. Granby's fellows would naturally support him, and their hostility could only make Laurence's circumstances unpleasant.

But there had been no alternative; open disrespect could not be borne, and Granby had known very well that his behavior was beyond the pale. Laurence was still downcast when he turned back inside; his spirits rose only as he walked into the courtyard and found Temeraire awake and waiting for him. "I am sorry to have abandoned you so long," Laurence said, leaning against his side and petting him, more for his own comfort than Temeraire's. "Have you been very bored?"

"No, not at all," Temeraire said. "There were a great many people who came by and spoke to me; some of them measured me for a new harness. Also, I have been talking to Maximus here, and he tells me we are to train together."

Laurence nodded a greeting to the Regal Copper, who had acknowledged the mention of his name by opening a sleepy eye; Maximus lifted his massive head enough to return the gesture, and then sank back down. "Are you hungry?" Laurence asked, turning back to Temeraire. "We must be up early to fly for Celeritas—that is the training master here," he added, "so you will likely not have time in the morning."

"Yes, I would like to eat," Temeraire said; he seemed wholly unsurprised to have a dragon as training master, and in the face of his pragmatic response, Laurence felt a little silly for his own first shock; of course Temeraire would see nothing strange in it.

Laurence did not bother strapping himself back on completely for the short hop to the ledge, and there he dismounted to let Temeraire hunt without a passenger. The uncomplicated pleasure of watching the dragon soar and dive so gracefully did a great deal to ease Laurence's mind. No matter how the aviators should respond to him, his position was secure in a way that no sea captain could hope for; he had experience in managing unwilling men, if it came to that in his crew, and at least Martin's example showed that not all the officers would be prejudiced against him from the beginning.

There was some other comfort also: as Temeraire swooped and snatched a lumbering shaggy-haired cow neatly off the ground and settled down to eat it, Laurence heard enthusiastic murmuring and looked up to see a row of small heads poking out of the windows above. "That is the Imperial, sir, is he not?" one of the boys, sandy-haired and round-faced, called out to him.

"Yes, that is Temeraire," Laurence answered. He had always made an effort towards the education of his young gentlemen, and his ship had been considered a prime place for a squeaker; he had many family and service friends to do favors for, so he had fairly extensive experience of boys, most of it favorable. Unlike many grown men, he was not at all uncomfortable in their company, even if these were younger than most of his midshipmen ever had been.

"Look, look, how smashing," another one, smaller and darker, cried and pointed; Temeraire was skimming low to the ground and collecting up all three sheep that had been released for him, before stopping to eat again.

"I dare say you all have more experience of dragon-flight than I; does he show to advantage?" he asked them.

"Oh, yes," was the general and enthusiastic response. "Corners on a wink and a nod," the sandy-haired boy said, adopting a professional tone, "and splendid extension; not a wasted wingbeat. Oh, ripping," he added, dissolving back into a small boy, as Temeraire back-winged to take the last cow.

"Sir, you haven't picked your runners yet, have you?" another dark-haired one asked hopefully, which at once set up a clamor among all the others; all of them announcing their worthiness for what Laurence gathered was some position to which particularly favored cadets were assigned, in a dragon-crew.

"No; and I imagine when I do it will be on the advice of your instructors," he said, with mock severity. "So I dare say you ought to mind them properly the next few weeks. There, have you had enough?" he asked, as Temeraire rejoined him on the ledge, landing directly on the edge with perfect balance.

"Oh yes, they were very tasty; but now I am all over blood, may we go and wash up?" Temeraire said.

Laurence realized belatedly this had been omitted from his tour; he glanced up at the children. "Gentlemen, I must ask you for direction; shall I take him to the lake for bathing?"

They all stared down at him with round surprised eyes. "I have never heard of bathing a dragon," one of them said.

The sandy-haired one added, "I mean, can you imagine trying to wash a Regal? It would take ages. Usually they lick their chops and talons clean, like a cat."

"That does not sound very pleasant; I like being washed, even if it is a great deal of work," Temeraire said, looking at Laurence anxiously.

Laurence suppressed an exclamation and said equably, "Certainly it is a great deal of work, but so are many other things that ought to be done; we shall go to the lake at once. Only wait here a moment, Temeraire; I will go and fetch some linens."

"Oh, I will bring you some!" The sandy-haired boy vanished from the windows; the rest immediately followed, and scarcely five minutes later the whole half a dozen of them had come spilling out onto the ledge with a pile of imperfectly folded linens whose provenance Laurence suspected.

He took them anyway, thanking the boys gravely, and climbed back aboard, making a mental note of the sandy-haired fellow; it was the sort of initiative he liked to see and considered the making of an officer.

"We could bring our carabiner belts tomorrow, and then we could ride along and help," the boy added now, with a too-guileless expression.

Laurence eyed him and wondered if this was forwardness to discourage, but he was secretly cheered by the enthusiasm, so he contented himself with saying firmly, "We shall see."

They stood watching from the ledge, and Laurence saw their eager faces until Temeraire came around the castle and they passed out of sight. Once at the lake, he let Temeraire swim about to clean off the worst of the gore, then wiped him down with particular care. It was appalling to a man raised to daily holystoning of the deck that aviators should leave their beasts to keep themselves clean, and as he rubbed down the sleek black sides, he suddenly considered the harness. "Temeraire, does this chafe you at all?" he asked, touching the straps.

"Oh, not very often now," Temeraire said, turning his head to look. "My hide is getting a great deal tougher; and when it does bother me I can shift it a little, and then it is better straightaway."

"My dear, I am covered with shame," Laurence said. "I ought never have kept you in it; from now on you shall not wear it for an instant while it is not necessary for our flying together."

"But is it not required, like your clothing?" Temeraire said. "I would not like anyone to think I was not civilized."

"I shall get you a larger chain to wear about your neck, and that will serve," Laurence said, thinking of the golden collar Celeritas wore. "I am not going to have you suffering for a custom that so far as I can tell is nothing but laziness; and I am of a mind to complain of it in the strongest terms to the next admiral I see."

He was as good as his word and stripped the harness from Temeraire the moment they landed in the courtyard. Temeraire looked a little nervously at the other dragons, who had been watching with interest from the moment the two of them had returned with Temeraire still dripping from the lake. But none of them seemed shocked, only curious, and once Laurence had detached the gold-and-pearl chain and wrapped it around one of Temeraire's talons, rather like a ring, Temeraire relaxed entirely and settled back down on the warm flagstones. "It is more pleasant not to have it on; I had not realized how it would be," he confided quietly to Laurence, and scratched at a darkened spot on his hide where a buckle had rested and crushed together several scales into a callus.

Laurence paused in cleaning the harness and stroked him in apology. "I do beg your forgiveness," he said, looking at the galled spot with remorse. "I will try and find a poultice for these marks."

"I want mine off, too," chirped one of the Winchesters suddenly, and flitted down from Maximus's back to land in front of Laurence. "Will you, please?"

Laurence hesitated; it did not seem right to him to handle another man's beast. "I think perhaps your own handler is the only one who ought to remove it," he said. "I do not like to give offense."

"He has not come for three days," the Winchester said sadly, his small head drooping; he was only about the size of a couple of draft horses, and his shoulder barely topped Laurence's head. Looking more closely, Laurence could see his hide was marked with streaks of dried blood, and the harness did not look particularly clean or well-kept, unlike those of the other dragons; it bore stains and rough patches.

"Come here, and let me have a look at you," Laurence said quietly, as he took up the linens, still wet from the lake, and began to clean the little dragon.

"Oh, thank you," the Winchester said, leaning happily into the cloth. "My name is Levitas," he added shyly.

"I am Laurence, and this is Temeraire," Laurence said.

"Laurence is my captain," Temeraire said, the smallest hint of belligerence in his tone, and an emphasis on the possessive; Laurence looked up at him in surprise, and paused in his cleaning to pat Temeraire's side. Temeraire subsided, but watched with his pupils narrowed to thin slits while Laurence finished.

"Shall I see if I cannot find what has happened to your handler?" he told Levitas with a final pat. "Perhaps he is not feeling well, but if so I am sure he will be well soon."

"Oh, I do not think he is sick," Levitas said, with that same sadness. "But that feels much better already," he added, and rubbed his head gratefully against Laurence's shoulder.

Temeraire gave a low displeased rumble and flexed his talons against the stone; with an alarmed chirp, Levitas flew straightaway up to Maximus's back and nestled down small against the other Winchester again. Laurence turned to Temeraire. "Come now, what is this jealousy?" he said softly. "Surely you cannot begrudge him a little cleaning when his handler is neglecting him."

"You are mine," Temeraire said obstinately. After a moment, however, he ducked his head in a shamefaced way and added in a smaller voice, "He would be easier to clean."

"I would not give up an inch of your hide were you twice Laetificat's size," Laurence said. "But perhaps I will see if some of the boys would like to wash him, tomorrow."

"Oh, that would be good," Temeraire said, brightening. "I do not quite understand why his handler has not come; you would never stay away so long, would you?"

"Never in life, unless I was kept away by force," Laurence said. He did not understand it himself; he could imagine that a man harnessed to a dim beast would not necessarily find the creature's company satisfying intellectually, but at the least he would have expected the easy affection with which he had seen James treat Volatilus. And though even smaller, Levitas was certainly more intelligent than Volly. Perhaps it was not so strange that there would be less dedicated men among aviators as well as in any other branch of the service, but with the shortage of dragons, it seemed a great pity to see one of them reduced to unhappiness, which could not help but affect the creature's performance.

Laurence carried Temeraire's harness with him out of the castle yard and over to the large sheds where the ground crews worked; though it was late in the day, there were several men still sitting out in front, smoking comfortably. They looked at him curiously, not saluting, but not unfriendly, either. "Ah, you'd be Temeraire's," one of them said, reaching out to take the harness. "Has it broken? We'll be having a proper harness ready for you in a few days, but we can patch it up in the meantime."

"No, it merely needs cleaning," Laurence said.

"You haven't a harness-tender yet; we can't be assigning you your ground crew till we know how he's to be trained," the man said. "But we'll see to it; Hollin, give this a rub, would you?" he called, catching the attention of a younger man who was working on a bit of leatherwork inside.

Hollin came out, wiping grease off onto his apron, and took the harness in big, capable-looking hands. "Right you are; will he give me any trouble, putting it back on him after?" he asked.

"That will not be necessary, thank you; he is more comfortable without it, so merely leave it beside him," Laurence said firmly, ignoring the looks this won him. "And Levitas's harness requires attention as well."

"Levitas? Well now, I'd say that's for his captain to speak to his crew about," the first man said, sucking on his pipe thoughtfully.

That was perfectly true; nevertheless, it was a poor-spirited answer. Laurence gave the man a cold, steady look, and let silence speak for him. The men shifted a little uncomfortably under his glare. He said, very softly, "If they need to be rebuked to do their duty, then it must be arranged; I would not have thought any man in the Corps would need to hear anything but that a dragon's well-being was at risk to seek to amend the situation."

"I'll do it along of dropping off Temeraire's," Hollin said hurriedly. "I don't mind; he's so small it won't take me but a few shakes."

"Thank you, Mr. Hollin; I am glad to see I was not mistaken," Laurence said, and turned back to the castle; he heard the murmur behind him of "Regular Tartar, he is; wouldn't fancy being on his crew." It was not a pleasant thing to hear, at all; he had never been considered a hard captain, and he had always prided himself on ruling his men by respect rather than fear or a heavy hand; many of his crew had been volunteers.

He was conscious, too, of guilt: by speaking so strongly, he had indeed gone over the head of Levitas's captain, and the man would have every right to complain. But Laurence could not quite bring himself to regret it; Levitas was clearly neglected, and it in no way fit his sense of duty to leave the creature in discomfort. The informality of the Corps might for once be of service to him; with any luck the hint might not be taken as direct interference, or as truly outrageous as it would have been in the Navy.

It had not been an auspicious first day; he was both weary and discouraged. There had been nothing truly unacceptable as he had feared, nothing so bad he could not bear it, but also nothing easy or familiar. He could not help but long for the comforting strictures of the Navy which had encompassed all his life, and wish impractically that he and Temeraire might be once again on the deck of the *Reliant*, with all the wide ocean around them.

Chapter 6

THE SUN WOKE him, streaming in through the eastern windows. The forgotten cold plate had been waiting for him the night before when he had finally climbed back up to his room, Tolly evidently being as good as his word. A couple of flies had settled on the food, but that was nothing to a seaman; Laurence had waved them off and devoured it to the crumbs. He had meant only to rest awhile before supper and a bath; now he blinked stupidly up at the ceiling for the better part of a minute before getting his bearings.

Then he remembered the training; he scrambled up at once. He had slept in his shirt and breeches, but fortunately he had a second of each, and his coat was reasonably fresh. He would have to remember to find a tailor locally where he could order another. It was a bit of a struggle to get into it alone, but he managed, and felt himself in good order when at last he descended.

The senior officers' table was nearly empty. Granby was not there, but Laurence felt the effect of his presence in the sideways glances the two young men sitting together at the lower end of the table gave him. Nearer the head of the room, a big, thickset man with a florid face and no coat on was eating steadily through a heaped plate of eggs and black pudding and bacon; Laurence looked around uncertainly for a sideboard.

"Morning, Captain; coffee or tea?" Tolly was at his elbow, holding two pots.

"Coffee, thank you," Laurence said gratefully; he had the cup drained and held out for more before the man even turned away. "Do we serve ourselves?" he asked.

"No, here comes Lacey with eggs and bacon for you; just mention if you like something else," Tolly said, already moving on.

The maidservant was wearing coarse homespun, and she said, "Good morning!" cheerfully instead of staying silent, but it was so pleasant to see a friendly face that Laurence found himself returning the greeting. The plate she was carrying was so hot it steamed, and he had not a fig to give for propriety once he had tasted the splendid bacon: cured with some unfamiliar smoke, and full of flavor, and the yolks of his eggs almost bright orange. He ate quickly, with an eye on the squares of light traveling across the floor where the sun struck through the high windows.

"Don't choke," said the thickset man, eyeing him. "Tolly, more tea," he bellowed; his voice was loud enough to carry through a storm. "You Laurence?" he demanded, as his cup was refilled.

Laurence finished swallowing and said, "Yes, sir; you have the advantage of me."

"Berkley," the man said. "Look here, what sort of nonsense have you been filling your dragon's head with? My Maximus has been muttering all morning about wanting a bath, and his harness removed; absurd stuff."

"I do not find it so, sir, to be concerned with the comfort of my dragon," Laurence said quietly, his hands tightening on the cutlery.

Berkley glared straight back at him. "Why damn you, are you suggesting I neglect Maximus? No one has ever washed dragons; they don't mind a little dirt, they have hide."

Laurence reined in his temper and his voice; his appetite was gone, however, and he set down knife and fork. "Evidently your dragon disagrees; do you suppose yourself a better judge than he of what gives him discomfort?"

Berkley scowled at him fiercely, then abruptly he snorted. "Well, you are a fire-breather, make no mistake; and here I thought you Navy fellows were all so stiff and cautious-like." He drained his teacup and stood up from the table. "I will be seeing you later; Celeritas wants to pace Maximus and Temeraire out together." He nodded, apparently in all friendliness, and left.

Laurence was a little dazed by this abrupt reversal; then he realized he was near to being late, and he had no more time to think over the incident. Temeraire was waiting impatiently, and now Laurence found himself paying for his virtue, as the harness had to be put back on; even with the help of two ground crewmen he called over, they barely reached the courtyard in time.

Celeritas was not yet in the courtyard as they landed, but only a short while after their arrival, Laurence saw the training master emerge from one of the openings carved into the cliff wall: evidently these were private quarters, perhaps for older or more honored dragons. Celeritas shook out his wings and flew over to the courtyard, landing neatly on his rear legs, and he looked Temeraire over thoroughly. "Hm, yes, excellent depth of chest. Inhale, please. Yes, yes." He sat back down on all fours. "Now then. Let us have a look at you. Two full circuits of the valley, first circuit horizontal turns, then backwing on the second. Go at an easy pace, I wish to assess your conformation, not your speed." He made a nudging gesture with his head.

Temeraire leapt back aloft at full speed. "Gently," Laurence called, tugging at the reins to remind him, and Temeraire slowed reluctantly to a more moderate pace. He soared easily through the turns, and then the loops; Celeritas called out, "Now again, at speed," as they came back around. Laurence bent low to Temeraire's neck as the wings beat with great frantic thrusts about him, and the wind whistled at a high pitch past his ears. It was faster than they had ever gone before, and as exhilarating; he could not resist, and gave a small whoop for Temeraire's ears only as they went racing into the turn.

The second circuit completed, they winged back towards the courtyard again; Temeraire was scarcely breathing fast. But before they crossed half the valley there came a sudden tremendous roaring from overhead, and a vast black shadow fell over them: Laurence looked up in alarm to see Maximus barreling down towards their path as though he meant to ram them. Temeraire jerked to an abrupt stop and hovered in place, and Maximus went flying past and swept back up just short of the ground.

"What the devil do you mean by this, Berkley?" Laurence roared at the top of his lungs, standing in the harness; he was in a fury, his hands shaking but for his grip on the reins. "You will explain yourself, sir, this instant—"

"My God! How can he do that?" Berkley was shouting back at him, conversationally, as though they had not done anything out of the ordinary at all; Maximus was flying sedately back up towards the courtyard. "Celeritas, do you see that?"

"I do; pray come in and land, Temeraire," Celeritas said, calling out from the courtyard. "They were flying at you on orders, Captain; do not be agitated," he said to Laurence as Temeraire landed neatly on the edge. "It is of utmost importance to test the natural reaction of a dragon to being startled from above, where we cannot see; it is an instinct that often cannot be overcome by any training."

Laurence was still very ruffled, and Temeraire as well: "That was very unpleasant," he said to Maximus reproachfully.

"Yes, I know, it was done to me also when we started training," Maximus said, cheerful and unrepentant. "How do you just hang in the air like that?"

"I never gave it much thought," Temeraire said, mollified a little; he craned his neck over to examine himself. "I suppose I just beat my wings the other way."

Laurence stroked Temeraire's neck comfortingly as Celeritas peered closely at Temeraire's wing-joints. "I had assumed it was a common ability, sir; is it unusual, then?" Laurence asked.

"Only in the sense of it being entirely unique in my two hundred years' experience," Celeritas said dryly, sitting back. "Anglewings can maneuver in tight circles, but not hover in such a manner." He scratched his forehead. "We will have to give some thought to the applications of the ability; at the least it will make you a very deadly bomber."

Laurence and Berkley were still discussing it as they went in to dinner, as well as the approach to matching Temeraire and Maximus. Celeritas had kept them working all the rest of the day, exploring Temeraire's maneuvering capabilities and pacing the two dragons against each other. Laurence had already felt, of course, that Temeraire was extraordinarily fast and handy in the air; but there was a great deal of pleasure and satisfaction at hearing Celeritas say so, and to have Temeraire easily outdistance the older and larger Maximus.

Celeritas had even suggested they might try and have

Temeraire fly double-pace, if he proved to retain his maneuverability even as he grew: that he might be able to fly a strafing run along the length of the entire formation and come back to his position in time to fly a second along with the rest of the dragons.

Berkley and Maximus had taken it in good part to have Temeraire fly rings around them. Of course Regal Coppers were the first-rates of the Corps, and Temeraire would certainly never equal Maximus for sheer weight and power, so there was no real basis for jealousy; still, after the tension of his first day, Laurence was inclined to take an absence of hostility as a victory. Berkley himself was an odd character, a little old to be a new captain and very queer in his manners, with a normal state of extreme stolidity broken by occasional explosions.

But in his strange way he seemed a steady and dedicated officer, and friendly enough. He told Laurence abruptly, as they sat at the empty table waiting for the other officers to join them, "You will have to face down a damned sight of jealousy, of course, for not having to wait for a prime 'un as much as anything. I was six years waiting for Maximus; it was well worth it, but I don't know that I would be able not to hate you if you were prancing about in front of me with an Imperial while he was still in the shell."

"Waiting?" Laurence said. "You were assigned to him before he was even hatched?"

"The moment the egg was cool enough to touch," Berkley said. "We get four or five Regal Coppers in a generation; Aerial Command don't leave it to chance who mans 'em. I was grounded the moment I said yes-thank-you, and here I sat staring at him in the shell and lecturing squeakers, hoping he wouldn't take too much bloody time about it, which by God he did." Berkley snorted and drained his glass of wine.

Laurence had already formed a high opinion of Berkley's skill in the air after their morning's work, and he did indeed seem the sort of man who could be entrusted with a rare and valuable dragon; certainly he was very fond of Maximus and showed it in a bluff way. As they had parted from Maximus and Temeraire in the courtyard, Laurence had overheard him telling the big dragon, "I suppose I will get no peace until you have your harness taken off too, damn you," while ordering his ground crew to see to it, and Maximus nearly knocking him over with a caressing nudge.

The other officers were beginning to file into the room; most of them were much younger than himself or Berkley, and the hall quickly grew noisy with their cheerful and often high-pitched voices. Laurence was a little tense at first, but his fears did not materialize; a few more of the lieutenants did look at him dubiously, and Granby sat as far away as possible, but other than this no one seemed to pay him much notice.

A tall, blond man with a sharp nose said quietly, "I beg your pardon, sir," and slipped into the chair beside him. Though all the senior officers were in coats and neckcloths for dinner, the newcomer was noticeably different in having his neckcloth crisply folded, and his coat pressed. "Captain Jeremy Rankin, at your service," he said courteously, offering a hand. "I believe we have not met?"

"No, I am just arrived yesterday; Captain Will Laurence, at yours," Laurence answered. Rankin had a firm grip, and a pleasant and easy manner; Laurence found him very easy to talk to, and learned without surprise that Rankin was a son of the Earl of Kensington.

"My family have always sent third sons to the Corps, and in the old days before the Corps were formed and dragons reserved to the Crown, my however-many-great-grandfather used to support a pair," Rankin said. "So I have no difficulties going home; we still maintain a small covert for fly-overs, and I was often there even during my training. It is an advantage I wish more aviators could have," he added, low, glancing around the table.

Laurence did not wish to say anything that might be construed as critical; it was all right for Rankin to hint at it, being one of them, but from his own lips it could only be offensive. "It must be hard on the boys, leaving home so early," he said, with more tact. "In the Navy we—that is, the Navy does not take lads before they are twelve, and even then they are set on shore between cruises, and have time at home. Did you find it so, sir?" he added, turning to Berkley.

"Hm," Berkley said, swallowing; he looked a little hard at Rankin before answering Laurence. "Can't say that I did; squalled a little, I suppose, but one gets used to it, and we run the squeakers about to keep them from getting too homesick." He turned back to his food with no attempt to keep the conversation going, and Laurence was left to turn back and continue his discussion with Rankin.

"Am I late—oh!" It was a slim young boy, his voice not yet broken but tall for that age, hurrying to the table in some disarray; his long red hair was half coming out of his plaited queue. He halted abruptly at the table's edge, then slowly and reluctantly took the seat on Rankin's other side, which was the only one left vacant. Despite his youth, he was a captain: the coat he wore had the double golden bars across the shoulders.

"Why, Catherine, not at all; allow me to pour you some wine," Rankin said. Laurence, already looking in surprise at the boy, thought for a moment he had misheard; then saw he had not, at all: the boy was indeed a young lady. Laurence looked around the table blankly; no one else seemed to think anything of it, and it was clearly no secret: Rankin was addressing her in polite and formal tones, serving her from the platters.

"Allow me to present you," Rankin added, turning. "Captain Laurence of Temeraire, Miss—oh, no, I forget; that is, Captain Catherine Harcourt of, er, Lily."

"Hello," the girl muttered, not looking up.

Laurence felt his face going red; she was sitting there in breeches that showed every inch of her leg, with a shirt held closed only by a neckcloth; he shifted his gaze to the unalarming top of her head and managed to say, "Your servant, Miss Harcourt."

This at least caused her to raise her head. "No, it is *Captain* Harcourt," she said; her face was pale, and her spray of freckles stood out prominently against it, but she was clearly determined to defend her rights; she gave Rankin a strangely defiant look as she spoke.

Laurence had used the address automatically; he had not meant to offend, but evidently he had. "I beg your pardon, Captain," he said at once, bowing his head in apology. It was indeed difficult to address her so, however, and the title felt strange and awkward on his tongue; he was afraid he sounded unnaturally stiff. "I meant no disrespect." And now he recognized the dragon's name as well; it had struck him as unusual yesterday, but with so much else to consider, that one detail had slipped his mind. "I believe you have the Longwing?" he said politely.

"Yes, that is my Lily," she said, an involuntary warmth coming into her voice as she spoke her dragon's name.

"Perhaps you were not aware, Captain Laurence, that Longwings will not take male handlers; it is some odd quirk of theirs, for which we must be grateful, else we would be deprived of such charming company," Rankin said, inclining his head to the girl. There was an ironic quality to his voice that made Laurence frown; the girl was very obviously not at ease, and Rankin did not seem to be making her more so. She had dropped her head again, and was staring at her plate with her lips pale and pressed together into an unhappy line.

"It is very brave of you to undertake such a duty, M— Captain Harcourt; a glass—that is to say, to your health," Laurence said, amending at the last moment and making the toast a sip; he did not think it appropriate to force a slip of a girl to drink an entire glass of wine.

"It is no more than anyone else does," she said, muttering; then belatedly she took her own glass and raised it in return. "I mean: and to yours."

Silently he repeated her title and name to himself; it would be very rude of him to make the mistake again, having been corrected once, but it was so strange he did not entirely trust himself yet. He took care to look at her face and not elsewhere. With her hair pulled back so tightly she did look boyish, which was some help, along with the clothes that had allowed him to mistake her initially; he supposed that was why she went about in male dress, appalling and illegal though it was.

He would have liked to talk to her, although it would have been difficult not to ask questions, but he could not be steadily talking over Rankin. He was left to wonder at it in the privacy of his own thoughts; to think that every Longwing in service was captained by a woman was shocking. Glancing at her slight frame, he wondered how she supported the work; he himself felt battered and tired after the day's flying, and though perhaps a proper harness would reduce the strain, he still found it hard to believe a woman could manage it day after day. It was cruel to ask it of her, but of course Longwings could not be spared. They were perhaps the most deadly English dragons, to be compared only with Regal Coppers, and without them the aerial defenses of England would be hideously vulnerable.

With this object of curiosity to occupy his thoughts, and Rankin's civil conversation as well, his first dinner passed more pleasantly than he had to some extent expected, and he rose from the table encouraged, even though Captain Harcourt and Berkley had been silent and uncommunicative throughout. As they stood, Rankin turned to him and said, "If you are not otherwise engaged, may I invite you to join me in the officers' club for some chess? I rarely have the chance of a game, and I confess that since you mentioned that you play, I have been eager to seize upon the opportunity."

"I thank you for the invitation; it would give me great pleasure as well," Laurence said. "For the moment I must beg to be excused, however; I must see to Temeraire, and then I have promised to read to him."

"Read to him?" Rankin said, with an expression of amusement that did not hide his surprise at the idea. "Your dedication is admirable, and all that is natural in a new handler. However, allow me if I may to assure you that for the most part dragons are quite capable of managing on their own. I know several of our fellow captains are in the habit of spending all their free time with their beasts, and I would not wish you based on their example to think it a necessity, or a duty to which you must sacrifice the pleasure of human company."

"I thank you kindly for your concern, but I assure you it is misplaced in my case," Laurence said. "For my own part, I could desire no better society than Temeraire's, and it is as much for my own sake as for his that we are engaged. But I would be very happy to join you later this evening, unless you keep early hours."

"I am very happy to hear it, on both counts," Rankin said. "As for my hours, not at all; I am not in training, of course, only here on courier duty, so I need not keep to a student's schedule. I am ashamed to admit that on most days I am not to be found downstairs until shortly before noon, but on the other hand that grants me the pleasure of expecting to see you this evening."

With this they parted, and Laurence set out to find Temeraire. He was amused to find three of the cadets lurking just outside the dining hall door: the sandy-haired boy and two others, each clutching a fistful of clean white rags. "Oh, sir," the boy said, jumping up as he saw Laurence coming out. "Would you need any more linens, for Temeraire?" he asked eagerly. "We thought you might, so we brought some, when we saw him eating."

"Here now, Roland, what d'you think you're about, there?" Tolly, carrying a load of dishes from the dining hall, stopped on seeing the cadets accost Laurence. "You know better'n to pester a captain."

"I'm not, am I?" the boy said, looking hopefully at Laurence. "I only thought, perhaps we could help a little. He is very big, after all, and Morgan and Dyer and I all have our carabiners; we can lock on without any trouble at all," he said earnestly, displaying an odd harness that Laurence had not even noticed before: it was a thick leather belt laced tightly around his waist, with an attached pair of straps ending in what looked at first glance like a large chain link made of steel. On closer examination, Laurence saw that this had a piece which could be folded in, and thus open the link to be hooked on to something else.

Straightening, Laurence said, "As Temeraire does not yet have a proper harness, I do not think you can lock on to the straps with these. However," he added, hiding a smile at their downcast looks, "come along, and we shall see what can be done. Thank you, Tolly," he said, nodding to the servant. "I can manage them."

Tolly was not bothering to hide his grin at this exchange. "Right you are," he said, carrying on with his duties.

"Roland, is it?" Laurence asked the boy, as he walked on to the courtyard with the three children trotting to keep up.

"Yes, sir, Cadet Emily Roland, at your service." Turning to her companions, and thus remaining blithely unconscious of Laurence's startled expression, she added, "And these are Andrew Morgan and Peter Dyer; we are all in our third year here."

"Yes, indeed, we would all like to help," Morgan said, and Dyer, smaller than the other two and with round eyes, only nodded.

"Very good," Laurence managed, looking surreptitiously down at the girl. Her hair was cut bowl-fashion, just like the two boys', and she had a sturdy, stocky build; her voice was scarcely pitched higher than theirs: his mistake had not been unnatural. Now that he gave a moment's thought to the matter, it made perfect sense; the Corps would naturally train up a few girls, in anticipation of needing them as Longwings hatched, and likely Captain Harcourt was herself the product of such training. But he could not help wondering what sort of parent would hand over a girl of tender years to the rigor of the service.

They came out into the courtyard and were met by a scene of raucous activity: a great confusion of wings and dragon voices filling the air. Most if not all of the dragons had just come from feeding and were now being attended by members of their crews, who were busy cleaning the harnesses. Despite Rankin's words, Laurence scarcely saw a dragon whose captain was not standing by its head and petting or talking to it; this evidently was a common interlude during the day when dragons and their handlers were at liberty.

He did not immediately see Temeraire; after searching the busy courtyard for a few moments, he realized that Temeraire had settled outside the exterior walls, likely to avoid the bustle and noise. Before going out to him, Laurence took the cadets over to Levitas: the little dragon was curled up alone just inside the courtyard walls, watching the other dragons with their officers. Levitas was still in his harness, but it looked much better than it had on the previous day: the leather looked as though it had been worked over and rubbed with oil to make it more supple, and the metal rings joining the straps were brightly polished.

Laurence now guessed that the rings were intended to provide a place for the carabiners to latch on; though Levitas was small compared with Temeraire, he was still a large creature, and Laurence thought he could easily sustain the weight of the three cadets for the short journey. The dragon was eager and happy for the attention, his eyes brightening as Laurence made the suggestion.

"Oh yes, I can carry you all easily," he said, looking at the three cadets, who looked back at him with no less eagerness. They all scrambled up as nimbly as squirrels, and each of them locked on to two separate rings in an obviously well-practiced motion.

Laurence tugged on each strap; they seemed secure enough. "Very well, Levitas; take them down to the shore, and Temeraire and I will meet you there shortly," he said, patting the dragon's side.

Having seen them off, Laurence wove through the other dragons and made his way out of the gate. He stopped short on his first clear look at Temeraire; the dragon looked strangely downcast, a marked difference from his happy attitude at the conclusion of the morning's work, and Laurence hurried to his side. "Are you not feeling well?" Laurence asked, inspecting his jaws, but Temeraire was bloodstained and messy from his meal, and looked to have eaten well. "Did something you ate disagree with you?"

"No, I am perfectly well," Temeraire said. "It is only— Laurence, I am a proper dragon, am I not?"

Laurence stared; the note of uncertainty in Temeraire's voice was wholly new. "As proper a dragon as there is in the world; what on earth would make you ask such a question? Has anyone said anything unkind to you?" A quick surge of temper was rising in him already at the mere possibility; the aviators might look at him askance and say what they liked, but he was not going to tolerate anyone making remarks to Temeraire.

"Oh, no," Temeraire said, but in a way that made Laurence doubt the words. "No one was unkind, but they could not help noticing, while we were all feeding, that I do not look quite like the rest of them. They are all much more brightly colored than I am, and their wings do not have so many joins. Also, they have those ridges along their backs, and mine is plain, and I have more talons on my feet." He turned and inspected himself as he catalogued these differences. "So they looked at me a little oddly, but no one was unkind. I suppose it is because I am a Chinese dragon?"

"Yes, indeed, and you must recall that the Chinese are counted the most skilled breeders in the world," Laurence said firmly. "If anything, the others should look to you as their ideal, not the reverse, and I beg you will not for a moment doubt yourself. Only consider how well Celeritas spoke of your flying this morning."

"But I cannot breathe fire, or spit acid," Temeraire said, settling back down, still with an air of dejection. "And I am not as big as Maximus." He was quiet for a moment, then added, "He and Lily ate first; the rest of us had to wait until after they were done, and then we were allowed to hunt as a group."

Laurence frowned; it had not occurred to him that dragons would have a system of rank among themselves. "My dear, there has never been a dragon of your breed in England, so your precedence has not yet been established," he said, trying to find an explanation which would console Temeraire. "Also, perhaps it has something to do with the rank of their captains, for you must recall that I have less seniority than any other captain here."

"That would be very silly; you are older than most of them are, and have a great deal of experience," Temeraire said, losing some of his unhappiness in indignation over the idea of a slight to Laurence. "You have won battles, and most of them are only still in training."

"Yes, though at sea, and things are very different aloft," Laurence said. "But it is quite true that precedence and rank are not guarantors of wisdom or good breeding; pray do not take it so to heart. I am sure that when we have been in service a year or two, you will be acknowledged as you deserve. But for the moment, did you get enough to eat? We shall return to the feeding grounds at once if not."

"Oh, no, there was no shortage," Temeraire said. "I was able to catch whatever I wanted, and the others did not get in my way very much at all."

He fell silent, and was clearly still inclined to be dismal; Laurence said, "Come, we must see about getting you bathed."

Temeraire brightened at the prospect, and after the better part of an hour spent playing with Levitas in the lake and then being scrubbed by the cadets, his spirits were greatly restored. Afterwards, he curled happily about Laurence in the warm courtyard when they settled down together to read, apparently much happier. But Laurence still saw Temeraire looking at his gold-and-pearl chain more often, and touching it with the tip of his tongue; he was beginning to recognize the gesture as a desire for reassurance. He tried to put affection in his voice as he read, and stroked the foreleg on which he was comfortably seated.

He was still frowning with concern later that evening, as he came into the officers' club; a left-handed blessing, for the momentary hush that fell when he came into the room bothered him far less than it might otherwise have done. Granby was standing at the pianoforte near the door, and he pointedly touched his forehead in salute and said, "Sir," as Laurence came in.

It was an odd sort of insolence that could hardly be reprimanded; Laurence chose to answer as if it had been sincere, and said politely, "Mr. Granby," with a nod that he made a general gesture to the room, and walked on with what haste was reasonable. Rankin was sitting far back in a corner of the room by a small table, reading a newspaper; Laurence joined him, and in a few moments the two of them had set up the chessboard which Rankin had taken down from a shelf.

The buzz of conversation had already resumed; between moves, Laurence observed the room as well as he could without making himself obvious. Now that his eyes were opened, he could see a few female officers scattered in the crowd here, also. Their presence seemed to place no restraint on the general company; the conversation though good-natured was not wholly refined, and it was made noisy and confused by interruptions.

Nevertheless there was a clear sense of good-fellowship throughout the room, and he could not help feeling a little wistful at his natural exclusion from it; both by their preference and his own he did not feel that he was fitted for participation, and it could not but give him a pang of loneliness. But he dismissed it almost at once; a Navy captain had to be used to a solitary existence, and often without such companionship as he had in Temeraire. And also, he might now look forward to Rankin's company as well; he returned his attention to the chessboard, and looked no more at the others.

Rankin was perhaps out of practice a little, but not

unskilled, and as the game was not one of Laurence's favorite pastimes they were reasonably well-matched. While they played, Laurence mentioned his concern for Temeraire to Rankin, who listened with sympathy. "It is indeed shameful that they should have not given him precedence, but I must counsel you to leave the remedy to him," Rankin said. "They behave that way in the wild; the deadlier breeds demand first fruits of the hunt, and the weaker give way. He must likely assert himself among the other beasts to be given more respect."

"Do you mean by offering some sort of challenge? But surely that cannot be a wise policy," Laurence said, alarmed at the very idea; he had heard the old fantastic stories of wild dragons fighting among themselves, and killing one another in such dueling. "To allow battle among such desperately valuable creatures, for so little purpose?"

"It rarely comes to an actual battle; they know one another's capabilities, and I promise you, once he feels certain of his strength, he will not tolerate it, nor will he meet with any great resistance," Rankin said.

Laurence could not have great confidence in this; he was certain it was no lack of courage that prevented Temeraire from taking precedence, but a more delicate sensibility, which had unhappily enabled him to sense the lack of approbation of the other dragons. "I would still like to find some means of reassuring him," Laurence said sadly; he could see that henceforth all the feedings would be a source of fresh unhappiness to Temeraire, and yet they could not be avoided, save by feeding him at different times, which would only make him feel still more isolated from the others.

"Oh, give him a trinket and he will settle down," Rankin said. "It is amazing how it restores their spirits; whenever my beast becomes sulky, I bring him a bauble and he is at once all happiness again; just like a temperamental mistress."

Laurence could not help smiling at the absurdity of this joking comparison. "I have been meaning to get him a collar, as it happens," he said, more seriously, "such as the one Celeritas wears, and I do believe it would make him very happy. But I do not suppose there is anywhere here where such an item may be commissioned."

"I can offer you a remedy for that, at any rate. I go to Edinburgh regularly on my courier duties, and there are several excellent jewelers there; some of them even carry ready-made items for dragons, as there are many coverts here in the north within flying distance. If you care to accompany me, I would be happy to bear you there," Rankin said. "My next flight will be this Saturday, and I can easily have you back by suppertime if we leave in the morning."

"Thank you; I am very much obliged to you," Laurence said, surprised and pleased. "I will apply to Celeritas for permission to go."

Celeritas frowned at the request, made the next morning, and looked at Laurence narrowly. "You wish to go with Captain Rankin? Well, it will be the last day of liberty you have for a long time, for you must and will be here for every moment of Temeraire's flight training."

He was almost fierce about it, and Laurence was surprised by his vehemence. "I assure you I have no objection," he said, wondering in astonishment if the training master thought he meant to shirk his duties. "Indeed, I had not imagined otherwise, and I am well aware of the need for urgency in his training. If my absence would cause any difficulty, I beg you to have no hesitation in refusing the request."

Whatever the source of his initial disapproval, Celeritas was mollified by this statement. "As it happens, the ground crewmen will need a day to fit Temeraire out with his new gear, and it will be ready by then," he said, in less stern tones. "I suppose we can spare you, as long as Temeraire is not finicky about being harnessed without you there, and you may as well have a final excursion."

Temeraire assured Laurence he did not mind, so the plan was settled, and Laurence spent part of the next few evenings making measurements of his neck, and of Maximus's, thinking the Regal Copper's current size might be a good approximation for what Temeraire could reach in future. He pretended to Temeraire that these were for the harness; he looked forward to giving the present as a surprise, and seeing it take away some of the quiet distress that lingered, casting a pall over the dragon's usually high spirits.

Rankin looked with amusement at his sketches of possible designs. The two of them had already formed the settled habit of playing chess together in the evenings, and sitting together at dinner. Laurence so far had little conversation with the other aviators; he regretted it, but could see little point in trying to push himself forward when he was comfortable enough as he was, and in the absence of any sort of invitation. It seemed clear to him that Rankin was as outside the common life of the aviators as he was, perhaps set aside by the elegance of his manners, and if they were both outcast for the same reason, they might at least have the pleasure of each other's society for compensation.

He and Berkley met at breakfast and training every day, and he continued to find the other captain an astute airman and aerial tactician; but at dinner or in company Berkley was silent. Laurence was not sure either that he wished to draw the man into intimacy, or that a gesture in that direction would be welcome, so he contented himself with being civil, and discussing technical matters; so far they had known each other only a few days, and there would be time enough to take a better measure of the man's real character.

He had steeled himself to react properly on meeting Captain Harcourt again, but she seemed shy of his company; he saw her almost only at a distance, though Temeraire was soon to be flying in company with her dragon, Lily. One morning however she was at table when he arrived for breakfast, and in an attempt to make natural conversation, he asked how her dragon came to be called Lily, thinking it might be a nickname like Volly's. She flushed to her roots again and said very stiffly, "I liked the name; pray how did you come to name Temeraire?"

"To be perfectly honest, I did not have any idea of the proper way of naming a dragon, nor any way of finding out at the time," Laurence said, feeling he had made a misstep; no one had remarked on Temeraire's unusual name before, and only now that she had brought him to task for it did he guess that perhaps he had raised a sore point with her. "I called him after a ship: the first *Téméraire* was captured from the French, and the one presently in service is a ninety-eight-gun three-decker, one of our finest line-of-battle ships."

When he had made this confession, she seemed to grow more easy, and said with more candor, "Oh; as you have said as much, I do not mind admitting that it was nearly the same with me. Lily was not properly expected to hatch for another five years at the earliest, and I had no notion of a name. When her egg hardened, they woke me in the middle of the night at Edinburgh covert and flung me on a Winchester, and I barely managed to reach the baths before she broke the shell. I simply gaped when she invited me to give her a name, and I could not think of anything else."

"It is a charming name, and perfectly suits her, Catherine," Rankin said, joining them at the table. "Good morning, Laurence; have you seen the paper? Lord Pugh has finally managed to marry off his daughter; Ferrold must be desperately hard up." This piece of gossip, concerning as it did people whom Harcourt did not know at all, left her outside the conversation. Before Laurence could change the subject, however, she excused herself and slipped away from the table, and he lost the opportunity to further the acquaintance.

The few days remaining in the week before the excursion passed swiftly. The training as yet was still more a matter of testing Temeraire's flying abilities, and seeing how best he and Maximus could be worked into the formation centered on Lily. Celeritas had them fly endless circuits around the training valley, sometimes trying to minimize the number of wingbeats, sometimes trying to maximize their speed, and always trying to keep them in line with one another. One memorable morning was spent almost entirely upside down, and Laurence found himself dizzy and red-faced at the end of it. The stouter Berkley was huffing as he staggered off Maximus's back after the final pass, and Laurence leapt forward to ease him down to the ground as his legs gave out from under him.

Maximus hovered anxiously over Berkley and rumbled in distress. "Stop that moaning, Maximus; nothing more ridiculous than a creature of your size behaving like a mother hen," Berkley said as he fell into the chair that the servants had hurriedly brought. "Ah, thank you," he said, taking the glass of brandy Laurence offered him, and sipped at it while Laurence loosened his neckcloth.

"I am sorry to have put you under such a strain," Celeritas said, when Berkley was no longer gasping and scarlet. "Ordinarily these trials would be spread over half a month's time. Perhaps I am pressing on too quickly."

"Nonsense, I will be well in a trice," Berkley said at once. "I know damned well we cannot spare a moment, Celeritas, so do not be holding us back on my account."

"Laurence, why are matters so urgent?" Temeraire asked that evening after dinner, as they once again settled down together outside the courtyard walls to read. "Is there to be a great battle soon, and we are needed for it?"

Laurence folded the book closed, keeping his place with a finger. "No; I am sorry to disappoint you, but we are too raw to be sent by choice directly into a major action. Still, it is very likely that Lord Nelson will not be able to destroy the French fleet without the help of one of the Longwing formations presently stationed in England; our duty will be to take their place, so they may go. That will indeed be a great battle, and though we will not participate in it directly, I assure you our part is by no means unimportant."

"No, though it does not sound very exciting," Temeraire said. "But perhaps France will invade us, and then we will have to fight?" He sounded rather more hopeful than anything else.

"We must hope not," Laurence said. "If Nelson destroys their fleet, it will pretty well put paid to any chance of Bonaparte's bringing his army across. Though I have heard he has something like a thousand boats to carry his men, they are only transports, and the Navy would sink them by the dozens if they tried to come across without the protection of the fleet."

Temeraire sighed and put his head down over his forelegs. "Oh," he said.

Laurence laughed and stroked his nose. "How bloodthirsty you are," he said with amusement. "Do not fear; I promise you we will see enough action when your training is done. There is a great deal of skirmishing over the Channel, for one thing; and then we may be sent in support of a naval operation, or perhaps sent to harass the French shipping independently." This heartened Temeraire greatly, and he turned his attention to the book with restored good humor.

Friday they spent in an endurance trial, trying to see how long both dragons could stay aloft. The formation's slowest members would be the two Yellow Reapers, so both Temeraire and Maximus had to be kept to that slower pace for the test, and they went around and around the training valley in an endless circle, while above them the rest of the formation performed a drill under Celeritas's supervision.

A steady rain blurred all the landscape below into a grey monotony and made the task still more boring. Temeraire often turned his head to inquire, a little plaintively, how long he had been flying, and Laurence was generally obliged to inform him that scarcely a quarter of an hour had passed since the last query. Laurence at least could watch the formation wheeling and diving, their bright colors marked against the pale grey sky; poor Temeraire had to keep his head straight and level to maintain the best flying posture.

After perhaps three hours, Maximus began to fall off the pace, his great wings beating more slowly and his head drooping; Berkley took him back in, and Temeraire was left all alone, still going around. The rest of the formation came spiraling down to land in the courtyard, and Laurence saw the dragons nodding to Maximus, inclining their heads respectfully. At this distance he could not make out any words, but it was clear they were all conversing easily among themselves while their captains milled about and Celeritas gathered them together to review their performance. Temeraire saw them as well, and sighed a little, though he said nothing; Laurence leaned forward and stroked his neck, and silently vowed to bring him back the most elegant jewels he could find in the whole of Edinburgh, if he had to draw out half his capital to do so.

Laurence came out into the courtyard early the next morning to say farewell to Temeraire before his trip with Rankin. He stopped short as he emerged from the hall: Levitas was being put under gear by a small ground crew, with Rankin at his head reading a newspaper and paying little attention to the proceedings. "Hello, Laurence," the little dragon said to him happily. "Look, this is my captain, he has come! And we are flying to Edinburgh today."

"Have you been talking with him?" Rankin said to Laurence, glancing up. "I see you were not exaggerating, and that you do indeed enjoy dragon society; I hope you will not find yourself tiring of it. You will be taking Laurence along with myself today; you must make an effort to show him a good pace," he told Levitas.

"Oh, I will, I promise," Levitas said at once, bobbing his head anxiously.

Laurence made some civil answer and walked quickly to Temeraire's side to cover his confusion; he did not know what to do. There was no possible way to avoid the journey now without being truly insulting; but he felt almost ill. Over the last few days he had seen more evidence than he liked of Levitas's unhappiness and neglect: the little dragon watched anxiously for a handler who did not come, and if he or his harness had been given more than a cursory wipe, it was because Laurence had encouraged the cadets to see to him, and asked Hollin to continue attending to his harness. To find Rankin the one responsible for such neglect was bitterly disappointing; to see Levitas behaving with such servility and gratitude for the least cold attention was painful.

Perceived through the lens of his neglect of his dragon,

Rankin's remarks on dragons took on a character of disdain that could only be strange and unpleasant in an aviator; and his isolation from his fellow officers also, rather than an indication of nice taste. Every other aviator had introduced himself with his dragon's name ready to his lips; Rankin alone had considered his family name of more importance, and left Laurence to find out only by accident that Levitas was assigned to him. But Laurence had not seen through any of this, and now he found he had, in the most unguarded sort of way, encouraged the acquaintance of a man he could never respect.

He petted Temeraire and made him some reassurances meant mostly for his own comfort. "Is anything wrong, Laurence?" Temeraire said, nosing at him gently with concern. "You do not seem well."

"No, I am perfectly well, I assure you," he said, making an effort to sound normal. "You are quite certain you do not mind my going?" he asked, with a faint hope.

"Not at all, and you will be back by evening, will you not?" Temeraire asked. "Now that we have finished Duncan, I was hoping perhaps you could read me something more about mathematics; I thought it was very interesting how you explained that you could tell where you are, when you have been sailing for a long time, only through knowing the time and some equations."

Laurence had been very glad to leave behind mathematics after having forced the basics of trigonometry into his head. "Certainly, if you like," he said, trying to keep dismay out of his voice. "But I thought perhaps you would enjoy something about Chinese dragons?"

"Oh, yes, that would be splendid too; we could read that next," Temeraire said. "It is very nice how many books there are, indeed; and on so many subjects."

If it would give Temeraire something to think about

and keep him from becoming distressed, Laurence was prepared to go as far as to bring his Latin up to snuff and read him *Principia Mathematica* in the original; so he only sighed privately. "Very well, then I leave you in the hands of the ground crew; I see them coming now."

Hollin was leading the party; the young crewman had attended so well to Temeraire's harness and seen to Levitas with such goodwill that Laurence had spoken of him to Celeritas, and asked to have him assigned to lead Temeraire's ground crew. Laurence was pleased to see the request had been granted; because this step was evidently a promotion of some significance, there had been some uncertainty about the matter. He nodded to the young man. "Mr. Hollin, will you be so good as to present me to these other men?" he asked.

When he had been given all their names and repeated them silently over to fix them in his memory, he deliberately met their eyes in turn and said firmly, "I am sure Temeraire will give you no difficulty, but I trust you will make a point of consulting his comfort as you make the adjustments. Temeraire, please have no hesitation about informing these men if you notice the least discomfort or restriction upon your movement."

Levitas's case had provided him with evidence that some crewmen might neglect their assigned dragon's gear if a captain was not watchful, and indeed anything else was hardly to be expected. Though he had no fear of Hollin's neglecting his work, Laurence meant to put the other men on notice that he would not tolerate any such neglect where Temeraire was concerned; if such severity fixed his reputation as a hard captain, so be it. Perhaps in comparison with other aviators he was; he would not neglect what he considered his duty for the sake of being liked.

A murmur of "Very good" and "Right you are" came in response; he was able to ignore the raised eyebrows and exchanged glances. "Carry on, then," he said with a final nod, and turned away with no small reluctance to join Rankin.

All his pleasure in the expedition was gone; it was distasteful in the extreme to stand by while Rankin snapped at Levitas and ordered him to hunch down uncomfortably for them to board. Laurence climbed up as quickly as he could, and did his best to sit where his weight would give Levitas the least difficulty.

The flight was brief, at least; Levitas was very swift, and the ground rolled away at a tremendous pace. He was glad to find the speed of their passage made conversation nearly impossible, and he was able to give brief answers to the few remarks Rankin ventured to shout. They landed less than two hours after they had left, at the great walled covert which spread out beneath the watchful looming eye of Edinburgh Castle.

"Stay here quietly; I do not want to hear that you have been pestering the crew when I return," Rankin said sharply to Levitas, after dismounting; he threw the reins of his harness around a post, as if Levitas were a horse to be tethered. "You can eat when we return to Loch Laggan."

"I do not want to bother them, and I can wait to eat, but I am a little thirsty," Levitas said in a small voice. "I tried to fly as fast as I could," he added.

"It was very fast indeed, Levitas, and I am grateful to you. Of course you must have something to drink," Laurence said; this was as much as he could bear. "You there," he called to the ground crewmen lounging around the edges of the clearing; none of them had stirred when Levitas had landed. "Bring a trough of clean water at once, and see to his harness while you are about it."

The men looked a little surprised, but they set to work under Laurence's hard eye. Rankin did not make any objection, although as they climbed up the stairs away from the covert and onto the streets of the city he said, "I see you are a little tender-hearted towards them. I am hardly surprised, as that is the common mode among aviators, but I must tell you that I find discipline answers far better than the sort of coddling more often seen. Levitas for instance must always be ready for a long and dangerous flight; it is good for him to be used to going without."

Laurence felt all the awkwardness of his situation; he was here as Rankin's guest, and he would have to fly back with the man in the evening. Nevertheless, he could not restrain himself from saying, "I will not deny having the warmest sentiments towards dragons as a whole; in my experience thus far I have found them uniformly appealing and worthy of nothing but respect. However, I must disagree with you very strongly that providing ordinary and reasonable care in any way constitutes coddling, and I have always found that deprivation and hardship, when necessary, can be better endured by men who have not been subjected to them previously for no cause."

"Oh, dragons are not men, you know; but I will not argue with you," Rankin said easily. Perversely it made Laurence even angrier; if Rankin had been willing to defend his philosophy, it could have been a sincere if wrongheaded position. But clearly it was not; Rankin was only consulting his own ease, and these remarks were merely excuses for the neglect he performed.

Fortunately they were at the crossroads where their paths were to diverge. Laurence did not have to endure Rankin's company any longer, as the man had to go on rounds to the military offices in the city; they had agreed to meet back at the covert before their departure, and he escaped gladly.

He wandered around the city for the next hour without direction or purpose, solely to clear his mind and temper. There was no obvious way to ameliorate Levitas's situation, and Rankin was clearly inured to disapproval: Laurence now recalled Berkley's silence, Harcourt's evident discomfort, the avoidance of the other aviators in general, and Celeritas's disapproval. It was unpleasant to think that by showing such an evident partiality for Rankin's company, he had given himself the character of approving the man's behavior.

Here was something for which he had rightly earned the cold looks of the other officers. It was of no use to say he had not known: he ought to have known. Instead of putting himself to the trouble of learning the ways of his new comrades-in-arms, he had been happy enough to throw himself into the company of one they avoided and looked at askance. He could hardly excuse himself by saying he had not consulted or trusted their general judgment.

He calmed himself only with difficulty. He could not easily undo the damage he had done in a few unthinking days, but he could and would alter his behavior henceforth. By putting forth the dedication and effort that was only Temeraire's due in any case, he could prove that he neither approved nor intended to practice any sort of neglect. By courtesy and attention to those aviators with whom he would be training, like Berkley and the other captains of the formation, he could show that he did not hold himself above his company. These small measures would take a great deal of time to repair his reputation, but they were all he could do. The best he could do was resolve upon them at once, and prepare to endure however long it would take.

Having finally drawn himself from his self-recrimination, he now took his bearings and hurried on to the offices of the Royal Bank. His usual bankers were Drummonds, in London, but on learning that he was to be stationed at

Loch Laggan, he had written to his prize-agent to direct the funds from the capture of the *Amitié* here. As soon as he had given his name, he at once saw that the instructions had been received and obeyed; for he was instantly conducted to a private office and greeted with particular warmth.

The banker, a Mr. Donnellson, was happy to inform him, on his inquiry, that the prize-money for the *Amitié* had included a bounty for Temeraire equal to the value that would have been placed on an unhatched egg of the same breed. "Not that a number could easily be settled upon, as I understand it, for we have no notion of what the French paid for it, but at length it was held equal to a Regal Copper egg in value, and I am happy to say that your two-eighths share of the entire prize comes to nearly fourteen thousand pounds," he finished, and struck Laurence dumb.

Having recovered over a glass of excellent brandy, Laurence soon perceived the self-serving efforts of Admiral Croft behind this extraordinary assessment. But he hardly objected; after a brief discussion which ended in his authorizing the Bank to invest perhaps half of the money into the Funds for him, he shook Mr. Donnellson's hand with enthusiasm and took away a handful of banknotes and gold, along with a generously offered letter which he might show to merchants to establish his credit. The news restored his spirits to some extent, and he soothed them further by purchasing a great many books and examining several different pieces of valuable jewelry, and imagining Temeraire's happiness at receiving them both.

He settled finally upon a broad pendant of platinum almost like a breastplate, set with sapphires around a single enormous pearl; the piece was designed to fasten about the dragon's neck with a chain that could be extended as Temeraire grew. The price was enough to make him swallow, but he recklessly signed the cheque regardless, and then waited while a boy ran to certify the amount with the Bank so he could immediately bear away the well-wrapped piece, with some difficulty due to its weight.

From there he went straight back to the covert, even though there was another hour to the appointed meeting time. Levitas was lying unattended in the same dusty landing ground, his tail curled around himself; he looked tired and lonely. There was a small herd of sheep kept penned in the covert; Laurence ordered one killed and brought for him, then sat with the dragon and talked to him quietly until Rankin returned.

The flight back was a little slower than the one out, and Rankin spoke coldly to Levitas when they landed. Past the point of caring if it seemed rude, Laurence interrupted with praise and patted Levitas. It was little enough, and he felt miserable to see the little dragon huddled silently in a corner of the courtyard after Rankin had gone inside. But Aerial Command had given Levitas to Rankin; Laurence had no authority to correct the man, who was senior to him.

Temeraire's new harness was neatly assembled upon a couple of benches by the side of the courtyard, the broad neck-brace marked with his name in silver rivets. Temeraire himself was sitting outside again, looking over the quiet lake valley that was gradually fading into shadow as the late-afternoon sun sank in the west, his eyes thoughtful and a little sad. Laurence went to his side at once, carrying the heavy packages.

Temeraire's joy in the pendant was so great as to rescue Laurence's mood as well as his own. The silver metal looked dazzling against his black hide, and once it was on he tilted the piece up with a forehand to look at the great pearl in enormous satisfaction, his pupils widening tremendously so he could better examine it. "And I do

so like pearls, Laurence," he said, nuzzling at him gratefully. "It is very beautiful; but was it not dreadfully
expensive?"

"It is worth every penny to see you looking so handsome," Laurence said, meaning that it was worth every
penny to see him so happy. "The prize-money for the
Amitié has come in, so I am well in pocket, my dear. Indeed, it is quite your due, you know, for the better part
of it comes from the bounty for our having taken your
egg from the French."

"Well, that was none of my doing, although I am very
glad it happened," Temeraire said. "I am sure I could
not have liked any French captain half so much as you.
Oh, Laurence, I am so very happy, and none of the others have anything nearly so nice." He cuddled himself
around Laurence with a deep sigh of satisfaction.

Laurence climbed into the crook of one foreleg and
sat there petting him and enjoying his continued quiet
gloating over the pendant. Of course, if the French ship
had not been so delayed and then captured, some French
aviator would have had Temeraire by now; Laurence
had previously given little thought to what might have
been. Likely the man was somewhere cursing his luck;
the French certainly would have learned that the egg had
been captured by now, even if they did not know that it
had hatched an Imperial, or that Temeraire had been
successfully harnessed.

He looked up at his preening dragon and felt the rest
of his sorrow and anxiety leave him; whatever else happened, he could hardly complain of the turn fate had
served him, in comparison with that poor fellow. "I
have brought you some books as well," he said. "Shall I
begin on Newton for you? I have found a translation of
his book on the principles of mathematics, although I
will warn you at once that I am wholly unlikely to be
able to make sense of what I read for you; I am no great

hand at mathematics beyond what my tutors got into my head for sailing."

"Please do," Temeraire said, looking away from his new treasure for a moment. "I am sure we will be able to puzzle it out together, whatever it is."

Chapter 7

❧

LAURENCE ROSE EARLY the next morning and breakfasted alone, to have a little time before the training would begin. He had examined the new harness carefully last night, looking over each neat stitch and testing all the solid rings; Temeraire had also assured him that the new gear was very comfortable, and that the crewmen had been attentive to his wishes. He felt some gesture was due, and so having made some calculations in his head, he now walked out to the workshops.

Hollin was already up and working in his stall, and he stepped out at once on catching sight of Laurence. "Morning to you, sir; I hope there is nothing wrong with the harness?" the young man asked.

"No; on the contrary, I commend you and your colleagues highly," Laurence said. "It looks splendid, and Temeraire tells me he is very happy in it; thank you. Kindly tell the others for me that I will be having an additional half-crown for each man disbursed with their pay."

"Why, that is very kind of you, sir," Hollin said, looking pleased but not terribly surprised; Laurence was very glad to see his reaction. An extra ration of rum or grog was of course not a desirable reward to men who could buy liquor easily from the village below, and soldiers and aviators were paid better than sailors, so he had puzzled over an appropriate amount: he wanted to reward their diligence, but he did not want to seem as though he were trying to purchase the men's loyalty.

"I also wish to commend you personally," Laurence added, more relaxed now. "Levitas's harness looks in much better order, and he seems more comfortable. I am obliged to you: I know it was not your duty."

"Oh! Nothing to it," Hollin said, smiling broadly now. "The little fellow was made so happy, I was right glad to have done it. I'll give him a look over now and again to make sure he's staying in good order. Seems to me he's a little lonely," he added.

Laurence would never go so far as to criticize another officer to a crewman; he contented himself with saying merely, "I think he was certainly grateful for the attention, and if you should have the time, I would be glad of it."

It was the last moment that he had time to spare concern for Levitas, or anything beyond the tasks immediately before him. Celeritas had satisfied himself that he understood Temeraire's flying capabilities, and now that Temeraire had his fine new harness, their training began in earnest. From the beginning, Laurence was staggering straight to bed after supper, and having to be woken by the servants at the first light of morning; he could barely muster any sort of conversation at the dinner table, and he spent every free moment either dozing with Temeraire in the sun or soaking in the heat of the baths.

Celeritas was merciless and tireless both. There were countless repetitions of this wheeling turn, or that pattern of swoops and dives; then flying short bombing runs at top speed, during which the bellmen hurled practice bombs down at targets on the valley floor. Long hours of gunnery-practice, until Temeraire could hear a full volley of eight rifles go off behind his ears without so much as blinking; crew maneuvers and drills until he no longer twitched when he was clambered upon or his harness shifted; and to close every day's work, another long stretch of endurance training, sending him around and around until he had nearly doubled the amount of time he could spend aloft at his quickest pace.

Even while Temeraire was sprawled panting in the training courtyard and getting his wind back, the training master had Laurence practice moving about the harness both on Temeraire's back and upon rings hung over the cliff wall, to increase his skill at a task that other aviators had been doing from their earliest years in the service. It was not too unlike moving about the tops in a gale, if one imagined a ship moving at a pace of thirty miles in an hour and turning completely sideways or upside down at any moment; his hands slipped free constantly during the first week, and without the paired carabiners he would have plummeted to his death a dozen times over.

And as soon as they were released from the day's flight training, they were handed straight over to an old captain, Joulson, for drilling in aerial signaling. The flag and flare signals for communicating general instructions were much the same as in the Navy, and the most basic gave Laurence no difficulty; but the need to coordinate quickly between dragons in mid-air made the usual technique of spelling out more unusual messages impractical. As a result, there was a vastly longer list of signals, some requiring as many as six flags, and all of these had to be beaten into their heads, for a captain could not rely solely upon his signal-officer. A signal seen and acted upon even a moment more quickly might make all the difference in the world, so both captain and dragon must know them all; the signal-officer was merely a safeguard, and his duty more to send signals for Laurence and call his attention to new signals in battle than to be the sole source of translation.

To Laurence's embarrassment, Temeraire proved quicker to learn the signals than himself; even Joulson was more than a little taken aback at the dragon's proficiency. "And he is old to be learning them, besides," he told Laurence. "Usually we start them on the flags the very day after hatching. I did not like to say so before, not to be discouraging, but I expected him to have a good deal of trouble. If a dragonet is a bit slow and does not learn all the signals by the end of their fifth or sixth week, he struggles with the last ones sadly; but here Temeraire is already older than that, and learning them as though he were fresh from the egg."

But though Temeraire had no exceptional difficulty, the effort of memorization and repetition was still as tiring as their more physical duties. Five weeks of rigorous work passed this way, without even a break on Sundays; they progressed together with Maximus and Berkley through the increasingly complex maneuvers that had to be learned before they could join the formation, and all the time the dragons were growing enormously. By the end of this period, Maximus had almost reached his full adult size, and Temeraire was scarcely one man's height less in the shoulder, though much leaner, and his growth was now mostly in bulk and in his wings rather than his height.

He was beautifully proportionate throughout: his tail was long and very graceful; his wings fit elegantly against his body and looked precisely the right size when fanned out. His colors had intensified, the black hide turning hard and glossy save for the soft nose, and the blue and pale grey markings on the edges of his wings spreading and becoming opalescent. To Laurence's partial eye, he was the handsomest dragon in the

entire covert, even without the great shining pearl bla-
zoned upon his chest.

The constant occupation, along with the rapid
growth, had at least temporarily eased Temeraire's unhappiness. He was now larger than any of the other
dragons but Maximus; even Lily was shorter than he
was, though her wingspan was still greater. Though
Temeraire did not push himself forward and was not
given precedence by the feeders, Laurence saw on the
occasions when he observed that most of the other dragons did unconsciously give way to him at feeding times,
and if Temeraire did not come to be friendly with any of
them, he seemed too busy to pay it mind, much as Laurence himself with the other aviators.

For the most part, they were company for each other;
they were rarely apart except while eating or sleeping, and Laurence honestly felt little need of other society. Indeed, he was glad enough for the excuse, which
enabled him to avoid Rankin's company almost entirely.
By answering with reserve on all occasions when he
was not able to do so, he felt he had at least halted
the progress of their acquaintance, if not partly undone
it. His and Temeraire's acquaintance with Maximus
and Berkley progressed, at least, which kept them
from being wholly isolated from their fellows, though
Temeraire continued to prefer sleeping outside on the
grounds, rather than in the courtyard with the other
dragons.

They had already been assigned Temeraire's ground
crew: besides Hollin as the head, Pratt and Bell, armorer
and leatherworker respectively, formed the core, along
with the gunner Calloway. Many dragons had no more,
but as Temeraire continued to grow, the masters were
somewhat grudgingly granted assistants: first one and
then a second for each, until Temeraire's complement
was only a few men short of Maximus's. The harness-

master's name was Fellowes; he was a silent but dependable man, with some ten years of experience in his line, and more to the point skillful at coaxing additional men out of the Corps; he managed to get Laurence eight harness-men. They were badly wanted, as Laurence persisted in having Temeraire out of the gear whenever possible; he needed the full harness put on and off far more often than most dragons.

Save for these hands, the rest of Temeraire's crew would be composed entirely of officers, gentlemen born; and even the hands were the equivalent of warrant officers or their mates. It was strange to Laurence, used to commanding ten raw landsmen to every able seaman. There was none of the bosun's brutal discipline here; such men could not be struck or started, and the worst punishment was to turn a man off. Laurence could not deny he liked it better, though he felt unhappily disloyal at admitting of any fault in the Navy, even to himself.

Nor was there any fault to be found in the caliber of his officers, as he had imagined; at least, not more than in his prior experience. Half of his riflemen were completely raw midwingmen who had barely yet learned which end of a gun to hold; however, they seemed willing enough, and were improving quickly: Collins was overeager but had a good eye, and if Donnell and Dunne still had some difficulty in finding the target, they were at least quick in reloading. Their lieutenant, Riggs, was somewhat unfortunate: hasty-tempered and excitable, given to bellowing at small mistakes; he was himself a fine shot, and knew his work, but Laurence would have preferred a steadier man to guide the others. But he did not have free choice of men; Riggs had seniority and had served with distinction, so at least merited his position, which made him superior to several officers with whom Laurence had been forced to serve in the Navy.

The permanent aerial crew, the topmen and bellmen

responsible for managing Temeraire's equipage during
flight, and the senior officers and lookouts, were not yet
settled. Most of the currently unassigned junior officers
at the covert would first be given a chance to take positions upon Temeraire during the course of his training
before final assignment was made; Celeritas had explained that this was a common technique used to ensure that the aviators practiced handling as many types
of dragon as possible, as the techniques varied greatly
depending on the breed. Martin had done well in his
stint, and Laurence had hopes that he might be able to
get the young midwingman a permanent berth; several
other promising young men had also recommended
themselves to him.

The only matter of real concern to him was the question of his first lieutenant. He had been disappointed in
the first three candidates assigned him: all were adequate, but none of them struck him as gifted, and he was
particular for Temeraire's sake, even if he would not
have been for his own. More unpleasantly, Granby had
just been assigned in his turn, and though the lieutenant
was executing his duties in perfect order, he was always
addressing Laurence as "sir" and pointedly making his
obedience at every turn; it was an obvious contrast with
the behavior of the other officers, and made them all uneasy. Laurence could not help but think with regret of
Tom Riley.

That aside, he was satisfied, though increasingly eager
to be done with maneuver drills; fortunately Celeritas
had pronounced Temeraire and Maximus almost ready
to join the formation. There were only the last complex
maneuvers to be mastered, those flown entirely upside
down; the two dragons were in the midst of practicing
these in a clear morning when Temeraire remarked to
Laurence, "That is Volly over there, coming towards

us," and Laurence lifted his head to see a small grey speck winging its way rapidly to the covert.

Volly sailed directly into the valley and landed in the training courtyard, a violation of the covert rules when a practice was in session, and Captain James leapt off his dragon's back to talk to Celeritas. Interested, Temeraire righted himself and stopped in mid-air to watch, tumbling about all the crew except Laurence, who was by now used to the maneuver; Maximus kept going a little longer until he noticed that he was alone, then turned and flew back despite Berkley's roared protests.

"What do you suppose it is?" Maximus asked in his rumbling voice; unable to hover himself, he was obliged to fly in circles.

"Listen, you great lummox; if it is any of your affair you will be told," Berkley said. "Will you get back to maneuvers?"

"I do not know; perhaps we could ask Volly," Temeraire said. "And there is no sense in our doing maneuvers anymore; we already know all of these," he added. He sounded so mulish that Laurence was startled; he leaned forward, frowning, but before he could speak, Celeritas called them in, urgently.

"There has been an air battle in the North Sea, off Aberdeen," he said with no preliminaries, when they had scarcely landed. "Several dragons of the covert outside Edinburgh responded to distress signals from the city; though they drove off the French attack, Victoriatus was wounded. He is very weak and having difficulty staying in the air: the two of you are large enough to help support him and bring him in more quickly. Volatilus and Captain James will lead you; go at once."

Volly took the lead and flew off at a tearing speed, showing them his heels easily: he kept only just within the limits of their sight. Maximus could not keep up even with Temeraire, however, so with flag-signals and some hasty shouting back and forth through the speaking-trumpets, Berkley and Laurence agreed that Temeraire would go on ahead, and his crew would send up regular flares to mark the direction for Maximus.

The arrangements made, Temeraire pulled away very rapidly; going, Laurence thought, a little too fast. The distance was not very great as the dragon flew; Aberdeen was some 120 miles distant, and the other dragons would be coming towards them, closing the distance from the other side. Still, they would need to be able to fly the same distance again to bring Victoriatus in, and even though they would be flying over land, not ocean, they could not land and rest with the wounded dragon leaning upon them: there would be no getting him off the ground again. Some moderation of speed would be necessary.

Laurence glanced down at the chronometer strapped down to Temeraire's harness, waited for the minute hand to shift, then counted wingbeats. Twenty-five knots: too high. "Gently, if you please, Temeraire," he called. "We have a good deal of work ahead of us."

"I am not tired at all," Temeraire said, but he slowed regardless; Laurence made his new speed as fifteen knots: a good pace, and one that Temeraire could sustain almost indefinitely.

"Pass the word for Mr. Granby," Laurence said; shortly, the lieutenant clambered forward to Laurence's position at the base of Temeraire's neck, swapping carabiners quickly to move himself along. "What is your estimate of the best rate the injured dragon can be maintaining?" Laurence asked him.

For once, Granby did not respond with cold formality, but thoughtfully; all the aviators had immediately become very grave on the moment of hearing of the injured dragon. "Victoriatus is a Parnassian," he said. "A large mid-weight: heavier than a Reaper. They don't have heavy-combat dragons at Edinburgh, so the others supporting him must be mid-weights; they cannot be making more than twelve miles per hour."

Laurence paused to convert between knots and miles, then nodded; Temeraire was going almost twice as quickly, then. Taking into account Volly's speed in bringing the message, they had perhaps three hours before they would need to start looking for the other party. "Very good. We may as well use the time; have the topmen and bellmen exchange places for practice, and then I think we will try some gunnery."

He felt quite calm and settled himself, but he could feel Temeraire's excitement transmitting itself through a faint twitching along the back of his neck; of course this was Temeraire's first action, of any sort, and Laurence stroked the twitching ridge soothingly. He swapped around his carabiners and turned to observe the maneuvers he had ordered. In sequence, a topman climbed down to the belly-rigging at the same time as a bellman climbed up to the back on the other side, the two weights balancing each other. As the man who had just climbed up locked himself into place, he tugged on the signal-strap, colored in alternating sections of black and white, and pulled it ahead a section; in a moment it advanced again, indicating that the man below had locked himself in as well. All went smoothly: Temeraire was presently carrying three topmen and three bellmen, and the exchange took less than five minutes all told.

"Mr. Allen," Laurence said sharply, calling one of the lookouts to order: an older cadet, soon to be made ensign, neglecting his duty to watch the other men at their work. "Can you tell me what is in the upper north-west? No, do not turn round and look; you must be able to answer that question the moment it is asked. I will speak with your instructor; mind your work now."

The riflemen took up their positions, and Laurence nodded to Granby to give the order; the topmen began throwing out the flat ceramic disks used for targeting, and the riflemen took turns attempting to shoot them out of the air as they flew past. Laurence watched and frowned. "Mr. Granby, Mr. Riggs, I make twelve targets out of twenty; you concur? Gentlemen, I hope I need not say that this will not do against French sharpshooters. Let us begin again, at a slower rate: precision first, speed second, Mr. Collins, so pray do not be so hasty."

He kept them at it for a full hour, then had the hands go through the complicated harness adjustments for storm flying; afterwards he himself went down below and observed the men stationed below while they reverted to fair-weather rigging. They did not have the tents aboard, so he could not have them practice going to quarters and breaking down full gear, but they did well enough at the rigging changes, and he thought they would have done well even with the additional equipment.

Temeraire occasionally glanced around to watch throughout these maneuvers, his eyes bright; but for the most part he was intent on his flying, rising and falling in the air to catch the best currents, driving himself forward with great steady beats, each thrust fully carried through. Laurence laid his hand upon the long, ropy muscles of Temeraire's neck, feeling them move smoothly as though oiled beneath the skin, and was not tempted to distract him with conversation; there was no need. He knew without speaking that Temeraire shared his satisfaction at putting their joint training to real purpose at last. Laurence had not wholly realized his own sense of quiet frustration to have been in some sense demoted from a serving officer to a schoolboy, until he now found himself again engaged in active duty.

The three hours were nearly up by the chronometer,

and it was time to begin preparing to give support to the injured dragon; Maximus was perhaps half an hour behind them, and Temeraire would have to carry Victoriatus alone until the Regal Copper caught up. "Mr. Granby," Laurence said, as he latched himself back in to his normal position at the base of the neck, "let us clear the back; all the men below, save for the signal-ensign and the forward lookouts."

"Very good, sir," Granby said, nodding, and turned at once to arrange it. Laurence watched him work with mingled satisfaction and irritation. For the first time in the past week, Granby had been going about his duties without that air of stiff resentment, and Laurence could easily perceive the effects: the speed of nearly every operation improved; myriad small defects in harness placement and crew positioning, previously invisible to his own inexperienced eye, now corrected; the atmosphere among the men more relaxed. All the many ways in which an excellent first lieutenant could improve the life of a crew, and Granby was now proven capable of them all, but that only made his earlier attitude more regrettable.

Volatilus turned and came flying back towards them only shortly after they had cleared the top; James pulled him about and cupped his hands around his mouth to call to Laurence. "I've sighted them, two points to the north and twelve degrees down; you'll need to drop to come up under them, for I don't think he can get any more elevation." He signaled the numbers with hand gestures as he spoke.

"Very good," Laurence called back, through his speaking-trumpet, and had the signal-ensign wave a confirmation with flags; Temeraire was large enough now that Volly could not get so close as to make verbal communication certain.

Temeraire stooped into a dive at his quick signal, and

very soon Laurence saw a speck on the horizon rapidly enlarge into the group of dragons. Victoriatus was instantly identifiable; he was larger by half than either of the two Yellow Reapers struggling to keep him aloft. Though the injuries were already under thick bandages applied by his crew, blood had seeped through showing the slashing marks where the dragon had evidently taken blows from the enemy beasts. The Parnassian's own claws were unusually large, and stained with blood as well; his jaws also. The smaller dragons below looked crowded, and there was no one aboard the injured dragon but his captain and perhaps half a dozen men.

"Signal the two supporters: prepare to stand aside," Laurence said; the young signal-ensign waved the colored flags in rapid sequence, and a prompt acknowledgment came back. Temeraire had already flown around the group and positioned himself properly: he was just below and to the back of the second supporting dragon.

"Temeraire, are you quite ready?" Laurence called. They had practiced this maneuver in training, but it would be unusually difficult to carry out here: the injured dragon was barely beating his wings, and his eyes were half-shut with pain and exhaustion; the two supporters were clearly worn out themselves. They would have to drop out of the way smoothly, and Temeraire dart in very quickly, to avoid having Victoriatus collapse into a deadly plummet that would be impossible to arrest.

"Yes; please let us hurry, they look so very tired," Temeraire said, glancing back. His muscles were tightly gathered, they had matched the others' pace, and nothing more could be gained by waiting.

"Signal: exchange positions on lead dragon's mark," Laurence said. The flags waved; the acknowledgment came. Then on both sides of the foremost of the two supporting dragons, the red flags went out, and then were swapped for the green.

The rear dragon dropped and peeled aside swiftly as Temeraire lunged. But the forward dragon went a little too slowly, his wings stuttering, and Victoriatus began to tilt forward as the Reaper tried to descend away and make room. "Dive, damn you, dive!" Laurence roared at the top of his lungs; the smaller dragon's lashing tail was dangerously near Temeraire's head, and they could not move into place.

The Reaper gave up the maneuver and simply folded his wings; he dropped out of the way like a stone. "Temeraire, you must get him up a little so you can come forward," Laurence shouted again, crouched low against the neck; Victoriatus's hindquarters had settled over Temeraire's shoulders instead of further back, and the great belly was less than three feet overhead, barely kept up by the injured dragon's waning strength.

Temeraire showed with a bob of his head that he had heard and understood; he beat up rapidly at an angle, pushing the slumping Parnassian back up higher through sheer strength, then snapped his wings closed. A brief, sickening drop: then his wings fanned out again. With a single great thrust, Temeraire had himself properly positioned, and Victoriatus came heavily down upon them again.

Laurence had a moment of relief; then Temeraire cried out in pain. He turned and saw in horror that in his confusion and agony, Victoriatus was scrabbling at Temeraire, and the great claws had raked Temeraire's shoulder and side. Above, muffled, he heard the other captain shouting; Victoriatus stopped, but Temeraire was already bleeding, and straps of the harness were hanging loose and flapping in the wind.

They were losing elevation rapidly; Temeraire was struggling to keep flying under the other dragon's weight. Laurence fought with his carabiners, yelling at the signal-ensign to let the men below know. The boy scrambled partway down the neck-strap, waving the white-and-red flag wildly; in a moment Laurence gratefully saw Granby climbing up with two other men to bandage the wounds, reaching the gashes more quickly than he could. He stroked Temeraire, called reassurance to him in a voice that struggled not to break; Temeraire did not spare the effort to turn and reply, but bravely kept beating his wings, though his head was drooping with the strain.

"Not deep," Granby shouted, from where they worked to pad the gashes, and Laurence could breathe and think clearly again. The harness was shifting upon Temeraire's back; aside from a great deal of lesser rigging, the main shoulder-strap had been nearly cut through, saved only by the wires that ran through it. But the leather was parting, and as soon as it went the wires would break under the strain of all the men and gear currently riding below.

"All of you; take off your harnesses and pass them to me," Laurence said to the signal-ensign and the lookouts; the three boys were the only ones left above, besides him. "Take a good grip on the main harness and get your arms or legs tucked beneath." The leather of the personal harnesses was thick, solidly stitched, well-oiled; the carabiners were solid steel: not quite as strong as the main harness, but nearly so.

He slung the three harnesses over his arm and clambered along the back-strap to the broader part of the shoulders. Granby and the two midwingmen were still working on the injuries to Temeraire's side; they spared him a puzzled look, and Laurence realized they could not see the nearly severed shoulder-band: it was hidden from their view by Temeraire's foreleg. There was no time to call them forward to help in any case; the band was rapidly beginning to give way.

He could not come at it normally; if he tried to put his weight on any of the rings along the shoulder-band, it would certainly break at once. Working as quickly as he could under the roaring pressure of the wind, he hooked two of the harnesses together by their carabiners, then looped them around the back-strap. "Temeraire, stay as level as you can," he shouted; then, clinging to the ends of the harnesses, he unlocked his own carabiners and climbed carefully out onto the shoulder, held by nothing more secure than his grip on the leather.

Granby was shouting something at him; the wind was tearing it away, and he could not make out the words. Laurence tried to keep his eyes fixed on the straps; the ground below was the beautiful, fresh green of early spring, strangely calm and pastoral: they were low enough that he could see white dots of sheep. He was in arm's reach now; with a hand that shook slightly, he latched the first carabiner of the third loose harness onto the ring just above the cut, and the second onto the ring just below. He pulled on the straps, throwing his weight against them as much as he dared; his arms ached and trembled as if with high fever. Inch by inch, he drew the small harness tighter, until at last the portion between the carabiners was the same size as the cut portion of the band and was taking much of its weight: the leather stopped fraying away.

He looked up; Granby was slowly climbing towards him, snapping onto rings as he came. Now that the harness was in place, the strain was not an immediate danger, so Laurence did not wave him off, but only shouted, "Call up Mr. Fellowes," the harness-master, and pointed to the spot. Granby's eyes widened as he came over the foreleg and saw the broken strap.

As Granby turned to signal below for help, bright

sunlight abruptly fell full on his face; Victoriatus was shuddering above them, wings convulsing, and the Parnassian's chest came heavily down on Temeraire's back. Temeraire staggered in mid-air, one shoulder dipping under the blow, and Laurence was sliding along the linked harness straps, wet palms giving him no purchase. The green world was spinning beneath him, and his hands were already tired and slick with sweat; his grip was failing.

"Laurence, hold on!" Temeraire called, head turned to look back at him; his muscles and wing-joints were shifting as he prepared to snatch Laurence out of the air.

"You must not let him fall," Laurence shouted, horrified; Temeraire could not try to catch him except by tipping Victoriatus off his back, and sending the Parnassian to his death. "Temeraire, you must not!"

"Laurence!" Temeraire cried again, his claws flexing; his eyes were wide and distressed, and his head waved back and forth in denial. Laurence could see he did not mean to obey. He struggled to keep hold of the leather straps, to try and climb up; if he fell, it was not only his own life which would be forfeit, but the injured dragon and all his crew still aboard.

Granby was there suddenly, seizing Laurence's harness in both his hands. "Lock onto me," he shouted. Laurence saw at once what he meant. With one hand still clinging to the linked harnesses, he locked his loose carabiners onto the rings of Granby's harness, then transferred his grip to Granby's chest-straps. Then the midwingmen reached them; all at once there were many strong hands grabbing at them, drawing Laurence and Granby back up together to the main harness, and they held Laurence in place while he locked his carabiners back onto the proper rings.

He could scarcely breathe yet, but he seized his speaking-trumpet and called urgently, "All is well." His voice was hardly audible; he pulled in a deep breath and tried again, more clearly this time: "I am fine, Temeraire; only keep flying." The tense muscles beneath them unwound slowly, and Temeraire beat up again, regaining a little of the elevation they had lost. The whole process had lasted perhaps fifteen minutes; he was shaking as if he had been on deck throughout a three-day gale, and his heart was thundering in his breast.

Granby and the midwingmen looked scarcely more composed. "Well done, gentlemen," Laurence said to them, as soon as he trusted his voice to remain steady. "Let us give Mr. Fellowes room to work. Mr. Granby, be so good as to send someone up to Victoriatus's captain and see what assistance we can provide; we must take what precautions we can to keep him from further starts."

They gaped at him a moment; Granby was the first to recover his wits, and began issuing orders. By the time Laurence had made his way, very cautiously, back to his post at the base of Temeraire's neck, the midwingmen were wrapping Victoriatus's claws with bandages to prevent him from scratching Temeraire again, and Maximus was coming into sight in the distance, hurrying to their assistance.

The rest of the flight was relatively uneventful, if the effort involved in supporting a nearly unconscious dragon through the air were ever to be considered ordinary. As soon as they landed Victoriatus safely in the courtyard, the surgeons came hurrying to see to both him and Temeraire; to Laurence's great relief, the cuts indeed proved quite shallow. They were cleaned and inspected, pronounced minor, and a loose pad placed over them to keep the torn hide from being irritated; then Temeraire was set loose and Laurence told to let him sleep and eat as much as he liked for a week.

It was not the most pleasant way to win a few days of liberty, but the respite was infinitely welcome. Laurence immediately walked Temeraire to an open clearing near the covert, not wanting to strain him by another leap aloft. Though the clearing was upon the mountain, it was relatively level, and covered in soft green grass; it faced south, and the sun came into it nearly the entire day. There the two of them slept together from that afternoon until late in the next, Laurence stretched out upon Temeraire's warm back, until hunger woke them both.

"I feel much better; I am sure I can hunt quite normally," Temeraire said; Laurence would not hear of it. He walked back up to the workshops and roused the ground crew instead. Very shortly they had driven a small group of cattle up from the pens and slaughtered them; Temeraire devoured every last scrap and fell directly back to sleep.

Laurence a little diffidently asked Hollin to arrange for the servants to bring him some food; it was enough like asking the man for personal service to make Laurence uncomfortable, but he was reluctant to leave Temeraire. Hollin took no offense; but when he returned, Lieutenant Granby was with him, along with Riggs and a couple of the other lieutenants.

"You should go and have something hot to eat, and a bath, and then sleep in your own bed," Granby said quietly, having waved the others off a little distance. "You are all over blood, and it is not warm enough yet for you to sleep outside without risk to your health. I and the other officers will take it in turns to stay with him; we will fetch you at once if he wakes, or if any change should occur."

Laurence blinked and looked down at himself; he had not even noticed that his clothes were spattered and streaked with the near-black of dragon blood. He ran a hand over his unshaven face; he was clearly presenting a rather horrible picture to the world. He looked up at Temeraire; the dragon was completely unaware of his surroundings, sides rising and falling with a low, steady rumble. "I dare say you are right," he said. "Very well; and thank you," he added.

Granby nodded; and with a last look up at the sleeping Temeraire, Laurence took himself back to the castle. Now that it had been brought to mind, the sensation of dirt and sweat was unpleasant upon his skin; he had gotten soft, with the luxury of daily bathing at hand. He stopped by his room only long enough to exchange his stained clothes for fresh, and went straight to the baths.

It was shortly after dinner, and many of the officers had a habit of bathing at this hour; after Laurence had taken a quick plunge into the pool, he found the sweatroom very crowded. But as he came in, several fellows made room for him; he gladly took the opened place, and returned the nods of greeting around the room before he laid himself down. He was so tired that it only occurred to him after his eyes were closed in the blissful heat that the attention had been unusual, and marked; he almost sat up again with surprise.

"Well flown; very well flown, Captain," Celeritas told him that evening, approvingly, when he belatedly came to report. "No, you need not apologize for being tardy. Lieutenant Granby has given me a preliminary account, and with Captain Berkley's report I know well enough what happened. We prefer a captain be more concerned for his dragon than for our bureaucracy. I trust Temeraire is doing well?"

"Thank you, sir, yes," Laurence said gratefully. "The surgeons have told me there is no cause for alarm, and he says he is quite comfortable. Have you any duties for me during his recovery?"

"Nothing other than to keep him occupied, which

you may find enough of a challenge," Celeritas said, with the snort that passed for a chuckle with him. "Well, that is not quite true; I do have one task for you. Once Temeraire is recovered, you and Maximus will be joining Lily's formation straightaway. We have had nothing but bad news from the war, and the latest is worse: Villeneuve and his fleet have slipped out of Toulon under cover of an aerial raid against Nelson's fleet; we have lost track of them. Under the circumstances, and given this lost week, we cannot wait any longer. Therefore it is time to assign your flight crew, and I would like your requests. Consider the men who have served with you these last weeks, and we will discuss the matter tomorrow."

Laurence walked slowly back out to the clearing after this, deep in thought. He had begged a tent from the ground crews and brought along a blanket; he thought he would be quite comfortable once he had pitched it by Temeraire's side, and he liked the idea better than spending the whole night away. He found Temeraire still sleeping peacefully, the flesh around the bandaged area only ordinarily warm to the touch.

Having satisfied himself on this point, Laurence said, "A word with you, Mr. Granby," and led the lieutenant some short distance away. "Celeritas has asked me to name my officers," he said, looking steadily at Granby; the young man flushed and looked down. Laurence continued, "I will not put you in the position of refusing a post; I do not know what that means in the Corps, but I know in the Navy it would be a serious mark against you. If you would have the least objection, speak frankly; that will be an end to the matter."

"Sir," Granby began, then shut his mouth abruptly, looking mortified: he had used the term so often in veiled insolence. He started over again. "Captain, I am well aware I have done little enough to deserve such consideration; I can only say that if you are willing to overlook what my past behavior has been, I would be very glad of the opportunity." This speech was a little stilted in his mouth, as if he had tried to rehearse it.

Laurence nodded, satisfied. His decision had been a near thing; if it had not been for Temeraire's sake, he was not sure he could have borne to thus expose himself to a man who had behaved disrespectfully towards him, despite Granby's recent heroics. But Granby was so clearly the best of the lot that Laurence had decided to take the risk. He was well-pleased with the reply; it was fair enough and respectful even if awkwardly delivered. "Very good," he said simply.

They had just begun walking back when Granby suddenly said, "Oh, damn it; I may not be able to word it properly, but I cannot just leave things at that: I have to tell you how very sorry I am. I know I have been playing the scrub."

Laurence was surprised by his frankness, but not displeased, and he could never have refused an apology offered with so much sincerity and feeling as was obvious in Granby's tone. "I am very happy to accept your apology," he said, quietly but with real warmth. "For my part, all is forgotten, I assure you, and I hope that henceforth we may be better comrades than we have been."

They stopped and shook hands; Granby looked both relieved and happy, and when Laurence tentatively inquired for his recommendations for other officers, he answered with great enthusiasm, as they made their way back towards Temeraire's side.

Chapter 8

EVEN BEFORE THE pad of bandages had come off, Temeraire began to make plaintive noises about wanting to be bathed again; by the end of the week, the cuts were scabbed over and healing, and the surgeons gave grudging approval. Having rounded up what he already thought of as his cadets, Laurence came out to the courtyard to take the waiting Temeraire down, and found him talking with the female Longwing whose formation they would be joining.

"Does it hurt when you spray?" Temeraire was asking inquisitively. Laurence could see that Temeraire was inspecting the pitted bone spurs on either side of her jaw, evidently where the acid was ejected.

"No, I do not feel it in the least," Lily answered. "The spray will only come out if I am pointing my head down, so I do not splash myself, either; although of course you all must be careful to avoid it when we are in formation."

The enormous wings were folded against her back, looking brown with the translucent folds of blue and orange overlapping each other; only the black-and-white edges stood out against her sides. Her eyes were slit-pupiled, like Temeraire's, but orange-yellow, and the exposed bone spurs showing on either side of her jaw gave her a very savage appearance. But she stood with perfect patience while her ground crew scrambled over her, polishing and cleaning every scrap of harness with great attention; Captain Harcourt was walking back and forth around her and inspecting the work.

Lily looked down at Laurence as he came to Temeraire's side; her alarming eyes gave her stare a baleful quality, although she was only curious. "Are you Temeraire's captain? Catherine, shall we not go to the lake with them? I am not sure I want to go in the water, but I would like to see."

"Go to the lake?" Captain Harcourt was drawn from her inspection of the harness by the suggestion, and she stared at Laurence in open astonishment.

"Yes; I am taking Temeraire to bathe," Laurence said firmly. "Mr. Hollin, let us have the light harness, if you please, and see if we cannot rig it to keep the straps well away from these cuts."

Hollin was working on cleaning Levitas's harness; the little dragon had just come back from eating. "You'll be going along?" he asked Levitas. "If so, sir, maybe there's no need to put any gear on Temeraire?" he added to Laurence.

"Oh, I would like to," Levitas said, looking at Laurence hopefully, as if for permission.

"Thank you, Levitas," Laurence said, by way of answer. "That will be an excellent solution; gentlemen, Levitas will take you down again this time," he told the cadets; he had long since given up trying to alter his address on Roland's behalf; as she seemed perfectly able to count herself included regardless, it was easier to treat her just as the others. "Temeraire, shall I ride with them, or will you carry me?"

"I will carry you, of course," Temeraire said.

Laurence nodded. "Mr. Hollin, are you otherwise occupied? Your assistance would be helpful, and Levitas can certainly manage you if Temeraire carries me."

"Why, I would be happy, sir, but I haven't a harness," Hollin said, eyeing Levitas with interest. "I have never been up before; I mean, not outside the ground-crew rigging, that is. I suppose I can cobble something together out of a spare, though, if you give me a moment."

While Hollin was working on rigging himself out, Maximus descended into the courtyard, shaking the ground as he landed. "Are you ready?" he asked Temeraire, looking pleased; Berkley was on his back, along with a couple of midwingmen.

"He has been moaning about it so long I have given in," Berkley said, in answer to Laurence's amused and questioning look. "Damned foolish idea if you ask me, dragons swimming; great nonsense." He thumped Maximus's shoulder affectionately, belying his words.

"We are coming also," Lily said; she and Captain Harcourt had held a quiet discussion while the rest of the party assembled, and now she lifted Captain Harcourt aboard onto her harness. Temeraire picked Laurence up carefully; despite the great talons Laurence had not the least concern. He was perfectly comfortable in the enclosure of the curving fingers; he could sit in the palm and be as protected as in a metal cage.

Once down by the shore, only Temeraire went directly into the deep water and began to swim. Maximus came tentatively into the shallows, but went no further than he could stand, and Lily stood on the shore watching, nosing at the water but not going in. Levitas, as was his habit, first wavered on the shore, and then dashed out all at once, splashing and flapping wildly with his eyes tightly shut until he got out to the deeper water and began to paddle around enthusiastically.

"Do we need to go in with them?" one of Berkley's midwingmen asked, with a certain tone of alarm.

"No, do not even contemplate it," Laurence said. "This lake is runoff from the mountain snows, and we would turn blue in a moment. But the swim will take away the worst of the dirt and blood from their feeding, and the rest will be much easier to clean once they have soaked a little."

"Hm," Lily said, listening to this, and very slowly crept out into the water.

"Are you quite sure it is not too cold for you, dearest?" Harcourt called after her. "I have never heard of a dragon catching an ague; I suppose it is out of the question?" she said to Laurence and Berkley.

"No, cold just wakes 'em up, unless it is freezing weather; that they don't care for," Berkley said, then raised his voice to bellow, "Maximus, you great coward, go in if you mean to; I am not going to stand here all day."

"I am not afraid," Maximus said indignantly, and lunged forward, sending out a great wave that briefly swamped Levitas and washed over Temeraire. Levitas came up with a splutter, and Temeraire snorted and ducked his head into the water to splash at Maximus; in a moment the two were engaged in a royal battle that bid fair to make the lake look like the Atlantic in a full gale.

Levitas came fluttering out of the lake, dripping cold water onto all of the waiting aviators. Hollin and the cadets set to wiping him down, and the little dragon said, "Oh, I do like swimming so; thank you for letting me come again."

"I do not see why you cannot come as often as you like," Laurence said, glancing at Berkley and Harcourt to see how they would take this; neither of them seemed to give it the slightest thought, or to think his interference officious.

Lily had at last gone in deep enough to be mostly submerged, or at least as much as her natural buoyancy would allow. She stayed well away from the splashing pair of younger dragons, and scrubbed at her own hide with the side of her head. She came out next, more interested in being washed than in the swimming, and rumbled in pleasure as she pointed out spots and had them carefully cleaned by Harcourt and the cadets.

Maximus and Temeraire finally had enough, and came out to be wiped down as well. Maximus required all the exertions of Berkley and his two grown midwingmen. Working on the delicate skin of Temeraire's face while the cadets scrambled all over his back, Laurence could not hide a smile at Berkley's grumbling over his dragon's size.

He stepped back from his work a moment to simply enjoy the scene: Temeraire was speaking with the other dragons freely, his eyes bright and his head held proudly, with no more signs of self-doubt; and even if this strange, mixed company was not anything Laurence would once have sought out for himself, the easy camaraderie warmed him through. He was conscious of having proven himself and having helped Temeraire to do the same, and of the deep satisfaction of having found a true and worthy place, for the both of them.

The pleasure lasted until their return to the courtyard. Rankin was standing by the side of the courtyard, wearing evening dress and tapping the straps of his personal harness against the side of his leg in very obvious irritation, and Levitas gave a little alarmed hop as he landed. "What do you mean by flying off like this?" Rankin said, not even waiting for Hollin and the cadets to climb down. "When you are not feeding, you are to be here and waiting, do you understand me? And you there, who told you that you could ride him?"

"Levitas was kind enough to bear them to oblige me,

Captain Rankin," Laurence said, stepping out of Temeraire's hand and speaking sharply to draw the man's attention away. "We have only been down at the lake, and a signal would have fetched us in a moment."

"I do not care to be running after signal-men to have my dragon available, Captain Laurence, and I will thank you to mind your own beast and leave mine to me," Rankin said, very coldly. "I suppose you are wet now?" he added to Levitas.

"No, no; I am sure I am mostly dry, I was not in for very long at all, I promise," Levitas said, hunching himself very small.

"Let us hope so," Rankin said. "Bend down, hurry up about it. And you lot are to stay away from him from now on," he told the cadets as he climbed up in their place, nearly shouldering Hollin aside.

Laurence stood watching Levitas fly away with Rankin on his back; Berkley and Captain Harcourt were silent, as were the other dragons. Lily abruptly turned her head and made an angry spitting noise; only a few droplets fell, but they sizzled and smoked upon the stone, leaving deep black pockmarks.

"Lily!" Captain Harcourt said, but there was a quality of relief in her voice at the break in the silence. "Pray bring some harness oil, Peck," she said to one of her ground crewmen, climbing down; she poured it liberally over the acid droplets, until smoke ceased rising. "There, cover it with some sand, and tomorrow it should be safe to wash."

Laurence was also glad for the small distraction; he did not immediately trust himself to speak. Temeraire nuzzled him gently, and the cadets looked at him in worry. "I oughtn't ever have suggested it, sir," Hollin said. "I'm sure I beg your pardon, and Captain Rankin's."

"Not in the least, Mr. Hollin," Laurence said; he could hear his own voice, cold and very stern, and he tried to mitigate the effect by adding, "You have done nothing wrong whatsoever."

"I don't see any reason why we ought to stay away from Levitas," Roland said, low.

Laurence did not hesitate for a moment in his response; it was as strong and automatic as his own helpless anger against Rankin. "Your superior officer has given you orders to do so, Miss Roland; if that is not reason enough you are in the wrong service," he snapped. "Let me never hear you make another such remark. Take these linens back to the laundry at once, if you please. You will pardon me, gentlemen," he added to the others, "I will go for a walk before supper."

Temeraire was too large to successfully creep after him, so the dragon resorted instead to flying past and waiting for him in the first small clearing along his path. Laurence had thought he wanted to be alone, but he found he was very glad to come into the dragon's encircling forearms and lean upon his warm bulk, listening to the almost musical thrumming of his heart and the steady reverberation of his breathing. The anger slipped away, but it left misery in its place. He would have desperately liked to call Rankin out.

"I do not know why Levitas endures it; even if he is small, he is still much bigger than Rankin," Temeraire said eventually.

"Why do you endure it when I ask you to put on a harness, or perform some dangerous maneuver?" Laurence said. "It is his duty, and it is his habit. From the shell he has been raised to obey, and has suffered such treatment. He likely does not contemplate any alternative."

"But he sees you, and the other captains; no one else is treated so," Temeraire said. He flexed his claws; they dug furrows in the ground. "I do not obey you because it is a habit and I cannot think for myself; I do it because I know you are worthy of being obeyed. You would never treat me unkindly, and you would not ask me to do something dangerous or unpleasant without cause."

"No, not without cause," Laurence said. "But we are in a hard service, my dear, and we must sometimes be willing to bear a great deal." He hesitated, then added gently, "I have been meaning to speak to you about it, Temeraire: you must promise me in future not to place my life above that of so many others. You must surely see that Victoriatus is far more necessary to the Corps than I could ever be, even if there were not his crew to consider also; you should never have contemplated risking their lives to save mine."

Temeraire curled more closely around him. "No, Laurence, I cannot promise such a thing," he said. "I am sorry, but I will not lie to you: I could not have let you fall. You may value their lives above your own; I cannot do so, for to me you are worth far more than all of them. I will not obey you in such a case, and as for duty, I do not care for the notion a great deal, the more I see of it."

Laurence was not sure how to answer this; he could not deny that he was touched by the degree to which Temeraire valued him, yet it was also alarming to have the dragon express so plainly that he would follow orders or not as his own judgment decreed. Laurence trusted that judgment a great deal, but he felt again that he had made an inadequate effort to teach Temeraire the value of discipline and duty. "I wish I knew how to explain it to you properly," he said, a little despairingly. "Perhaps I will try and find you some books on the subject."

"I suppose," Temeraire said, for once dubious about reading something. "I do not think anything would persuade me to behave differently. In any case, I would much rather just avoid it ever happening again. It was very dreadful, and I was afraid I might not be able to catch you."

Laurence could smile at this. "On that point at least we are agreed, and I will gladly promise you to do my best to avoid any repetition."

Roland came running to fetch him the next morning; he had slept by Temeraire's side again in the little tent. "Celeritas wants you, sir," she said, and went back to the castle by his side, once he had put his neckcloth back on and restored his coat. Temeraire gave him a sleepy murmur of farewell, barely opening one eye before going back to sleep. As they walked, she ventured, "Captain, are you still angry at me?"

"What?" he said, blankly; then he remembered, and said, "No, Roland; I am not angry with you. You do understand why you were wrong to speak so, I hope."

"Yes," she said, and he was able to ignore that it came out a little doubtfully. "I did not speak to Levitas; but I could not help seeing he does not look very well this morning."

Laurence glanced at the Winchester as they walked through the courtyard; Levitas was curled in the back corner, far from the other dragons, and despite the early hour, he was not sleeping but staring dully at the ground. Laurence looked away; there was nothing to be done.

"Run along, Roland," Celeritas said, when she had brought Laurence to him. "Captain, I am sorry to have called you so early; first, is Temeraire well enough to resume his training, do you think?"

"I believe so, sir; he is healing very quickly, and yesterday he flew down to the lake and back with no difficulty," Laurence said.

"Good, good." Celeritas fell silent, and then he sighed. "Captain, I am obliged to order you not to interfere with Levitas any further," he said.

Laurence felt hot color come to his face. So Rankin had complained of him. And yet it was no more than he deserved; he would never have brooked such officious involvement in the running of his ship, or his management of Temeraire. The thing had been wrong, whatever justifications he had given himself, and anger was quickly subsumed in shame. "Sir, I apologize that you should have been put to the necessity of telling me so; I assure you it will not arise again."

Celeritas snorted; having delivered his rebuke, he seemed at no great pains to reinforce it. "Give me no assurances; you would lower yourself in my eyes if you could mean them with real honesty," he said. "It is a great pity, and I am at fault as much as anyone. When I could not tolerate him myself, Aerial Command thought he might do as a courier, and set him to a Winchester; for his grandfather's sake I could not bring myself to speak against it, though I knew better."

Comforting as it was to have the reprimand softened, Laurence was curious to understand what Celeritas meant by not being able to tolerate him; surely Aerial Command would never have proposed a fellow like Rankin as a handler to a dragon as extraordinary as the training master. "Did you know his grandfather well?" he asked, unable to resist making the tentative inquiry.

"My first handler; his son also served with me," Celeritas said briefly, turning his head aside; his head drooped. He recovered after a moment and added, "Well, I had hopes for the boy, but at his mother's insistence he was not raised here, and his family gave him strange notions; he ought never have been an aviator, much less a captain. But now he is, and while Levitas obeys him, so he remains. I cannot allow you to interfere. You can imagine what it would mean if we allowed officers to meddle with one another's beasts: lieutenants desperate to be captains could hardly resist the temptation to seduce away any dragon who was not blissfully happy, and we would have chaos."

Laurence bowed his head. "I understand perfectly, sir."

"In any case, I will be giving you more pressing matters to attend to, for today we will begin your integration into Lily's formation," Celeritas said. "Pray go and fetch Temeraire; the others will be here shortly."

Walking back out, Laurence was thoughtful. He had known, of course, that the larger breeds would outlive their handlers, when they were not killed in battle together; he had not considered that this would leave the dragons alone and without a partner afterwards, nor how they or Aerial Command would manage the situation. Of course it was in Britain's best interests to have the dragon continue in service, with a new handler, but he also could not help but think the dragon himself would be happier so, with duties to occupy his thoughts and keep him from the kind of sorrow that Celeritas obviously still felt.

Arriving once again at the clearing, Laurence looked at the sleeping Temeraire with concern. Of course there were many years before them, and the fortunes of war might easily make all such questions moot, but Temeraire's future happiness was his responsibility, heavier by far to him than any estate could have been, and some time soon he would have to consider what provisions he could make to ensure it. A well-chosen first lieutenant, perhaps, might step into his place, with Temeraire brought to the notion over the course of several years.

"Temeraire," he called, stroking the dragon's nose; Temeraire opened his eyes and made a small rumble.

"I am awake; are we flying again today?" he said, yawning enormously up at the sky and twitching his wings a little.

"Yes, my dear," Laurence said. "Come, we must get you back into your harness; I am sure Mr. Hollin will have it ready for us."

The formation ordinarily flew in a wedge-shaped block that resembled nothing more than a flock of migrating geese, with Lily at the head. The Yellow Reapers Messoria and Immortalis filled the key flanking positions, providing the protective bulk to keep Lily from close-quarters attack, while the ends were held by the smaller but more agile Dulcia, a Grey Copper, and a Pascal's Blue called Nitidus. All were full-grown, and all but Lily had previous combat experience; they had been especially chosen for this critical formation to support the young and inexperienced Longwing, and their captains and crews were rightly proud of their skill.

Laurence had cause to be thankful for the endless labor and repetition of the last month and a half; if the maneuvers they had practiced for so long had not become by now second nature for Temeraire and Maximus, they could never have kept up with the practiced, effortless acrobatics of the others. The two larger dragons had been added into position so as to form a back row behind Lily, closing the formation into a triangle shape. In battle, their place would be to fend off any attempts to break up the formation, to defend it against attack from other heavy-combat-class dragons, and to carry the great loads of bombs that their crews would drop below upon those targets that had already been weakened by Lily's acid.

Laurence was very glad to see Temeraire admitted fully to the company of the other dragons of the formation, although none of the older dragons had the energy for much play outside their work. For the most part they lazed about during the scant idle hours, and only observed in tolerant amusement while Temeraire and Lily and Maximus talked and occasionally went aloft for a game of aerial tag. For his own part, Laurence also felt a great deal more welcome among the other aviators now, and discovered that he had without noticing it adjusted to the informality of their relations: the first time he found himself addressing Captain Harcourt as simply "Harcourt," in a post-training discussion, he did not even realize he had done so until after the words were out of his mouth.

The captains and first lieutenants generally held such discussions of strategy and tactics at dinnertime, or during the late evenings after the dragons had all fallen asleep. Laurence's opinion was rarely solicited in these conversations, but he did not take that greatly to heart: though he was quickly coming to grasp the principles of aerial warfare, he still considered himself a newcomer to the art, and he could hardly take offense at the aviators doing the same. Save when he could contribute some information about Temeraire's particular capabilities, he remained quiet and made no attempt to insinuate himself into the conversations, rather listening for the purpose of educating himself.

The conversation did turn, from time to time, to the more general subject of the war; out of the way as they were, their information was several weeks out of date, and speculation irresistible. Laurence joined them one evening to find Sutton saying, "The French fleet could be bloody well anywhere." Sutton was Messoria's captain and the senior among them, a veteran of four wars, and somewhat given to both pessimism and colorful language. "Now they have slipped out of Toulon, for all we know the bastards are already on their way across the Channel; I wouldn't be surprised to find the army of invasion on our doorstep tomorrow."

Laurence could hardly let this pass. "You are mistaken, I assure you," he said, taking his seat. "Villeneuve and his fleet have slipped out of Toulon, yes, but he is not engaged in any grand operation, only in flight: Nelson has been in steady pursuit all along."

"Why, have you heard something, Laurence?" Chenery, Dulcia's captain, asked, looking up from the desultory game of vingt-et-un that he and Little, Immortalis's captain, were playing.

"I have had some letters, yes; one from Captain Riley, of the *Reliant*," Laurence said. "He is with Nelson's fleet: they have chased Villeneuve across the Atlantic, and he writes that Lord Nelson has hopes of catching the French in the West Indies."

"Oh, and here we are without any idea of what is going on!" Chenery said. "For Heaven's sake, fetch it here and read it to us; you are not very good to be keeping this all to yourself while we are all in the dark."

He spoke with too much eagerness for Laurence to take offense; as the sentiments were repeated by the other captains, he sent a servant to his room to bring him the scant handful of letters he had received from former colleagues who knew his new direction. He was obliged to omit several passages commiserating with him on his change in situation, but he managed to elide them gracefully enough, and the others listened with great hunger to his bits and pieces of news.

"So Villeneuve has seventeen ships, to Nelson's twelve?" Sutton said. "I don't think much of the blighter for running, then. What if he turns about? Racing across the Atlantic like this, Nelson cannot have any aerial force; no transport could keep up the pace, and we do not have any dragons stationed in the West Indies."

"I dare say the fleet could take him with fewer ships still," Laurence said, with spirit. "You are to remember the Nile, sir, and before that the battle of Cape St. Vincent: we have often been at some numerical disadvantage and still carried the day; and Lord Nelson himself has never lost a fleet action." With some difficulty, he restrained himself and stopped here; he did not wish to seem an enthusiast.

The others smiled, but not in any patronizing manner, and Little said in his quiet way, "We must hope he can bring them to account, then. The sad fact of the matter is, while the French fleet remains in any way intact, we are in deadly danger. The Navy cannot always be catching them, and Napoleon only need hold the Channel for two days, perhaps three, to ferry his army across."

This was a lowering thought, and they all felt its weight. Berkley at last broke the resulting silence with a grunt and took up his glass to drain it. "You can all sit about glooming; I am for bed," he said. "We have enough to do without borrowing trouble."

"And I must be up early," Harcourt said, sitting up. "Celeritas wants Lily to practice spraying upon targets in the morning, before maneuvers."

"Yes, we all ought to get to sleep," Sutton said. "We can hardly do better than to get this formation into order, in any case; if any chance of flattening Bonaparte's fleet offers, you may be sure that one of the Longwing formations will be wanted, either ours or one of the two at Dover."

The party broke up, and Laurence climbed to his tower room thoughtfully. A Longwing could spit with tremendous accuracy; in their first day of training Laurence had seen Lily destroy targets with a single quick spurt from nearly four hundred feet in the air, and no cannon from the ground could ever fire so far straight up. Pepper guns might hamper her, but her only real danger would come from aloft: she would be the target of every enemy dragon in the air, and the formation as a whole was designed to protect her. The group would be a formidable presence upon any battlefield, Laurence could easily see; he would not have liked to be beneath them in a ship, and the prospect of doing so much good for England gave him fresh interest for the work.

Unfortunately, as the weeks wore on, he saw plainly that Temeraire found it harder going to keep up his own interest. The first requirement of formation flying was precision, and holding one's position relative to the others. Now that Temeraire was flying with the group, he was limited by the others, and with speed and maneuverability so far beyond the general, he soon began to feel the constraint. One afternoon, Laurence overheard him asking, "Do you ever do more interesting flying?" to Messoria; she was an experienced older dragon of thirty years, with a great many battle-scars to render her an object of admiration.

She snorted indulgently at him. "Interesting is not very good; it is hard to remember interesting in the middle of a battle," she said. "You will get used to it, never fear."

Temeraire sighed and went back to work without anything more like a complaint; but though he never failed to answer a request or to put forth an effort, he was not enthusiastic, and Laurence could not help worrying. He did his best to console Temeraire and provide him with other subjects to engage his interest; they continued their practice of reading together, and Temeraire listened with great interest to every mathematical or scientific article that Laurence could find. He followed them all without difficulty, and Laurence found himself in the strange position of having Temeraire explain to him the material which he was reading aloud.

Even more usefully, perhaps a week after they had resumed training a parcel arrived for them in the mail from Sir Edward Howe. It was addressed somewhat whimsically to Temeraire, who was delighted to receive a piece of mail of his very own; Laurence unwrapped it for him and found within a fine volume of dragon stories from the Orient, translated by Sir Edward himself, and just published.

Temeraire dictated a very graceful note of thanks, to which Laurence added his own, and the Oriental tales became the set conclusion to their days: whatever other reading they did, they would finish with one of the stories. Even after they had read them all, Temeraire was perfectly happy to begin over again, or occasionally request a particular favorite, such as the story of the Yellow Emperor of China, the first Celestial dragon, on whose advice the Han dynasty had been founded; or the Japanese dragon Raiden, who had driven the armada of Kublai Khan away from the island nation. He particularly liked the last because of the parallel with Britain, menaced by Napoleon's Grande Armée across the Channel.

He listened also with a wistful air to the story of Xiao Sheng, the emperor's minister, who swallowed a pearl from a dragon's treasury and became a dragon himself; Laurence did not understand his attitude, until Temeraire said, "I do not suppose that is real? There is no way that people can become dragons, or the reverse?"

"No, I am afraid not," Laurence said slowly; the notion that Temeraire might have liked to make a change was distressing to him, suggesting as it did a very deep unhappiness.

But Temeraire only sighed and said, "Oh, well; I thought as much. It would have been nice, though, to be able to read and write for myself when I liked, and also then you could fly alongside me."

Laurence laughed, reassured. "I am sorry indeed we cannot have such a pleasure; but even if it were possible, it does not sound a very comfortable process from the story, nor one which could be reversed."

"No, and I would not like to give up flying at all, not even for reading," Temeraire said. "Besides, it is very pleasant to have you read to me; may we have another one? Perhaps the story about the dragon who made it rain, during the drought, by carrying water from the ocean?"

The stories were obviously myths, but Sir Edward's translation included a great many annotations, describing the realistic basis for the legends according to the best modern knowledge. Laurence suspected even these might be exaggerated slightly; Sir Edward was very clearly enthusiastic towards Oriental dragons. But they served their purpose admirably: the fantastic stories made Temeraire only more determined to prove his similar merit, and gave him better heart for the training.

The book also proved useful for another reason, for only a little while after its arrival, Temeraire's appearance diverged yet again from the other dragons, as he began to sprout thin tendrils round his jaws, and a ruff of delicate webbing stretched between flexible horns around his face, almost like a frill. It gave him a dramatic, serious look, not at all unbecoming, but there was no denying he looked very different from the others, and if it had not been for the lovely frontispiece of Sir Edward's book, an engraving of the Yellow Emperor which showed that great dragon in possession of the same sort of ruff, Temeraire would certainly have been unhappy at being yet again marked apart from his fellows.

He was still anxious at the change in his looks, and shortly after the ruff had come in, Laurence found him studying his reflection in the surface of the lake, turning his head this way and that and rolling his eyes back in his head to see himself and the ruff from different angles.

"Come now, you are like to make everyone think you are a vain creature," Laurence said, reaching up to pet the waving tendrils. "Truly, they look very well; pray give them no thought."

Temeraire made a small, startled noise, and leaned in towards the stroking. "That feels strange," he said.

"Am I hurting you? Are they so tender?" Laurence stopped at once, anxious. Though he had not said as much to Temeraire, he had noticed from reading the stories that the Chinese dragons, at least the Imperials and Celestials, did not seem to do a great deal of fighting, except in moments of the greatest crisis for their nations. They seemed more famed for beauty and wisdom, and if the Chinese bred for such qualities first, it would not be impossible that the tendrils might be of a sensitivity which could make them a point of vulnerability in battle.

Temeraire nudged him a little and said, "No, they do not hurt at all. Pray do it again?" When Laurence very carefully resumed the stroking, Temeraire made an odd purring sort of sound, and abruptly shivered all over. "I think I quite like it," he added, his eyes growing unfocused and heavy-lidded.

Laurence snatched his hand away. "Oh, Lord," he said, glancing around in deep embarrassment; thankfully no other dragons or aviators were about at the moment. "I had better speak to Celeritas at once; I think you are coming into season for the first time. I ought to have realized, when they sprouted; it must mean you have reached your full growth."

Temeraire blinked. "Oh, very well; but must you stop?" he asked plaintively.

"It is excellent news," Celeritas said, when Laurence had conveyed this intelligence. "We cannot breed him yet, for he cannot be spared for so long, but I am very pleased regardless: I am always anxious when sending an immature dragon into battle. And I will send word to the breeders; they will think of the best potential crosses to make. The addition of Imperial blood to our lines can only be of the greatest benefit."

"Is there anything—some means of relief—" Laurence stopped, not quite sure how to word the question in a way which would not seem outrageous.

"We will have to see, but I think you need not worry," Celeritas said dryly. "We are not like horses or dogs; we can control ourselves at least as well as you humans."

Laurence was relieved; he had feared that Temeraire might find it difficult now to be in close company with Lily or Messoria, or the other female dragons, though he rather thought Dulcia was too small to be a partner of interest to him. But he expressed no interest of that sort in them; Laurence ventured to ask him, once or twice, in a hinting way, and Temeraire seemed mostly baffled at the notion.

Nevertheless there were some changes, which became perceptible by degrees. Laurence first noticed that Temeraire was more often awake in the mornings without having to be roused; his appetites changed also, and he ate less frequently, though in greater quantities, and might voluntarily go so long as two days without eating at all.

Laurence was somewhat concerned that Temeraire was starving himself to avoid the unpleasantness of not being given precedence, or the sideways looks of the other dragons at his new appearance. However, his fears were relieved in dramatic fashion, scarcely a month after the ruff had developed. He had just landed Temeraire at the feeding grounds and stood off from the mass of assembled dragons to observe, when Lily and Maximus were called onto the grounds. But on this occasion, another dragon was called down with them: a newcomer of a breed Laurence had never before seen, its wings patterned like marble, veins of orange and yellow and brown shot through a nearly translucent ivory, and very large, but not bigger than Temeraire.

The other dragons of the covert gave way and watched them go down, but Temeraire unexpectedly made a low rumbling noise, not quite a growl, from deep in his throat; very like a croaking bullfrog if a frog of some twelve tons might be imagined, and he leapt down after them uninvited.

Laurence could not see the faces of the herders, so far below, but they milled about the fences as if taken aback; it was quite clear however that none of them liked to try and shoo Temeraire away, not surprising considering that he was already up to his chops in the gore of his first cow. Lily and Maximus made no objection, the strange dragon of course did not even notice it as a change, and after a moment the herders released half a dozen more beasts into the grounds, that all four dragons might eat their fill.

"He is of a splendid conformity; he is yours, is he not?" Laurence turned to find himself addressed by a stranger, wearing thick woolen trousers and a plain civilian's coat, both marked with dragon-scale impressions: he was certainly an aviator and an officer besides, his carriage and voice gentleman-like, but he spoke with a heavy French accent, and Laurence was puzzled momentarily by his presence.

The Frenchman was not alone; Sutton was keeping

him company, and now he stepped forward to make the introductions: the Frenchman's name was Choiseul.

"I have come from Austria only last night, with Praecursoris," Choiseul said, gesturing at the marbled dragon below, who was daintily taking another sheep, neatly avoiding the blood spurting from Maximus's third victim.

"He has some good news for us, though he makes a long face over it," Sutton said. "Austria is mobilizing; she is coming into the war with Bonaparte again, and I dare say he will have to turn his attention to the Rhine instead of the Channel, soon enough."

Choiseul said, "I hope I do not discourage your hopes in any way; I would be desolate to give you unnecessary concern. But I cannot say that I have great confidence in their chances. I do not wish to sound ungrateful; the Austrian corps was generous enough to grant myself and Praecursoris asylum during the Revolution, and I am most deeply in their debt. But the archdukes are fools, and they will not listen to the few generals of competence they have. Archduke Ferdinand to fight the genius of Marengo and Egypt! It is an absurdity."

"I cannot say that Marengo was so brilliantly run as all that," Sutton said. "If the Austrians had only brought up their second aerial division from Verona in time, we would have had a very different ending; it was as much luck as anything."

Laurence did not feel himself sufficiently in command of land tactics to offer his own comment, but this seemed perilously close to bravado; in any case, he had a healthy respect for luck, and Bonaparte seemed to attract a greater share than most generals.

For his part, Choiseul smiled briefly and did not contradict, saying only, "Perhaps my fears are excessive; still, they have brought us here, for our position in a defeated Austria would be untenable. There are many men in my former service who are very savage against me for having taken so valuable a dragon as Praecursoris away," he explained, in answer to Laurence's look of inquiry. "Friends warned me that Bonaparte means to demand our surrender as part of any terms that might be made, and to place us under a charge of treason. So again we have had to flee, and now we cast ourselves upon your generosity."

He spoke with an easy, pleasant manner, but there were deep lines around his eyes, and they were unhappy; Laurence looked at him with sympathy. He had known French officers of his sort before, naval men who had fled France after the Revolution, eating their hearts out on England's shores; their position was a sad and bitter one: worse, he felt, than the merely dispossessed noblemen who had fled to save their lives, for they felt all the pain of sitting idle while their nation was at war, and every victory celebrated in England was a wrenching loss for their own service.

"Oh yes, it is uncommon generous of us, taking in a Chanson-de-Guerre like this," Sutton said, with heavy but well-meant raillery. "After all, we have so very many heavyweights we can hardly squeeze in another, particularly so fine and well-trained a veteran."

Choiseul bowed slightly in acknowledgment and looked down at his dragon with affection. "I gladly accept the compliment for Praecursoris, but you have already many fine beasts here; that Regal Copper looks prodigious, and I see from his horns he is not yet at his full growth. And your dragon, Captain Laurence, surely he is some new breed? I have not seen his like."

"No, nor are you likely to again," Sutton said, "unless you go halfway round the world."

"He is an Imperial, sir, a Chinese breed," Laurence said, torn between not wishing to show off and an undeniable pleasure in doing just so. Choiseul's astonished reaction, though decently restrained, was highly satisfying, but then Laurence was obliged to explain the circumstances of Temeraire's acquisition, and he could not help but feel somewhat awkward when relating the triumphant capture of a French ship and a French egg to a Frenchman.

But Choiseul was clearly used to the situation and heard the story with at least the appearance of complaisance, though he offered no remark. Though Sutton was inclined to dwell on the French loss a little smugly, Laurence hurried on to ask what Choiseul would be doing in the covert.

"I understand there is a formation in training, and that Praecursoris and I are to join in the maneuvers: some notion I believe of our serving as a relief, when circumstances allow," Choiseul said. "Celeritas hopes also that Praecursoris may be of some assistance in the training of your heaviest beasts for formation flying: we have always flown in formation, for close on fourteen years now."

A thundering rush of wings interrupted their conversation as the other dragons were called to the hunting grounds, the first four having finished their meal, and Temeraire and Praecursoris both made an attempt to land at the same convenient outcropping nearby: Laurence was startled to see Temeraire bare his teeth and flare his ruff at the older dragon. "I beg you to excuse me," he said hastily, and hurried to find another place, calling Temeraire, and with relief saw him wheel away and follow.

"I would have come to you," Temeraire said, a little reproachfully, casting a narrowed eye at Praecursoris, who was now occupying the contested perch and speaking quietly with Choiseul.

"They are guests here; it is only courteous to give

way," Laurence said. "I had no notion that you were so fierce in matters of precedence, my dear."

Temeraire furrowed the ground before him with his claws. "He is not any bigger than I am," he said. "And he is not a Longwing, so he does not spit poison, and there are no fire-breathing dragons in Britain; I do not see why he is any better than I am."

"He is not one jot better, not at all," Laurence said, stroking the tensed foreleg. "Precedence is merely a matter of formality, and you are perfectly within your rights to eat with the others. Pray do not be quarrelsome, however; they have fled the Continent, to be away from Bonaparte."

"Oh?" Temeraire's ruff smoothed out gradually against his neck, and he looked at the strange dragon with more interest. "But they are speaking French; if they are French, why are they afraid of Bonaparte?"

"They are royalists, loyal to the Bourbon kings," Laurence said. "I dare say they left after the Jacobins put the King to death; it was very dreadful in France for a while, I am afraid, and though Bonaparte is at least not chopping people's heads off anymore, he is scarcely much better in their eyes; I assure you they despise him worse than we do."

"Well, I am sorry if I was rude," Temeraire murmured, and straightened up to address Praecursoris. *"Veuillez m'excuser, si je vous ai dérangé,"* he said, to Laurence's astonishment.

Praecursoris turned around. *"Mais non, pas du tout,"* he answered mildly, and inclined his head. *"Permettez que je vous présente Choiseul, mon capitaine,"* he added.

"Et voici Laurence, le mien," Temeraire said. "Laurence, pray bow," he added, in an undertone, when Laurence only stood staring.

Laurence at once made his leg; he of course could not interrupt the formal exchange, but he was bursting with curiosity, and as soon as they were winging their way down to the lake for Temeraire's bath, he demanded, "But how on earth do you come to speak French?"

Temeraire turned his head about. "What do you mean? Is it very unusual to speak French? It was not at all difficult."

"Well, it is prodigious strange; so far as I know you have never heard a word of it: certainly not from me, for I am lucky if I can say my bonjours without embarrassing myself," Laurence said.

"I am not surprised that he can speak French," Celeritas said, when Laurence asked him later that afternoon, at the training grounds, "but only that you should not have heard him do so before; do you mean to say Temeraire did not speak French when he first cracked the shell? He spoke English directly?"

"Why, yes," Laurence said. "I confess we were surprised, but only to hear him speak at all so soon. Is it unusual?"

"That he spoke, no; we learn language through the shell," Celeritas said. "And as he was aboard a French vessel in the months before his hatching, I am not surprised at all that he should know that tongue. I am far more surprised that he was able to speak English after only a week aboard. Fluently?"

"From the first moment," Laurence said, pleased at this fresh evidence of Temeraire's unique gifts. "You have been forever surprising me, my dear," he added, patting Temeraire's neck, making him preen with satisfaction.

But Temeraire continued somewhat more prickly, particularly where Praecursoris was concerned: no open animosity, nor any particular hostility, but he was clearly anxious to show himself an equal to the older dragon, particularly once Celeritas began to include the Chanson-de-Guerre in their maneuvers.

Praecursoris was not, Laurence was secretly glad to see, as fluid or graceful in the air as Temeraire; but his experience and that of his captain counted for a great deal, and they knew and had mastered many of the formation maneuvers already. Temeraire grew very intent on his work; Laurence sometimes came out from dinner and found his dragon flying alone over the lake, practicing the maneuvers he had once found so boring, and on more than one occasion he even asked to sacrifice part of their reading time to additional work. He would have worked himself to exhaustion daily if Laurence had not restrained him.

At last Laurence went to Celeritas to ask his advice, hoping to learn some way of easing Temeraire's intensity, or perhaps persuading Celeritas to separate the two dragons. But the training master listened to his objections and said calmly, "Captain Laurence, you are thinking of your dragon's happiness. That is as it should be, but I must think first of his training, and the needs of the Corps. Do you argue he is not progressing quickly, and to great levels of skill, since Praecursoris arrived?"

Laurence could only stare; the idea that Celeritas had deliberately promoted the rivalry to encourage Temeraire was first startling, then almost offensive. "Sir, Temeraire has always been willing, has always put forth his best efforts," he began angrily, and only stopped when Celeritas snorted to interrupt him.

"Pull up, Captain," he said, with a rough amusement. "I am not insulting him. The truth is, he is a little too intelligent to be an ideal formation fighter. If the situation were different, we would make him a formation leader or an independent, and he would do very well. But as matters stand, given his weight, we must have him in formation, and that means he must learn rote maneuvers. They are simply not enough to hold his attention. It is not a very common complaint, but I have seen it before, and the signs are unmistakable."

Laurence unhappily could offer no argument; there was perfect truth in Celeritas's remarks. Seeing that Laurence had fallen silent, the training master continued, "This rivalry adds enough spice to overcome a natural boredom which would shortly progress to frustration. Encourage him, praise him, keep him confident in your affection, and he will not suffer from a bit of squabbling with another male; it is very natural, at his age, and better he should set himself against Praecursoris than Maximus; Praecursoris is old enough not to take it seriously."

Laurence could not be so sanguine; Celeritas did not see how Temeraire fretted. Yet neither could Laurence deny that his remarks were motivated from a selfish perspective: he disliked seeing Temeraire driving himself so hard. But of course he needed to be driven hard; they all did.

Here in the placid green north, it was too easy to forget that Britain was in great danger. Villeneuve and the French navy were still on the loose; according to dispatches, Nelson had chased them all the way to the West Indies only to be eluded again, and now was desperately seeking them in the Atlantic. Villeneuve's intention was certainly to meet with the fleet out of Brest and then attempt to seize the straits of Dover; Bonaparte had a vast number of transports cramming every port along the French coast, waiting only for such a break in the Channel defenses to ferry over the massive army of invasion.

Laurence had served on blockade-duty for many long months, and he knew well how difficult it was to maintain discipline through the endless, unvarying days with no enemy in sight. The distractions of more company, a wider landscape, books, games: these things made the duty of training more pleasant by far, but he now recognized that in their own way they were as insidious as monotony.

So he only bowed, and said, "I understand your design, sir; thank you for the explanation." But he returned to Temeraire still determined to curb the almost obsessive practicing, and if possible to find an alternative means of engaging the dragon's interest in the maneuvers.

These were the circumstances which first gave him the notion of explaining formation tactics to Temeraire. He did so more for Temeraire's sake than his own, hoping to give the dragon some more intellectual interest in the maneuvers. But Temeraire followed the subject with ease, and shortly the lessons became real discussion, as valuable to Laurence as to Temeraire, and more than compensating for his lack of participation in the debates which the captains held among themselves.

Together they embarked on designing a series of their own maneuvers, taking advantage of Temeraire's unusual flying capabilities, which could be fitted into the slower and more methodical pace of the formation. Celeritas himself had spoken of designing such maneuvers, but the pressing need for the formation had forced him to put aside the plan for the immediate future.

Laurence salvaged an old flight-table from the attics, recruited Hollin's help to repair its broken leg, and set it up in Temeraire's clearing under his dragon's interested eyes. It was a sort of vast diorama set upon a table, with a latticework on top; Laurence did not have a set of the proper scale figures of dragons to hang from it, but he substituted whittled and colored bits of wood, and by tying these with bits of thread from the lattice, they were able to display three-dimensional positions for each other's consideration.

Temeraire from the beginning displayed an intuitive grasp of aerial movement. He could instantly declare whether a maneuver was feasible or not, and describe the movements necessary to bring it about if so; the initial inspiration for a new maneuver was most often his. Laurence in turn could better assess the relative military strengths of various positions, and suggest such modifications as would improve the force which might be brought to bear.

Their discussions were lively and vocal, and attracted the attention of the rest of his crew; Granby tentatively asked to observe, and when Laurence gave leave, was shortly followed by the second lieutenant, Evans, and many of the midwingmen. Their years of training and experience gave them a foundation of knowledge which both Laurence and Temeraire lacked, and their suggestions further refined the design.

"Sir, the others have asked me to propose to you that perhaps we might try some of the new maneuvers," Granby said to him, some few weeks into the project. "We would be more than happy to sacrifice our evenings to the work; it would be infamous not to have a chance of showing what he can do."

Laurence was deeply moved, not merely by their enthusiasm, but by seeing that Granby and the crew felt the same desire to see Temeraire acknowledged and approved. He was very glad indeed to find the others as proud of and for Temeraire as he himself was. "If we have enough hands present tomorrow evening, perhaps we may," Laurence said.

Every officer from his three runners on up was present ten minutes early. Laurence looked over them a little bemused as he and Temeraire descended from their daily trip to the lake; he only now realized, with all of them lined up and waiting, that his aerial crew wore their full uniforms, even now in this impromptu session. The other crews were often to be seen without coats or neckcloths, particularly in the recent heat; he could not help but take this as a compliment to his own habit.

Mr. Hollin and the ground crew were also ready and waiting; even though Temeraire was inclined to fidget in his excitement, they swiftly had him in his combat-duty harness, and the aerial crew came swarming aboard.

"All aboard and latched on, sir," Granby said, taking up his own launch position on Temeraire's right shoulder.

"Very well. Temeraire, we will begin with the standard clear-weather patrol pattern twice, then shift to the modified version on my signal," Laurence said.

Temeraire nodded, his eyes bright, and launched himself into the air. It was the simplest of their new maneuvers, and Temeraire had little difficulty following it; the greater problem, Laurence saw at once, as Temeraire pulled out of the last corkscrewing turn and back into his standard position, would be in accustoming the crew. The riflemen had missed at least half their targets, and Temeraire's sides were stained where the lightly weighted sacks full of ash that stood for bombs in practice had hit him instead of falling below.

"Well, Mr. Granby, we have some work ahead of us before we can make a creditable showing of it," Laurence said, and Granby nodded ruefully.

"Indeed, sir; perhaps if he flew a little slower at first?" Granby said.

"I think perhaps we must adjust our thinking as well," Laurence said, studying the pattern of ash marks. "We cannot be hurling bombs during these quick turns he makes, there is no way we can be sure of missing him. So we cannot work steadily: we must wait and release the equivalent of a full broadside in the moments when he is level. We will be at greater risk of missing a target entirely, but that risk can be borne; the other cannot."

Temeraire flew in an easy circuit while the topmen

and bellmen hastily adjusted their bombing gear; this time, when they attempted the maneuver again, Laurence saw the sacks falling away, and there were no fresh marks to be seen on Temeraire's sides. The riflemen, also waiting for the level parts of the run, improved their record as well, and after half a dozen repetitions, Laurence was well-satisfied with the results.

"When we can deliver our full allotment of bombs and achieve perhaps an eighty percent success rate in our gunnery, on this and the other four new maneuvers, I will consider our work worth bringing to Celeritas's attention," Laurence said, when they had all dismounted and the ground crew were stripping Temeraire and polishing the dust and grime off his hide. "And I think it eminently achievable: I commend all of you, gentlemen, on a most creditable performance."

Laurence had previously been sparing with his praise, not wishing to seem as though he was courting the crew's affections, but now he felt he could scarcely be overly enthusiastic, and he was pleased to see the heartfelt response of his officers to the approval. They were uniformly eager to continue, and after another four weeks of practice, Laurence was indeed beginning to think them ready to perform for a wider audience when the decision was taken from his hands.

"That was an interesting variation you were flying last evening, Captain," Celeritas said to him at the end of the morning session, as the dragons of the formation landed and the crews disembarked. "Let us see you fly it tomorrow in formation." With that he nodded and dismissed them, and Laurence was left to call together his crew and Temeraire for a hasty final practice.

Temeraire was inclined to be anxious, late that evening, after the others had gone back inside and he and Laurence were sitting quietly together in the dark, too tired to do more than rest in each other's company.

"Come, do not let yourself fret," Laurence said. "You will do very well tomorrow; you have mastered all of the maneuvers from beginning to end. We have been holding back only to give the crew better mastery."

"I am not very worried about the flying, but what if Celeritas does not approve of the maneuvers?" Temeraire said. "We would have wasted all our time to no purpose."

"If he thought the maneuvers wholly unwise, he would never have solicited us," Laurence said. "And in any case our time has not been wasted in the least; the crew have all learned their work a good deal better for having to give more attention and thought to their tasks, and even if Celeritas disapproved entirely I would still count all these evenings of ours profitably spent."

He at last soothed Temeraire to sleep and himself dozed off by the dragon's side; though it was early September, the summer's warmth was lingering, and he took no chill. Despite all his reassurances to Temeraire, Laurence himself was up and alert by first light, and he could not wholly repress a degree of anxiety in his own breast. Most of his crew were at the breakfast table as early as he was, so he made a point of speaking with several of them, and eating heartily; he would rather have not taken anything but coffee.

When he came out into the training courtyard he found Temeraire there already in his gear and looking over the valley; his tail was lashing the air uneasily. Celeritas was not yet there; fifteen minutes passed before any of the other dragons of the formation arrived, and by then Laurence had taken Temeraire and his crew out to fly a few circuits of the area. The younger ensigns and midwingmen were particularly inclined to be shrill, and he had the hands go through exchanging places to settle their nerves.

Dulcia landed, and Maximus after her; the full formation was now assembled, and Laurence brought Temeraire back in to the courtyard. Celeritas had still not yet arrived. Lily was yawning widely; Praecursoris was quietly speaking with Nitidus, the Pascal's Blue, who also spoke French, his egg having been purchased from a French hatchery many years before the start of the war, when relations had been amicable enough to permit such exchanges. Temeraire still looked at Praecursoris with a brooding eye, but for once Laurence did not mind, if it would provide some distraction.

A bright flurry of wings caught his eye; looking up, he saw Celeritas coming in to land, and beyond him the rapidly dwindling forms of several Winchesters and Greylings, going away in various directions. Lower in the sky, two Yellow Reapers were heading south in company with Victoriatus, though the wounded Parnassian's convalescence was not properly over. All the dragons came alert, sitting up; the captains' voices died away; the crews fell into a heavy and expectant silence, all before Celeritas even reached the ground.

"Villeneuve and his fleet have been caught," Celeritas said, raising his voice to be heard over the noise. "They have been penned up in the port of Cadiz, with the Spanish navy also." Even as he spoke, the servants were running out of the hall, carrying hastily packed bags and boxes; even the maids and cooks had been pressed into duty. Without being ordered, Temeraire rose to all four legs, just as did the other dragons; the ground crews were already unrolling the belly-netting and climbing up to rig the tents.

"Mortiferus has been sent to Cadiz; Lily's formation must go to the Channel at once to take the place of his wing. Captain Harcourt," Celeritas said, turning to her, "Excidium remains at the Channel, and he has eighty years' experience; you and Lily must train with him in every free moment you have. I am giving Captain Sutton

command of the formation for the moment; this is no reflection upon your work, but with this abbreviation of
your training, we must have more experience in the
role."

It was more usual for the captain of the lead dragon of
a formation to be the commander, largely because that
dragon had to lead off every maneuver, but she nodded
without any sign of offense. "Yes, certainly," she said;
her voice came out a little high, and Laurence glanced at
her with quick sympathy: Lily had hatched unexpectedly early, and Harcourt had become a captain barely
out of her own training; this might well be her first action, or very nearly so.

Celeritas gave her an approving nod. "Captain Sutton, you will naturally consult with Captain Harcourt
as far as possible."

"Of course," Sutton said, bowing to Harcourt from
his position aboard Messoria's back.

The baggage was already pulled down tight, and
Celeritas took a moment to inspect each of the harnesses
in turn. "Very good: try your loads. Maximus, begin."

One by one, the dragons all rose to their hind legs,
wind tearing across the courtyard as they beat their
wings and tried to shake the rigging loose; one by one
they dropped and reported, "All lies well."

"Ground crews aboard," Celeritas said, and Laurence
watched while Hollin and his men hurried into the belly-
rigging and strapped themselves in for the long flight.
The signal came up from below, indicating they were
ready, and he nodded to his signal-ensign, Turner, who
raised the green flag. Maximus's and Praecursoris's
crews raised their flags only a moment later; the smaller
dragons were already waiting.

Celeritas sat back onto his haunches, surveying them
all. "Fly well," he said simply.

There was nothing more, no other ceremony or preparation; Captain Sutton's signal-ensign raised the flag for *formation go aloft,* and Temeraire sprang into the air with the others, falling into position beside Maximus. The wind was in the north-west, almost directly behind them, and as they rose through the cloud cover, far to the east Laurence could see the faint glimmer of sunlight on water.

III

Chapter 9

THE RIFLE-BALL PASSED so close it stirred Laurence's hair; the crack of return fire sounded behind him, and Temeraire slashed out at the French dragon as they swept past, raking the deep blue hide with long gashes even as he twisted gracefully to avoid the other dragon's talons.

"It's a Fleur-de-Nuit, sir, the coloring," Granby shouted, wind whipping away at his hair, as the blue dragon pulled away with a bellow and wheeled about for another attempt at the formation, its crew already clambering down to stanch the bleeding: the wounds were not disabling.

Laurence nodded. "Yes. Mr. Martin," he called, more loudly, "get the flash-powder ready; we will give them a show on their next pass." The French breed were heavily built and dangerous, but they were nocturnal by nature, and their eyes sensitive to sudden flashes of bright light. "Mr. Turner, the flash-powder warning signal, if you please."

A quick confirmation came from Messoria's signal-ensign; the Yellow Reaper was herself engaged in fending off a spirited attack against the front of the formation by a French middleweight. Laurence reached out to pat Temeraire's neck, catching his attention. "We are going to give the Fleur-de-Nuit a dose of flash-powder," he shouted. "Hold this position, and wait for the signal."

"Yes, I am ready," Temeraire said, a deep note of excitement ringing in his voice; he was almost trembling.

"Pray be careful," Laurence could not help adding; the French dragon was an older one, judging by its scars, and he did not want Temeraire to be hurt through over-confidence.

The Fleur-de-Nuit arrowed towards them, trying once again to barrel between Temeraire and Nitidus: the goal was clearly to split apart the formation, injuring one or the other dragon in the process, which would leave Lily vulnerable to attack from behind on a subsequent pass. Sutton was already signaling a new maneuver which would bring them about and give Lily an angle of attack against the Fleur-de-Nuit, which was the largest of the French assailants, but before it could be accomplished this next run had to be deflected.

"All hands at the ready; stand by on the powder," Laurence said, using the speaking-trumpet to amplify his orders, as the massive blue-and-black creature came roaring towards them. The speed of the engagement was far beyond anything Laurence had ever before experienced. In the Navy, an exchange of fire might last five minutes; here a pass was over in less than one, and then a second came almost immediately. This time the French dragon was angling closer towards Nitidus, wanting nothing more to do with Temeraire's claws; the smaller Pascal's Blue would not be able to hold his position against the great bulk. "Hard to larboard; close with him!" he shouted to Temeraire.

Temeraire answered at once; his great black wings abruptly swiveled and tilted them towards the Fleur-de-Nuit, and Temeraire closed more swiftly than a typical heavy-combat dragon would have been able to do. The enemy dragon jerked and looked at them in reflex, and Laurence shouted, "Light the powder," as he caught a glimpse of the pale white eyes.

He only just closed his own eyes in time; the brilliant flash was visible even through his eyelids, and the Fleur-de-Nuit bellowed in pain. Laurence opened his eyes again to find Temeraire slashing fiercely at the other dragon, carving deep strokes into its belly, and his riflemen strafing the bellmen on the other side. "Temeraire, hold your position," Laurence called; Temeraire was in danger of falling behind in his enthusiasm for fighting off the other dragon.

With a start, Temeraire beat his wings in a flurry and lunged back into his place in the formation; Sutton's signal-ensign raised the green flag, and as a unit they all wheeled around in a tight loop, Lily already opening her jaws and hissing: the Fleur-de-Nuit was still flying blind, and streaming blood into the air as its crew tried to guide it away.

"Enemy above! Enemy above!" Maximus's larboard lookout was pointing frantically upwards; even as the boy shrilled, a terrible thick roaring like thunder sounded in their ears and drowned him out: a Grand Chevalier came plummeting down towards them. The dragon's pale belly had allowed it to blend into the heavy cloud cover undetected by the lookouts, and now it descended towards Lily, great claws opening wide; it was nearly twice her size, and outweighed even Maximus.

Laurence was shocked to see Messoria and Immortalis both suddenly drop; he realized belatedly it was the reflex which Celeritas had warned them of, so long ago: a reaction to being startled from above. Nitidus had given a startled jerk of his wings, but recovered, and Dulcia had kept her position, but Maximus had put on a burst of speed and overshot the others, and Lily herself was wheeling around in instinctive alarm. The formation had dissolved into chaos, and she was wholly exposed.

"Ready all guns; straight at him!" he roared, signaling frantically to Temeraire; it was unnecessary, for after a moment's hovering, Temeraire had already launched himself to Lily's defense. The Chevalier was too close to deflect him entirely, but if they could strike him before he was able to latch on to Lily, they could still save her from a fatal mauling, and give her time to strike back.

The four other French dragons were all coming about again. Temeraire put on a burst of sudden speed and just barely slid past the reaching claws of the Pêcheur-Couronné, and collided with the great French beast with all his claws outstretched even as the Chevalier slashed at Lily's back.

She shrieked in pain and fury, thrashing; the three dragons were all entangled now, beating their wings furiously in opposite directions, clawing and slashing. Lily could not spit upwards; they had to somehow get her loose, but Temeraire was much smaller than the Chevalier, and Laurence could see the enormous dragon's claws sinking deeper into Lily's flesh, even though her crew were hacking at the iron-hard talons with axes.

"Get a bomb up here," Laurence snapped to Granby; they would have to try and hurl one into the Chevalier's belly-rigging, despite the danger of missing and striking Temeraire or Lily.

Temeraire kept slashing away in a blind passion, his sides belling out for breath; he roared so tremendously that his body vibrated with the force and Laurence's ears ached. The Chevalier shuddered with pain; somewhere on his other side, Maximus also roared, blocked from Laurence's sight by the French dragon's bulk. The attack had its effect: the Chevalier bellowed in his deep hoarse voice, and his claws sprang free.

"Cut loose," Laurence shouted. "Temeraire, cut loose; get between him and Lily." In answer, Temeraire pulled himself free and dropped. Lily was moaning, streaming blood, and she was losing elevation rapidly. Having driven off the Chevalier was not enough: the other dragons were now as great a danger to her until she could get back aloft into fighting position. Laurence heard Captain Harcourt calling orders whose words he could not make out; abruptly Lily's belly-rigging fell away like a great net sinking down through the clouds, and bombs, supplies, baggage, all went tumbling down and vanished into the waters of the Channel below; her ground crew were all tying themselves to the main harness instead.

Thus lightened, Lily shuddered and made a great effort, beating back up into the sky; the wounds were being packed with white bandages, but even at a distance Laurence could see she would need stitching. Maximus had the Chevalier engaged, but the Pêcheur-Couronné and the Fleur-de-Nuit were falling into a small wedge formation with the other French middleweight, preparing to take a dash at Lily again. Temeraire maintained position just above Lily and hissed threateningly, his bloody claws flexing; but she was climbing too slowly.

The battle had turned into a wild melee; though the other British dragons had now recovered from their initial fright, they were in no sort of order. Harcourt was wholly occupied with Lily's difficulties, and the last French dragon, a Pêcheur-Rayé, was fighting Messoria far below. Clearly the French had identified Sutton as the commander, and were keeping him out of the way; a strategy Laurence could grimly admire. He had no authority to take command, he was the most junior captain in the party, but something had to be done.

"Turner," he said, catching his signal-ensign's attention; but before he gave any order, the other British dragons were already wheeling around and in motion.

"Signal, sir, *form up around leader*," Turner said, pointing.

Laurence looked back and saw Praecursoris swinging into Maximus's usual place with signal-flags waving: not being limited to the formation's pace, Choiseul and the big dragon had gone on ahead of them, but his lookouts had evidently caught sight of the battle and he had now returned. Laurence tapped Temeraire's shoulder to draw his attention to the signal. "I see it," Temeraire called back, and at once backwinged and settled into his proper position.

Another signal flashed out, and Laurence brought Temeraire up and in closer; Nitidus also pulled in more tightly, and together they closed the gap in the formation where Messoria would normally have been. *Formation rise together*, the next signal came, and with the other dragons around her, Lily took heart and was able to beat up more strongly: the bleeding had stopped at last. The trio of French dragons had separated; they could no longer hope to succeed with a collective charge, not straight into Lily's jaws, and the formation would be up to the level of the Chevalier in a moment.

Maximus break away, the signal flashed: Maximus was still engaged in close quarters with the Chevalier, and rifles were cracking away on both sides. The great Regal Copper gave a final slash of his claws and pushed away: just a fraction too soon, for the formation was not yet high enough, and another few moments were necessary before Lily would be able to strike.

The Chevalier's crew now saw his fresh danger and sent the big dragon back aloft, a great deal of shouting going on aboard in French. Though he was bleeding from many wounds, the Chevalier was so large that these did not hamper him severely, and he was still able to climb quicker than the injured Lily. After a moment, Choiseul signaled, *Formation hold elevation,* and they gave up the pursuit.

The French dragons came together at a distance into a loose cluster, wheeling around as they considered their next attack. But then they all turned as one and fled rapidly north-east, the Pêcheur-Rayé disengaging from Messoria also. Temeraire's lookouts were all calling out and pointing to the south, and when Laurence looked over his shoulder he saw ten dragons flying towards them at great speed, British signals flashing out from the Longwing in the lead.

The Longwing was indeed Excidium; he and his formation accompanied them along the rest of the journey to the Dover covert, the two heavyweight Chequered Nettles among them taking it in turn to support Lily on the way. She was making reasonable progress, but her head was drooping, and she made a very heavy landing, her legs trembling so that the crew only barely managed to scramble off before she crumpled to the ground. Captain Harcourt's face was streaked with unashamed tears, and she ran to Lily's head and stood there caressing her and murmuring loving encouragement while the surgeons began their work.

Laurence directed Temeraire to land on the very edge of the covert's landing ground, so the injured dragons might have more room. Maximus, Immortalis, and Messoria had all taken painful if not dangerous wounds in the battle, though nothing like what Lily had suffered, and their low cries of pain were very difficult to hear. Laurence repressed a shudder and stroked Temeraire's sleek neck; he was deeply grateful for Temeraire's quickness and grace, which had preserved him from the others' fate. "Mr. Granby, let us unload at once, and then if you please, let us see what we can spare for the comfort of Lily's crew; they have no baggage left, it looks to me."

"Very good, sir," Granby said, turning to give the orders at once.

It took several hours to settle the dragons down and get them unpacked and fed; fortunately the covert was a very large one, covering perhaps one hundred acres when including the cattle pastures, and there was no difficulty about finding a comfortably large clearing for Temeraire. Temeraire was wavering between excitement at having seen his first battle and deep anxiety for Lily's sake; for once he ate only indifferently, and Laurence finally told the crew to take away the remainder of the carcasses. "We can hunt in the morning, there is no need to force yourself to eat," he said.

"Thank you; I truly do not feel very hungry at the moment," Temeraire said, settling down his head. He was quiet while they cleaned him, until the crewmen had gone and left him alone with Laurence. His eyes were closed to slits, and for a moment Laurence wondered if he had fallen asleep; then he opened them a little more and asked softly, "Laurence, is it always so, after a battle?"

Laurence did not need to ask what he meant; Temeraire's weariness and sorrow were apparent. It was hard to know how to answer; he wanted so very much to reassure. Yet he himself was still tense and angry, and while the sensation was familiar, its lingering was not. He had been in many actions, no less deadly or dangerous, but this one had differed in the crucial respect: when the enemy took aim at his charge, they were threatening not his ship, but his dragon, already the dearest creature to him in the world. Nor could he contemplate injury to Lily or Maximus or any of the members of the formation with any sort of detachment; they might not be his own Temeraire, but they were full comrades-in-arms as well. It was not at all the same, and the surprise attack had caught him unprepared in his mind.

"It is often difficult afterwards, I am afraid, particularly when a friend has been injured, or perhaps killed," he said finally. "I will say that I find this action especially hard to bear; there was nothing to be gained, for our part, and we did not seek it out."

"Yes, that is true," Temeraire said, his ruff drooping low upon his neck. "It would be better if I could think we had all fought so hard, and Lily had been hurt, for some purpose. But they only came to hurt us, so we did not even protect anyone."

"That is not true at all; you protected Lily," Laurence said. "And consider: the French made a very clever and skillful attack, taking us wholly by surprise, with a force equal to our own in numbers and superior in experience, and we defeated it and drove them off. That is something to be proud of, is it not?"

"I suppose that is true," Temeraire said; his shoulders settled as he relaxed. "If only Lily will be all right," he added.

"Let us hope so; be sure that all that can be done for her, will be," Laurence said, stroking his nose. "Come now, you must be tired. Will you not sleep? Shall I read to you a little?"

"I do not think I can sleep," Temeraire said. "But I would like you to read to me, and I will lie quietly and rest." He yawned as soon as he had finished saying this, and was asleep before Laurence had even taken the book out. The weather had finally turned, and the warm, even breaths rising from his nostrils made small puffs of fog in the crisp air.

Leaving him to sleep, Laurence walked quickly back to the covert headquarters; the path through the dragon-fields was lit with hanging lanterns, and in any case he could see the windows up ahead. An easterly wind was carrying the salt air in from the harbor, mingled with the coppery smell of the warm dragons, already familiar and hardly noticed. He had a warm room on the second floor, with a window that looked out onto the back gardens, and his baggage had already been unpacked. He looked at the wrinkled clothes ruefully; evidently the servants at the covert had no more notion of packing than the aviators themselves did.

There was a great noise of raised voices as he came into the senior officers' dining room, despite the late hour; the other captains of the formation were assembled at the long table where their own meal was going largely untouched.

"Is there any word about Lily?" he asked, taking the empty chair between Berkley and Dulcia's captain, Chenery; Captain Harcourt and Captain Little of Immortalis were the only ones not present.

"He cut her to the bone, the great coward, but that is all we know," Chenery said. "They are still sewing her up, and she hasn't taken anything to eat."

Laurence knew that was a bad sign; injured dragons usually became ravenous, unless they were in very great pain. "Maximus and Messoria?" he asked, looking at Berkley and Sutton.

"Ate well, and fast asleep," Berkley said; his usually placid face was drawn and haggard, and he had a streak of dark blood running across his forehead into his bristly hair. "That was damned quick of you today, Laurence; we'd have lost her."

"Not quick enough," Laurence said quietly, forestalling the murmur of agreement; he had not the least desire to be praised for this day's work, though he was proud of what Temeraire had done.

"Quicker than the rest of us," Sutton said, draining his glass; from the looks of his cheeks and nose, it was not his first. "They caught us properly flat-footed, damned Frogs. What the devil they were doing to have a patrol there, I would like to know."

"The route from Laggan to Dover isn't much of a secret, Sutton," Little said, coming to the table; they dragged chairs about to make room for him at their end of the table. "Immortalis is settled and eating, by the by; speaking of which, please give me that chicken here." He wrenched off a leg with his hands and tore into it hungrily.

Looking at him, Laurence felt the first stirrings of appetite; the other captains seemed to feel the same way, and for the next ten minutes there was silence while they passed the plates around and concentrated on their food; they had none of them eaten since a hasty breakfast before dawn at the covert near Middlesbrough. The wine was not very good, but Laurence drank several glasses anyway.

"I expect they've been lurking about between Felix-stowe and Dover, just waiting to get a drop on us," Little said after a while, wiping his mouth and continuing his earlier thought. "By God, if you ever catch me taking Immortalis that way again; overland it is for us from now on, unless we're looking for a fight."

"Right you are," Chenery said, with heartfelt agreement. "Hello, Choiseul; pull up a chair." He shuffled over a little more, and the royalist captain joined them.

"Gentlemen, I am very happy to say that Lily has begun to eat; I have just come from Captain Harcourt," he said, and raised a glass. "To their health, may I propose?"

"Hear, hear," Sutton said, refilling his own glass; they all joined in the toast, and there was a general sigh of relief.

"Here you all are, then; eating, I hope? Good, very good." Admiral Lenton had come up to join them; he was the commander-in-chief of the Channel Division, and thus all those dragons at the Dover covert. "No, don't be fools, don't get up," he said impatiently, as Laurence and Choiseul began to rise, and the others belatedly followed. "After the day you've had, for Heaven's sake. Here, pass that bottle over, Sutton. So, you all know that Lily is eating? Yes, the surgeons hope she will be flying short distances in a couple of weeks, and in the meantime you have at least nicely mauled a couple of their heavy-combat beasts. A toast to your formation, gentlemen."

Laurence was at last beginning to feel his tension and distress ease; knowing Lily and the others were out of danger was a great relief, and the wine had loosened the tight knot in his throat. The others seemed to feel much the same way, and conversation grew slow and fragmented; they were all much inclined to nod over their cups.

"I am quite certain that the Grand Chevalier was Triumphalis," Choiseul was telling Admiral Lenton quietly. "I have seen him before; he is one of France's most dangerous fighters. He was certainly at the Dijon covert, near the Rhine, when Praecursoris and I left Austria, and I must represent to you, sir, that it bears out all my worst fears: Bonaparte would not have brought him here if he was not wholly confident of victory against Austria, and I am sure more of the French dragons are on their way to assist Villeneuve."

"I was inclined to agree with you before, Captain; now I am sure of it," Lenton said. "But for the moment, all we can do is hope Mortiferus reaches Nelson before the French dragons reach Villeneuve, and that he can do the job; we cannot spare Excidium if we do not have Lily. I would not be surprised if that was what they intended by this strike; it is the clever sort of way that damned Corsican thinks."

Laurence could not help thinking of the *Reliant,* perhaps even now under the threat of a full-scale French aerial attack, and the other ships of the great fleet currently blockading Cadiz. So many of his friends and acquaintances; even if the French dragons did not arrive first, there would be a great naval battle to be fought, and how many would be lost without his ever hearing another word from them? He had not devoted much time to correspondence in the last busy months; now he regretted the neglect deeply.

"Have we had any dispatches from the blockade at Cadiz?" he asked. "Have they seen any action?"

"Not that I have heard of," Lenton said. "Oh, that's right, you're our fellow from the Navy, aren't you? Well, I will be starting those of you with uninjured beasts on patrolling over the Channel Fleet anyway while the others recover; you can touch down for a bit by the flagship and hear the news. They'll be damned glad to see you; we haven't been able to spare anyone long enough to bring them the post in a month."

"Will you want us tomorrow, then?" Chenery asked, stifling a yawn, not entirely successfully.

"No, I can spare you a day. See to your dragons, and enjoy the rest while it lasts," Lenton said, with a sharp, braying laugh. "I'll be having you rousted out of bed at dawn the day after."

Temeraire slept very heavily and late the next morning, leaving Laurence to occupy himself for some hours after breakfast. He met Berkley at the table, and walked back with him to see Maximus. The Regal Copper was still eating, a procession of fresh-slaughtered sheep going down his gullet one after another, and he only rumbled a wordless, mouth-full greeting as they came to the clearing.

Berkley brought out a bottle of rather terrible wine, and drank most of it himself while Laurence sipped at his glass to be polite, as they told over the battle again with diagrams scratched in the dirt and pebbles representing the dragons. "We would do very well to add a light-flyer, a Greyling if one can be spared, to fly lookout above the formation," Berkley said, sitting back heavily upon a rock. "It is all our big dragons being young; when the big ones panic in that way, the little ones will have a start even if they know better."

Laurence nodded. "Although I hope this misadventure will at least have given them some experience in dealing with the fright," he said. "In any event, the French cannot count on having such ideal circumstances often; without the cloud cover they should never have managed it."

"Gentlemen; are you looking over the plan of yesterday?" Choiseul had been walking past towards the headquarters; he joined them and crouched down beside the diagram. "I am very sorry to have been away at the beginning." His coat was dusty and his neckcloth was stained badly with sweat: he looked as though he had not shifted his clothes since yesterday, and a thin tracery of red veins stood out in the whites of his eyes; he rubbed his face as he looked down.

"Have you been up all night?" Laurence asked.

Choiseul shook his head. "No, but I took it in turns with Catherine—with Harcourt—to sleep a little, by Lily; she would not rest otherwise." He shut his eyes in an enormous yawn, and nearly fell over. "*Merci,*" he said, grateful for Laurence's steadying hand, and pushed himself slowly to his feet. "I will leave you; I must get Catherine some food."

"Pray go and get some rest," Laurence said. "I will bring her something; Temeraire is asleep, and I am at liberty."

Harcourt herself was wide awake, pale with anxiety but steady now, giving orders to the crew and feeding Lily with chunks of still-steaming beef from her own hand, a constant stream of encouragement coming from her lips. Laurence had brought her some bread with bacon; she would have taken the sandwich in her bloody hands, unwilling to interrupt, but he managed to coax her away long enough to wash a little and eat while a crewman took her place. Lily kept eating, with one golden eye resting on Harcourt for reassurance.

Choiseul came back before Harcourt had quite fin-

ished, his neckcloth and coat gone and a servant following with a pot of coffee, strong and hot. "Your
lieutenant is looking for you, Laurence; Temeraire begins to stir," he said, sitting down again heavily beside
her. "I cannot manage to sleep; the coffee has done me
well."

"Thank you, Jean-Paul, if you are not too tired, I
would be very grateful for your company," she said, already drinking her second cup. "Pray have no hesitation, Laurence, I am sure Temeraire must be anxious. I
am obliged to you for coming."

Laurence bowed to them both, though he had a sense
of awkwardness for the first occasion since he had
grown used to Harcourt. She was leaning with no appearance of consciousness against Choiseul's shoulder, and he was looking down at her with undisguised
warmth; she was quite young, after all, and Laurence
could not help feeling the absence of any suitable chap-
erone.

He consoled himself that nothing could happen with
Lily and the crew present, even if they had not both been
so obviously done in; in any case, he could hardly stay
under the circumstances, and he hurried away to Temeraire's clearing.

The rest of the day he spent gratefully in idleness,
seated comfortably in his usual place in the crook of
Temeraire's foreleg and writing letters; he had formed
an extensive correspondence while at sea, with all the
long hours to fill, and now many of his acquaintance
were owed responses. His mother, too, had managed
to write him several hasty and short letters, evidently
kept from his father's knowledge; at least they were
not franked, so Laurence was obliged to pay to receive
them.

Having gorged himself to compensate for his lack of

appetite the night before, Temeraire then listened to the letters Laurence was writing and dictated his own contributions, sending greetings to Lady Allendale, and to Riley. "And do ask Captain Riley to give my best wishes to the crew of the *Reliant*," he said. "It seems so very long ago, Laurence, does it not? I have not had fish in months now."

Laurence smiled at this measure of time. "A great deal has happened, certainly; it is strange to think it has not even been a year," he said, sealing the envelope and writing the direction. "I only hope they are all well." It was the last, and he laid it upon the substantial pile with satisfaction; he was a great deal easier in his conscience now. "Roland," he called, and she came running up from where the cadets were playing a game of jacks. "Go take this to the dispatch post," he said, handing her the stack.

"Sir," she said, a little nervously, accepting the letters, "when I am done, might I have liberty for the evening?"

He was startled by the request; several of the ensigns and midwingmen had put in for liberty, and had it granted, that they might visit the city, but the idea of a ten-year-old cadet wandering about Dover alone was absurd, even if she were not a girl. "Would this be for yourself alone, or will you be going with one of the others?" he asked, thinking she might have been invited to join one of the older officers in a respectable excursion.

"No, sir, only for me," she said; she looked so very hopeful that Laurence thought for a moment of granting it and taking her himself, but he could not like to leave Temeraire alone to brood over the previous day.

"Perhaps another time, Roland," he said gently. "We will be here in Dover for a long time now, and I promise you will have another opportunity."

"Oh," she said, downcast. "Yes, sir." She went away drooping so that Laurence felt guilty.

Temeraire watched her go and inquired, "Laurence, is there something particularly interesting in Dover, and might we go and see it? So many of our crew seem to be making a visit."

"Oh dear," Laurence said; he felt rather awkward explaining that the main attraction was the abundance of harbor prostitutes and cheap liquor. "Well, a city has a great many people in it, and thus various entertainments provided in close proximity," he tried.

"Do you mean such as more books?" Temeraire said. "But I have never seen Dunne or Collins reading, and they were so very excited to be going: they talked of nothing else all yesterday evening."

Laurence silently cursed the two unfortunate young midwingmen for complicating his task, already planning their next week's duties in a vengeful spirit. "There is also the theater, and concerts," he said lamely. But this was carrying concealment too far: the sting of dishonesty was unpleasant, and he could not bear to feel he had been deceitful to Temeraire, who after all was grown now. "But I am afraid that some of them go there to drink, and keep low company," he said more frankly.

"Oh, you mean whores," Temeraire said, startling Laurence so greatly he nearly fell from his seat. "I did not know they had those in cities, too, but now I understand."

"Where on earth had you heard of them?" Laurence asked, steadying himself; now relieved of the burden of explanation, he felt irrationally offended that someone else had chosen to enlighten Temeraire.

"Oh, Victoriatus at Loch Laggan told me, for I wondered why the officers were going down to the village when they did not have family there," Temeraire said. "But you have never gone; are you sure you would not like to?" he added, almost hopefully.

"My dear, you must not say such things," Laurence said, blushing and shaking with laughter at the same time. "It is not a respectable subject for conversation, at all, and if men cannot be prevented from indulging the habit, they at least ought not to be encouraged. I shall certainly speak with Dunne and Collins; they ought not to be bragging about it, and especially not where the ensigns might hear."

"I do not understand," Temeraire said. "Vindicatus said that it was prodigiously nice for men, and also desirable, for otherwise they might like to get married, and that did not sound very pleasant at all. Although if you very much wished to, I suppose I would not mind." He made this last speech with very little sincerity, looking at Laurence sideways, as if to gauge the effect.

Laurence's mirth and embarrassment both faded at once. "I am afraid you have been given some very incomplete knowledge," he said gently. "Forgive me; I ought to have spoken of these matters to you before. I must beg you to have no anxiety: you are my first charge and will always be, even if I should ever marry, and I do not suppose I will."

He paused a moment to reflect if speaking further would give Temeraire more worry, but in the end he decided to err on the side of full confidence, and added, "There was something of an understanding between myself and a lady, before you came to me, but she has since set me at liberty."

"Do you mean she has refused you?" Temeraire said, very indignantly, by way of demonstrating that dragons might be as contrary as men. "I am very sorry, Laurence;

if you like to get married, I am sure you can find someone else, much nicer."

"This is very flattering, but I assure you, I have not
the least desire to seek out a replacement," Laurence
said.

Temeraire ducked his head a little, and made no further demurrals, quite evidently pleased. "But Laurence—"
he said, then halted. "Laurence," he asked, "if it is not a
fit subject, does that mean I ought not speak of it anymore?"

"You must be careful to avoid it in any wider company, but you may always speak of anything you like to
me," Laurence said.

"I am merely curious, now, if that is all there is in
Dover," Temeraire said. "For Roland is too young for
whores, is she not?"

"I am beginning to feel the need of a glass of wine to
fortify myself against this conversation," Laurence said
ruefully.

Thankfully, Temeraire was satisfied with some further
explanation of what the theater and concerts might be,
and the other attractions of a city; he turned his attention willingly to a discussion of the planned route for
their patrol, which a runner had brought over that
morning, and even inquired about the possibility of
catching some fish for dinner. Laurence was glad to see
him so recovered in spirit after the previous day's mis-
fortunes, and had just decided that he would take
Roland to the town after all, if Temeraire did not object,
when he saw her returning in the company of another
captain: a woman.

He had been sitting upon Temeraire's foreleg in what
he was abruptly conscious was a state of disarray; he
hurriedly climbed down on the far side so that he was

briefly hidden by Temeraire's body. There was no time to put back his coat, which was hung over a tree limb some distance away in any case, but he tucked his shirt back into his trousers and tied his neckcloth hastily back round his neck.

He came around to make his bow, and nearly stumbled as he saw her clearly; she was not unhandsome, but her face was marred badly by a scar that could only have been made by a sword; the left eye drooped a little at the corner where the blade had just missed it, and the flesh was drawn along an angry red line all the way down her face, fading to a thinner white scar along her neck. She was his own age, or perhaps a little older; the scar made it difficult to tell, but in any case she wore the triple bars which marked her as a senior captain, and a small gold medal of the Nile in her lapel.

"Laurence, is it?" she said, without waiting for any sort of introduction, while he was still busy striving to conceal his surprise. "I am Jane Roland, Excidium's captain; I would take it as a personal favor if I might have Emily for the evening—if she can possibly be spared." She glanced pointedly at the idle cadets and ensigns; her tone was sarcastic, and she was clearly offended.

"I beg your pardon," Laurence said, realizing his mistake. "I had thought she wanted liberty to visit the town; I did not realize—" And here he barely caught himself; he was quite sure they were mother and daughter, not only because of the shared name but also a certain similarity of feature and expression, but he could not simply make the assumption. "Certainly you may have her," he finished instead.

Hearing his explanation, Captain Roland unbent at once. "Ha! I see, what mischief you must have imagined her getting into," she said; her laugh was curiously hearty and unfeminine. "Well, I promise I shan't let her run wild, and to have her back by eight o'clock. Thank you; Excidium and I have not seen her in almost a year, and we are in danger of forgetting what she looks like."

Laurence bowed and saw them off; Roland hurrying to keep up with her mother's long, mannish stride, speaking the whole time in obvious excitement and enthusiasm, and waving her hand towards her friends as she went away. Watching them go, Laurence felt a little foolish; he had at last grown used to Captain Harcourt, and should have been able to draw the natural conclusion. Excidium was after all another Longwing; presumably he too insisted on a female captain just as did Lily, and with his many years of service, his captain could scarcely have avoided battle. Yet Laurence had to own he was surprised, and not a little shocked, to see a woman so cut about and so forward; Harcourt, his only other example of a female captain, was by no means missish, but she was still quite young and conscious of her early promotion, which perhaps made her less assured.

With the subject of marriage so fresh in his mind after his discussion with Temeraire, he also could not help wondering about Emily's father; if marriage was an awkward proposition for a male aviator, it seemed nearly inconceivable for a female one. The only thing he could imagine was that Emily was natural-born, and as soon as the idea occurred to him he scolded himself to be entertaining such thoughts about a perfectly respectable woman he had just met.

But his involuntary guess proved entirely correct, in the event. "I am afraid I have not the slightest idea; I have not seen him in ten years," she said, later that evening; she had invited him to join her for a late supper at the officers' club after bringing Emily back, and after a few glasses of wine he had not been able to resist making a tentative inquiry after the health of Emily's father. "It is not as though we were married, you know; I do not believe he even knows Emily's name."

She seemed wholly unconscious of any shame, and after all Laurence had privately felt any more legitimate situation would have been impossible. But he was uncomfortable nevertheless; thankfully, though she noticed, she did not take any offense at it for herself, but rather said kindly, "I dare say our ways are still odd to you. But you *can* marry, if you like, it is not held against you at all in the Corps. It is only that it is rather hard on the other person, always taking second place to a dragon. For my own part, I have never felt anything wanting; I should never have desired children if it were not for Excidium's sake, although Emily is a dear, and I am very happy to have her. But it was sadly inconvenient, for all that."

"So Emily is to follow you as his captain?" Laurence said. "May I ask you, are the dragons, the long-lived ones, I mean, always inherited this way?"

"When we can manage it; they take it very hard, you see, losing a handler, and they are more likely to accept a new one if it is someone they have some connection to, and whom they feel shares their grief," she said. "So we breed ourselves as much as them; I expect they will be asking you to manage one or two for the Corps yourself."

"Good Lord," he said, startled by the idea; he had discarded the thought of children with his plans of marriage, from the very moment of Edith's refusal, and still further gone now that he was aware of Temeraire's objections; he could not immediately imagine how he might arrange the matter.

"I suppose it must be rather shocking to you, poor fellow. I am sorry," she said. "I would offer, but you ought to wait until he is at least ten years old; and in any case I cannot be spared just now."

Laurence required a moment to understand what she meant, then he snatched up his wineglass with an unsteady hand and endeavored to conceal his face behind it; he could feel color rising in his cheeks despite all the will in the world to prevent it. "Very kind," he said into the cup, strangled half between mortification and laughter; it was not the sort of offer he had ever envisioned receiving, even if it had only half been made.

"Catherine might do for you by then, however," Roland went on, still in that appallingly practical tone. "That might do nicely, indeed; you could have one each for Lily and Temeraire."

"Thank you!" he said, very firmly, in desperation trying to change the subject. "May I bring you a glass of something to drink?"

"Oh, yes; port would be splendid, thank you," she said. By this time he was beyond being shocked; and when he returned with two glasses and she offered him an already-lit cigar, he shared it with her willingly.

He stayed talking with her for several hours more, until they were the only ones left in the club and the servants were beginning to pointedly stop concealing their yawns. They climbed the stairs together. "It is not so very late as all that," she said, looking at the handsome great clock at the end of the upper landing. "Are you very tired? We might have a hand or two of piquet in my rooms."

By this time he had begun to be so easy with her that he thought nothing of the suggestion. When he left her at last, very late, to return to his own rooms, a servant was walking down the hall and glanced at him; only then did he consider the propriety of his behavior and suffer a qualm. But the damage, if any, had already been done; he put it from his mind, and sought his bed at last.

Chapter 10

❧

HE WAS SUFFICIENTLY experienced to no longer be very surprised, the next morning, when he found that their late night had led to no gossip. Instead, Captain Roland hailed him warmly at breakfast and introduced him to her lieutenants without the slightest consciousness, and they walked out to their dragons together.

Laurence saw Temeraire finishing off a hearty breakfast of his own, and took a moment to have a private and forceful word with Collins and Dunne about their indiscretion. He did not mean to go on like a blue-light captain, preaching chastity and temperance all day; still, he did not think it prudish if he preferred his youngsters to have a respectable example before them in the older officers. "If you must keep such company, I do not propose to have you making whoremongers of yourselves, and giving the ensigns and cadets the notion that this is how they ought to behave," he said, while the two midwingmen squirmed. Dunne even opened his mouth and looked as though he would rather like to protest, but subsided under Laurence's very cold stare: that was a degree of insubordination he did not intend to permit.

But having finished the lecture and dismissed them to their work, he found himself a trifle uneasy as he recalled that his own behavior of the previous night was not above reproach. He consoled himself by the reminder that Roland was a fellow-officer; her company could hardly be compared to that of whores, and in any case they had not created any sort of public spectacle, which was at the heart of the matter. However, the rationalization rang a little hollow, and he was glad to distract himself with work: Emily and the two other runners were already waiting by Temeraire's side with the heavy bags of post that had accumulated for the blockading fleet.

The very strength of the British fleet left the ships on the blockade in strangely isolated circumstances. It was rarely necessary for a dragon to be sent to their assistance; they received all but their most urgent dispatches and supplies by frigate, and so had little opportunity to hear recent news or receive their post. The French might have twenty-one ships in Brest, but they did not dare come out to face the far more skilled British sailors. Without naval support, even a full French heavy-combat wing would not risk a strafing run with the sharpshooters always ready in the tops and the harpoon and pepper guns primed upon the deck. Occasionally there might be an attack at night, usually made by a single nocturnal-breed dragon, but the riflemen often gave as good as they got in such circumstances, and if a full-scale attack were ever launched, a flare signal could easily be seen by the patrolling dragons to the north.

Admiral Lenton had decided to reorder the uninjured dragons of Lily's formation as necessary from day to day, to both keep the dragons occupied and patrol a somewhat greater extent. Today he had ordered Temeraire to fly point, with Nitidus and Dulcia flanking him: they would trail Excidium's formation on the first leg of Channel patrol, then break off for a pass over the main squadron of the Channel Fleet, currently just off Ushant and blockading the French port of Brest. Aside from the more martial benefits, their visit would furnish the ships of the fleet with at least a little break in the lonely monotony of their blockade-duty.

The morning was so cold and crisp no fog had gathered, the sky sharply brilliant and the water below almost black. Squinting against the glare, Laurence would have liked to imitate the ensigns and midwingmen, who were rubbing black kohl under their eyes, but as pointleader, he would be in command of the small group while they were detached, and he would likely be asked aboard to see Admiral Lord Gardner when they landed at the flagship.

Thanks to the weather, it was a pleasant flight, even if not a very smooth one: wind currents seemed to vary unpredictably once they had moved out over the open water, and Temeraire followed some unconscious instinct in rising and falling to catch the best wind. After an hour's patrol, they reached the point of separation; Captain Roland raised a hand in farewell as Temeraire angled away south and swept past Excidium; the sun was nearly straight overhead, and the ocean glittered beneath them.

"Laurence, I see the ships ahead," Temeraire said, perhaps half an hour later, and Laurence lifted his telescope, having to cup a hand around his eye and squint against the sun before he could see the sails on the water.

"Well sighted," Laurence called back, and said, "Give them the private signal if you please, Mr. Turner." The signal-ensign began running up the pattern of flags that would mark them as a British party; less of a formality in their case, thanks to Temeraire's unusual appearance.

Shortly they were sighted and identified; the leading British ship fired a handsome salute of nine guns, more perhaps than was strictly due to Temeraire, as he was not an official formation leader. Whether it was misunderstanding or generosity, Laurence was pleased by the attention, and had the riflemen fire off a return salute as they swept by overhead.

The fleet was a stirring sight, with the lean and elegant cutters already leaping across the water to cluster around the flagship in anticipation of the post, and the great ships-of-the-line tacking steadily into the northerly wind to keep their positions, white sails brilliant against the water, colors flying in proud display from every mainmast. Laurence could not resist leaning forward to watch over Temeraire's shoulder, so far that the carabiner straps drew taut.

"Signal from the flagship, sir," Turner said, as they drew near enough for the flags to be readable. "Captain come aboard on landing."

Laurence nodded; no less than he had anticipated. "Pray acknowledge, Mr. Turner. Mr. Granby, I think we will do a pass over the rest of the fleet to the south, while they make ready for us." The crew of the *Hibernia* and the neighboring *Agincourt* had begun casting out the floating platforms that would be lashed together to form a landing surface for the dragons, and a small cutter was already moving among them, gathering up the towlines. Laurence knew from experience that the operation required some time, and would go no quicker with the dragons circling directly overhead.

By the time they had completed their sweep and returned, the platforms were ready. "Bellmen up above, Mr. Granby," Laurence ordered; the crew of the lower rigging quickly came scrambling up onto Temeraire's back. The last few sailors hastily cleared off the deck as Temeraire made his descent, with Nitidus and Dulcia following close upon him; the platform bobbed and sank lower in the water as Temeraire's great weight came upon it, but the lashings held secure. Nitidus and Dulcia landed at opposite corners once Temeraire had settled himself, and Laurence swung himself down.

"Runners, bring the post," he said, and himself took the sealed envelope of dispatches from Admiral Lenton to Admiral Gardner.

Laurence climbed easily into the waiting cutter, while his runners Roland, Dyer, and Morgan hurried to hand the bags of post over to the outstretched hands of the sailors. He went to the stern; Temeraire was sprawled low to better preserve the balance of the platform, with his head resting upon the edge of the platform very close to the cutter, much to the discomfort of that vessel's crew. "I will return presently," Laurence told him. "Pray give Lieutenant Granby the word if you require anything."

"I will, but I do not think I will need to; I am perfectly well," Temeraire answered, to startled looks from the cutter's crew, which only increased as he added, "But if we could go hunting afterwards, I would be glad of it; I am sure I saw some splendid large tunnys on our way."

The cutter was an elegant, clean-lined vessel, and she bore Laurence to the *Hibernia* at a pace which he would once have thought the height of speed; now he stood looking out along her bowsprit, running before the wind, and the breeze in his face seemed barely anything.

They had rigged a bosun's chair over the *Hibernia*'s side, which Laurence ignored with disdain; his sea-legs had scarcely deserted him, and in any case climbing up the side presented him with no difficulty. Captain Bedford was waiting to greet him, and started in open surprise as Laurence climbed aboard: they had served together in the *Goliath* at the Nile.

"Good Lord, Laurence; I had no notion of your being here in the Channel," he said, formal greeting forgotten, and meeting him instead with a hearty handshake. "Is that your beast, then?" he asked, staring across the water at Temeraire, who was in his bulk not much smaller than the seventy-four-gun *Agincourt* behind him. "I thought he had only just hatched a sixmonth gone."

Laurence could not help a swelling pride; he hoped that he concealed it as he answered, "Yes, that is Temeraire. He is not yet eight months old, yet he does have nearly his full growth." With difficulty he restrained himself from boasting further; nothing, he was sure, could be more irritating, like one of those men who could not stop talking of the beauty of their mistress, or the cleverness of their children. In any case, Temeraire did not require praising; any observer looking at him could hardly fail to mark his distinctive and elegant appearance.

"Oh, I see," Bedford said, looking at him with a bemused expression. Then the lieutenant at Bedford's shoulder coughed meaningfully. Bedford glanced at the fellow and then said, "Forgive me; I was so taken aback to see you that I have been keeping you standing about. Pray come this way, Lord Gardner is waiting to see you."

Admiral Lord Gardner had only lately come to his position as commander in the Channel, on Sir William Cornwallis's retirement; the strain of following so successful a leader in so difficult a position was telling upon him. Laurence had served in the Channel Fleet several years before, as a lieutenant; they had never been introduced previously, but Laurence had seen him several times, and his face was markedly aged.

"Yes, I see, Laurence, is it?" Gardner said, as the flag-lieutenant presented him, and murmured a few words which Laurence could not hear. "Pray be seated; I must read these dispatches at once, and then I have a few words to give you to carry back for me to Lenton," he said, breaking the seal and studying the contents. Lord Gardner grunted and nodded to himself as he read through the messages; from his sharp look, Laurence knew when he reached the account of the recent skirmish.

"Well, Laurence, you have already seen some sharp action, I gather," he said, laying aside the papers at last. "It is just as well for you all to get some seasoning, I expect; it cannot be long before we see something more from them, and you must tell Lenton so for me. I have been sending every sloop and brig and cutter I dare to risk close in to the shore, and the French are busy as bees inland outside Cherbourg. We cannot tell with what, precisely, but they can hardly be preparing for anything but invasion, and judging by their activity, they mean it to be soon."

"Surely Bonaparte cannot have more news of the fleet in Cadiz than do we?" Laurence said, disturbed by this intelligence. The degree of confidence augured by such preparations was frighteningly high, and though Bonaparte was certainly arrogant, his arrogance had rarely proven to be wholly unfounded.

"Not of immediate events, no, of that I am now thankfully certain. You have brought me confirmation that our dispatch-riders have been coming back and forth steadily," Gardner said, tapping the sheaf of papers on his desk. "However, he cannot be so wild as to imagine he can come across without his fleet, and that suggests he expects them soon."

Laurence nodded; that expectation might still be ill-founded or wishful, but that Bonaparte had it at all meant Nelson's fleet was in imminent danger.

Gardner sealed the packet of returning dispatches and handed them over. "There; I am much obliged to you, Laurence, and for your bringing the post to us. Now I trust you will join us for dinner, and of course your fellow captains as well?" he said, rising from his desk. "Captain Briggs of the *Agincourt* will join us as well, I think."

A lifetime of naval training had inculcated in Laurence the precept that such an invitation from a superior officer was as good as a command, and though Gardner was no longer strictly his superior, it remained impossible to even think of refusing. But Laurence could not help but consider Temeraire with some anxiety, and Nitidus with even more. The Pascal's Blue was a nervous creature who required a great deal of careful management from Captain Warren under ordinary circumstances, and Laurence was certain that he would be distressed at the prospect of remaining aboard the makeshift floating platform without his handler and no officer above the rank of lieutenant anywhere to be seen.

And yet dragons did wait under such conditions all the time; if there had been a greater aerial threat against the fleet, several might even have been stationed upon platforms at all times, with their captains frequently called upon to join the naval officers in planning. Laurence could not like subjecting the dragons to such a wait for no better cause than a dinner engagement, but neither could he honestly say there was any actual risk to them.

"Sir, nothing could give me greater pleasure, and I am sure I speak for Captain Warren and Captain Chenery as well," he said: there was nothing else to be done. Indeed Gardner could hardly be said to be waiting for an answer; he had already gone to the door to call in his lieutenant.

However, only Chenery came over in response to the signaled invitation, bearing sincere but mild regrets. "Nitidus will fret if he is left alone, you see, so Warren thinks it much better if he does not leave him," was all the explanation he offered, made to Gardner very cheerfully; he seemed unconscious of the deep solecism he was committing.

Laurence privately winced at the startled and somewhat offended looks this procured, not merely from Lord Gardner but from the other captains and the flag-lieutenant as well, though he could not help but feel relieved. Still the dinner began awkwardly, and continued so.

The admiral was clearly oppressed by thoughts of his work, and there were long periods between his remarks. The table would have been a silent and heavy one, save that Chenery was in his usual form, high-spirited and quick to make conversation, and he spoke freely in complete disregard of the naval convention that reserved the right of starting conversation to Lord Gardner.

When addressed directly, the naval officers would pause very pointedly before responding to him, as briefly as possible, before dropping the subject. Laurence was at first agonized on his behalf, and then began to grow angry. It must have been clear to even the most sensitive temper that Chenery was speaking in ignorance; his chosen subjects were innocuous, and to sit in sullen and reproachful silence seemed to Laurence a far greater piece of rudeness.

Chenery could not help but notice the cold response; as yet he was only beginning to look puzzled, not offended, but that would hardly last. When he gamely tried once more, this time Laurence deliberately volunteered a reply. The two of them carried the discussion along between them for several minutes, and then Gardner, his attention drawn from his brown study, glanced up and contributed a remark. The conversation was thus blessed, and the other officers joined in at last; Laurence made a great effort, and kept the topic running throughout the rest of the meal.

What ought to have been a pleasure thus became a chore, and he was very glad when the port was taken off the table, and they were invited to step up on deck for cigars and coffee. Taking his cup, he went to stand by the larboard taffrail to better see the floating platform: Temeraire was sleeping quietly with the sun beating on his scales, one foreleg dangling over the side into the water, and Nitidus and Dulcia were resting against him.

Bedford came to stand and look with him, in what Laurence took as companionable silence; after a moment Bedford said, "I suppose he is a valuable animal and we must be glad to have him, but it is appalling you should be chained to such a life, and in such company."

Laurence could not immediately command the power of speech in response to this remark so full of sincere pity; half a dozen answers all crowded to his lips. He drew a breath that shook in his throat and said in a low, savage voice, "Sir, you will not speak to me in such terms, either of Temeraire or of my colleagues; I wonder that you could imagine such an address acceptable."

Bedford stepped back from his vehemence. Laurence turned away and left his coffee cup clattering upon the steward's tray. "Sir, I think we must be leaving," he said to Gardner, keeping his voice even. "As this is Temeraire's first flight along this course, best were we to return before sunset."

"Of course," Gardner said, offering a hand. "Godspeed, Captain; I hope we will see you again shortly."

Despite this excuse, Laurence did not find himself back at the covert until shortly after nightfall. Having seen Temeraire snatch several large tunnys from the water, Nitidus and Dulcia expressed the inclination to try fishing themselves, and Temeraire was perfectly happy to continue demonstrating. The younger crewmen were not entirely prepared for the experience of being on board while their dragon hunted; but after the first plummeting drop had accustomed them to the experience, the startled yells vanished, and they rapidly came to view the process as a game.

Laurence found that his black mood could not survive their enthusiasm: the boys cheered wildly each time Temeraire rose up with yet another tunny wriggling in his claws, and several of them even sought permission to climb below, the better to be splashed as Temeraire made his catch.

Thoroughly glutted and flying somewhat more slowly back towards the coast, Temeraire hummed in happiness and contentment, turned his head around to look at Laurence with bright-eyed gratitude, and said, "Has this not been a pleasant day? It has been a long time since we have had such splendid flying," and Laurence found that he had no anger left to conceal in making his reply.

The lamps throughout the covert were just coming alight, like great fireflies against the darkness of the scattered trees, the ground crews moving among them with their torches even as Temeraire made his descent. Most of the younger officers were still soaking wet and beginning to shiver as they climbed down from Temeraire's warm bulk; Laurence dismissed them to their rest and stood watch with Temeraire himself while the ground crew finished unharnessing him. Hollin looked at him a little reproachfully as the men brought down the neck and shoulder harnesses, encrusted with fish scales, bones, and entrails, and already beginning to stink.

Temeraire was too pleased and well-fed for Laurence to feel apologetic; he only said cheerfully, "I am afraid we have made some heavy work for you, Mr. Hollin, but at least he will not need feeding tonight."

"Aye, sir," Hollin said gloomily, and marshaled his men to the task.

The harness removed and his hide washed down by the crew, who by this time had formed the technique of passing buckets along rather like a fire brigade to clean him after his meals, Temeraire yawned enormously, belched, and sprawled out upon the ground with so self-satisfied an expression that Laurence laughed at him. "I must go and deliver these dispatches," he said. "Will you sleep, or shall we read this evening?"

"Forgive me, Laurence, I think I am too sleepy," Temeraire said, yawning again. "Laplace is difficult to follow even when I am quite awake, and I do not want to risk misunderstanding."

As Laurence had enough difficulty for his own part merely in pronouncing the French of Laplace's treatise on celestial mechanics well enough for Temeraire to comprehend, without making any effort to himself grasp the principles he was reading aloud, he was perfectly willing to believe this. "Very well, my dear; I will see you in the morning, then," he said, and stood stroking Temeraire's nose until the dragon's eyes had slid shut, and his breathing had evened out into slumber.

Admiral Lenton received the dispatches and the verbal message with frowning concern. "I do not like it in the least, not in the least," he said. "Working inland, is he? Laurence, could he be building more boats on shore, planning to add to his fleet without our knowing?"

"Some awkward transports he might perhaps be able to make, sir, but never ships-of-the-line," Laurence said at once, with perfect certainty on the subject. "And he already has a great many transports, in every port along the coastline; it is difficult to conceive that he might require more."

"And all this is around Cherbourg, not Calais, though the distance is greater, and our fleet is closer by. I cannot account for it, but Gardner is quite right; I am damned sure he means mischief, and he cannot very well do it until his fleet is here." Abruptly he stood and walked straight from the office; unsure whether to take this as a dismissal, Laurence followed him through the headquarters and outside, to the clearing where Lily was lying in her recovery.

Captain Harcourt was sitting by Lily's head, stroking her foreleg, over and over; Choiseul was with her and reading quietly to them both. Lily's eyes were still dull with pain, but in a more encouraging sign, she had evidently just eaten whole food at last, for there was a great heap of cracked bones still being cleared away by the ground crew.

Choiseul put down his book and said a quiet word to Harcourt, then came to them. "She is almost asleep; I beg you not to stir her," he said, very softly.

Lenton nodded and beckoned him and Laurence both further away. "How does she progress?" he asked.

"Very well, sir, according to the surgeons; they say she heals as quickly as could be hoped," Choiseul said. "Catherine has not left her side."

"Good, good," Lenton said. "Three weeks, then, if their original estimate holds true. Well, gentlemen, I have changed my mind; I am going to send Temeraire out on patrol every day during her recovery, rather than giving him and Praecursoris turn and turn about. You do not need the experience, Choiseul, and Temeraire does; you will have to keep Praecursoris exercised independently."

Choiseul bowed, with no hint of dissatisfaction, if he felt any. "I am happy to serve in any way I can, sir; you need merely direct me."

Lenton nodded. "Well, and for now, stay with Harcourt as much as ever you can; I am sure you know what it is to have a wounded beast," he said. Choiseul rejoined her by the now-sleeping Lily, and Lenton led Laurence away again, scowling in private thought. "Laurence," he said, "while you patrol, I want you to try and run formation maneuvers with Nitidus and Dulcia; I know you have not been trained to small-formation work, but Warren and Chenery can help you there. I want him able to lead a pair of light-combatants in a fight independently, if need be."

"Very good, sir," Laurence said, a little startled; he wanted badly to ask for some explanation, and repressed his curiosity with some difficulty.

They came to the clearing where Excidium was just falling asleep; Captain Roland was speaking with her ground crewmen and inspecting a piece of the harness. She nodded to them both and came away with them; they walked back together towards the headquarters.

"Roland, can you do without Auctoritas and Crescendium?" Lenton asked abruptly.

She lifted an eyebrow at him. "If I have to, of course," she said. "What's this about?"

Lenton did not seem to object to being so directly queried. "We must begin to think about sending Excidium to Cadiz once Lily is flying well," he said. "I am not going to have the kingdom lost for want of one dragon in the right place; we can hold out against aerial raids a long time here, with the help of the Channel Fleet and the shore batteries, and that fleet must not be allowed to escape."

If Lenton did choose to send Excidium and his formation away, their absence would leave the Channel vulnerable to aerial attack; yet if the French and Spanish fleet escaped Cadiz and came north, to join with the ships in port at Brest and Calais, perhaps even a single day of so overwhelming an advantage would be enough for Napoleon to ferry over his invasion force.

Laurence did not envy Lenton the decision; without knowing whether Bonaparte's aerial divisions were halfway to Cadiz overland or still along the Austrian border, the choice could only be half guess. Yet it would have to be made, if only through inaction, and Lenton was clearly prepared instead to take the risk.

Now Lenton's design with regard to Temeraire's orders was clear: the admiral wanted the flexibility of having a second formation on hand, even if a small and imperfectly trained one. Laurence thought that he recalled that Auctoritas and Crescendium were middleweight combat dragons, part of Excidium's supporting forces; perhaps Lenton intended to match them with Temeraire, to make a maneuverable strike force of the three of them.

"Trying to out-guess Bonaparte; the thought makes my blood run cold," Captain Roland said, echoing Laurence's sentiments. "But we will be ready to go whenever you want to send us; I will fly maneuvers without Auctor and Cressy as time allows."

"Good, see to it," Lenton said, as they climbed the stairs to the foyer. "I will leave you now; I have another ten dispatches to read yet, more's the pity. Goodnight, gentlemen."

"Goodnight, Lenton," Roland said, and stretched out with a yawn when he was gone. "Ah well, formation flying would be deadly boring without a change-about every so often, any road. What do you say to some supper?"

They had some soup and toasted bread, and a nice Stilton after, with port, and once again settled in Roland's room for some piquet. After a few hands, and some idle conversation, she said, with the first note of diffidence he had ever heard from her, "Laurence, may I make so bold—"

The question made him stare, as she had never before hesitated to forge ahead on any subject whatsoever. "Certainly," he said, trying to imagine what she could possibly mean to ask him. Abruptly he was aware of his surroundings: the large and rumpled bed, less than ten steps away; the open throat of her dressing-gown, for which she had exchanged her coat and breeches, behind a screen, when they first came into the room. He looked down at his cards, his face heating; his hands trembled a little.

"If you have any reluctance, I beg you to tell me at once," she added.

"No," Laurence said at once, "I would be very happy to oblige you. I am sure," he added belatedly, as he realized she had not yet asked.

"You are very kind," she said, and a wide flash of a smile crossed her face, lopsidedly, the right side of her mouth turning up more than the scarred left. Then she went on, "And I would be very grateful if you would tell me, with real honesty, what you think of Emily's work, and of her inclination for the life."

He was hard-pressed not to turn crimson at his mistaken assumption, even as she added, "I know it is a wretched thing to ask you to speak ill of her to me, but I have seen what comes of relying too heavily upon the line of succession, without good training. If you have any cause to doubt her suitability, I beg you to tell me now, while there still may be time to repair the fault."

Her anxiety was very plain now, and thinking of Rankin and his disgraceful treatment of Levitas, Laurence could well understand it; sympathy enabled him to recover from his self-inflicted embarrassment. "I have seen the consequences of what you describe as well," he said, quick to reassure her. "I promise you I would speak frankly if I saw any such signs; indeed, I should never have taken her on as a runner if I were not entirely convinced of her reliability, and her dedication to her duty. She is too young for certainty, of course, but I think her very promising."

Roland blew out a breath gustily and sat back in her chair, letting her hand of cards drop as she stopped even pretending to be paying them attention. "Lord, how you relieve me," she said. "I hoped, of course, but I find I

cannot trust myself on the subject." She laughed with relief, and went to her bureau for a new bottle of wine.

Laurence held out his glass for her to fill. "To Emily's
success," he proposed, and they drank; then she reached
out, took the glass from his hand, and kissed him. He
had indeed been wholly mistaken; on this matter, she
proved not at all tentative.

Chapter 11

❦

LAURENCE COULD NOT help wincing at the haphazard way in which Jane threw her things out of the wardrobe and into heaps upon the bed. "May I help you?" he asked finally, out of desperation, and took possession of her baggage. "No, I beg you, permit me the liberty; you may consider your flight path as I do this," he said.

"Thank you, Laurence, that is very kind of you." She sat down with her maps instead. "It will be a straight-forward flight, I hope," she went on, scribbling calculations and moving the small bits of wood which she was using to represent the scattered dragon transport ships that would provide Excidium and his formation with resting places on their way to Cadiz. "So long as the weather holds, less than two weeks should see us there." With so much urgent need, the dragons would not be going by a single transport, but rather would fly from one transport to another, attempting to predict their locations based on the current and the wind.

Laurence nodded, though a little grimly; they were only a day shy of October, and there was every likelihood at this time of year that the weather would not hold. Then she would be faced with the dangerous choice of trying to find a transport that might easily have been blown off-course, or seeking shelter inland in the face of Spanish artillery. Presuming, of course, that the formation was not itself brought down by a storm: dragons were from time to time cast down by lightning or heavy winds, and if flung into a heavy ocean, they could easily drown with all their crew.

But there was no choice. Lily had recovered with great speed over the intervening weeks; she had led the formation through a full patrol only yesterday, and landed without pain or stiffness. Lenton had looked her over, spoken a few words with her and Captain Harcourt, and gone straightaway to give Jane her orders for Cadiz. Laurence had been expecting as much, of course, but he could not help feeling concern, both for the dragons going and for those remaining behind.

"There, that will do," she said, finishing her chart and throwing down her pen; he looked up from the baggage in surprise: he had fallen into a brown study and packed mechanically, without marking what he did; now he realized that he had been silent for nearly twenty minutes together, and that he had one of her stays in his hands. He hastily dropped it atop the neatly packed things in her small case, and closed the lid.

The sunlight was beginning to come in at the window; their time was gone. "There, Laurence, do not look so glum; I have made the flight to Gibraltar a dozen times," she said, coming to kiss him soundly. "You will have a worse time of it here, I am afraid; they will undoubtedly try some mischief once they know we are gone."

"I have every confidence in you," Laurence said, ringing the bell for the servants. "I only hope we have not misjudged." It was as much as he would say critical of Lenton, particularly on a subject where he could not be unbiased. Yet he felt that even if he had not had a personal objection to make to placing Excidium and his formation in danger, he would still have been concerned by the lack of further intelligence.

Volly had arrived three days before with a report full of fresh negatives. A handful of French dragons had arrived in Cadiz: enough to keep Mortiferus from forcing out the fleet, but not a tenth of the dragons which had been stationed along the Rhine. And in cause for more concern, even though nearly every light and quick dragon not wholly involved in dispatch service had been pressed into scouting and spying, they still knew nothing more of Bonaparte's work across the Channel.

He walked with her to Excidium's clearing and saw her aboard; it was strange, for he felt as though he ought to feel more. He would have put a bullet in his brains sooner than let Edith go to face danger while he remained behind himself, yet he could say his adieus to Roland without much more of a pang than in bidding farewell to any other comrade. She blew him a friendly kiss from atop Excidium's back, once her crew were all aboard. "I will see you in a few months, I am sure, or sooner if we can chase the Frogs out of harbor," she called down. "Fair winds, and mind you don't let Emily run wild."

He raised a hand to her. "Godspeed," he called, and stood watching as the enormous wings carried Excidium up, the other dragons of his formation rising to join him, until they had all dwindled out of sight to the south.

Although they kept a wary eye on the Channel skies, the first weeks after Excidium's departure were quiet. No raids came, and Lenton was of the opinion that the French still thought Excidium was in residence, and were correspondingly reluctant to make any venture. "The longer we can keep them thinking it, the better," he said to the assembled captains after another uneventful patrol. "Aside from the benefit to us, just as well if they don't realize another formation is nearing their precious fleet at Cadiz."

They all took a great measure of comfort from the news of Excidium's safe arrival, which Volly brought almost two weeks to the day from his departure. "They'd already begun when I left," Captain James told the other captains the next day, taking a hurried breakfast before setting out on his return journey. "You could hear the Spaniards howling for miles: their merchantmen are as quick to fall apart under dragon-spray as any ship-of-the-line, and their shops and houses as well. I expect they'll fire on the Frenchmen themselves if Villeneuve doesn't come out soon, alliance or not."

The atmosphere grew lighter after this encouraging news, and Lenton cut their patrol a little short and granted them all liberty for celebration, a welcome respite to men who had been working at a frenetic pace. The more energetic went into town; most seized a little sleep, as did the weary dragons.

Laurence took the opportunity to enjoy a quiet evening's reading with Temeraire; they stayed together late into the night, reading by the light of the lanterns. Laurence woke out of a light doze some time after the moon had risen: Temeraire's head was dark against the illuminated sky, and he was looking searchingly to the north of their clearing. "Is something the matter?" Laurence asked him. Sitting up, he could hear a faint noise, strange and high.

Even as they listened, the sound stopped. "Laurence, that was Lily, I think," Temeraire said, his ruff standing up stiffly.

Laurence slid down at once. "Stay here; I will return as quickly as I may," he said, and Temeraire nodded without ever looking away.

The paths through the covert were largely deserted and unlit: Excidium's formation gone, all the light dragons out on scouting duty, and the night cold enough to send even the most dedicated crews into the barracks buildings. The ground had frozen three days before; it was packed and hard enough for his heels to drum hollowly upon it as he walked.

Lily's clearing was empty; a faint murmur of noise from the barracks, whose lit windows he could see distantly, through the trees, and no one about the buildings. Lily herself was crouched motionless, her yellow eyes red-rimmed and staring, and she was clawing the ground silently. Low voices, and the sound of crying; Laurence wondered if he was intruding untimely, but Lily's evident distress decided him: he walked into the clearing, calling in a strong voice, "Harcourt? Are you there?"

"No further" came Choiseul's voice, low and sharp: Laurence came around Lily's head and halted in dreadful surprise: Choiseul was holding Harcourt by the arm, and there was an expression of complete despair on his face. "Make no sound, Laurence," he said; there was a sword in his hand, and behind him on the ground Laurence could see a young midwingman stretched out, dark bloodstains spreading over the back of his coat. "No sound at all."

"For God's sake, what do you think you are about?" Laurence said. "Harcourt, is it well with you?"

"He has killed Wilpoys," she said thickly; she was wavering where she stood, and as the torchlight came on her face he could see a bruise already darkening across half her forehead. "Laurence, never mind about me, you must go and fetch help; he means to do Lily a mischief."

"No, never, never," Choiseul said. "I mean no harm to her or you, Catherine, I swear it. But I will not be answerable if you interfere, Laurence; do nothing." He raised the sword; blood gleamed on its edge, not far from Harcourt's neck, and Lily made the thin eerie noise again, a high-pitched whining that grated against the ear. Choiseul was pale, his face taking on a greenish cast in the light, and he looked desperate enough to do anything; Laurence kept his position, hoping for a better moment.

Choiseul stood staring at him a moment longer, until satisfied Laurence did not mean to go, and then said, "We will go all of us together to Praecursoris; Lily, you will stay here, and follow when you see us go aloft: I promise you no harm will come to Catherine so long as you obey."

"Oh, you miserable, cowhearted traitor dog," Harcourt said, "do you think I am going to go to France with you, and lick Bonaparte's boots? How long have you been planning this?" She struggled to pull away from him, even staggering as she was, but Choiseul shook her and she nearly fell.

Lily snarled, half-rising, her wings mantling: Laurence could see the black acid glistening at the edges of her bone spurs. "Catherine!" she hissed, the sound distorted through her clenched teeth.

"Silence, enough," Choiseul said, pulling Harcourt up and close to his body, pinning her arms: the sword still held steady in his other hand, Laurence's eyes always upon it, waiting for a chance. "You will follow, Lily; you will do as I have said. We are going now; march, at once, monsieur, there." He gestured with the sword. Laurence did not turn around, but stepped backwards, and once beneath the shadow of the trees he moved more slowly still, so that Choiseul came unknowingly closer than he meant to do.

A moment of wild grappling: then they all three went to the ground in a heap, the sword flying and Harcourt caught between them. They struck the ground heavily, but Choiseul was beneath, and for a moment Laurence had the advantage; he was forced to sacrifice it to roll Harcourt free and out of harm's way, and Choiseul struck him across the face as soon as she was clear, throwing him off.

They rolled about on the ground, battering at each other awkwardly, both trying to reach for the sword even as they struggled. Choiseul was powerfully built and taller, and though Laurence had a far greater experience of close combat, the Frenchman's weight began to tell as they wrestled. Lily was roaring out loud now, voices calling in the distance, and despair gave Choiseul a burst of strength: he drove a fist into Laurence's stomach and lunged for the sword while Laurence curled gasping about the pain.

Then there was a tremendous roaring above them: the ground shuddered, branches tumbling down in a rain of dry leaves and pine needles, and an immense old tree was wrenched whole out of the ground beside them: Temeraire was above them, beating wildly as he tore away the cover. More bellowing, now from Praecursoris: the French dragon's pale marbled wings were visible in the dark, approaching, and Temeraire writhed around to face him, claws stretching out. Laurence dragged himself up and threw himself onto Choiseul, bearing him down to the ground with all his weight: he was retching even as they struggled, but Temeraire's danger spurred him on.

Choiseul managed to turn them over and force an arm against Laurence's throat, pressing hard; choking, Laurence caught only a glimpse of motion, and then Choiseul went limp: Harcourt had fetched an iron bar from Lily's gear and struck him upon the back of the head.

She was nearly fainting with the effort, Lily trying to crowd between the trees to reach her; the crew were rushing into the clearing now at last, however, and many hands helped Laurence up to his feet. "Stand over that man there, bring torches," Laurence said, gasping. "And get a full-voiced man here, with a speaking-trumpet; hurry, damn you," for above, Temeraire and Praecursoris were still circling each other, claws flashing.

Harcourt's first lieutenant was a big-chested man with a voice that needed no trumpet: as soon as he understood the circumstances he cupped his hands around his mouth and bellowed up at Praecursoris. The big French dragon broke off and flew in wild desperate circles for a moment as he peered down to where Choiseul was being secured, and then with drooping head he returned to the ground, Temeraire hovering watchfully until he had landed.

Maximus was housed not far off, and Berkley had come to the clearing on hearing the noise: he took charge now, setting men to chain Praecursoris, and others to bear Harcourt and Choiseul to the surgeons; still others to take away poor Wilpoys to be buried. "No, thank you, I can manage," Laurence said, shaking off the willing hands that would have carried him as well; his breath was returning, and he walked slowly over to the clearing where Temeraire had landed beside Lily, to comfort both the dragons and try to calm them.

Choiseul did not rouse for the better part of a day, and when he first woke he was thick-tongued and confused in his speech. Yet by the next morning, he was once again in command of himself, and at first refused to answer any questions whatsoever.

Praecursoris had been ringed round by all the other dragons, and ordered to remain on the ground under pain of Choiseul's death: a threat to the handler was the one thing which could hold an unwilling dragon, and the means by which Choiseul had intended to force Lily to defect to France were now used against him. Praecursoris made no attempt to defy the command, but huddled into a miserable heap beneath his chains, eating nothing, and occasionally keening softly.

"Harcourt," Lenton said at last, coming into the dining room and finding them all assembled and waiting, "I am damned sorry, but I must ask you to try: he has not spoken to anyone else, but if he has the honor of a yellow rat he must feel some explanation owed you. Will you ask him?"

She nodded, and then she drained her glass, but her face stayed so very pale that Laurence asked quietly, "Should you like me to accompany you?"

"Yes, if you please," she said at once, gratefully, and he followed her to the small, dark cell where Choiseul was incarcerated.

Choiseul could not meet her gaze, nor speak to her; he shook his head and shuddered, and even wept as she asked him questions in an unsteady voice. "Oh damn you," she cried at last, crackling with anger. "How could—how could you have a heart to do this? Every word you have said to me was a lie; tell me, did you even arrange that first ambush, on our way here? Tell me!"

Her voice was breaking, and he had dropped his face into his hands; now he raised it and cried to Laurence, "For God's sake, make her go; I will tell you anything you like, only send her out," and dropped it back down again.

Laurence did not in the least want to be his interrogator, but he could not prolong Harcourt's suffering unnecessarily; he touched her on the shoulder, and she fled at once. It was deeply unpleasant to have to ask Choiseul questions, still more unpleasant to hear that he had been a traitor since coming from Austria.

"I see what you think of me," Choiseul added, noting the look of disgust on Laurence's face. "And you have a right; but for me, there was no choice."

Laurence had been keeping himself strictly to questions, but this paltry attempt at excuse inflamed him beyond his resistance. With contempt, he said, "You might have chosen to be honest, and done your duty in the place you begged of us."

Choiseul laughed, with no mirth in the sound. "Indeed; and when Bonaparte is in London this Christmastime, what then? You may look at me that way if you like; I have no doubt of it, and I assure you if I thought any deed of mine could alter that outcome, I would have acted."

"Instead you have become a traitor twice over and helped him, when your first betrayal could only be excused if you had been sincere in your principles," Laurence said; he was disturbed by Choiseul's certainty, though he would never conceive of giving any sign as much.

"Ah, principles," Choiseul said; all his bravado had deserted him, and he seemed now only weary and resigned. "France is not so under-strength as are you, and Bonaparte has executed dragons for treason before. What do principles matter to me when I see the shadow of the guillotine hanging upon Praecursoris, and where was I to take him? To Russia? He will outlive me by two centuries, and you must know how they treat dragons there. I could hardly fly him to America without a transport. My only hope was a pardon, and Bonaparte offered it only at a price."

"By which you mean Lily," Laurence said coldly.

Surprisingly, Choiseul shook his head. "No, his price was not Catherine's dragon, but yours." At the blank look upon Laurence's face, he added, "The Chinese egg was sent as a gift for him from the Imperial Throne; he meant me to retrieve it. He did not know Temeraire was already hatched." Choiseul shrugged and spread his hands. "I thought perhaps if I killed him—"

Laurence struck him full across the face, with such

force as to knock him onto the stone floor of the cell; his chair rocked and fell over with a clatter. Choiseul coughed and blotted blood from his lip, and the guard opened the door and looked inside. "Everything all right, sir?" he asked, looking straight at Laurence; he paid not the slightest mind to Choiseul's injury.

"Yes, you may go," Laurence said flatly, wiping blood from his hand onto his handkerchief as the door closed once again. He would ordinarily have been ashamed to strike a prisoner, but in this moment he felt not the slightest qualm; his heart was still beating very quickly.

Choiseul slowly set his chair back upright and sat down once more. More quietly, he said, "I am sorry. I could not bring myself to it, in the end, and I thought instead—" He stopped, seeing the color rise again in Laurence's face.

The very notion that for all these months such malice had been lurking so close to Temeraire, averted only by some momentary quirk of conscience on Choiseul's part, was enough to make his blood run cold. With loathing, he said, "And so instead you tried to seduce a girl barely past her schoolroom years and abduct her."

Choiseul said nothing; indeed, Laurence could hardly imagine what defense he could have offered. After a moment's pause, Laurence added, "You can have no further pretensions to honor: tell me what Bonaparte plans, and perhaps Lenton will have Praecursoris sent to the breeding grounds in Newfoundland, if indeed your motive is for his life, and not your own miserable hide."

Choiseul paled, but said, "I know very little, but what I know I will tell you, if he gives his word to do as much."

"No," Laurence said. "You may speak and hope for a mercy you do not deserve if you choose; I will not bargain with you."

Choiseul bowed his head, and when he spoke he was

broken, so faint Laurence had to strain to hear him. "I do not know what he intends, precisely, but he desired me to urge the weakening of the covert here most particularly, to have as many sent south to the Mediterranean as could be arranged."

Laurence felt sick with dismay; this goal at least had been brilliantly accomplished. "Does he have some means for his fleet to escape Cadiz?" he demanded. "Does he suppose he can bring them here without facing Nelson?"

"Do you imagine Bonaparte confided in me?" Choiseul said, not lifting his head. "To him also I was a traitor; I was told the tasks I was to accomplish, nothing more."

Laurence satisfied himself with a few more questions that Choiseul truly knew nothing else; he left the room feeling both soiled and alarmed, and went at once to Lenton.

The news cast a heavy pall upon the whole covert. The captains had not broadcast the details, but even the lowliest cadet or crewman could tell that a shadow lay upon them. Choiseul had timed his attempt well: the dispatch-rider would not reach them again for six days, and from there two weeks or more would be required to see any portion of the forces from the Mediterranean restored to the Channel. Militia forces and several Army detachments had already been sent for; they would arrive within a few days, to begin emplacing additional artillery along the coastline.

Laurence, with additional cause for anxiety, had spoken to Granby and Hollin to raise their caution on Temeraire's behalf. If Bonaparte were jealous enough of having so personal a prize taken away, he might well send another agent, this one more willing to slay the dragon he could no longer claim. "You must promise me to be careful," he told Temeraire as well. "Eat nothing unless one of us is by, and has approved it; and if anyone whom I have not presented to you seeks to approach you, do not under any circumstances permit it, even if you must fly to another clearing."

"I will have a care, Laurence, I promise," said Temeraire. "I do not understand, though, why the French Emperor should want to have me killed; how could that improve his circumstances? He would do better to ask them for another egg."

"My dear, the Chinese would hardly condescend to give him a second where the first went so badly astray while in the keeping of his own men," he said. "I am still puzzled at their having given him even one, indeed; he must have some prodigiously gifted diplomat at their court. And I suppose his pride may be hurt, to think that a lowly British captain stands in the place which he had meant to occupy himself."

Temeraire snorted with disdain. "I am sure I would never have liked him in the least, even if I had hatched in France," he said. "He sounds a very unpleasant person."

"Oh, I cannot truly say. One hears a great deal of his pride, but there is no denying that he is a very great man, even if he is a tyrant," Laurence said reluctantly; he would have been a great deal happier to be able to convince himself that Bonaparte was a fool.

Lenton gave orders that patrols now were to be flown only by half the formation at a time, the rest kept back at the covert for intensive combat training. Under cover of night, several additional dragons were secretly flown down from the coverts at Edinburgh and Inverness, including Victoriatus, the Parnassian whom they had rescued what now seemed a long time ago. His captain, Richard Clark, made a nice point of coming to greet Laurence and Temeraire. "I hope you can forgive me for not paying you my respects and my gratitude sooner," he said. "I confess at Laggan I had very little thought for anything but his recovery, and we were shipped out again without warning, as I believe were you."

Laurence shook his hand heartily. "Pray do not give it a thought," he said. "I hope he is wholly recovered?"

"Entirely, thank Heaven, and none too soon, either," Clark said grimly. "I understand the assault is expected at any moment."

And yet the days stretched out, painfully long with anticipation, and no attack came. Three more Winchesters were brought down for additional scouting, but one and all they returned from their dangerous forays to the French shores to report heavy patrols at all hours along the enemy's coastline; there was no chance of penetrating far enough inland to acquire more information.

Levitas was among them, but the company was large enough that Laurence was not obliged to see much of Rankin, for which he was grateful. He tried not to see the signs of that neglect which he could do no more to cure; he felt he could not visit the little dragon further without provoking a quarrel which might be disastrous to the temper of the whole covert. However, he compromised with his conscience so far as to say nothing when he saw Hollin coming to Temeraire's clearing very early the next morning with a bucket full of dirty cleaning rags and a guilty expression.

A great coldness settled over the camp as night came on Sunday, the first week of waiting gone: Volatilus had not arrived as expected. The weather had been clear, certainly no cause for delay; it stayed so for two further days, and then a third; still he did not come. Laurence tried not to look to the skies, and ignored his men doing the same, until that night he found Emily crying quietly outside the clearing, having crept away from the barracks for a little privacy.

She was very ashamed to be caught at it, and pretended there was only some dust in her eyes. Laurence took her to his rooms and had some cocoa brought; he told her, "I was two years older than you are now when I first went to sea, and I blubbered at night for a week." She looked so very skeptical at this account that a laugh was drawn from him. "No, I am not inventing this for your benefit," he said. "When you are a captain, and find one of your own cadets in similar circumstances, I imagine you will tell them what I have just told you."

"I am not really afraid," she said, weariness and cocoa having combined to make her drowsy and unguarded. "I know Excidium will never let anything happen to Mother, and he is the finest dragon in all Europe." She woke up at having made this slip, and added anxiously, "Temeraire is very nearly as good, of course."

Laurence nodded gravely. "Temeraire is a great deal younger. Perhaps he will equal Excidium some day, when he has more experience."

"Yes, just so," she said, very relieved, and he concealed his smile. Five minutes later she was asleep; he laid her on the bed and went to sleep with Temeraire.

"Laurence, Laurence." He stirred and blinked upwards; Temeraire was nudging him awake urgently, though the sky was still dark. Laurence was dimly aware of a low roaring noise, a crowd of voices, and then the crack of gunfire. He started up at once: none of his crew were in the clearing, nor his officers. "What is it?" Temeraire asked, rising to his feet and unfurling his wings as Laurence climbed down. "Are we being attacked? I do not see any dragons aloft."

"Sir, sir!" Morgan came running into the clearing, nearly falling over himself in his haste and eagerness. "Volly is here, sir, and there has been a great battle, and Napoleon is killed!"

"Oh, does that mean the war is over already?" Temeraire asked, disappointed. "I have not even been in any real battles yet."

"Perhaps the news may have grown in the telling; I should be surprised to learn that Bonaparte is truly dead," Laurence said, but he had identified the noise as cheering, and certainly some good news had arrived, if not of quite such an absurd caliber. "Morgan, go and rouse Mr. Hollin and the ground crew with my apologies for the hour, and ask them to bring Temeraire his breakfast. My dear," he said, turning to Temeraire, "I will go and learn what I can, and return with the news soonest."

"Yes, please, and do hurry," Temeraire said urgently, rearing up on his back legs to see above the trees what might be in progress.

The headquarters was blazing with light; Volly was sitting on the parade grounds before the building tearing ravenously into a sheep, a couple of groundsmen with the dispatch service keeping off the growing crowd of men streaming from the barracks. Several of the young Army and militia officers were firing off their guns in their excitement, and Laurence was forced to nearly push his way through to reach the doors.

The doors to Lenton's office were closed, but Captain James was sitting in the officers' club, eating with scarcely less ferocity than his dragon, and already all the other captains were with him, having the news.

"Nelson told me to wait; said they'd come out of port before I had time to make another circuit," James was saying, out of the corner of his mouth and somewhat muffled by toast, while Sutton attempted to sketch the scene on a piece of paper. "I hardly believed him, but sure enough, by Sunday morning out they came, and we met them off Cape Trafalgar early on Monday."

He swallowed down a cup of coffee, all the company

waiting impatiently for him to finish, and pushed his plate aside for a moment to take the paper from Sutton. "Here, let me," he said, drawing little circles to mark the positions of the ships. "Twenty-seven and twelve dragons of ours, against thirty-three and ten."

"Two columns, breaking their line twice?" Laurence asked, studying the diagram with satisfaction: just the sort of strategy to throw the French into disarray, from which their ill-trained crews could hardly have recovered.

"What? Oh, the ships, yes, with Excidium and Laetificat over the weather column, Mortiferus over the lee," James said. "It was hot work at the head of the divisions, I can tell you; I couldn't see so much as a spar from above for the clouds of smoke. At one time I thought for sure *Victory* had blown up; the Spanish had one of those blasted little Flecha-del-Fuegos over there, dashing about quicker than our guns could answer. He had all her sails on fire before Laetificat sent him running with his tail between his legs."

"What were our losses?" Warren asked, his quiet voice cutting through the high spirits of their excitement.

James shook his head. "It was a proper bloodbath and no mistake," he said somberly. "I suppose we have near a thousand men killed; and poor Nelson himself came in a hairsbreadth of it: the fire-breather set alight one of *Victory*'s sails, and it came down upon him where he stood on the quarterdeck. A couple of quick-thinking fellows doused him with the scuttlebutt, but they say his medals were melted to his skin, and he will wear them all the time, now."

"A thousand men; God rest their souls," Warren said; conversation ceased, and when finally resumed it was at first subdued.

But excitement, joy gradually overcame what perhaps

were the more proper sentiments of the moment. "I hope you will excuse me, gentlemen," Laurence said, nearly shouting as the noise climbed to a fresh pitch; it precluded any chance of acquiring further intelligence for the moment. "I promised Temeraire to return at once. James, I suppose that the report of Bonaparte's demise is a false one?"

"Yes, more's the pity: unless he falls down in an apoplexy over the news," James called back, which roused a general shout of laughter that continued by natural progression into a round of "Hearts of Oak," and the singing followed Laurence out the door and even through the covert, as the song was taken up by the men outside.

By the time the sun rose, the covert was half empty. Scarcely a man had slept; the prevailing mood could not help but be joyful almost to the point of hysteria, as nerves which had been drawn to their limits abruptly relaxed. Lenton did not even attempt to call the men to order and looked the other way as they poured out of the covert into the city, to carry the news to those who had not yet heard and mingle their voices into the general rejoicing.

"Whatever scheme of invasion Bonaparte has been working towards, this must surely have put paid to it," Chenery said exultantly, later that evening, as they stood together on the balcony and watched the returning crowd still milling more slowly about in the parade grounds below, all the men thoroughly drunk but too happy for quarreling, snatches of song bursting out occasionally to float up towards them. "How I should like to see his face."

"I think we have been giving him too much credit," Lenton said; his cheeks were red with port and satisfaction, as well they might be: his judgment to send Excidium had proven sound and contributed materially to the victory. "I think it clear he does not understand the navy so well as the army and the aerial corps. An uninformed man might well imagine that thirty-three ships-of-the-line had no excuse to lose so thoroughly to twenty-seven."

"But how can it have taken his aerial divisions so long to reach them?" Harcourt said. "Only ten dragons, and from what James said, more than half of those Spanish—that is not a tenth of the strength he had in Austria. Perhaps he has not moved them from the Rhine after all?"

"I have heard the passes over the Pyrenees are damned difficult, though I have never tried them myself," Chenery said. "But I dare say he never sent them, thinking Villeneuve had what forces he needed, and they have all been lolling about in covert and getting fat. No doubt he has been thinking all this time that Villeneuve would sail straight through Nelson, perhaps losing one or two ships in the process: expecting them daily, and wondering where they were, and we here biting our nails meanwhile for no good reason."

"And now his army cannot come across," Harcourt said.

"Quoth Lord St. Vincent, 'I don't say they cannot come, but they cannot come by sea,'" Chenery said, grinning. "And if Bonaparte thinks to take Britain with forty dragons and their crews, he is very welcome to try, and we can give him a taste of those guns the militia fellows have been so busily digging-in. It would be a pity to waste all their hard work."

"I confess I would not mind a chance to give that rascal yet another dose of medicine," Lenton said. "But he will not be so foolish; we must be content with having done our duty, and let the Austrians have the glory of polishing him off. His hope of invasion is done." He swallowed the rest of his port and said abruptly, "There is no more putting it off, though, I am afraid; we cannot need anything more from Choiseul now."

In the silence that fell among them, Harcourt's drawn breath was almost a sob, but she made no protest, and her voice remained admirably steady as she merely asked, "Have you decided what you will do with Praecursoris?"

"We will send him to Newfoundland if he will go; they need another breeding sire there to fill out their complement, and it is not as though he were vicious," Lenton said. "The fault is with Choiseul, not him." He shook his head. "It is a damned pity, of course, and all our beasts will be creeping about miserable for days, but there is nothing else for it. Best to get it done with quickly; tomorrow morning."

Choiseul was given a few moments with Praecursoris, the big dragon nearly draped with chains and watched closely by Maximus and Temeraire on either side. Laurence felt the shudders go through Temeraire's body as they stood their unpleasant guard, forced to observe while Praecursoris swung his head from side to side in denial, and Choiseul made a desperate attempt to persuade him to accept the shelter Lenton had offered. At last the great head drooped in the barest hint of a nod, and Choiseul stepped close to lay his cheek against the smooth nose.

Then the guards stepped forward; Praecursoris tried to lash at them, but the entangling chains pulled him back, and as they led Choiseul away the dragon screamed: a dreadful sound. Temeraire hunched himself away from it, his wings flaring, and moaned softly; Laurence leaned forward and stretched himself fully against his neck, stroking over and over. "Do not look, my dear," he said, the words struggling to come through the thickening of his throat. "It will be over in a moment."

Praecursoris screamed once more, at the end; then he

fell to the ground heavily, as if all vital force had gone from his body. Lenton signaled that they might go, and Laurence touched Temeraire's side. "Away, away," he said, and Temeraire launched himself far from the scaffold at once, striking out over the clean, empty sea.

"Laurence, may I bring Maximus over here, and Lily?" Berkley asked, in his usual abrupt way, having come upon him without warning. "Your clearing is big enough, I think."

Laurence raised his head and stared at him dully. Temeraire was still huddled in misery, head hidden beneath his wings, inconsolable: they had flown for hours, just the two of them and the ocean below, until Laurence had at last begged him to turn back to land, out of fear that he would become exhausted. He himself felt almost bruised and ill, as if feverish. He had attended at hangings before, a grim reality of naval life, and Choiseul had been far more deserving of the fate than many a man Laurence had seen at the end of a rope; he could not say why he felt such anguish now.

"If you like," he said, without enthusiasm, letting his head sink again. He did not look up at the rush of wings and shadows as Maximus came over the clearing, his enormous bulk blotting out the sun until he landed heavily beside Temeraire; Lily followed after him. They huddled at once around each other and Temeraire; after a few moments, Temeraire unwound himself enough to entwine more thoroughly with them both, and Lily spread her great wings over them all.

Berkley led Harcourt over to where Laurence sat leaning against Temeraire's side, and pushed her unresisting to sit beside him; he lowered his stout frame awkwardly to the ground opposite them and handed about a dark bottle. Laurence took it and drank without curiosity: strong, unwatered rum, and he had not eaten anything all day; it went to his head very quickly, and he was glad for the muffling of all sensation.

Harcourt began to weep after a little while, and Laurence was horrified to find his own face wet even as he reached to grip her shoulder. "He was a traitor, nothing but a lying traitor," Harcourt said, scrubbing tears away with the back of her hand. "I am not sorry in the least; I am not sorry at all." She spoke with an effort, as though she were trying to convince herself.

Berkley handed her the bottle again. "It is not him; damned rotter, deserved it," he said. "You are sorry on account of the dragon, and so are they. They don't think much of King and country, you know; Praecursoris never knew a damned thing about it but where Choiseul told him to go."

"Tell me," Laurence said abruptly, "would Bonaparte have really executed the dragon for treason?"

"Likely enough; the Continentals do, once in a great while. More to scare the riders off the notion than because they blame the beasts," Berkley said.

Laurence was sorry to have asked; sorry to know that Choiseul had been telling the truth so far at least. "Surely the Corps would have granted him shelter in the colonies, if he had asked," he said angrily. "There is still no possible excuse. He desired his place in France restored; he was willing to risk Praecursoris to have it back, for we might just as easily have chosen to put his dragon to death."

Berkley shook his head. "Knew we are too hard up for breeders to do as much," he said. "Not to excuse the fellow; I dare say you are right. He thought Bonaparte was going to roll us up, and he did not like to go and live in the colonies." Berkley shrugged. "Still damned hard on the dragon, and he has not done anything wrong."

"That is not true; he has," Temeraire put in unexpectedly, and they looked up at him; Maximus and Lily raised their heads as well to listen. "Choiseul could not have forced him to fly away from France, nor to come here bent on hurting us. It does not seem to me that he is any less guilty at all."

"I suppose it is likely he did not understand what was being asked of him," Harcourt said tentatively to this challenge.

Temeraire said, "Then he ought to have refused until he did understand: he is not simple, like Volly. He might have saved his rider's life, then, and his honor too. I would be ashamed to let my rider be executed, and not me too, if I had done as much." He added venomously, his tail lashing the air, "And I would not let anyone execute Laurence anyway; I should like to see them try."

Maximus and Lily both rumbled in agreement. "I will never let Berkley commit treason, ever," Maximus said, "but if he did, I would step on anyone who tried to hang him."

"I would just take Catherine and go away, I think," Lily said. "But perhaps Praecursoris would have liked to do the same. I suppose he could not break all those chains, for he is smaller than either of you, and he cannot spray. Also, there was only one of him, and he was being guarded. I do not know what I would do, if I could not have escaped."

She finished softly, and they all began to slump down in fresh misery, huddling together again, until Temeraire stopped and said with sudden decision, "I will tell you what we shall do: if ever you need to rescue Catherine, or you Berkley, Maximus, I will help you, and you will do as much for me. Then we do not need to worry; I do not suppose anyone could stop all three of us, at least not before we could escape."

All three of them appeared immeasurably cheered by this excellent scheme; Laurence was now regretting the amount of rum he had consumed, for he could not properly form the protest he felt had to be made, and urgently.

"Enough of that, you damned conspirators; you will have us hanged a great deal sooner than we will," Berkley said, thankfully, on his behalf. "Will you have something to eat, now? We are not going to eat until you do, and if you are so busy to protect us, you may as well begin by saving us from starvation."

"I do not think you are in any danger of starving," Maximus said. "The surgeon said only two weeks ago that you are too fat."

"The devil!" Berkley said indignantly, sitting up, and Maximus snorted in amusement at having provoked him; but shortly the three dragons did allow themselves to be persuaded to take some food, and Maximus and Lily returned to their own clearings to be fed.

"I am still sorry for Praecursoris, even though he acted badly," Temeraire said presently, having finished his meal. "I do not see why they could not let Choiseul go off to the colonies with him."

"There must be a price for such things, or else men would do them more often, and in any case he deserved to be punished for it," Laurence said; his own head had cleared with some food and strong coffee. "Choiseul meant to make Lily suffer as much as Praecursoris does; only imagine if the French had me prisoner, and demanded that you fly for them against your friends and former comrades to save my life."

"Yes, I do see," Temeraire said, but with dissatisfaction in his tone. "Yet it still seems to me they might have punished him differently. Would it not have been better to keep him a prisoner and force Praecursoris to fly for us?"

"I see you have a nice sense of the appropriate," Laurence said. "But I do not know that I can see any lesser punishment for treason; it is too despicable a crime to be punished by mere imprisonment."

"And yet Praecursoris is not to be punished the same way, only because it is not practical, and he is needed for breeding?" Temeraire said.

Laurence considered the matter and could not find an answer for this. "I suppose, in all honesty, being aviators ourselves we cannot like the idea of putting a dragon to death, and so we have found an excuse for letting him live," he said finally. "And as our laws are meant for men, perhaps it is not wholly fair to enforce them upon him."

"Oh, *that* I can well agree with," Temeraire said. "Some of the laws which I have heard make very little sense, and I do not know that I would obey them if it were not to oblige you. It seems to me that if you wish to apply laws to us, it were only reasonable to consult us on them, and from what you have read to me about Parliament, I do not think any dragons are invited to go there."

"Next you will cry out against taxation without representation, and throw a basket of tea into the harbor," Laurence said. "You are indeed a very Jacobin at heart, and I think I must give up trying to cure you of it; I can but wash my hands and deny responsibility."

Chapter 12

❦

$\mathcal{B}$Y THE NEXT morning Praecursoris had already gone, sent away to a dragon transport launching from Portsmouth for the small covert in Nova Scotia, whence he would be led to Newfoundland, and at last immured in the breeding grounds which had lately been started there. Laurence had avoided any further sight of the stricken dragon, and deliberately had kept Temeraire awake late the night before, so that he would sleep past the moment of departure.

Lenton had chosen his time as wisely as he could; the general rejoicing over the victory at Trafalgar continued, and served to counter the private unhappiness to some extent. That very day a display of fireworks was announced by pamphlets, to be held over the mouth of the Thames; and Lily, Temeraire, and Maximus, being the youngest of the dragons at the covert and the worst affected, were sent to observe by Lenton's orders.

Laurence was deeply grateful for the word as the brilliant displays lit the sky and the music from the barges drifted to them across the water: Temeraire's eyes were wide with excitement, the bright bursts of color reflecting in his pupils and his scales, and he cocked his head first one way then another, in an effort to hear more clearly. He talked of nothing but the music and the explosions and the lights, all the way back to the covert.

"Is that a concert, then, the sort they have in Dover?" he asked. "Laurence, cannot we go again, and perhaps a little closer next time? I could sit very quietly, and I would not disturb anyone."

"I am afraid fireworks such as those are a special occasion, my dear; concerts are only music," Laurence said, avoiding an answer; he could well imagine the reaction of the city's inhabitants to a dragon's coming to take in a concert.

"Oh," Temeraire said, but he was not greatly dampened. "I would still like that extremely; I could not hear very well tonight."

"I do not know that there is any suitable accommodation which could be made in the city," Laurence said slowly and reluctantly, but happily a sudden inspiration came to him, and he added, "but perhaps I can hire some musicians to come to the covert and play for you, instead; that would be a great deal more comfortable, in any case."

"Yes, indeed, that would be splendid," Temeraire said eagerly. He communicated this idea to Maximus and Lily as soon as they had all once again landed, and the two of them professed equal interest.

"Damn you, Laurence, you had much better learn to say no; you will forever be getting us into these absurd starts," Berkley said. "Just see if any musicians will come here, for love or money."

"For love, perhaps not; but for a week's wages and a hearty meal, I am quite certain most musicians could be persuaded to play in the heart of Bedlam," Laurence said.

"It sounds a fine idea to me," Harcourt said. "I would quite like it myself. I have not been to a concert except once when I was sixteen; I had to put on skirts for it, and after only half an hour a dreadful fellow sat next to me and whispered impolite remarks until I poured a pot of coffee into his lap. It quite spoiled my pleasure, even though he went away straight after."

"Christ above, Harcourt, if I ever have reason to offend you, I will make damned sure you have nothing hot at hand," Berkley said; while Laurence struggled between nearly equal portions of dismay: at her having been subjected to such insult and at her means of repulsion.

"Well, I would have struck him, but I would have had to get up. You have no notion how difficult it is to arrange skirts when sitting down; it took me five minutes together the first time," she said reasonably. "So I did not want to have it all to do again. Then the waiter came by and I thought that would be easier, and anyway more like something a girl ought to do."

Still a little pale with the notion, Laurence bade them goodnight, and took Temeraire off to his rest. He slept once again in the small tent by his side, even though he thought Temeraire was well over his distress, and was rewarded in the morning by being woken early, Temeraire peering into the tent with one great eye and inquiring if perhaps Laurence would like to go to Dover and arrange for the concert today.

"I would like to sleep until a civilized hour, but as that is evidently not to be, perhaps I will ask leave of Lenton to go," Laurence said, yawning as he crawled from the tent. "May I have my breakfast first?"

"Oh, certainly," Temeraire said, with an air of generosity.

Muttering a little, Laurence pulled his coat back on and began to walk back to the headquarters. Halfway to the building, he nearly collided with Morgan, running to find him. "Sir, Admiral Lenton wants you," the boy said, panting with excitement, when Laurence had steadied him. "And he says, Temeraire is to go into combat rig."

"Very good," Laurence said, concealing his surprise. "Go tell Lieutenant Granby and Mr. Hollin at once, and then do as Lieutenant Granby tells you; mind you speak of this to no one else."

"Yes, sir," the boy said, and dashed off again to the barracks; Laurence quickened his pace.

"Come in, Laurence," Lenton said in reply to his knock; it seemed that every other captain in the covert was already crowded into the office as well. To Laurence's surprise, Rankin was at the front of the room, sitting by Lenton's desk. By wordless agreement, they had managed to avoid speaking to one another since Rankin's transfer from Loch Laggan, and Laurence had known nothing of his and Levitas's activities. These had evidently been more dangerous than Laurence might have imagined: a bandage around Rankin's thigh was visibly stained with blood, and his clothes also; his thin face was pale and set with pain.

Lenton waited only until the door had closed behind the last few stragglers to begin; he said grimly, "I dare say you already realize, gentlemen: we have been celebrating too soon. Captain Rankin has just returned from a flight over the coast; he was able to slip past their borders, and caught a look at what that damned Corsican has been working on. You may see for yourselves."

He pushed across his desk a sheet of paper, smudged with dirt and bloodstains that did not obscure an elegantly drafted diagram in Rankin's precise hand. Laurence frowned, trying to puzzle the thing out: it looked rather like a ship-of-the-line, but with no railings at all around her upper deck, and no masts shipped, with strange thick beams protruding from both sides fore and aft, and no gunports.

"What is it for?" Chenery said, turning it around. "I thought he already had boats?"

"Perhaps it will become clearer if I explain that he had

dragons carrying them about over the ground," Rankin said. Laurence understood at once: the beams were intended to give the dragons a place to hold; Napoleon meant to fly his troops over the Navy's guns entirely, while so many of Britain's aerial forces were occupied at the Mediterranean.

Lenton said, "We are not certain how many men he will have in each—"

"Sir, I beg your pardon; may I ask, how long are these vessels?" Laurence asked, interrupting. "And is this to scale?"

"To my eye, yes," Rankin said. "The one which I saw in mid-air had two Reapers to a side, and room to spare; perhaps two hundred feet from front to back."

"They will be three-deckers inside, then," Laurence said grimly. "If they sling hammocks, he can fit as many as two thousand men apiece, for a short journey, if he means to carry no provisions."

A murmur of alarm went around the room. Lenton said, "Less than two hours to cross each way, even if they launch from Cherbourg, and he has sixty dragons or more."

"He could land fifty thousand men by midmorning, good God," said one of the captains Laurence did not know, a man who had arrived only recently; the same calculation was running in all their heads. It was impossible not to look about the room and tally their own side: less than twenty men, a good quarter of whom were the scout and courier captains whose beasts could do very little in combat.

"But surely the things must be hopeless to manage in the air, and can the dragons carry such a weight?" Sutton asked, studying the design further.

"Likely he has built them from light wood; he only needs them to last a day, after all, and they need not be watertight," Laurence said. "He needs only an easterly wind to carry him over; with that narrow framing they will offer very little resistance. But they will be vulnerable in the air, and surely Excidium and Mortiferus are already on their way back?"

"Four days away, at best, and Bonaparte must know that as well as do we," Lenton said. "He has spent nearly his entire fleet and the Spanish as well to buy himself freedom from their presence; he is not going to waste the chance." The obvious truth of this was felt at once; a grim and expectant silence fell upon the room. Lenton looked down at his desk, then stood up, uncharacteristically slow; Laurence for the first time noticed that his hair was grey and thin.

"Gentlemen," Lenton said formally, "the wind is in the north today, so we may have a little grace if he chooses to wait for a better wind. All of our scouts will be flying in shifts just off Cherbourg; we will have an hour's warning at least. I do not need to tell you we will be hopelessly outnumbered; we can only do our best, and delay if we cannot prevent."

No one spoke, and after a moment he said, "We will need every heavy- and middleweight beast on independent duty; your task will be to destroy these transports. Chenery, Warren, the two of you will take midwing positions in Lily's formation, and two of our scouts will take the wing-tip positions. Captain Harcourt, undoubtedly Bonaparte will reserve some dragons for defense; your task is to keep those defenders occupied as best you can."

"Yes, sir," she said; the others nodded.

Lenton took a deep breath and rubbed his face. "There is nothing else to be said, gentlemen; go to your preparations."

There was no sense in keeping it from the men; the French had nearly caught Rankin on his way back and already knew that their secret at last was out. Laurence quietly told his lieutenants, then sent them about their work; he could see the passage of the news through the ranks: men leaning in to hear from one another, their faces hardening as they grasped the situation, and the ordinary idle conversation of a morning vanishing quite away. He was proud to see even the youngest officers take it with great courage and go straight back to their work.

This was the first time Temeraire would ever use the complete accoutrements of heavy combat outside of practice; for patrol a much lighter set of gear was used, and their previous engagement had been under traveling harness. Temeraire stood very straight and still, only his head turned about so he could watch with great excitement as the men rigged him out with the heaviest leather harness, triple-riveted, and began hooking in the enormous panels of chain-mesh that would serve as armor.

Laurence began his own inspection of the equipment and belatedly realized that Hollin was nowhere to be seen; he looked three times through the whole clearing before he quite believed the man's absence, and then called the armorer Pratt away from his work on the great protective plates which would shield Temeraire's breast and shoulders during the fighting. "Where is Mr. Hollin?" he asked.

"Why, I don't believe I've seen him this morning, sir," Pratt said, scratching his head. "He was in last night, though."

"Very good," Laurence said, and dismissed him. "Roland, Dyer, Morgan," he called, and when the three runners came, he said, "Go and see if you can find Mr. Hollin, and then tell him I expect him here at once, if you please."

"Yes, sir," they said almost in unison, and dashed off in different directions after a hurried consultation.

He returned to watching the men work, a deep frown on his face; he was astonished and dismayed to find the man failing in his duty at all, and under these circumstances most particularly; he wondered if Hollin could have fallen ill and gone to the surgeons: it seemed the only excuse, but the man would surely have told one of his crewmates.

More than an hour went by, and Temeraire was in full rig with the crew practicing boarding maneuvers under Lieutenant Granby's severe eye, before young Roland came hurrying back to the clearing. "Sir," she said, panting and unhappy. "Sir, Mr. Hollin is with Levitas, please do not be angry," she said, all in one rushing breath.

"Ah," Laurence said, a little embarrassed; he could hardly admit to Roland that he had been turning a blind eye to Hollin's visits, so she naturally was reluctant to be a tale-bearer on a fellow aviator. "He will have to answer for it, but that can wait; go and tell him he is needed at once."

"Sir, I told him so, but he said he cannot leave Levitas, and he told me to go away at once, and to tell you that he begs you to come, if only you can," she said, very quickly, and eyeing him nervously to see how he would take this insubordination.

Laurence stared; he could not account for the extraordinary response, but after a moment, his estimate of Hollin's character decided him. "Mr. Granby," he called, "I must go for a moment; I leave things in your hands. Roland, stay here and come fetch me at once if anything occurs," he told her.

He walked quickly, torn between temper and concern, and reluctance to once again expose himself to a complaint from Rankin, particularly under the circumstances. No one could deny the man had done his duty bravely, just now, and to offer him insult directly after would be an extraordinary piece of rudeness. And at the same time, Laurence could not help but grow angry at the man as he followed Roland's directions: Levitas's clearing was one of the small ones nearest the headquarters, undoubtedly chosen for Rankin's convenience rather than his dragon's; the grounds were poorly tended, and when Levitas came into view, Laurence saw he was lying in a circle of bare sandy dirt, with his head in Hollin's lap.

"Well, Mr. Hollin, what's all this?" Laurence said, irritation making his tone sharp; then he came around and saw the great expanse of bandages that covered Levitas's flank and belly, hidden from the other side, and already soaked through with the near-black blood. "My God," he said involuntarily.

Levitas's eyes opened a little at the sound and turned up to look at him hopefully; they were glazed and bright with pain, but after a moment recognition came into them, and the little dragon sighed and closed them again, without a word.

"Sir," Hollin said, "I'm sorry, I know I've my duty, but I couldn't leave him. The surgeon's gone; says there's nothing more to be done for him, and it won't be long. There is no one here at all, not even to send for some water." He stopped, and said again, "I couldn't leave him."

Laurence knelt beside him and put his hand on Levitas's head, very lightly for fear of causing him more pain. "No," he said. "Of course not."

He was glad now to find himself so close to the headquarters. There were some crewmen idling by the door talking of the news, so he could send them to Hollin's assistance, and Rankin was in the officers' club, easily found. He was drinking wine, his color already greatly improved and having shifted his bloodstained clothing for fresh; Lenton and a couple of the scout captains were sitting with him and discussing positions to hold along the coastline.

Coming up to him, Laurence told him very quietly, "If you can walk, get on your feet; otherwise I will carry you."

Rankin put down his glass and stared at him coldly. "I beg your pardon?" he said. "I gather this is some more of your officious—"

Laurence paid no attention, but seized the back of his chair and heaved. Rankin fell forward, scrabbling to catch himself on the floor; Laurence took him by the scruff of his coat and dragged him up to his feet, ignoring his gasp of pain.

"Laurence, what in God's name—" Lenton said in astonishment, rising to his feet.

"Levitas is dying; Captain Rankin wishes to make his farewells," Laurence said, looking Lenton squarely in the eye and holding Rankin up by the collar and the arm. "He begs to be excused."

The other captains stared, half out of their chairs. Lenton looked at Rankin, then very deliberately sat back down again. "Very good," he said, and reached for the bottle; the other captains slowly sank back down as well.

Rankin stumbled along in his grip, not even trying to free himself, shrinking a little from Laurence as they went; outside the clearing, Laurence stopped and faced him. "You will be generous to him, do you understand me?" he said. "You will give him every word of praise he has earned from you and never received; you will tell him he has been brave, and loyal, and a better partner than you have deserved."

Rankin said nothing, only stared as if Laurence were a dangerous lunatic; Laurence shook him again. "By God, you will do all this and more, and hope that it is enough to satisfy me," he said savagely, and dragged him on.

Hollin was still sitting with Levitas's head in his lap, a bucket now beside him; he was squeezing water from a clean cloth into the dragon's open mouth. He looked at Rankin without bothering to hide his contempt, but then he bent over and said, "Levitas, come along now; look who's come."

Levitas's eyes opened, but they were milky and blind. "My captain?" he said uncertainly.

Laurence thrust Rankin forward and down onto his knees, none too gently; Rankin gasped and clutched at his thigh, but he said, "Yes, I am here." He looked up at Laurence and swallowed, then added awkwardly, "You have been very brave."

There was nothing natural or sincere in the tone; it was as ungraceful as could be imagined. But Levitas only said, very softly, "You came." He licked at a few drops of water at the corner of his mouth. The blood was still welling sluggishly from beneath the dressing, thick enough to slightly part the bandages one from the other, glistening and black. Rankin shifted uneasily; his breeches and stockings were being soaked through, but he looked up at Laurence and did not try to move away.

Levitas gave a low sigh, and then the shallow movement of his sides ceased. Hollin closed his eyes with one rough hand.

Laurence's hand was still heavy on the back of Rankin's neck; now he lifted it away, rage gone, and only tight-lipped disgust left. "Go," he said. "We who valued him will make the arrangements, not you." He did not even look at the man as Rankin left the clearing. "I cannot stay," he said quietly to Hollin. "Can you manage?"

"Yes," Hollin said, stroking the little head. "There can't be anything, with the battle coming and all, but I'll see he's taken and buried proper. Thank you, sir; it meant a great deal to him."

"More than it ought," Laurence said. He stood looking down at Levitas a short while longer; then he went back to the headquarters and found Admiral Lenton.

"Well?" Lenton asked, scowling, as Laurence was shown into his office.

"Sir, I apologize for my behavior," Laurence said. "I am happy to bear any consequences you should think appropriate."

"No, no, what are you talking about? I mean Levitas," Lenton said impatiently.

Laurence paused, then said, "Dead, with a great deal of pain, but he went easily at the end."

Lenton shook his head. "Damned pity," he said, pouring a glass of brandy for Laurence and himself. He finished his own glass in two great swallows and sighed heavily. "And a wretched time for Rankin to become unharnessed," he said. "We have a Winchester hatching unexpectedly at Chatham: any day now, by the hardening of the shell. I have been scrambling to find a fellow in range worthy of the position and willing to be put to a Winchester; now here he is on the loose and having made himself a hero bringing us this news. If I don't send him and the beast ends up unharnessed, we will have a yowl from his entire damned family, and a question taken up in Parliament, like as not."

"I would rather see a dragon dead than in his hands," Laurence said, setting down his glass hard. "Sir, if you want a man who will be a credit to the service, send Mr. Hollin; I would vouch with my life for him."

"What, your ground-crew master?" Lenton frowned at him, but thoughtfully. "That is a thought, if you think him suited for the task; he could not feel he was hurting his career by such a step. Not a gentleman, I suppose."

"No, sir, unless by gentleman you mean a man of honor rather than breeding," Laurence said.

Lenton snorted at this. "Well, we are not so stiff-necked a lot we must pay that a great deal of mind," he said. "I dare say it will answer nicely; if we are not all dead or captured by the time the egg cracks, at any rate."

Hollin stared when Laurence relieved him of his duties, and said a little helplessly, "My own dragon?" He had to turn away and hide his face; Laurence pretended not to see. "Sir, I don't know how to thank you," he said, whispering to keep his voice from breaking.

"I have promised you will be a credit to the service; see to it you do not make me a liar, and I will be content," Laurence said, and shook his hand. "You must go at once; the hatching is expected at almost any day, and there is a carriage waiting to take you to Chatham."

Looking dazed, Hollin accepted Laurence's hand, and the bag with his few possessions which his fellows on the ground crew had hastily packed for him, then allowed himself to be led off towards the waiting carriage by young Dyer. The crew were beaming upon him as they went; he was obliged to shake a great many hands, until Laurence, fearing he would never get under way, said, "Gentlemen, the wind is still in the north; let us get some of this armor off Temeraire for the night," and put them to work.

Temeraire watched him go a little sadly. "I am very glad that the new dragon will have him instead of Rankin, but I wish they had given him to Levitas sooner, and perhaps Hollin would have kept him from dying," he said to Laurence, as the crew worked on him.

"We cannot know what would have happened," Laurence said. "But I am not certain Levitas could ever have been happy with such an exchange; even at the end he only wanted Rankin's affection, as strange as that seems to us."

Laurence slept with Temeraire again that evening, close and sheltered in his arms and wrapped in several woolen blankets against the early frost. He woke just before first light to see the barren tree-tops bending away from the sunrise: an easterly wind, blowing from France.

"Temeraire," he called quietly, and the great head rose up above him to sniff the air.

"The wind has changed," Temeraire said, and bent down to nuzzle him.

Laurence allowed himself the indulgence of five minutes, lying warm and embraced, with his hands resting on the narrow, tender scales of Temeraire's nose. "I hope I have never given you cause for unhappiness, my dear," he said softly.

"Never, Laurence," Temeraire said, very low.

The ground crew came hurrying from the barracks the moment he touched the bell. The chain-mesh had been left in the clearing, under a cloth, and Temeraire had slept in the heavy harness for this once. He was quickly fitted out, while at the other side of the clearing Granby reviewed every man's harness and carabiners. Laurence submitted to his inspection as well, then took a moment to clean and reload his pistols fresh, and belt on his sword.

The sky was cold and white, a few darker grey clouds scudding like shadows. No orders had come yet. At Laurence's request, Temeraire lifted him up to his shoulder and reared onto his hind legs; he could see the dark line of the ocean past the trees, and the ships bobbing in the harbor. The wind came strongly into his face, cold and salt. "Thank you, Temeraire," he said, and Temeraire set him down again. "Mr. Granby, we will get the crew aboard," Laurence said.

The ground crew put up a great noise, more a roar than a cheer, as Temeraire rose into the air; Laurence could hear it echoed throughout the covert as the other great beasts beat up into the sky. Maximus was a great blazing presence in his red-gold brilliance, dwarfing the others; Victoriatus and Lily also stood out against the crowd of smaller Yellow Reapers.

Lenton's flag was streaming from his dragon Obversaria, the golden Anglewing; she was only a little larger than the Reapers, but she cut through the crowd of dragons and took the lead with effortless grace, her wings rotating almost as did Temeraire's. As the larger dragons had been set on independent duty, Temeraire did not need to keep to the formation's speed; he quickly negotiated a position near the leading edge of the force.

The wind was in their faces, cold and damp, and the low whistling shriek of their passage carried away all noise, leaving only the leathery snap of Temeraire's wings, each beat like a sail going taut, and the creaking of the harness. Nothing else broke the unnatural, heavy silence of the crew. They were already drawn in sight: at this distance the French dragons seemed a cloud of gulls or sparrows, so many were they, and wheeling so in unison.

The French were keeping at a considerable height, some nine hundred feet above the surface of the water, well out of range of even the longest pepper guns. Below them, a lovely and futile spread of white sail: the Channel Fleet, many of the ships wreathed in smoke where they had tried a hopeless shot. More of the ships had taken up positions nearer the land, despite the terrible danger of placing themselves so close to a leeward shore; if the French could be forced to land very near the edge of the cliffs, they might yet come into range of the long guns, if briefly.

Excidium and Mortiferus were racing back from

Trafalgar at frantic speed with their formations, but they could not hope to arrive before the end of the week. There was not a man among them but had known to a nicety the numbers which the French could muster against them. Rationally, there had never been any cause for hope.

Even so, it was a different thing to see those numbers made flesh and wing: fully twelve of the light wooden transports which Rankin had spied out, each carried by four dragons, and defended by as many more besides. Laurence had never heard of such a force in modern warfare; it was the stuff of the Crusades, when dragons had been smaller and the country more wild, the more easily to feed them.

This occurring to him, Laurence turned to Granby and said calmly, loud enough to carry back to the men, "The logistics of feeding so many dragons together must be impractical for any extended period; he will not be able to try this again soon."

Granby only stared at him a moment, then with a start he said hurriedly, "Just so; right you are. Should we give the men a little exercise? I think we have at least half an hour's grace before we meet them."

"Very good," Laurence said, pushing himself up to his feet; the force of the wind was great, but braced against his straps he was able to turn around. The men did not quite like to meet his eyes, but there was an effect: backs straightened, whispers stopped; none of them cared to show fear or reluctance to his face.

"Mr. Johns, exchange of positions, if you please," Granby called through his speaking-trumpet; shortly the topmen and bellmen had run through their exchange under the direction of their lieutenants, and the men were warmed up against the biting wind; their faces looked a little less pinched. They could not engage in true gunnery-practice with the other crews so close, but with a commendable show of energy, Lieutenant Riggs had his riflemen fire blanks to loosen their fingers. Dunne had long, thin hands, at present bled white with cold; as he struggled to reload, his powder-horn slipped out of his fingers and nearly went over the side. Collins only saved it by leaning nearly straight out from Temeraire's back, just barely catching the cord.

Temeraire glanced back once as the shots went off, but straightened himself again without any reminder. He was flying easily, at a pace which he could have sustained for the better part of a day; his breathing was not labored or even much quickened. His only difficulty was an excess of high spirits: as the French dragons came more closely into view, he succumbed to excitement and put on a burst of speed; but at the touch of Laurence's hand, he drew back again into the line.

The French defenders had formed into a loosely woven line-of-battle, the larger dragons above, with the smaller ones beneath in a darting unpredictable mass, forming a wall shielding the transport vessels and their carriers. Laurence felt if only they could break through the line, there might be some hope. The carriers, most of them of the middle-weight Pêcheur-Rayé breed, were laboring greatly: the unaccustomed weight was telling on them, and he was sure they would be vulnerable to an attack.

But they had twenty-three dragons to the French forty-and-more defenders, and almost a quarter of the British force was made up of Greylings and Winchesters, no proper match for the combat-weight dragons. Getting through the line would be nearly impossible; and once through, any attacker would immediately be isolated and vulnerable in turn.

On Obversaria, Lenton sent up the flags for attack: *Engage the enemy more closely.* Laurence felt his own heart begin beating faster, with the tremble of excite-

ment that would fade only after the first moments of
battle. He raised the speaking-trumpet and called forward, "Choose your target, Temeraire; if ever you can
get us alongside a transport, you cannot do wrong." In
the confusion of the enormous crowd of dragons, he
trusted Temeraire's instincts better than his own; if there
was a gap in the French line, Laurence was sure that
Temeraire would see it.

By way of answer, Temeraire struck out immediately
for one of the outlying transports, as if he meant to go
straight at it; abruptly he folded his wings and dived,
and the three French dragons who had closed ranks in
front of him dashed in pursuit. Swiveling his wings,
Temeraire halted himself in mid-air while the three went
flashing past; with a few mighty wing-strokes he was
now flying directly up towards the unprotected belly of
the first carrier on the larboard side, and now Laurence
could see that this dragon, a smaller female Pêcheur-
Rayé, was visibly tired: her wings laboring, even though
her pace was still regular.

"Ready bombs," Laurence shouted. As Temeraire
came hurtling past the Pêcheur-Rayé and slashed at the
French dragon's side, the crew hurled the bombs onto
the deck of the transport. The crack of gunfire came
from the Pêcheur's back, and Laurence heard a cry behind him: Collins threw up his arms and went limp in
his harness, his rifle tumbling away into the water
below. A moment later the body followed: he was dead,
and one of the others had cut him loose.

There were no guns on the transport itself, but the
deck was built slanting like a roof: three of the bombs
rolled off before they could burst, drifting smoke as they
fell uselessly. However, two exploded in time: the whole
transport sagged in mid-air as the shock briefly threw
the Pêcheur off her pace, gaping holes torn in the
wooden planking. Laurence caught a single glimpse of a

pale, staring face inside, smudged with dirt and inhuman with terror; then Temeraire was angling away.

Blood was dripping from somewhere below, a thin black stream; Laurence leaned to check, but saw no injury; Temeraire was flying well. "Granby," he shouted, pointing.

"From his claws—the other beast," Granby shouted back, after a moment, and Laurence nodded.

But there was no opportunity for a second pass: two more French dragons were coming at them directly. Temeraire beat up quickly into the sky, the enemy beasts following; they had seen his trick of maneuvering and were coming at a more cautious pace so as not to overrun him.

"Double back, straight down and at them," Laurence called to Temeraire.

"Guns ready," Riggs shouted behind him, as Temeraire drew a deep, swelling breath and neatly turned back on himself in mid-air. No longer at war with gravity, he plummeted towards the French dragons, roaring furiously. The tremendous volume rattled Laurence's bones even in the face of the wind; the dragon in the lead recoiled, shrieking, and entangled the head of the second in its wings.

Temeraire flew straight down between them, through the bitter smoke of the enemy gunfire, the British rifles speaking in answer; several of the enemy dead were already cut loose and falling. Temeraire lashed out and carved a gash along the second dragon's flank as they went past; the spurting blood splashed Laurence's trousers, fever-hot against his skin.

They were away, and the two attackers were still struggling to right themselves: the first was flying very badly and making shrill noises of pain. Even as Laurence glanced behind them he saw the dragon being turned back for France: with their advantage in numbers, Bonaparte's aviators had no need to push their dragons past injury.

"Bravely done," Laurence called, unable to keep jubilation, pride out of his voice, as absurd as it was to indulge in such sentiments at the height of so desperate a battle. Behind him, the crew cheered wildly as the second of the French dragons pulled away to find another opponent, not daring to attempt Temeraire alone. At once Temeraire was winging back towards their original target, head raised proudly: he was still unmarked.

Their formation-partner Messoria was at the transport: thirty years of experience made her and Sutton wily, and they too had won past the line-of-battle, to continue the attack on the already-weakened Pêcheur whom Temeraire had injured. A pair of the smaller Poux-de-Ciel were defending the Pêcheur; together they were more than Messoria's weight, but she was making use of every trick she had, skillfully baiting them forward, trying to make an opening for a dash at the Pêcheur. More smoke was pouring from the transport's deck: Sutton's crew had evidently managed to land a few more bombs upon it.

Flank to larboard, Sutton signaled from Messoria's back as they approached. Messoria made a dash at the two defenders to keep their attention on her, while Temeraire swept forward and lashed at the Pêcheur's side, his claws tearing through the chain-mesh with a hideous noise; dark blood spurted. Bellowing, instinctively trying to lash out at Temeraire in defense, the Pêcheur let go the beam with one foreleg; it was secured to the dragon's body by many heavy chains, but even so the transport listed visibly down, and Laurence could hear the men inside yelling.

Temeraire made an ungraceful but effective fluttering hop and avoided the strike, still closely engaged; he tore away more of the chain-mesh and clawed the Pêcheur again. "Prepare volley," Riggs bellowed, and the riflemen strafed the Pêcheur's back cruelly. Laurence saw one of the French officers taking aim at Temeraire's head; he fired his own pistols, and with the second shot, the man went down clutching his leg.

"Sir, permission to board," Granby called forward. The Pêcheur's topmen and riflemen had suffered heavy losses; its back was largely cleared, and the opportunity was ideal; Granby was standing at the ready with a dozen of the men, all of them with swords drawn and hands ready to unlock their carabiners.

Laurence had been dreading this possibility of all things; it was only with deep reluctance that he gave Temeraire the word and laid them alongside the French dragon. "Boarders away," he shouted, waving Granby his permission with a low, sinking feeling in his belly; nothing could have been more unpleasant than to watch his men make that terrifying unharnessed leap into the waiting enemy's hands, while he himself had to remain at his station.

A terrible ululating cry in the near distance: Lily had just struck a French dragon full in the face, and it was scrabbling and clawing at its own face, jerking in one direction and then the next, frenzied with the pain. Temeraire's shoulders hunched with sympathy just as the Pêcheur's did; Laurence flinched himself from the intolerable sound. Then the screaming stopped, abruptly; a sickening relief: the captain had crept out along the neck and put a bullet into his own dragon's head rather than see the creature die slowly as the acid ate through the skull and into the brain. Many of his crew had leapt to other dragons for safety, some even to Lily's back, but he had sacrificed the opportunity; Laurence saw him falling alongside the tumbling dragon, and they plunged into the ocean together.

He wrenched himself from the horrible fascination of

the sight; the bloody struggle aboard the Pêcheur's back was going well for them, and he could already see a couple of the midwingmen working on the chains that secured the transport to the dragon. But the Pêcheur's distress had not gone unnoticed: another French dragon was coming towards them at speed, and some exceptionally daring men were climbing out of the holes in the damaged transport, trying to make their way up the chains to the Pêcheur's back to provide assistance. Even as Laurence caught sight of them, a couple of them slipped on the sloping deck and fell; but there were more than a dozen making the attempt, and if they were to reach the Pêcheur, they would certainly turn the tide of battle against Granby and the boarders.

Messoria cried out then, a long shrill wail. "Fall back," Laurence heard Sutton shouting. She was streaming dark blood from a deep cut across her breastbone, another wound on her flank already being packed with white bandage; she dropped and wheeled away, leaving the two Poux-de-Ciel who had been attacking her at liberty. Though they were much smaller than Temeraire, he could not engage the Pêcheur while under attack from two directions: Laurence had either to call back the boarding party, or abandon them and hope they could take the Pêcheur, securing its surrender by seizing its captain alive.

"Granby!" Laurence shouted; the lieutenant looked around, wiping blood from a cut on his face, and nodded as soon as he saw their position, waving them off. Laurence touched Temeraire's side and called to him; with a last parting slash across the Pêcheur's flank that laid white bone bare, Temeraire spun away, gaining some distance, and hovered to permit them to survey. The two smaller French dragons did not pursue, but remained hovering close to the Pêcheur; they did not dare try to get close enough to send men over, for Temeraire could easily overwhelm them if they put themselves in so exposed a position.

Yet Temeraire himself was also in some danger. The riflemen and half the bellmen had gone for the boarding party; well worth the risk, for if they took the Pêcheur, the transport could not very well continue on; if it did not fall entirely, at least the three remaining dragons would likely be forced to turn back for France. But that meant Temeraire was now undermanned, and they were vulnerable to boarding themselves: they could not risk another close engagement.

The boarding party was making steady progress now against the last men resisting aboard the Pêcheur's back; they would certainly outdistance the men from the transport. One of the Poux-de-Ciel dashed in and tried to lie alongside the Pêcheur; "At them," Laurence called, and Temeraire dived instantly, his raking claws and teeth sending the smaller beast into a hurried retreat. Laurence had to send Temeraire winging away again, but it had been enough. The French had lost their chance, and the Pêcheur was crying out in alarm, twisting her head around: Granby was standing at the French dragon's neck with a pistol aimed at a man's head—they had taken the captain.

At Granby's order, the chains were flung off the Pêcheur, and they turned the captured French dragon's head towards Dover. She flew unwillingly and slowly, head turning back every few moments in anxiety for her captain; but she went, and the transport was left hanging wildly askew, the three remaining dragons struggling desperately under its weight.

Laurence had little opportunity to enjoy the triumph: two fresh dragons came diving at them: a Petit Chevalier considerably larger than Temeraire despite the name, and a middleweight Pêcheur-Couronné who dashed to seize the sagging support beam. The men still clinging to the roof threw the dangling chains to the fresh dragon's crew, and in moments the transport was righted and under way again.

The Poux-de-Ciel were coming at them again from opposite sides, and the Petit Chevalier was angling round from behind: their position was exposed, and growing rapidly hopeless. "Withdraw, Temeraire," Laurence called, bitter though the order was to give. Temeraire turned away at once, but the pursuing dragons drew nearer; he had been fighting hard now for nearly half an hour, and he was tiring.

The two Poux-de-Ciel were working in concert, trying to herd Temeraire towards the big dragon, darting across his path of flight to slow him. The Petit Chevalier suddenly put on a burst of speed, and as he drew alongside them a handful of men leapt over. " 'Ware boarders," Lieutenant Johns shouted in his hoarse baritone, and Temeraire looked round in alarm. Fear gave him fresh energy to draw away from the pursuit; the Chevalier fell behind, and after Temeraire lashed out and caught one of the Poux-de-Ciel, they too abandoned the chase.

However, there were eight men already crossed over and latched on; Laurence grimly reloaded his pistols, thrusting them into his belt, then lengthened his carabiner straps and stood. The five topmen under Lieutenant Johns were trying to hold the boarders at the middle of Temeraire's back. Laurence made his way back as quickly as he dared. His first shot went wide, his second took a Frenchman directly in the chest; the man fell coughing blood and dangled limply from the harness.

Then it was hot, frantic sword-work, with the sky whipping past too quickly to see anything but the men before him. A French lieutenant was standing in front of him; the man saw his gold bars and aimed a pistol at him; Laurence barely heard the speech the man tried to make him, and paid no attention, but knocked the gun away with his sword-arm and clubbed the Frenchman on the temple with his pistol-butt. The lieutenant fell; the man behind him lunged, but the wind of their passage was against him, and the sword-thrust scarcely penetrated the leather coat Laurence wore.

Laurence cut the man's harness-straps and kicked him off with a boot to the middle, then looked around for more boarders; but by good fortune the others were all dead or disarmed, and for their part only Challoner and Wright had fallen, except for Lieutenant Johns, who was hanging from his carabiners, blood welling up furiously from a pistol-wound in his chest; before they could try to tend him, he gave a final rattling gasp and also was still.

Laurence bent down and closed Johns's dead, staring eyes, and hung his own sword back on his belt. "Mr. Martin, take command of the top, acting lieutenant. Get these bodies cleared away."

"Yes, sir," Martin said, panting; there was a bloody gash across his cheek, and red splashes of blood in his yellow hair. "Is your arm all right, Captain?"

Laurence looked; blood was seeping a little through the rent in the coat, but he could move the arm easily, and he felt no weakness. "Only a scratch; I will tie it up directly."

He clambered over a body and back to his station at the neck and latched himself in tight, then pulled loose his neckcloth to wrap around the wound. "Boarders repelled," he called, and the nervous tension left Temeraire's shoulders. Temeraire had drawn away from the battlefield, as proper when boarded; now he turned back around, and when Laurence looked up he could see the whole extent of the field of battle, where it was not obscured by smoke and dragon wings.

All but three of the transports were under no sort of attack at all: the British dragons were being heavily engaged by the French defenders. Lily was flying virtually alone; only Nitidus remained with her, the others of their formation nowhere in Laurence's sight. He looked for Maximus and saw him engaged closely with their old enemy, the Grand Chevalier; the intervening two months of growth had brought Maximus closer to his size, and the two of them were tearing at each other in a terrible savagery.

At this distance the sound of the battle was muffled; instead he could hear a more fatal one entirely: the crash of the waves, breaking upon the foot of the white cliffs. They had been driven nearly to shore, and he could see the red-and-white coats of the soldiers formed up on the ground. It was not yet midday.

Abruptly a phalanx of six heavy-weight dragons broke off from the French line and dived towards the ground, all of them roaring at the top of their lungs while their crews threw bombs down. The thin ranks of redcoats wavered as in a breeze, and the mass of militia in the center almost broke, men falling to their knees and covering their heads, though scarcely any real damage was done. A dozen guns were fired off, wildly: shots wasted, Laurence thought in despair, and the leading transport could make its descent almost unmolested.

The four carriers drew closer together, flying in a tight knot directly above the transport, and let the keel of the vessel carve a resting place in the ground with its own momentum. The British soldiers in the front ranks threw up their arms as an immense cloud of dirt burst into their faces, and then almost at once half of them fell dead: the whole front of the transport had unhinged like a barn door, and a volley of rifle-fire erupted from inside to mow down the front lines.

A shout of *"Vive l'Empereur!"* went up as the French

soldiers poured out through the smoke: more than a thousand men, dragging a pair of eighteen-pounders with them; the men formed into lines to protect the guns as the artillery-men hurried to bring their charges to bear. The redcoats fired off an answering volley, and a few moments later the militia managed a ragged one of their own, but the Frenchmen were hardened veterans; though dozens fell dead, the ranks shut tight to fill in their places, and the men held their ground.

The four dragons who had carried the transport were flinging off their chains. Free of their burden, they rose again to join the fight, leaving the British aerial forces even more outnumbered than before. In a moment another transport would land under this increased protection, and its own carriers worsen the situation further.

Maximus roared furiously, clawed free of the Grand Chevalier and made a sudden desperate stoop towards the next transport as it began to descend; no art or maneuver, he only flung himself down. Two smaller dragons tried to bar his way, but he had committed his full weight to the dive; though he took raking blows from their claws and teeth, he bowled them apart by sheer force. One was only knocked aside; the other, a red-and-blue-barred Honneur-d'Or, tumbled against the cliffs with one wing splayed helplessly. It scrabbled at the ragged stone face, sending powdery chalk flying as it tried to get purchase and climb up onto the cliff-top.

A light frigate of some twenty-four guns, with a shallow draft, had been daring to stay near the coast; now she leapt at the chance: before the dragon could get up over the cliff's edge, her full double-shotted broadside roared out like thunder. The French dragon screamed once over the noise and fell, broken; the unforgiving surf pounded its corpse and the remnants of its crew upon the rocks.

Above, Maximus had landed on the second transport

and was clawing at the chains; his weight was too much for the carriers to support, but they were struggling valiantly, and with a great heave in unison they managed to get the transport over the edge of the cliff as he finally broke the supports. The wooden shell fell twenty feet through the air and cracked open like an egg, spilling men and guns everywhere, but the distance was not great enough. Survivors were staggering to their feet almost at once, and they were safely behind their own already-established line.

Maximus had landed heavily behind the British lines: his sides were steaming in the cold air, blood running freely from a dozen wounds and more, and his wings were drooped to the ground: he struggled to beat them again, to get aloft, and could not, but fell back onto his haunches trembling in every limb.

Three or four thousand men already on the ground, and five guns; the British troops massed here only twenty thousand, and most of those militia, who were plainly unwilling to charge in the face of dragons above: many men were already trying to run. If the French commander had any sense at all, he would scarcely wait for another three or four transports to launch his own charge, and if his men overran the gun emplacements they could turn the artillery against the British dragons and clear the approaches completely.

"Laurence," Temeraire said, turning his head around, "two more of those vessels are going in to land."

"Yes," Laurence said, low. "We must try and stop them; if they land, the battle on the ground is lost."

Temeraire was quiet a moment, even as he turned his path of flight onto an angle that would bring him ahead of the leading transport. Then he said, "Laurence, we cannot succeed, can we?"

The two forward lookouts, young ensigns, were listening also, so that Laurence had to speak as much to them as to Temeraire. "Not forever, perhaps," Laurence said. "But we may yet do enough to help protect England: if they are forced to land one at a time, or in worse positions, the militia may be able to hold them for some time."

Temeraire nodded, and Laurence thought he understood the unspoken truth: the battle was lost, and even this was only a token attempt. "And we must still try, or we would be leaving our friends to fight without us," Temeraire said. "I think this is what you have meant by duty, all along; I do understand, at least this much of it."

"Yes," Laurence said, his throat aching. They had outstripped the transports and were over the ground now, with the militia a blurred sea of red below. Temeraire was swinging about to face the first of the transports head-on; there was only just enough time for Laurence to put his hand on Temeraire's neck, a silent communion.

The sight of land was putting heart into the French dragons: their speed was increasing. There were two Pêcheurs at the fore of the transport; roughly equal in size, and neither injured: Laurence left it to Temeraire to decide which would be his target, and reloaded his own pistols.

Temeraire stopped and hovered in mid-air before the oncoming dragons, spreading his wings as if to bar the way; his ruff raised instinctively up, the webbed skin translucent grey in the sunlight. A slow, deep shudder passed along his length as he drew breath and his sides swelled out even further against his massive rib cage, making the bones stand out in relief: there was a strange stretched-tight quality to his skin, so that Laurence began to be alarmed: he could feel the air moving beneath, echoing, resonating, in the chambers of Temeraire's lungs.

A low reverberation seemed to build throughout

Temeraire's flesh, like a drum-beat rolling. "Temeraire," Laurence called, or tried to; he could not hear himself speak at all. He felt a single tremendous shudder travel forward along Temeraire's body, all the gathered breath caught up in that motion: Temeraire opened his jaws, and what emerged was a roar that was less sound than force, a terrible wave of noise so vast it seemed to distort the air before him.

Laurence could not see for a moment through the brief haze; when his vision cleared, he at first did not understand. Ahead of them, the transport was shattering as if beneath the force of a full broadside, the light wood cracking like gunfire, men and cannon spilling out into the broken surf far below at the foot of the cliffs. His jaw and ears were aching as if he had been struck on the head, and Temeraire's body was still trembling beneath him.

"Laurence, I think I did that," Temeraire said; he sounded more shocked than pleased. Laurence shared his sentiments: he could not immediately bring himself to speak.

The four dragons were still attached to the beams of the ruined transport, and the fore dragon to larboard was bleeding from its nostrils, choking and crying in pain. Hurrying to save the dragon, its crew cast off the chains, letting the fragment fall away, and it managed the last quarter mile to land behind the French lines. The captain and crew leapt down at once; the injured dragon was huddled and pawing at its head, moaning.

Behind them, a wild cheer was going up from the British ranks, and gunfire from the French: the soldiers on the ground were shooting at Temeraire. "Sir, we are in range of those cannon, if they get them loaded," Martin said urgently.

Temeraire heard and dashed out over the water, for the moment beyond their reach, and hovered in place.

The French advance had halted for a moment, several of the defenders milling about, wary of coming closer and as confused as Laurence and Temeraire himself were. But in a moment the French captains above might understand, or at least collect themselves; they would make a concerted attack on Temeraire and bring him down. There was only a little time left in which to make use of the surprise.

"Temeraire," he called urgently, "fly lower and try if you can striking at those transports from below, at cliff-height. Mr. Turner," he said, turning to the signal-ensign, "give those ships below a gun and show them the signal for *engage the enemy more closely;* I believe they will take my meaning."

"I will try," Temeraire said uncertainly, and dived lower, gathering himself and once again taking that tremendous swelling breath. Curving back upwards, he roared once again, this time at the underside of one of the transports still over the water. The distance was greater, and the vessel did not wholly shatter, but great cracks opened in the planks of the hull; the four dragons above were at once desperately occupied in keeping it from breaking open all the rest of the way.

An arrow-head formation of French dragons came diving directly towards them, some six heavyweight dragons behind the Grand Chevalier in the lead. Temeraire darted away and at Laurence's touch dropped lower over the water, where half a dozen frigates and three ships-of-the-line lay in wait. As they swept past their long guns spoke in a rolling broadside, one gun after another, scattering the French dragons into shrill confusion as they tried to avoid the flying grapeshot and cannonballs.

"Now, quickly, the next one," Laurence called to Temeraire, though the order was scarcely necessary: Temeraire had already doubled back upon himself. He went directly at the underside of the next transport in line: the largest, flown by four heavyweight dragons, and with ensigns of golden eagles flying from the deck.

"Those are his flags, are they not?" Temeraire called back. "Bonaparte is on there?"

"More likely one of his Marshals," Laurence shouted over the wind, but he felt a wild excitement anyway. The defenders were forming up again at a higher elevation, ready to come after them once more; but Temeraire beat forward with ferocious zeal and outdistanced them. This larger transport, made of heavier wood, did not break as easily; even so, the wood cracked like the sound of pistol-shot, splinters flying everywhere.

Temeraire dived down to attempt a second pass; suddenly Lily was flying alongside them, and Obversaria on their other side, Lenton bellowing through his speaking-trumpet, "Go at them, just go at them; we will take care of those damned buggers—" and the two of them whirled to intercept the French defenders coming after Temeraire again.

But even as Temeraire began his climb, fresh signals went up from the damaged transport. The four dragons who were carrying it together wheeled around and began to pull away; and across the battlefield all the transports still aloft gave way and turned, for the long and weary flight back in retreat to France.

Epilogue

"LAURENCE, BE A good fellow and bring me a glass of wine," Jane Roland said, all but falling into the chair beside his, without the slightest care for the ruin she was making of her skirts. "Two sets is more than enough dancing for me; I am not getting up from this table again until I leave."

"Should you prefer to go at once?" he asked, rising. "I am happy to take you."

"If you mean I am so ungainly in a dress that you think I cannot walk a quarter of a mile over even ground without falling down, you may say so, and then I will knock you on the head with this charming reticule," she said, with her deep laugh. "I have not got myself up in this fashion to waste it by running away so soon. Excidium and I will be back at Dover in a week, and then Lord knows how long it will be before I have another chance to see a ball, much less one supposedly in our honor."

"I will fetch and carry with you, Laurence. If they are not going to feed us anything more than these French tidbits, I am going to get more of them," Chenery said, getting up from his chair as well.

"Hear, hear," Berkley said. "Bring the platter."

They were parted at the tables by the crush of the crowd, which was growing extreme as the hour drew on; London society was still nearly delirious with joy over the joint victories at Trafalgar and Dover, and temporarily as happy to enthuse over the aviators as it had been to disdain them before. His coat and bars won him enough smiles and gestures of precedence that Laurence managed to acquire the glass of wine without great difficulty. Reluctantly he gave up the notion of taking a cigar for himself; it would have been the height of rudeness to indulge while Jane and Harcourt could not. He took a second glass instead; he imagined someone at the table would care for it.

Both his hands thus occupied, he was happily not forced to do more than bow slightly when he was addressed on his way back to the table. "Captain Laurence," Miss Montagu said, smiling with a great deal more friendliness than she had shown him in his parents' house; she looked disappointed to not be able to give him her hand. "How splendid it is to see you again; it has been ages since we were all together at Wollaton Hall. How is dear Temeraire? My heart was in my throat when I heard of the news; I was sure you should be in the thick of the battle, and so of course it was."

"He is very well, thank you," Laurence said, as politely as he could manage; *dear Temeraire* rankled extremely. But he was not going to be openly rude to a woman he had met as one of his parents' guests, even if his father had not yet been softened by society's new approbation; there was no sense in aggravating the quarrel and perhaps needlessly making his mother's situation more difficult.

"May I present you to Lord Winsdale?" she said, turning to her companion. "This is Captain Laurence; Lord Allendale's son, you know," she added, in an undertone that Laurence could barely hear.

"Certainly, certainly," Winsdale said, offering a very slight nod, what he appeared to think a piece of great condescension. "Quite the man of the hour, Laurence; you are to be highly commended. We must all count ourselves fortunate that you were able to acquire the animal for England."

"You are too kind to say so, Winsdale," Laurence said, deliberately forward to the same degree. "You must excuse me; this wine will grow too warm shortly."

Miss Montagu could hardly miss the shortness of his tone now; she looked angry for a moment, then said, with great sweetness, "Of course! Perhaps you are going to see Miss Galman, and can bear her my greetings? Oh, but how absurd of me; I must say Mrs. Woolvey, now, and she is not in town any longer, is she?"

He regarded her with dislike; he wondered at the combination of perception and spite that had enabled her to ferret out the former connection between himself and Edith. "No, I believe she and her husband are presently touring the lake country," he said, and bowed himself away, deeply grateful that she had not had the opportunity of surprising him with the news.

His mother had given him intelligence of the match in a letter sent only shortly after the battle, and reaching him still at Dover; she had written, after conveying the news of the engagement, "I hope what I write does not give you too much pain; I know you have long admired her, and indeed I have always considered her charming, although I cannot think highly of her judgment in this matter."

The true blow had fallen long before the letter came; news of Edith's marriage to another man could not be unexpected, and he had been able to reassure his mother with perfect sincerity. Indeed, he could not fault Edith's judgment: in retrospect he saw how very disastrous the match would have been, on both sides; he could not have spared her so much as a thought for the last nine months or more. There was no reason Woolvey should not make Edith a perfectly good husband. He himself certainly could not have, and he thought that he would truly be able to wish her happy, if he saw her again.

But he was still irritated by Miss Montagu's insinuations, and his face had evidently set into somewhat forbidding lines; as he came back to the table, Jane took the glasses from him and said, "You were long enough about it; was someone pestering you? Do not pay them any mind; take a turn outside, and see how Temeraire is enjoying himself: that will put you in a better frame of mind."

The notion appealed immensely. "I think I will, if you will pardon me," he said, with a bow to the company.

"Look in on Maximus for me, see if he wants any more dinner," Berkley called after him.

"And Lily!" Harcourt said, then looked guiltily about to see if any of the guests at the nearby tables had overheard: naturally the company did not realize that the women with the aviators were themselves captains, and assumed them rather wives, though Jane's scarred face had earned several startled looks, which she ignored with perfect ease.

Laurence left the table to their noisy and spirited discussion, making his way outdoors. The ancient covert near London had long ago been encroached upon by the city and given up by the Corps, save for use by couriers, but for the occasion it had been briefly reclaimed, and a great pavilion established at the northern edge where the headquarters had once stood.

By the aviators' request, the musicians had been set at the very edge of the pavilion, where the dragons could gather around outside to listen. The musicians had been at first somewhat distressed by the notion and inclined to edge their chairs away, but as the evening wore on and the dragons proved a more appreciative audience than the noisy crowd of society, their fear was gradually overcome by their vanity. Laurence came out to find the first violinist having abandoned the orchestra entirely and playing snatches of various airs in a rather didactic manner for the dragons, demonstrating the work of different composers.

Maximus and Lily were among the interested group, listening with fascination and asking a great many questions. Laurence saw after a moment, with some surprise, that Temeraire was instead curled up in a small clearing beyond the others, off to the side and talking with a gentleman whose face Laurence could not see.

He skirted the group and approached, calling Temeraire's name softly; the man turned, hearing him. With a start of pleasant surprise, Laurence recognized Sir Edward Howe, and hurried forward to greet him.

"I am very happy indeed to see you, sir," Laurence said, shaking his hand. "I had not heard that you were back in London, although I made a point of inquiring after you when we first arrived."

"I was in Ireland when the news reached me; I have only just come to London," Sir Edward said, and Laurence only then noticed that he was still in traveling-clothes, and his boots were dust-stained. "I hope you will forgive me; I presumed on our acquaintance to come despite the lack of a formal invitation, in hopes of speaking with you at once. When I saw the crowd inside, I thought it best to come and stay with Temeraire until you appeared rather than try to seek you within."

"Indeed, I am in your debt for putting yourself to so much trouble," Laurence said. "I confess I have been very anxious to speak with you ever since discovering Temeraire's ability, which I expect is the news which has brought you. All he can tell us is that the sensation is the same as that of roaring; we cannot account for how mere sound might produce so extraordinary an effect, and none of us have ever heard of anything like."

"No, you would not have," Sir Edward said. "Laurence—" He stopped and glanced at the crowd of dragons between them and the pavilion, all now rumbling in approval at the close of the first performance. "Might we speak somewhere in more privacy?"

"We can always go to my own clearing, if you would like to be somewhere quieter," Temeraire said. "I am happy to carry you both, and it will not take me a moment to fly there."

"Perhaps that would be best, if you have no objection?" Sir Edward asked Laurence, and Temeraire brought them over carefully in his foreclaws, setting them down in the deserted clearing before settling himself comfortably. "I must beg your pardon for putting you to such trouble, and interrupting your evening," Sir Edward said.

"Sir, I assure you I am very happy to have it interrupted in this cause," Laurence said. "Pray have no concern on that score." He was impatient to learn what Sir Edward might know; a concern over Temeraire's safety from some possible agent of Napoleon's lingered with him, perhaps even increased by the victory.

"I will keep you in suspense no longer," Sir Edward said. "Although I do not in the least pretend to understand the mechanical principles by which Temeraire's ability operates, the effects are described in literature, and so I may identify it for you: the Chinese, and the Japanese, for that matter, call it by the name *divine wind*. This tells you little beyond what you already know from example, I am afraid, but the true importance lies in this: it is an ability unique to one breed and one breed alone—the Celestial."

The name hung in silence for long moments; Laurence did not immediately know what to think. Temeraire looked between them uncertainly. "Is that very different from an Imperial?" he asked. "Are they not both Chinese breeds?"

"Very different indeed," Sir Edward answered him. "Imperial dragons are rare enough; but the Celestials are given only to the Emperors themselves, or their nearest kin. I should be surprised if there were more than a few score in all the world."

"The Emperors themselves," Laurence repeated, in wonder and slowly growing comprehension. "You will not have heard this, sir, but we took a French spy at the covert in Dover shortly before the battle: he revealed to us that Temeraire's egg was meant not merely for France, but for Bonaparte himself."

Sir Edward nodded. "I am not surprised to hear as much. The Senate voted Bonaparte the crown in May before last; the time of your encounter with the French vessel suggests the Chinese gave him the egg as soon as they learned. I cannot imagine why they should have made him such a gift; they have given no other signs of allying themselves with France, but the timing is too exact for any other explanation."

"And if they had some notion of when to expect the hatching, that might well explain the mode of transport as well," Laurence finished for him. "Seven months from China to France, around Cape Horn: the French could hardly have hoped to manage it except with a fast frigate, regardless of the risk."

"Laurence," Sir Edward said with pronounced unhappiness, "I must heartily beg your forgiveness for having so misled you. I cannot even plead the excuse of ignorance: I have read descriptions of Celestials, and seen many drawings of them. It simply never occurred to me that the ruff and tendrils might not develop save with maturity; in body and wing-shape they are identical to the Imperials."

"I beg you not to refine upon it, sir; no forgiveness is

called for, in the least," Laurence said. "It could scarcely have made much difference to his training, and in the event, we have learned of his ability in very good time." He smiled up at Temeraire, and stroked the sleek foreleg beside him, while Temeraire snorted in happy agreement. "So, my dear, you are a Celestial; I should not be surprised at all. No wonder Bonaparte was in such a taking to lose you."

"I imagine he will continue angry," Sir Edward said. "And what is worse, we may have the Chinese on our necks over it, when they learn; they are prickly to an extreme, where the Emperor's standing may be said to be concerned, and I do not doubt they will be annoyed to see a British serving officer in possession of their treasure."

"I do not see how it concerns either Napoleon or them in the least," Temeraire said, bristling. "I am no longer in the shell, and I do not care if Laurence is not an emperor. We defeated Napoleon in battle and made him fly away even though he is one; I cannot see that there is anything particularly nice about the title."

"Never fret, my dear; they have no grounds on which to make objection," Laurence said. "We did not take you from a Chinese vessel, arguably a neutral, but from a French man-of-war; they chose to hand your egg to our enemy, and you were wholly lawful prize."

"I am glad to hear it," Sir Edward said, though he looked doubtful. "They may still choose to be quarrelsome about it; their regard for the laws of other nations is very small, and vanishes entirely where it conflicts with their own notions of proper behavior. Pray have you any notion of how they stand with respect to us?"

"They could make a pretty loud noise, I suppose," Laurence said uncertainly. "I know they have no navy to speak of, but one hears a great deal of their dragons. I will bring the news to Admiral Lenton, though, and I am sure he will know better than I do how to meet any possible difference of opinion with them over the matter."

A rushing sound of wings came overhead, and the ground shook with impact: Maximus had come flying back to his own clearing, only a short distance away; Laurence could see his red-gold hide visible through the trees. Several smaller dragons flew past overhead also, going back to their own resting places: the ball was evidently breaking up, and Laurence realized from the low-burning lanterns that the hour had grown late.

"You must be tired from your journey," he said, turning back to Sir Edward. "I am once again deeply obliged to you, sir, for bringing me this intelligence. May I ask you, as a further favor, to join me for dinner tomorrow? I do not wish to keep you standing about in this cold, but I confess I have a great many questions on the subject I should like to put to you, and I would be happy to learn anything more you know of Celestials."

"It will be my pleasure," Sir Edward said, and bowed to both of them. "No, I thank you; I can find my own way out," he said, when Laurence would have accompanied him. "I grew up in London, and would often come wandering about here as a boy, dreaming of dragons; I dare say I know the place better than do you, if you have only been here a few days." He bade them farewell, having arranged the appointment.

Laurence had meant to stay the night at a nearby hotel where Captain Roland had taken a room, but he found he was disinclined to leave Temeraire; instead he searched out some old blankets in the stable being used by the ground crew, and made himself a somewhat dusty nest in Temeraire's arms, his coat rolled up to serve as a pillow. He would make his apologies in the morning; Jane would understand.

"Laurence, what is China like?" Temeraire asked idly, after they had settled down together, his wings sheltering them from the wintry air.

"I have never been, my dear; only to India," he said. "But I understand it is very splendid; it is the oldest nation in the world, you know; it even predates Rome. And certainly their dragons are the finest in the world," he added, and saw Temeraire preen with satisfaction.

"Well, perhaps we may visit, when the war is over and we have won. I would like to meet another Celestial someday," Temeraire said. "But as for their sending me to Napoleon, that is great nonsense; I am never going to let anyone take you from me."

"Nor I, my dear," Laurence said, smiling, despite all the complications which he knew might arise if China did object. In his heart he shared the simplicity of Temeraire's view of the matter, and he fell asleep almost at once in the security of the slow, deep rushing of Temeraire's heartbeat, so very much like the endless sound of the sea.

From the Sketchbook of
Sir Edward Howe

Yellow Reaper and Crew

at London Covert,
November 1805

Pascal's
Blue

Longwing

Celestial

Regal
Copper

Selected extracts from
*Observations on the Order Draconia in Europe,
with Notes on the Oriental Breeds*

By Sir Edward Howe, F.R.S.

LONDON
JOHN MURRAY, ALBEMARLE STREET
1796

Prefatory Note from the Author on the Measure of Dragon Weights

INCREDULITY IS THE likely response of most of my readers to the figures which appear hereinafter to describe the weight of various dragon breeds, as being wholly disproportionate to those which have hitherto been reported. The estimate of 10 tonnes for a full-grown Regal Copper is commonly known, and such prodigious bulk must already strain the imagination; what then must the reader think, when I report this a vast understatement and claim a figure closer to 30 tonnes, indeed reaching so high as 50 for the largest of this breed?

For explanation I must direct the reader to the recent work of M. Cuvier. In his latest anatomical studies of the air-sacs which enable draconic flight, M. Cuvier has drawn in turn upon the work of Mr. Cavendish and his successful isolation of those peculiar gases, lighter than the general composition of the air, which fill the sacs, and has correspondingly proposed a new system of measurement, which by compensating for the weight displaced by the air-sacs provides a better degree of comparison between the weight of dragons and that of other large land animals, lacking in these organs.

Those who have never seen a dragon in the flesh, and most particularly never one of the very largest breeds, in whom this discrepancy shall appear the most pronounced, may be sceptical; those who have had the opportunity, as I have, of seeing a Regal Copper side by side with the very largest of the Indian elephants, who have been measured at some 6 tonnes themselves, will I hope join me in greatly preferring a scheme of measurement which does not ridiculously suggest that the one, who could devour the other nearly in a bite, should weigh less than twice as much.

SIR EDWARD HOWE
December 1795

Chapter V

Breeds native to the British Isles—Common breeds—Relation to Continental breeds—The effect of modern diet upon size—Heredity of Regal Copper—Venomous and Vitriolic breeds.

. . . IT IS AS well to recollect that Yellow Reapers, so often unjustly regarded with that contempt engendered by familiarity, are to be found everywhere because of their many excellent qualities: generally hardy and not fastidious in their diet, untroubled by all but the worst extremes of heat or cold, almost invariably good-humoured in character, they have contributed to almost every bloodline in these Isles. These dragons fall squarely into the middle-weight range, though they range more widely within the breed than most, from a weight of some 10 tonnes to as many as 17, in a recent large specimen.

Ordinarily they fall between 12 and 15 tonnes, with a length generally of 50 feet, and a nicely proportioned wingspan of 80 feet.

Malachite Reapers are most easily distinguished from their more common cousins by colouration: while Yellow Reapers are mottled yellow, sometimes with white tiger-striping along their sides and wings, Malachite Reapers are a more muted yellow-brown with pale green markings. They are generally believed to be the result of unguided interbreeding during the Anglo-Saxon conquests between Yellow Reapers and Scandinavian Lindorms. Preferring cooler climes, they are generally to be found in north-eastern Scotland.

From hunting records and bone collections, we know that the Grey Widowmaker breed was once very nearly as common as the Reapers, though now they are rarely to be found; this breed being so violently intractable and given to stealing domesticated cattle has been made nearly extinct through hunting, though some individuals may be found living wild even to this day in isolated mountainous regions, particularly in Scotland, and a few more have been coaxed into breeding grounds to preserve as basic stock. They are small and aggressive by nature, rarely exceeding 8 tonnes, and their colouration of mottled grey is ideal for concealment while flying, which inspired their cross-breeding with the more even-tempered Winchesters to produce the Greyling breed.

The most common French breeds, the Pêcheur-Couronné and Pêcheur-Rayé, are more closely related to the Widowmaker breed than to the Reapers, if we may judge by wing conformation and the structure of the breast-bone, which in both breeds is keeled and fused with the clavicle. This anatomical peculiarity renders them both more useful for breeding down into light-combat and courier breeds, rather than into heavy-combat breeds. . . .

Cross-breeding with Continental species is also the source of all the heavy-weight breeds now to be found in Britain, none of which can be considered properly native to our shores. Most likely this is due to climate: heavier dragons greatly prefer warm environs, where their air-sacs can more easily compensate for their tremendous weight. It has been suggested that the British Isles cannot support herds vast enough to sustain the largest breeds; the flaws to this chain of reasoning may be shown by consideration of the very wide variations in diet to be tolerated among dragons insofar as quantity is concerned.

In the wild, it is well known, dragons eat so infrequently as once every two weeks, particularly in summer when they prefer to sleep a great deal and their natural prey are at their fattest; it will then come as no surprise to learn that dragons in the wild do not begin to approach the sizes which can be found among their domesticated cousins, fed daily and more, particularly during the early years so critical to growth.

By way of example we have only to consider the barren desert regions of Almería in the south-east of Spain, scantly inhabited by goats, which are the native grounds of the fierce Cauchador Real, part ancestor of our own Regal Copper; in domestication this breed reaches a fighting weight of some 25 tonnes, but in the wild is scarcely to be found over 10 or 12 tonnes. . . .

The Regal Copper exceeds in size all other breeds presently known, reaching in maturity as many as 50 tonnes in weight and 120 feet in length. They are dramatic in colour, shading from red to yellow with much variation between individuals. The male of the species is on the average slightly smaller than the female and develops forehead horns in maturity; both sexes have a marked spiny column along the back, which renders them particularly hazardous targets for boarding operations.

These great beasts are unquestionably the greatest triumph of the British breeding grounds, the product of some ten generations' labour and careful cross-breeding, and illustrative of the unanticipated benefits which may be yielded by matings not perhaps of obvious value. It was Roger Bacon who first proposed the notion of breeding females of the smaller Bright Copper species to the great sire Conquistador, brought to England as part of the dowry of Eleanor of Castile. Though his suggestions were founded in the erroneous supposition of the time, which thought colour to be indicative of some elemental influence, and the shared orange colour of the two breeds a sign of underlying congruence, the cross was a fruitful one,

leading to offspring even larger than their prodigious sire, and
better able to sustain flight over distance.

Mr. Josiah Colquhoun of Glasgow has suggested that the
disproportionate size of the air-sacs of the Bright Copper, relative to their frame, properly deserves the credit for this success,
and it is certain that Regal Coppers share this trait of their female progenitors. M. Cuvier's anatomical studies suggest that
indeed the vast bulk of the Regal Copper would crush the very
breath out of the dragons' lungs, if unsupported by aught but
their surprisingly delicate skeletal systems. . . .

While no pyrogenic species are to be found in the British
Isles, despite many attempts on the part of our breeders to induce this most valuable trait, so deadly to our shipping in the
persons of the French Flamme-de-Gloire and the Spanish
Flecha-del-Fuego, the native Sharpspitter breed is notable for
producing a venom to incapacitate its prey. Though the Sharpspitter itself is too small and low-flying to be of great value as
a fighting beast, cross-breeding with the French Honneur-
d'Or, for size, and with the Russian Ironwing, another venomous species, yielded several valuable crosses: better fliers,
middle-weight in size, with more potent venom.

Interbreeding among these, with frequent infusions from the
parent breeds, culminated in the successful hatching of the first
dragon which can properly be termed a Longwing, during the
reign of Henry VII. In this breed, the venom had become so
potent as to be more properly termed acid, and of a strength
which could be turned not only against other beasts, but
against targets upon the ground. The only other truly vitriolic
breeds known to us at present are the Copacati, an Incan
breed, and the Ka-Riu of Japan.

Longwings are unfortunately instantly identifiable upon the
battlefield and impossible to decoy, due to the unusual proportions for which they are named; though they rarely exceed 60
feet in length, wingspans of 120 feet are not uncommon
among them, and their wing colouration is particularly dramatic, shading from blue to orange, with vivid black-and-white
striations at the rims. They possess the same yellow-orange
eyes as their progenitor the Sharpspitter, which are exceptionally good. Though the breed was first considered intractable,

and indeed some consideration was given to their destruction, as too dangerous to be left unharnessed, during the reign of Elizabeth I new methods of harnessing were developed which secured the general domestication of the breed, and they were instrumental in the destruction of the Armada. . . .

Chapter XVII

Comparison of Oriental and Western breeds—Antiquity of the Oriental breeds—Known Breeds native to the Empires of China and Japan—Distinguishing characteristics of the Imperial—A note on the Celestial.

. . . THE SECRETS OF the Imperial breeding programme are most jealously guarded, as the national treasures which they assuredly are, and transmitted strictly through word of mouth among a trusted line and through documents encoded by closely held ciphers. Very little is therefore known in the West, and indeed anywhere outside the precincts of the imperial capital, about these breeds.

Brief observations by travellers have yielded only a handful of incomplete details; we know that the Imperial and Celestial are distinguished by the number of talons on their claws, which are five, unlike virtually every other draconic breed, being four-fingered; similarly, their wings have six spines rather than the five common to European breeds. In the Orient, these breeds are popularly supposed to be highly superior in intelligence, retaining into adulthood that remarkable facility of memory and linguistic ability which dragons ordinarily lose early in life.

For the veracity of this claim we have but one recent witness, though a reliable one: M. le Comte de la Pérouse encountered an Imperial dragon at the Korean court, who through their close relations to the court of China have been often granted the privilege of an Imperial egg. The first Frenchman to attend at this court in recent memory, he was asked for lessons in his native tongue, and by his reports, the dragon though full-grown was well able to hold a conversation by the time of his departure, some one month later, an achievement hardly to be scorned even by a gifted linguist. . . .

That the Celestial is closely related to the Imperial may be inferred from the few illustrations we in the West have managed to obtain of this breed, but very little else is known of them. The divine wind, that most mysterious of draconic abilities, is known to us only by hearsay, which would have us believe that the Celestials are able to produce earthquakes or storms, capable of leveling a city. Plainly the effects have been heartily exaggerated, but there is considerable practical respect for the ability among the Oriental nations, which cautions against any rash dismissal of this gift as pure phantasy. . . .

Acknowledgments

I OWE THANKS FIRST and foremost to the group of beta readers who saw *His Majesty's Dragon* through to completion, from the very first chapter to the last, and who gave me not only an enthusiastic audience to write for but enormous quantities of excellent advice: Holly Benton, Dana Dupont, Doris Egan, Diana Fox, Laura Kanis, Shelley Mitchell, L. Salom, Micole Sudberg, and Rebecca Tushnet; and to Francesca Coppa, for telling me to do it in the first place. Thanks also to Sara Rosenbaum and everyone else on livejournal who contributed title suggestions.

I've been lucky enough to have the help of a wonderful agent, Cynthia Manson, who is also a friend; and the advice of not one but two terrific editors, Betsy Mitchell at Del Rey and Jane Johnson at HarperCollins UK. Many other friends and readers gave me encouragement and advice along the way, and helped with everything from title suggestions to catching out-of-period words; I wish I could list them all but will settle for saying a general and heartfelt thank-you. I'd also like to thank several people who went out of their way to help with my research: Susan Palmer at the Soane Museum in London, Fiona Murray and the volunteer staff at the Georgian House in Edinburgh, and Helen Roche at the Merrion Hotel in Dublin.

To my mother and father and Sonia, much love and gratitude; and last and most important: this book is dedicated to my husband, Charles, who has given me so many gifts that I can't even begin to mention them all, the first and best of which is joy.

Here is an excerpt from the second adventure
in the Temeraire series

Throne of Jade

Naomi Novik

Published by
Del Rey Books

$\mathcal{T}$HE DAY WAS unseasonably warm for November, but in some misguided deference to the Chinese embassy, the fire in the Admiralty boardroom had been heaped excessively high, and Laurence was standing directly before it. He had dressed with especial care, in his best uniform, and all throughout the long and unbearable interview, the lining of his thick bottle-green broadcloth coat had been growing steadily more sodden with sweat.

Over the doorway, behind Lord Barham, the official indicator with its compass arrow showed the direction of the wind over the Channel: in the north-north-east today, fair for France; very likely even now some ships of the Channel Fleet were standing in to have a look at Napoleon's harbors. His shoulders held at attention, Laurence fixed his eyes upon the broad metal disk and tried to keep himself distracted with such speculation; he did not trust himself to meet the cold, unfriendly gaze fixed upon him.

Barham stopped speaking and coughed again into his fist; the elaborate phrases he had prepared sat not at all in his sailor's mouth, and at the end of every awkward, halting line, he stopped and darted a look over at the Chinese with a nervous agitation that approached obsequity. It was not a very creditable performance, but under ordinary circumstances, Laurence would have felt a degree of sympathy for Barham's position: some sort of formal message had been anticipated, even perhaps an envoy, but no one had ever imagined that the Emperor of China would send his own brother halfway around the world.

Prince Yongxing could, with a word, set their two nations at war; and there was besides something inherently awful in his presence: the impervious silence with which he met Barham's every remark; the overwhelming splendor of his dark yellow robes, embroidered thickly with dragons; the slow and relentless tapping of his long, jewel-encrusted fingernail against the arm of his chair. He did not even look at Barham: he only stared directly across the table at Laurence, grim and thin-lipped.

His retinue was so large they filled the boardroom to the corners, a dozen guards all sweltering and dazed in their quilted armor and as many servants besides, most with nothing to do, only attendants of one sort or another, all of them standing along the far wall of the room and trying to stir the air with broad-paneled fans. One man, evidently a translator, stood behind the prince, murmuring when Yongxing lifted a hand, generally after one of Barham's more involved periods.

Two other official envoys sat to Yongxing's either side. These men had been presented to Laurence only perfunctorily, and they had neither of them said a word, though the younger, called Sun Kai, had been watching all the proceedings, impassively, and following the translator's words with quiet attention. The elder, a big, round-bellied man with a tufted grey beard, had gradually been overcome by the heat: his head had sunk forward onto his chest, mouth half-open for air, and his hand was barely even moving his fan towards his face. They were robed in dark blue silk, almost as elaborately as the prince himself, and together they made an imposing façade: certainly no such embassy had ever been seen in the West.

A far more practiced diplomat than Barham might have been pardoned for succumbing to some degree of servility, but Laurence was scarcely in any mood to be forgiving; though he was nearly more furious with himself, at having hoped for anything better. He had come expecting to plead his case, and privately in his heart he had even imagined a reprieve; instead he had been scolded in terms he would have scrupled to use to a raw lieutenant, and all in front of a foreign prince and his retinue, assembled like a tribunal to hear his crimes. Still he held his tongue as long as he could manage, but when Barham at last came about to saying, with an air of great condescension, "Naturally, Captain, we have it in mind that you shall be put to another hatchling, afterwards," Laurence had reached his limit.

"No, sir," he said, breaking in. "I am sorry, but no: I will not do it, and as for another post, I must beg to be excused."

Sitting beside Barham, Admiral Powys of the Aerial Corps had remained quite silent through the course of the meeting; now he only shook his head, without any appearance of surprise, and folded his hands together over his ample belly. Barham gave him a furious look and said to Laurence, "Perhaps I am not clear, Captain; this is not a request. You have been given your orders, you will carry them out."

"I will be hanged first," Laurence said flatly, past caring that he was speaking in such terms to the First Lord of the Admiralty: the death of his career if he had still been a naval officer, and it could scarcely do him any good even as an aviator. Yet if they meant to send Temeraire away, back to China, his career as an aviator was finished: he would never accept a position with any other dragon. None other would ever compare, to Laurence's mind, and he would not subject a hatchling to being second-best when there were men in the Corps lined up six-deep for the chance.

Yongxing did not say anything, but his lips tightened; his attendants shifted and murmured among themselves in their own language. Laurence did not think he was imagining the hint of disdain in their tone, directed less at himself than at Barham; and the First Lord evidently shared the impression, his face growing mottled and choleric with the effort of preserving the appearance of calm. "By God, Laurence; if you imagine you can stand here in the middle of Whitehall and mutiny, you are wrong; I think perhaps you are forgetting that your first duty is to your country and your King, not to this dragon of yours."

"No, sir; it is you who are forgetting. It was for duty I put Temeraire into harness, sacrificing my naval rank, with no knowledge then that he was any breed truly out of the ordinary, much less a Celestial," Laurence said. "And for duty I took him through a difficult training and into a hard and dangerous service; for duty I have taken him into battle, and asked him to hazard his life and happiness. I will not answer such loyal service with lies and deceit."

"Enough noise, there," Barham said. "Anyone would think you were being asked to hand over your firstborn. I am sorry if you have made such a pet of the creature you cannot bear to lose him—"

"Temeraire is neither my pet nor my property, sir," Laurence snapped. "He has served England and the King as much as I have, or you yourself, and now, because he does not choose to go back to China, you stand there and ask me to lie to him. I cannot imagine what claim to honor I should have if I agreed to it. Indeed," he added, unable to restrain himself, "I wonder that you should even have made the proposal; I wonder at it greatly."

"Oh, your soul to the devil, Laurence," Barham said, losing his last veneer of formality; he had been a serving sea-officer for years before joining Government, and he was still very little a politician when his temper was up. "He is a Chinese dragon, it stands to reason he will like China better; in any case, he belongs to them, and there is an end to it. The name of thief is a very unpleasant one, and His Majesty's Government does not propose to invite it."

"I know how I am to take that, I suppose." If Laurence had not already been half-broiled, he would have flushed. "And I utterly reject the accusation, sir. These gentlemen do not deny they had given the egg to France; we seized it from a French man-of-war; the ship and the egg were condemned as lawful prize out of hand in the Admiralty courts, as you very well know. By no possible understanding does Temeraire belong to them; if they were so anxious about letting a Celestial out of their hands, they ought not have given him away in the shell."

Yongxing snorted and broke into their shouting match. "*That* is correct," he said; his English was thickly accented, formal and slow, but the measured cadences only lent all the more effect to his words. "From the first it was folly to let the second-born egg of Lung Tien Qian pass over sea. *That,* no one can now dispute."

It silenced them both, and for a moment no one spoke, save the translator quietly rendering Yongxing's words for the rest of the Chinese. Then Sun Kai unexpectedly said something in their tongue which made Yongxing look around at him sharply. Sun kept his head inclined deferentially, and did not look up, but still it was the first suggestion Laurence had seen that their embassy might perhaps not speak with a single voice. But Yongxing snapped a reply, in a tone which did not allow of any further comment, and Sun did not venture to make one. Satisfied that he had quelled his subordinate, Yongxing turned back to them and added, "Yet regardless of the evil chance that brought him into your hands, Lung Tien Xiang was meant to go to the French Emperor, not to be made beast of burden for a common soldier."

Laurence stiffened; *common soldier* rankled, and for the first time he turned to look directly at the prince, meeting that cold, contemptuous gaze with an equally steady one. "We are at war with France, sir; if you choose to ally yourself with our enemies and send them material assistance, you can hardly complain when we take it in fair fight."

"Nonsense!" Barham broke in, at once and loudly. "China is by no means an ally of France, by no means at all; we certainly do not view China as a French ally. You are not here to speak to His Imperial Highness, Laurence; control yourself," he added, in a savage undertone.

But Yongxing ignored the attempt at interruption. "And now you make piracy your defense?" he said, contemptuous. "We do not concern ourselves with the customs of barbaric nations. How merchants and thieves agree to pillage one another is not of interest to the Celestial Throne, except when they choose to insult the Emperor as you have."

"No, Your Highness, no such thing, not in the least," Barham said hurriedly, even while he looked pure venom at Laurence. "His Majesty and his Government have nothing but the deepest affection for the Emperor; no insult would ever willingly be offered, I assure you. If we had only known of the extraordinary nature of the egg, of your objections, this situation would never have arisen—"

"Now, however, you are well aware," Yongxing said,

"and the insult remains: Lung Tien Xiang is still in harness, treated little better than a horse, expected to carry burdens and exposed to all the brutalities of war, and all this, with a mere captain as his companion. Better had his egg sunk to the bottom of the ocean!"

Appalled, Laurence was glad to see this callousness left Barham and Powys as staring and speechless as himself. Even among Yongxing's own retinue, the translator flinched, shifting uneasily, and for once did not translate the prince's words back into Chinese.

"Sir, I assure you, since we learned of your objections, he has not been under harness at all, not a stitch of it," Barham said, recovering. "We have been at the greatest of pains to see to Temeraire's—that is, to Lung Tien Xiang's—comfort, and to make redress for any inadequacy in his treatment. He is no longer assigned to Captain Laurence, that I can assure you: they have not spoken these last two weeks."

The reminder was a bitter one, and Laurence felt what little remained of his temper fraying away. "If either of you had any real concern for his comfort, you would consult his feelings, not your own desires," he said, his voice rising, a voice which had been trained to bellow orders through a gale. "You complain of having him under harness, and in the same breath ask me to trick him into chains, so you might drag him away against his will. I will not do it; I will never do it, and be damned to you all."

Judging by his expression, Barham would have been glad to have Laurence himself dragged away in chains: eyes almost bulging, hands flat on the table, on the verge of rising; for the first time, Admiral Powys spoke, breaking in, and forestalled him. "Enough, Laurence, hold your tongue. Barham, nothing further can be served by keeping him. Out, Laurence; out at once: you are dismissed."

The long habit of obedience held: Laurence flung himself out of the room. The intervention likely saved him from an arrest for insubordination, but he went with no sense of gratitude; a thousand things were pent up in his throat, and even as the door swung heavily shut behind him, he turned back. But the Marines stationed to either side were gazing at him with thoughtlessly rude interest, as if he were a curiosity exhibited for their entertainment. Under their open, inquisitive looks he mastered his temper a little, and turned away before he could betray himself more fully.

Barham's words were swallowed by the heavy wood, but the inarticulate rumble of his still-raised voice followed Laurence down the corridor. He felt almost drunk with anger, his breath coming in short abrupt spurts and his vision obscured, not by tears, not at all by tears, except of rage. The antechamber of the Admiralty was full of sea-officers, clerks, political officials, even a green-coated aviator rushing through with dispatches. Laurence shouldered his way roughly to the doors, his shaking hands thrust deep into his coat pockets to conceal them from view.

He struck out into the crashing din of late-afternoon London, Whitehall full of workingmen going home for their suppers, and the bawling of the hackney drivers and chair-men over all, crying, "Make a lane, there," through the crowds. His feelings were as disordered as his surroundings, and he was navigating the street by instinct; he had to be called three times before he recognized his own name.

He turned only reluctantly: he had no desire to be forced to return a civil word or gesture from a former colleague. But with a measure of relief he saw it was Captain Roland, not an ignorant acquaintance. He was surprised to see her; very surprised, for her dragon, Excidium, was a formation-leader at the Dover covert. She could not easily have been spared from her duties, and in any case she could not come to the Admiralty openly, being a female officer, one of those whose existence was made necessary by the insistence of Longwings on female captains. The secret was but barely known outside the ranks of the aviators, and jealously kept against certain public disapproval; Laurence himself had found it difficult to accept the notion, at first, but he had grown so used to the idea that now Roland looked very odd to him out of uniform: she had put on skirts and a heavy cloak by way of concealment, neither of which suited her.

"I have been puffing after you for the last five minutes," she said, taking his arm as she reached him. "I was wandering about that great cavern of a building, waiting for you to come out, and then you went straight past me in such a ferocious hurry I could scarcely catch you. These clothes are a damned nuisance; I hope you appreciate the trouble I am taking for you, Laurence. But never mind," she added, her voice gentling. "I can see from your face that it did not go well: let us go and have some dinner, and you shall tell me everything."

"Thank you, Jane; I am glad to see you," he said, and let her turn him in the direction of her inn, though he did not think he could swallow. "How do you come to be here, though? Surely there is nothing wrong with Excidium?"

"Nothing in the least, unless he has given himself indigestion," she said. "No; but Lily and Captain Harcourt are coming along splendidly, and so Lenton was able to assign them a double patrol and give me a few days of liberty. Excidium took it as excuse to eat three fat cows at once, the wretched greedy thing; he barely cracked an eyelid when I proposed my leaving him with Sanders—that is my new first lieutenant—and coming to bear you company. So I put together a street-going rig and came up with the courier. Oh, hell: wait a minute, will you?" She stopped and kicked vigorously, shaking her skirts loose: they were too long, and had caught on her heels.

He held her by the elbow so she did not topple over, and afterwards they continued on through the London streets at a slower pace. Roland's mannish stride and scarred face drew enough rude stares that Laurence began to glare at the passersby who looked too long, though she herself paid them no mind; she noticed his behavior, however, and said, "You are ferocious out of temper; do not frighten those poor girls. What did those fellows say to you at the Admiralty?"

"You have heard, I suppose, that an embassy has come from China; they mean to take Temeraire back with them, and Government does not care to object. But evidently he will have none of it: tells them all to go hang themselves, though they have been at him for weeks now to go," Laurence said. As he spoke, a sharp sensation of pain, like a constriction just under his breastbone, made itself felt. He could picture quite clearly Temeraire kept nearly all alone in the old, worn-down London covert, scarcely used in the last hundred years, with neither Laurence nor his crew to keep him company, no one to read to him, and of his own kind only a few small courier-beasts flying through on dispatch service.

"Of course he will not go," Roland said. "I cannot believe they imagined they could persuade him to leave you. Surely they ought to know better; I have always heard the Chinese cried up as the very pinnacle of dragon-handlers."

"Their prince has made no secret he thinks very little of me; likely they expected Temeraire to share much the same opinion, and to be pleased to go back," Laurence said. "In any case, they grow tired of trying to persuade him; so that villain Barham ordered I should lie to him and say we were assigned to Gibraltar, all to get him aboard a transport and out to sea, too far for him to fly back to land, before he knew what they were about."

"Oh, infamous." Her hand tightened almost painfully on his arm. "Did Powys have nothing to say to it? I cannot believe he let them suggest such a thing to you; one cannot expect a naval officer to understand these things, but Powys should have explained matters to him."

"I dare say he can do nothing; he is only a serving officer, and Barham is appointed by the Ministry," Laurence said. "Powys at least saved me from putting my neck in a noose: I was too angry to control myself, and he sent me away."

They had reached the Strand; the increase in traffic made conversation difficult, and they had to pay attention to avoid being splashed by the questionable grey slush heaped in the gutters, thrown up onto the pavement by the lumbering carts and hackney wheels. His anger ebbing away, Laurence was increasingly low in his spirits.

From the moment of separation, he had consoled himself with the daily expectation that it would soon end: the Chinese would soon see Temeraire did not wish to go, or the Admiralty would give up the attempt to placate them. It had seemed a cruel sentence even so; they had not been parted a full day's time in the months since Temeraire's hatching, and Laurence had scarcely known what to do with himself, or how to fill the hours. But even the two long weeks were nothing to this, the dreadful certainty that he had ruined all his chances. The Chinese would not yield, and the Ministry would find some way of getting Temeraire sent off to China in the end: they plainly had no objection to telling him a pack of lies for the purpose. Likely enough Barham would never consent to his seeing Temeraire now even for a last farewell.

Laurence had not even allowed himself to consider what his own life might be with Temeraire gone. Another dragon was of course an impossibility, and the Navy would not have him back now. He supposed he could take on a ship in the merchant fleet, or a privateer; but he did not think he would have the heart for it, and he had done well enough out of prize-money to live on. He could even marry and set up as a country gentleman; but that prospect, once so idyllic in his imagination, now seemed drab and colorless.

Worse yet, he could hardly look for sympathy: all his former acquaintance would call it a lucky escape, his family would rejoice, and the world would think nothing of his loss. By any measure, there was something ridiculous in his being so adrift: he had become an aviator quite unwillingly, only from the strongest sense of duty, and less than a year had passed since his change in station; yet already he could hardly consider the possibility. Only another aviator, perhaps indeed only another captain, would truly be able to understand his sentiments, and with Temeraire gone, he would be as severed from their company as aviators themselves were from the rest of the world.

The front room at the Crown and Anchor was not quiet, though it was still early for dinner by town standards. The place was not a fashionable establishment, nor even genteel, its custom mostly consisting of countrymen used to a more reasonable hour for their food and drink. It was not the sort of place a respectable woman would have come, nor indeed the kind of place Laurence himself would have ever voluntarily frequented in earlier days. Roland drew some insolent stares, others only curious, but no one attempted any greater liberty: Laurence made an imposing figure beside her with his broad shoulders and his dress sword slung at his hip.

Roland led Laurence up to her rooms, sat him in an ugly armchair, and gave him a glass of wine. He drank deeply, hiding behind the bowl of the glass from her sympathetic look: he was afraid he might easily be unmanned. "You must be faint with hunger, Laurence," she said. "That is half the trouble." She rang for the maid; shortly a couple of manservants climbed up with a very good sort of plain single-course dinner: a roasted fowl, with greens and beef gravy sauce; some small cheese-cakes made with jam, calf's feet pie, a dish of red cabbage stewed, and a small biscuit pudding for relish. She had them place all the food on the table at once, rather than going through removes, and sent them away.

Laurence did not think he would eat, but once the food was before him he found he was hungry after all. He had been eating very indifferently, thanks to irregular hours and the low table of his cheap boardinghouse, chosen for its proximity to the covert where Temeraire was kept; now he ate steadily, Roland carrying the conversation nearly alone and distracting him with service gossip and trivialities.

"I was sorry to lose Lloyd, of course—they mean to put him to the Anglewing egg that is hardening at Kinloch Laggan," she said, speaking of her first lieutenant.

"I think I saw it there," Laurence said, rousing a little and lifting his head from his plate. "Obversaria's egg?"

"Yes, and we have great hopes of the issue," she said. "Lloyd was over the moon, of course, and I am very happy for him; still, it is no easy thing to break in a new premier after five years, with all the crew and Excidium himself murmuring about how Lloyd used to do things. But Sanders is a good-hearted, dependable fellow; they sent him up from Gibraltar, after Granby refused the post."

"What? Refused it?" Laurence cried, in great dismay: Granby was his own first lieutenant. "Not for my sake, I hope."

"Oh, Lord, you did not know?" Roland said, in equal dismay. "Granby spoke to me very pretty; said he was obliged, but he did not choose to shift his position. I was quite sure he had consulted you about the matter; I thought perhaps you had been given some reason to hope."

"No," Laurence said, very low. "He is more likely to end up with no position at all; I am very sorry to hear he should have passed up so good a place." The refusal could have done Granby no good with the Corps; a man who had turned down one offer could not soon expect another, and Laurence would shortly have no power at all to help him along.

"Well, I am damned sorry to have given you any more cause for concern," Roland said, after a moment. "Admiral Lenton has not broken up your crew, you know, for the most part: only gave a few fellows to Berkley out of desperation, he being so short-handed now. We were all sure that Maximus had reached his final growth; shortly after you were called here, he began to prove us wrong, and so far he has put on fifteen feet in length." She added this last in an attempt to recover the lighter tone of the conversation, but it was impossible: Laurence found that his stomach had closed, and he set down his knife and fork with the plate still half full.

Roland drew the curtains; it was already growing dark outside. "Do you care for a concert?"

"I am happy to accompany you," he said mechanically, and she shook her head.

"No, never mind; I see it will not do. Come to bed

then, my dear fellow; there is no sense in sitting about and moping."

They put out the candles and lay down together. "I have not the least notion what to do," he said quietly: the cover of dark made the confession a little easier. "I called Barham a villain, and I cannot forgive him asking me to lie; very ungentleman-like. But he is not a scrub; he would not be at such shifts if he had any other choice."

"It makes me quite ill to hear about him bowing and scraping to this foreign prince." Roland propped herself up on her elbow on the pillows. "I was in Canton Harbor once, as a mid, on a transport coming back the long way from India; those junks of theirs do not look like they could stand a mild shower, much less a gale. They cannot fly their dragons across the ocean without a pause, even if they cared to go to war with us."

"I thought as much myself, when I first heard," Laurence said. "But they do not need to fly across the ocean to end the China trade, and wreck our shipping to India also, if they liked; besides they share a border with Russia. It would mean the end of the coalition against Bonaparte, if the Tsar was attacked on his eastern borders."

"I do not see the Russians have done us very much good so far, in the war, and money is a low pitiful excuse for behaving like a bounder, in a man or a nation," Roland said. "The State has been short of funds before, and somehow we have scraped by and still blacked Bonaparte's eye for him. In any case, I cannot forgive them for keeping you from Temeraire. Barham still has not let you see him at all, I suppose?"

"No, not for two weeks now. There is a decent fellow at the covert who has taken him messages for me, and lets me know that he is eating, but I cannot ask him to let me in: it would be a court-martial for us both.

Though for my own part, I hardly know if I would let it stop me now."

He could scarcely have imagined even saying such a thing, a year ago; he did not like to think it now, but honesty put the words into his mouth. Roland did not cry out against it, but then she was an aviator herself. She reached out to stroke his cheek, and drew him down to such comfort as might be found in her arms.

Look for *Throne of Jade*
in bookstores everywhere.

And don't miss the exciting
third book in the series,
also from Del Rey,
Black Powder War